Praise for Gary Krist and *Bad Chemistry*

Also by Gary Krist

THE GARDEN STATE
BONE BY BONE

BAD
CHEMISTRY

GARY KRIST

BERKLEY BOOKS, NEW YORK

BAD CHEMISTRY

A Berkley Book / published by arrangement with
Random House, Inc.

PRINTING HISTORY
Random House hardcover edition / 1997
Berkley mass-market edition / January 2000

The Penguin Putnam Inc. World Wide Web site address is
http://www.penguinputnam.com

ISBN: 0-425-17300-3

BERKLEY®
Berkley Books are published by The Berkley Publishing Group,
a division of Penguin Putnam Inc.,
375 Hudson Street, New York, New York 10014.
BERKLEY and the "B" logo
are trademarks belonging to Penguin Putnam Inc.

PRINTED IN THE UNITED STATES OF AMERICA

10 9 8 7 6 5 4 3 2 1

For
Bill and Dennie Cheng
and
Harold and Joyce Krist
95 years of marriage

Prologue

The dreams were usually about deer. He would see them standing in the woods behind the house—skittish, secretive, their wet coats shining in the weak glow of the floodlights. He'd watch from a high window, his own ragged breath clouding the glass. The nearness of the deer, especially of their long, slick-muscled legs, unsettled him, filled him with an ache that tightened whenever he moved. Eventually, he'd wake up, feeling confused and ashamed. His cold, moonlit room would be spread out around him—the schoolbooks piled on a chair in the corner, the shadowy stretch of carpet, his hopelessly cluttered desk.

Sighing, he'd reach for the bedside lamp, ready for another sleepless night.

His name was Evan, and he was fourteen years old. His birthday had passed a few months before, and ever since then, as fall edged toward winter, he'd been feeling troubled and uneasy. He'd always been a thin and lanky boy, with feet too big for his skinny, small-boned frame and fine red hair pulled back into a short ponytail. But now he seemed to be getting taller by the day, and this growth struck him as a betrayal. It sapped his strength, undermined his feeling of control over himself. He felt that nothing, not even his own body, could be trusted anymore.

His mother and aunt—the two people closest to him—did little to help. Evan and the two women lived in that house together, ate meals together, even watched television together, but to him they were like a kind of insect life in the house. A nuisance. An infestation. They could only add to his troubles with their questions and concern, their clumsy efforts to understand what he was going through.

There were times, in fact, when he wanted to get rid of them. He imagined just wishing them away, making them disappear from his life. Although he knew he must love them. They were his only family.

Most of his time in the house was spent in his bedroom at the computer. Evan's mother and aunt didn't have a lot of money, but he had talked them into buying him a powerful, up-to-date desktop with a fast modem. He'd spend hours at the keyboard, the only light in his room the cold blue glow of the monitor. He'd play 3-D action games, download files and pictures from the Internet, eavesdrop on various on-line discussion groups—for recovering alcoholics, people with multiple sclerosis, Bible-beating evangelists, foot fetishists. Evan's mother and aunt could have no idea what he was doing for all those hours alone in his room, but they didn't limit his computer time. Evan's teacher, Ms. Curtis, had told them that his interest in computers should be encouraged. "Boys like Evan need a job skill they can rely on," he'd heard her telling his mother one night when he listened in on their telephone call. "Actually, we should all be relieved that he's taken an interest in *something*."

Besides the computer, the woods were what Evan liked

best. He would walk for hours through the woods behind his house. Sometimes he would head through the hawthorn thickets to a muddy stream out beyond their neighbor's property. He had a special place there—near a small, egg-shaped pool—where the bare branches of the trees formed a kind of skeletal dome overhead. He would climb onto a boulder above the pool and just sit quietly, tucking his long legs under him, pulling up the collar of his leather jacket against the chill. It was one of the few places he felt at home, under the bare oaks, while squirrels and birds nosed around in the brittle fallen leaves. He had other places, too—the small dump near the hardware store in town, the burned-out farmhouse where he'd found a roomful of maroon plastic chairs melted into outrageous shapes—but it was the egg-shaped pool that he went to most often. He could breathe there. He could picture it as the only place left in the world. He could imagine himself transformed there—an alien spirit hovering over the forest floor, sucking the life out of everything in sight.

And it was in that place, one cold afternoon in November, that he found the corpse.

At first, Evan wasn't sure what he was looking at. He'd been sitting on his boulder for an hour, sweeping the territory with his stare, pretending to be an animal of the forest—an owl or a hawk. But then his eye caught something white on the other side of the pool, a spot of brightness that was out of place against the browns and grays. He sat up and eased himself to the ground. From a distance, it looked to him like a toe, a human toe.

Evan tried to stay calm, but his excitement grew as he got closer. The white spot in the leaves was exactly what it seemed: a mud-caked, white-nailed human toe, sticking out of the stream bank.

Moving quickly, Evan picked up a short oak branch and began digging around the toe. He uncovered a long, narrow foot, unreal in its paleness. Evan threw the stick away, put on his dirty suede gloves, and began using his hands to dig. A hairless calf appeared in the wet, black dirt, then a thigh. He dug faster. As he cleared the top of the thigh, his gloved hand touched something spongy and bulblike. When he realized what it was, he fell back. He pivoted on his heel and sprang away, retreating to his place on the boulder.

Evan sat for a while and tried to catch his breath, careful not to touch his clothes with the contaminated gloves. Across the pool, the white leg stretched like a huge slug across the dirt, bleached and soft. He was disappointed that this wasn't the body of a girl, or, better, a young woman. Even so, he couldn't take his eyes off the leg. It reminded him of the legs of the deer in his dream, the perfect curves, the smoothness. The difference was that this body was dead, something entirely under his control. He'd found dead animals in the woods before—squirrels and chipmunks and even a cat once, its fur clotted with purple-black blood. But Fate had never presented him with anything as serious, as interesting, as this.

After a few more minutes, when his heartbeat and breathing were back to normal, Evan slid off the rock and walked toward the body again. He picked up the stick and started digging, more carefully this time, to avoid ripping the flesh with the jagged tip of the stick. It seemed clear to Evan that, for whatever reason, he had been chosen as the caretaker of this body, so he wanted to keep it perfect. But his excitement kept getting the better of him. Once or twice, as he was uncovering the second leg, he slipped, scraping the skin of the thigh in a way that should have drawn blood but somehow didn't.

Finally, giving in to his impatience, he threw the stick away again, grabbed the ankles, and just pulled. The body came loose more easily than he expected. He fell backward onto the mud, the stiff legs of the corpse falling on top of him. Shouting out in surprise, Evan rolled from under the legs and scrambled to his feet.

He saw then why the body had come out so easily. It wasn't whole. There were no hands at the end of the long arms, no head on the top of the neck.

Evan shook himself and turned away. He took off his gloves, put them on the ground, and then used his bare hands to brush the leaves from his jeans. He didn't know how to feel about this new development. He didn't know what it meant.

He turned back. The mutilated body lay in front of him, twisted on the bank of the stream, its whiteness streaked by mud and bits of leaves. It was a terrible thing, he thought. A terrible, scary, but beautiful thing.

He climbed up to his place on the boulder and decided just to look at it for a while. He rocked back and forth, his chin hooked over his knees. He had seen pictures of corpses like this on his computer. One night, while wandering Usenet, he'd found a newsgroup where police pictures of crime scenes were posted. The images were probably stolen, but Evan downloaded a few anyway and looked at them. They were mostly black-and-white: pictures of naked, dead bodies covered with dark blood, bodies riddled with bullet holes. There was even a shot of a woman whose throat had been cut and lay open for the camera like another, wider mouth. Evan was revolted by these pictures, but at the same time he was fascinated by them. After a day or two, he'd had to delete the files—to stop himself from thinking about the bodies every minute of the day.

But those had just been pictures. Here, now, as he sat fingering the little cross-shaped earring on his left earlobe, was a real corpse, and he couldn't turn his eyes away from it. The body's color seemed to change as he watched. With the light draining from the woods, the body seemed to take on a green shimmer, like one of those glow-in-

the-dark necklaces they sold at the football field on the
Fourth of July. It almost looked like something from another planet.

It was then—as he sat on that boulder, staring—that
Evan decided he would tell his mother and aunt nothing
about the body, at least for now. They would ruin everything if they knew, so he'd have to keep it a secret. He
could picture sitting with the two women at dinner, faking
interest as they discussed normal things—the new washing machine, or else Aunt Rita's hope for a promotion at
work. Evan would barely be able to keep himself from
laughing out loud. Imagine talking about a washing machine when there was a headless, handless corpse in the
woods less than a half mile away!

Evan closed his eyes and pressed them against his
knees. He knew it would be hard to keep this secret. He
would have to think carefully about everything he did and
said.

After a half hour or so, Evan's stomach began making
noises, and he realized it was time to go home for dinner.
He climbed down from the boulder and stepped carefully
across the stream. He pulled on his gloves, turned the
body straight again, and began to cover it with leaves. He
had no problem burying it; the leaves were soaked
through, and they stuck to the corpse like clay. When he
was done, he took off his gloves and hid them under a
rock nearby.

Evan stepped back and studied the small mound on the
forest floor, making sure that no part of the body could
be seen. The mound looked totally natural there beside
the stream, but he stopped and rearranged a few leaves
anyway, just to be safe.

Evan straightened up again. Yes, he told himself then:
yes, he would eventually have to tell somebody about this
corpse, maybe even the police. But not for a few days at
least. In the meantime, it would be his secret. He'd come

and visit it after school. All of the people he knew—his mother, his aunt, his teachers—would think that everything was normal. Only Evan would know that it wasn't, that life was different now, that he himself was different, changed by the knowledge of the body in the woods. The secret would give him power and energy; it would charge every minute of the day with importance. People would go on thinking it was the same person living among them in the body of Evan Potter. Only he would know otherwise.

Evan wiped his stiff, cold fingers on his jeans and started toward home. For the first time in many weeks, he felt completely happy.

PART ONE

1

Joel talked her into throwing a birthday party for the dog. A big one. He wanted every pet from the neighborhood to come, with owners in tow. The invitations would be delivered by Hermann himself, each one clipped to a red bandanna around his neck. BYOB, they would read: Bring Your Own Bone.

"Oh great," Kate said when Joel first told her about the idea, showing her the design for the invitations on his computer. "People might think we really think this is funny."

"True, they might," Joel answered. He smiled as he played with the fonts on the screen. "And that would be the funniest part of all, wouldn't it?"

Kate shook her head and leaned over to whisper in his ear. "You're bad, you know that, Joel?"

"I know that," he said, clicking away on his mouse.

On the afternoon of the party—a damp, cold Saturday in November—two dozen people crowded around the edges of the downstairs family room in Joel and Kate's four-bedroom colonial, trying to make their animals sit quietly at the picnic blanket. Joel stood at one end, ready to take what he called the official party picture. He was using a digital camera, some new toy he'd found that could be hooked up to his Macintosh. His plan, he told Kate, was to take a few shots, call up the images on the computer monitor, and print a copy for each guest.

But the animals weren't cooperating. Joel got off just one frame before a couple of the rowdier dogs, excited by the sight of all that food—or by the birthday hats clinging rakishly to the sides of their heads—broke free and ran around the blanket, trying to get at the cake. Things fell apart after that. Dogs howled, birds squawked, somebody cursed a broken video camera. Then the Websters' dachshund had an accident under the billiard table.

A dog party. It was a classic Joel idea, Kate thought. Although she had joked about it earlier, she really did wonder what kind of impression this party was making on their guests. Kate Baker—born Theodorus, from solid working-class Greek stock—had never felt totally sure of herself in her husband's choice of neighborhood, a rich D.C. exurb with winding roads, flowering cherries, and mailboxes labeled with names that could have come from the passenger list of the Mayflower. She always had the feeling there were unwritten rules in force, rules that had never made it to the old row house district of Chicago where she grew up. Would the idea of a dog party seem funny to these people instead of just corny? Kate had no idea.

Joel, on the other hand, never seemed to waste much time on questions like that. He was the only real nonconformist she'd ever met—a sixties student radical turned eighties entrepreneur turned nineties . . . what? Socially conscious businessman? Neocapitalist rebel? Kate didn't know what to call him. A lot of the virtues that her family had tried to drill into her from the day she was born—

duty, eagerness to please, concern for appearances—
didn't seem to interest Joel, and this fact about him, probably more than any other, intrigued Kate. She wished she
could be so confident.

It was her own stubborn sense of duty—as well as a
need to get away from a mind-numbing conversation
about Laura Ashley window treatments—that kept Kate
downstairs with the pets when Joel and the guests began
to wander up toward the drinks table. Even though Joel
had promised to do the cleaning up, Kate decided to stay
behind and deal with the three-legged Chihuahua, the macaw who bit, the mess. Not that she minded much. Kate
generally liked animals better than humans anyway, and
she felt that Joel deserved some indulgence right now.
He'd been putting in brutal hours at work for the past
month. There'd been a couple of freak currency fluctua-
tions in South America, and now a huge order of Malay-
sian vanilla beans was missing somewhere in the South
Pacific. Joel had been at the office until dawn three times
in the last week alone. In Kate's opinion, getting tanked
at a dog party was probably just what he needed.

After a few minutes, Kate managed to get the last of
the canine guests out the back door and into the fenced
yard. The macaw settled down, and the only cat invited
to the party came out from under the sofa to lap up the
crumbs left on the picnic blanket. Hermann—Kate and
Joel's own twelve-year-old German shepherd, the birthday dog—sat in a corner, giving Kate a dark stare.

"Well, don't look at me. They're your friends," she said
to him in her hoarse, raspy voice.

Hermann cocked his head to one side, his ears flattening
back against the thick black fur. He had such expressive
ears, Kate thought. She could read his ears the way other
people read human faces.

"Okay," she said, "so maybe this wasn't a great idea."

Hermann whimpered. He let Kate scratch him behind

those expressive ears, then gave her a quick, forgiving nuzzle and stalked off to the garage for a nap.

Kate stopped in the bathroom to see if she still looked all right after her struggle with the dogs. Her thick, raisin-black hair was pulled back into something like a French braid, though now stray hairs sprang from her head at every angle, giving her a wild, frazzled look. That hair, along with her intense green eyes and long, slightly crooked nose—inherited from a legendary Macedonian grandmother she'd never met—made her look a little like a crazy fortune-teller, she thought. And the effect was only strengthened by the small comma-shaped scar on the outside end of her right eyebrow, a childhood gift from her toy-throwing youngest brother. It made one eyebrow seem shorter than the other, and gave her whole face an off-center tilt. Kate frowned. At least her dress still looked good. It was tight, gray wool, belted at the waist—the kind of clingy thing she never wore before coming east. She liked the way it helped to fill out her too-narrow hips.

Deciding to leave the clutter on the picnic blanket for later, Kate went back upstairs and dove again into the noise of the party. Elena Drummond, her best friend, si-dled up to her with a drink in her hand. "Keep it under your hat, Kate, but I think there's something going on between Matilda Barnes and the Landons' weimaraner."

Kate grabbed Elena's drink and took a taste, letting a drop of gin fall to the floor like a tiny glass bead. "I always told you that woman was a bitch," she said.

Elena laughed. She seemed to love hearing Kate curse, though she would never say an off-color word herself. Elena was the only neighbor that Kate felt totally at ease with, and the two were inseparable, despite the fifteen-year difference in their ages and the even more extreme difference in their situations: Elena, fifty-one years old and living alone in the house next door to the Bakers, had two girls in college and an ex-husband whose monthly alimony check would occasionally show up with smiling holiday pictures of him and his new blond wife. To hear Elena tell it, she deposited the checks in the bank and gave the pictures to her macaw to shred.

"So how's my husband acting?" Kate asked her, giving back the drink.

"Joel? As bizarre and charming as usual." Elena took a quick sip. "Why?"

"Just checking." Kate looked across the room at her husband. Joel was standing near the CD player in the den, talking to Wayne and Allie Webster. He looked young for his forty-five years—sun-streaked brown hair, a square chin, mud-brown eyes, and a definite hint of adventurousness in his grin. Still a decently sexy man, Kate thought, better than I deserve. "It's just that things have been lousy at work," she continued. "He seems . . . I don't know, distracted lately."

"You worry too much," Elena said.

"Yeah, so you always tell me."

"And I'm always right."

Kate grabbed Elena's drink again. It was true that she was a worrier. There was no way she could be anything else, having been trained in worry from a young age. As the only daughter in a Greek family of seven, she'd had to look after four brothers and her father before she was even in her teens. Her mother, a tall, red-faced woman with ever-aching feet, would retreat into her bedroom most afternoons with a crossword puzzle and a magnum of cheap white wine. When her father came home from his job as a desk sergeant in the Chicago Police Department, it was Kate who had to have the meal on the table, the younger children bathed and in pajamas, the dog fed. Even years later, when she was a cop herself, she worried—about her widowed father's heart condition; about Vic, her partner, and his marital problems; about her brothers. She sometimes wondered if she hadn't left Chicago and come east just to escape this constant worry, to start over in a place where she could worry about herself for once.

Seeing an empty ice bucket on the drinks table, Kate excused herself, grabbed it, and pushed her way through the crowd. Her mind was racing now. It was at times like this—at a party, surrounded by the clever talk and laughter of her well-heeled Maryland neighbors—that she felt most self-conscious about her East Coast life. She remembered the parties her family used to give in Chicago. Their cramped row house with the sky-blue awnings would be overrun with screaming kids, gin-playing aunts, and dozens of off-duty cops drinking beer and eating homemade spanakopita off paper plates. Nowadays she gave parties like this—fancy affairs where people drank scotch and bottled mineral water and nobody would even think of bringing along a visiting cousin or a kid under sixteen. It still amazed her that she'd ended up in a place like Lewisburg. She'd come east to go to graduate school, to get away from cop work and do something better, worthier, something she could actually feel proud of. And Kate *was* proud of what she'd accomplished so far. She had her master's in social work and was counseling teenagers in the District as part of her early work toward a doctorate. Meeting and marrying a rich businessman wasn't part of her original plan, but it had happened. She couldn't help it if the people back home, especially her brothers, saw this part of her self-improvement as a little too convenient.

Kate went into the kitchen and put the bucket into the automatic ice maker. Her brothers. Even now, four years after leaving Chicago, she still found herself thinking about them, imagining their reactions to everything she said or did. She could just guess how they would roll their eyes at the thought of an automatic ice maker. "What's the deal, Katie," her oldest brother, Phil, would say. "Can't you be bothered to fill a few ice-cube trays?" The

Theodorus boys—three of them still cops, the youngest a contractor just starting his own business—were always skeptical about Joel and his fancy lifestyle. They tended to see anyone with money, especially ex-hippies with money, as automatically suspect. So they gave her a hard time about him, and about her new life in general. They kept telling her that she was getting soft out here, making nice with JDs in her spare time, living in her big suburban house. They warned her that she was—God forbid—turning feminine on them.

"Right, feminine," she'd answered back one year over Easter dinner. "Is that what you call it when you stop shooting at fifteen-year-old kids stealing televisions?"

"Oh, excuse me," Phil had answered. "Now she's got enough money to *buy* TVs for all those ghetto kids. And give them jobs in communes." He'd turned to Joel then and said, in all seriousness, "Hey, no offense."

Kate took the full ice bucket from the machine. Outside, the dogs were barking raucously. Kate wondered how smart it was to let half a dozen dogs run free in a fenced yard. She went over to the kitchen window to check on them. A few dime-sized flakes of snow were starting to fall out of the twilit sky, sticking to the coats of the longer-haired dogs. The animals seemed agitated—overtired and cranky, like children who had missed their naps. She was glad Hermann had stayed inside.

Then, just as she was turning away from the window, Kate saw something moving behind the row of cedars on the other side of the fence. At first she thought it was a man in a brown overcoat, but the figure had disappeared too fast for her to be sure. Maybe it was a neighbor attracted by all the barking. Or a deer, though it didn't seem likely that a deer would come within a mile of those baying hounds. She watched the spot for a few seconds, trying to see into the shadows behind the cedars, but it—he, whatever it was—had already gone.

Kate turned from the window and carried the ice bucket into the living room. The guests, who were making almost as much noise as their pets outside, were clustered at one end of the house, near the drinks and the music. Kate again looked over at Joel, who now seemed to be arguing with Don Fordham, the old college friend he'd taken on as a partner when he started his business—From the Rainforest Imports, Inc.—in the mid-seventies. The two stood off in a corner of the den, near the collection of Japanese prints. Joel had his hand on Don's shoulder and was saying something close to his ear. Don shook his head and looked uncomfortable, almost afraid. Kate was about to go over to them when Matilda Barnes plucked at her arm.

"A wonderful idea for a party!" she oozed, waving her drink. "And so nice for the dogs, too. They so rarely get together."

"Thank Joel for the idea," Kate shouted over the noise.

"I just love seeing them all together," Matilda went on. "And that weimaraner, who does he belong to?"

"The Landons."

"Such a handsome, handsome animal."

Kate bit her lower lip hard. "Excuse me a minute?" she said. She took the ice bucket over to the drinks table and then made her way across the busy room to Joel and Don. Whatever it was the two men were talking about, their argument was over by the time she reached them. They stood gloomily side by side, looking in opposite directions. Kate thought of bookends. "Everything okay here?" she said as she took her husband's arm.

"Have you seen Jeannette?" Don asked, before walking away to look for his wife.

Kate pinched Joel's arm. "Hey, take it easy," she said. "This is a party. You're not supposed to beat up on the guests. What was that all about?"

She could feel the anger knotting Joel's arm muscles. "Our usual philosophical differences," he said. "Don's acting like an old lady again." Then he turned to her with a strange smile on his face. He slipped his free hand around her, grazing her left breast, and pulled her face toward his. "I want to fuck you later," he whispered into her ear, then bit the lobe, her earring clicking against his teeth.

Kate felt suddenly breathless, ambushed. Joel quickly let her go and turned away, as if nothing had happened. Kate steadied herself. Normally, she would have been thrilled by her husband's little outburst—this kind of unexpected lewdness always aroused her more than she liked to admit—but she had a feeling that Joel was just trying to distract her, to end any discussion about the argument with Don. Feeling annoyed, Kate looked up at the man she had married just three years ago. There were lots of things—his evasiveness, for one—that she would change about him if she could. But what wife wouldn't say the same about her husband, or vice versa? I love this man, she told herself. That should be enough.

It was then that the dogs started howling.

The sound—an eerie, high-pitched wail—was almost like a chant. One by one, the guests became aware of it. The noise of the party shrank back, as if to make way for a more urgent sound.

"What on earth?" Elena said.

Kate was already moving. She elbowed past a few guests to get through the living room. Before anyone else had reacted, she was out the back door and down the steps to the fenced yard.

The dogs were circling the lawn in the twilight, sending nervous howls toward the sky. Kate saw the cause of the commotion immediately. It was impossible not to. In the middle of the yard, blazing like a comet, was an animal on fire.

Her jaw tightening, Kate watched the figure run from side to side, blue and yellow flames lapping silently

around its head and body. It was one of the dogs. She
recognized it as Pearlie, Don and Jeannette's Labrador.

"Quick, get me a blanket!" Kate shouted back at the
stunned guests who'd reached the back porch. "Or a
coat—who has a heavy coat?"

Kate remembered the picnic blanket in the family room.
She ran to the basement door and pulled it open. The
blanket—a thick wool comforter—lay there on the floor,
still covered with plates of half-eaten cake and dog bis-
cuits. Kate grabbed the nearest corner and pulled, sending
the plates flying. By the time she got back to the yard, a
few people had reached the bottom of the stairs, but they
stopped there, as if hypnotized by the sight of the writhing
animal on the lawn.

"Keep the other dogs away!" Kate shouted hoarsely.
Then, holding the blanket in front of her, she stepped
toward the burning dog. The Lab was moving fast, rolling
and jumping. She waited, then lunged with the blanket,
but the dog shot away and Kate skidded across the cold,
wet grass.

She got to her feet. People were shouting at her, but
she wouldn't let their words distract her. Turning, she
dove again at the dog. This time, she felt the quick heat
of the thing in her arms, the bone and tight muscle. Yellow flame seared her cheek as she locked her arms together, and her hair sizzled near her ears. She pulled the
dog's body under her and began rolling over on the slippery lawn, until finally her back hit the metal fence at the
edge of the yard. The dog, still panicky, broke free and
ran away, the blanket trailing from her collar. But Kate
could see that the flames were out.

Joel was kneeling at her side now. He took her head in
his hands. "Kate, damn it, are you all right? Talk to me."

Her cheeks and hands stung so sharply they seemed to
buzz. It was only then that she noticed the smell of kerosene.

"Somebody's calling an ambulance," Joel went on, checking her over. He was shaking. "You're out of your mind!"

"I'm okay," she said, her tongue thick in her mouth. She let him help her to her skinned knees, then to her feet. The howling had died down, but the dogs were still circling, their frantic silence as eerie as their noise had been. Kate could see Don on the other side of the yard, huddled over the burned dog, trying to keep her calm.

John Peters walked over to Kate and Joel with an open fuel can in his hands. "I found this in the grass over there. Yours?"

Joel nodded, looking grim. It was one of the kerosene cans they kept in the crawl space under the house—for the heater in his basement office.

"Who . . . ?" Kate started to ask, but her voice gave out before she could finish.

Joel shook his head. "Some kid, probably," he said.

Kate pushed away from Joel and went over to Don. He was trying to wrap the blanket around the Labrador, but Pearlie was jumpy—going into shock, probably. She snapped feebly at Don's wrists, her eyes still foggy with panic. "How does she look?" Kate asked.

Don's face was drained of color. "It's mostly around her shoulders and back," he said. "I don't know."

Suddenly, Jeannette was on top of them. "I can't believe this," she wailed. "Why would someone do this?" She shivered and held on to Kate as Don lifted the dog.

"I'll take her around to the driveway," Don said. "When the ambulance gets here, I'll see if they can do anything for her." Pearlie had settled down by now, and just lay wrapped in his arms, trembling. "Are you hurt?" he asked Kate.

"No, I'm okay. Really."

He stared at her for a second in the dim light. "I appreciate it," he said.

The ambulance arrived a few minutes later. At first, the two paramedics wouldn't do anything for Pearlie, but after seeing that Kate was all right, one of them agreed to treat the dog's burns and then take her to the animal hospital in town. The other paramedic sat Kate on a collapsed gurney in the back of the ambulance. He began dabbing her minor burns with antibiotic ointment, bandaging the two or three that were more serious. Neighbors and friends thronged outside the van. The spinning lights of the ambulance raked them all with a kind of disco strobe as they stood on the asphalt, looking nervous and awkward.

While Kate was being treated, a county police cruiser pulled up behind the ambulance in the driveway. The borough of Lewisburg had its own police department, but it was understaffed; it was the county police that usually responded to calls this far out of town. Kate saw the patrol officer, blond and built like a porn-magazine cliché, pull himself out of the car. He talked to one of the paramedics for a minute, then, notebook in hand, walked over to question Joel, Don, and the other guests.

Kate watched him with an uneasy fascination. She remembered exactly what this was like—arriving at a disturbance with nothing to go on, no way of knowing what had really happened. She could see the familiar look of skepticism in the patrolman's face. The ugliness of any crime had a way of tainting everyone it touched. Even victims were suspect. That feeling of constant distrust was one of the things she'd hated about being a cop.

The patrolman disappeared into the backyard and then, after a few minutes, came back to check on her. "How we doing in here?"

"I've been better," Kate said, giving him a weak smile as she read his name tag: Randall Briggs. One of the paramedics—a balding young black man with huge biceps—was kneeling beside her, winding gauze around her right wrist. "So, did you catch the perp yet?" she asked, trying for a lightness she couldn't really pull off.

"No, ma'am, not yet." He smiled, looking around the bright interior of the ambulance before continuing. "Tell you the truth, I'm not even sure what's been perpetrated here. Dog catches fire in somebody's backyard. What do you call that? Canine assault? Dog arson?"

"Criminal damage, number one," she said, feeling a quick jolt of anger. "Or cruelty to animals. It's a Class C misdemeanor."

Briggs looked straight at her then. The neutrality of his expression seemed forced, as if he'd practiced it in front of a mirror. "You want to tell me what happened?"

"It seems pretty clear, Officer Briggs. Some sicko pulled the kerosene out from the crawl space, threw some on the dog, and lit it."

"Okay, okay," he said. "But why would anybody do something like that, is what I want to know."

"It's what I want to know, too."

"Me, too," said the paramedic.

The patrolman paused for a second, pressing the eraser end of his pencil against his cheek. Another self-conscious gesture. "You see anything you think I oughta know about?" he asked then.

Kate was about to shake her head when she remembered what she'd seen behind the cedars, just a few minutes before the howling started. "Wait," she said, "I did see something—somebody—out back, a little before. I wasn't sure it was a person, though."

"Can you describe what you saw?"

"It was brown . . . ," she began. She tried to call the image back from memory, to reassemble it like a puzzle, but all she could come up with was a flash of brown and a definite feeling that what she'd seen was not an animal.

"It?"

"Maybe it was Bigfoot," said the paramedic as he ripped some tape off a roll.

"Just do your job, Mike," the patrolman said testily.

For a second, Kate wondered if they were lovers. "Sorry," she said finally. "I know it's nothing much to go on, but that's all I can say. No enemies that we know of, no feuds with the neighbors, and I saw what could have been a person in a brown overcoat. A few minutes before the dog . . . caught fire."

The patrolman pressed the pencil against his cheek again. He seemed relieved that she had no eyewitness evidence to give. "Well, it's more than anybody else here could tell me." He closed his notebook. "I'll see if the local department wants to assign somebody to this, whatever the hell they want to call it." He smiled. "In the meantime, you and your husband should consider not keeping flammables in an exposed crawl space like that. Things can happen."

A pause. "Yeah, I'll remember that," Kate said. And then, as the officer walked away, she added, under her breath, "Asshole."

"My sentiments exactly," the paramedic told her as he ripped off another piece of tape.

It was a couple of hours later—after the county cop and the paramedics had gone, after the last guest had trailed off toward home, after Kate had changed clothes and looked at her burn-slicked cheeks and charred hair in the bathroom mirror—that Joel announced he was going to the twenty-four-hour Safeway. He'd seemed restless and edgy all evening. Kate had talked him into making love after dinner, mainly because she thought it would help her feel normal again. And Joel had been sweet and slow and careful, whispering to her, coaxing her toward an orgasm that didn't want to arrive. But she could tell that he wasn't really with her. She wondered if he was upset that she'd put herself in danger—or embarrassed that he hadn't done anything himself to save the dog. And afterward, when she asked him again who could possibly douse a dog with kerosene and then set it on fire, he sounded more impatient than anything: "I wish I knew. It's crazy, it's sick. What else do you want me to say?"

But at eight o'clock, as he was leaving, Joel seemed to be coming out of his funk. He stopped to kiss Kate on the forehead, sparing her sore cheeks. "Hey, you're my hero, you know that?" he said. "You'll always be my one true hero."

He picked up his overcoat and his ridiculous gray fedora to keep the snow off his head.

"Don't forget the microwave popcorn," she told him as he left.

"Got it on the list."

It was the last time Kate was to see her husband in that house.

At nine o'clock, when he still hadn't come back from the supermarket, she started to worry. He'd said he was only going out for a few things. She wondered if he was having trouble with the car.

At ten o'clock, she started calling friends, guests at the party, to find out if Joel had stopped off to see any of them, maybe to talk over what had happened.

At eleven o'clock, she and Hermann were circling the parking lot of the all-night Safeway, looking for Joel's Saab wagon.

At midnight, for the second time that day, Kate was talking to the Hampton County Police.

2

Sometimes coffee is the only thing that keeps you alive.
Kate had always said this as a joke to her brothers and
other cops, but now, on the morning after Joel's disappearance, she could almost believe it. She and Elena were
sitting across the table from each other in the kitchen,
drinking coffee from Chicago White Sox mugs. It was
eight A.M. Kate had been up all night and was still wearing the jeans and black polo shirt she'd put on after Joel
left for the supermarket. She'd managed to make it until
seven before calling Elena and telling her what had happened. Seven, she figured, was reasonable; seven was not
panic.

"Maybe he was more upset about the dog than he let
on," Elena was saying. She'd come right over when Kate
called, not even stopping to brush her hair. Under her red
ski jacket she was still wearing an old flannel nightgown.
"Maybe it rattled him, and he's, well, taking some time
away."

"It doesn't sound like Joel," Kate replied. She took an-

other sip of hot black coffee. "But if there was some kind
of accident, I would have heard by now. He always carries
ID, even when he just goes out to walk Hermann." She
started pulling the gauze bandages off her hands and
wrists—so the hot cup would sting a little against the
places where her skin was burned. She thought the pain
would help her think.

"You called the hospitals?" Elena asked.

"Yeah, *and* the county police, *and* the Lewisburg police, but they won't lift a goddamn finger until he's offi-
cially a missing person. Even then, they'll drag their feet.
To them it's pretty obvious what happened here: He left
me. Moved on to greener pastures."

Elena hesitated before saying, "You're sure that's not
it?"

"Shit, you, too?" Kate said. With Joel gone, Elena was
her only close ally left, her only defense against cops and
neighbors and all their theories about why a middle-aged
husband would leave his wife without telling her. She
couldn't stand the thought that Elena might have doubts
about the marriage. "I don't know if that's the explanation," Kate said finally. She breathed in the steam from
her cup, then slowly let it out. "Who can ever say for
sure? But it just doesn't feel like that. I would have sensed
something."

Hermann got up from his place next to the stove and
pushed his snout into Kate's hand. She stroked his graying
black head. The idea of Joel carrying on a secret love
affair shook Kate deeply. She didn't think she was naive
about these things—she'd known a lot of straying cops in
her day—but she'd always felt that Joel was incapable of
anything like common infidelity. If he really fell for someone else, he would be honest with her about it. He
wouldn't sneak around and then run off without a word.
Joel had more dignity than that.

"No," she said then, shaking her head. "It's got to be something else."

Elena stared down into her cup, looking embarrassed. "He'll be back," she said softly.

Kate wished she could be so sure. She still had instincts—street instincts—and what they were telling her right now was not encouraging. Joel's disappearance alone was frightening enough, but the torching of the dog made it seem even more ominous to her. The fact that the two incidents happened only a few hours apart couldn't be a coincidence, Kate felt. But what was the connection? If there was a cause-and-effect here, why couldn't she figure it out?

Earlier that morning, at first light, she'd been out in the yard looking for clues. She knew that any investigation of the attack on Pearlie would come later, if at all—after Joel was missing for more than two days. By then, any evidence would have been trampled over, snowed on, or blown away. The county cop last night hadn't even bothered to cordon off the yard with yellow crime-scene tape. So Kate had decided to have a look around herself. First, she'd found the empty kerosene can, a rusty red five-gallon, sitting where John Peters had put it down the day before, near the open crawl space. Pulling on an old pair of gardening gloves, she slowly lifted the can by the sides, careful not to smudge any possible latent prints. She sniffed: the sweet, sharp smell of kerosene. "The accelerant," as she would have called it in earlier days. She took the can inside and put it in the basement until somebody could dust it.

Kate went back to the yard then to check for dropped items, footprints—anything. The cold air crept down her collar as she stopped to pick up what looked like a burnt match but turned out to be a piece of dry grass. She went over to the cedars where she'd seen the flash of brown during the party. She found a few broken branches at waist height, but that could have been from anything.

After a while she went inside, discouraged. She felt her energy flagging from lack of sleep, so she took a couple of ginseng pills from the medicine cabinet in the master bathroom. She looked at the label on the bottle. Joel, who'd studied botany at New Mexico State University, was a collector of exotic botanicals, smart drugs, traditional medicines, and just about anything else that made the FDA uncomfortable. He had accounts at four health food stores in the D.C. area, and always kept the house stocked with everything from echinacea, a flower extract that he swore could prevent colds, to L-glutamine, egg lecithin, and piracetam, all of which were supposed to "enhance cognitive ability." He wasn't against a joint now and then, either, and had even talked her into watching his back once during a little experiment with Ecstasy. Kate herself had become a regular user of two or three of his tamer herbs and drugs, enjoying more than anything else the sense they gave her of defying the puritanism of her cop upbringing. But even so, she always found herself going back to the basics: alcohol, her mother's drug of choice, and caffeine, the drug of everybody else in her family.

So it was caffeine that she had turned to when Elena came over at seven. And now, an hour later, as they sat at the kitchen table trying to make sense of everything that had happened, it was starting to have an effect. Four cups of mocha java were more than enough to make Kate jittery, but she couldn't bring herself to stop drinking it. If nothing else, she told herself, the jitteriness would keep her alert.

"Maybe he's gone out to Assateague or something," Elena was saying, still spinning out possible explanations. "Men like to look at the ocean when they're upset. It makes them feel deep."

Kate managed a smile. "Joel isn't a big fan of the beach. He can't even swim."

"Ha," Elena said, looking over at her. "You're joking, right?"

"He says he never got a chance to learn. His father died when he was four, and he didn't have any brothers or sisters to teach him. Besides, he grew up in the desert."

"You'd think a smart man like him would be able to figure it out on his own."

"Yeah, I'm sure he would figure it out if you pushed him into a swimming pool. Joel's a fast learner." This was a try at an offhand comment, but it brought an image to her mind—of the Saab wagon skidding off a bridge somewhere into a half-frozen reservoir; of Joel inside, his forehead bleeding, his mouth open, his palms spread white on the window of the car as it sank.

Kate stood up suddenly, just as the phone began to ring. She froze for a second, staring at Elena, then walked across the kitchen to answer it.

"Kate. Hi." The voice wasn't Joel's. "Any word yet?"

"No." Kate mouthed the word "Don" to Elena. "How's Pearlie?"

"They put her to sleep."

Kate felt her hip bump the edge of the kitchen counter. "Oh Don," she said. "Shit. She didn't seem all that bad when they took her."

"She was in a lot of pain. Second-degree burns, some third-degree. It would've been cruel to do anything else."

Kate put her hand out to feel for Hermann. He licked the burns around her knuckles.

"Anyway," Don went on, "we appreciate what you did. Tried to do."

"Listen, you don't think there's any connection between this thing with Joel and what happened to Pearlie, do you?"

"Connection?"

"It just seems so suspicious, you know? Both things happening on the same day?"

"You think the person who set fire to Pearlie took Joel or something?"

"Hell, I don't know what I think. I've been up all night." Kate looked out the window over the sink. A light snow was being whirled around by the wind, looking festive and hopeless at the same time. "Don, what were you and Joel arguing about yesterday?"

He waited too long before answering. "Some business. This problem with the vanilla shipment."

Kate knew he was putting her off—just the way Joel had done the day before. For a second, she considered digging in and demanding the truth. But she knew Don. She would only hurt her chances of ever getting any information from him if she pushed him now. And she couldn't imagine that he'd keep something from her if it could help explain Joel's disappearance.

"Just give me a call as soon as you hear any news," Don said. "And is there something we can do? I'd put Jeannette on the phone, but she's still shaken up."

"I'm okay," Kate told him. "Elena's with me. I'll be okay."

She hung up and turned to Elena. "They had to put Pearlie down," she said. "The burns were too bad."

Elena shook her head. She crossed her arms tightly across her chest. "God," she said.

Kate walked back to the table. "You know," she said, not looking at Elena, "back in Chicago once, there was this case, this missing-person case, that a detective friend of mine was working on. Some forty-year-old fireman, with a wife and two kids, and he went missing one day. The wife found a suicide note after he was gone, and then the guy's shoes and socks turned up on the shore of Lake Michigan somewhere. Everybody thought it was an open-and-shut case: suicide by drowning. Except the wife. She

said she was sure her husband didn't commit suicide. She
said she knew it, absolutely, in her heart."

"And?" Elena said, watching Kate closely. "She was
right, right?"

Kate shook her head. "No, she wasn't right. The husband washed up a few days later. No sign of foul play."
Kate rubbed her cold hands together. "The guy killed himself. As simple as that."

Kate turned to the stove. She looked down at her hands.
The burns were still red and slick, like swipes of lipstick
across her wrists and fingers. "As simple as that," she said
again, reaching for the coffeepot.

Kate sent Elena home after lunch. She spent most of the
afternoon making calls and pacing around the living room
and kitchen, compulsively eating peanuts and barbecue
potato chips left over from the dog party. Every time the
phone rang, Kate's mind sped through all kinds of pos-
sibilities—some of them hopeful, some not—but the call
was always another friend or neighbor, needing another
explanation from her.

Finally, she showered, changed into one of Joel's old
T-shirts and another pair of jeans, and brushed her hair.
It was now past three. Three o'clock was a deadline she'd
set for herself—the time when she'd have to admit that
Joel was really gone, that he wouldn't be walking in the
door with a sheepish look and an embarrassed explanation. Now that he had been missing for almost a full night
and day, she felt justified in violating his privacy.

Kate opened the door to the basement, turned on the
light, and went down to Joel's office, Hermann following
on her heels.

Joel was an organized man. His home office—just off
the downstairs family room, beyond the door that led to
the backyard—was immaculate. His Macintosh sat
squarely on a glass-topped desk, the cables to the printer

and the wall outlet held together neatly with the green
twist-ties he took from every newly opened box of gar-
bage bags. On the paneled walls around the desk were
pictures from his travels: a shot of Joel at the Great Wall
of China with some kind of official delegation, another of
Joel sitting on an elaborately jeweled elephant in India,
Joel at Angel's Falls in . . . where was it? Bolivia? Taped
to the monitor was a quotation clipped from *The New
York Times*: "The difference between computers and LSD
is that computers keep getting better and better and LSD
never got any better at all."

Kate pressed the red button on the surge protector. The
computer came to life with a reassuring chime. Hermann,
realizing that he was in for a long wait, flopped down on
the Chinese rug in the corner.

She went over to the beige file cabinet and pulled out
the top drawer. Inside were files and folders labeled with
the names of foreign businesses—names like Escalante
Exports, Chin Ho Liu Trading, Thiong Kai and Associ-
ates. She opened a couple of the folders and skimmed the
documents inside. They were mostly copies of invoices,
bills of sale, typical business correspondence. Kate sighed.
She had no idea what she was looking for. "Okay," she
told herself aloud. "Think like a cop."

She looked through the other file drawers. In the bottom
one, she found an Amnesty International date book. She
turned to the page for yesterday. Nothing. Nothing the
day before or the day after, either. In fact, it looked as if
Joel had stopped using this book sometime in the spring.
The earlier pages were filled with appointments, meetings,
lunches. But after April, there was nothing marked except
personal dates: their third wedding anniversary in May,
estimated-tax payment deadlines, the anniversary of his
mother's death (when, as part of some ritual he'd never
explained to her, he would carry orchids and a bottle of
tequila out to her grave in the cemetery near Alamo-

gordo). Kate assumed that he must have switched to a different date book. She rummaged through the rest of the files and then through the drawers of the desk but couldn't find one.

Finally, she turned to the computer. She grabbed the mouse and started scanning through the contents of the hard drive. Joel backed up his business correspondence every night, transferring files by modem from the computer at the office in D.C., printing out the important ones and putting them away in the cabinet. That's why there were folders on the hard drive with the same names as the paper files—Escalante, Chin Ho Liu—and many of the same documents in electronic versions. But there were lots of other folders, too, with names she didn't recognize. Sighing again, Kate sat down. She only wanted to do this once, so she wanted to do it right.

She searched for hours, stopping only to take Hermann out for a walk and to make more coffee. She moved from Joel's Word and Excel files to his Internet newsgroup and e-mail directories. She opened every message—on his desktop hard drive and on the hard drive of his laptop PowerBook. Most of the messages were personal; Joel had e-mail correspondents all over the world—people he'd met on trips, old friends from college, people he knew from the Internet and who shared his interests in computers, herbs, smart drugs, and strange third-world music. Kate skimmed through these letters, feeling guilty. If Joel had a mistress—someone he was in bed with now, not thinking of his wife—would they have exchanged hot, sexy e-mail? Would the evidence be here, in electronic form? Probably, she thought, feeling a surge of jealousy. But she wasn't finding anything even remotely suspicious.

Then, deep down in his received-mail folder on the desktop, she reached a few short messages with a blank field for the sender's name and an e-mail address for Joel that she'd never seen before. Most of these were full of

long series of numbers that could have been anything, but
there was one message that made her stop. It said: "4607
through BK unlocatable. Pursue your end. No communication." Then, a few skipped lines below that message,
was what seemed to be a quotation: "Note the following:
It is said that the effect of eating too much lettuce is soporific." Kate hit the PageUp key and looked through the
routing information at the top of the message for the
sender's address. She found it, though it didn't mean
much to her: X2YL9@bioper.com. She turned on the
printer and made a copy of the message.

It was now past nine o'clock. Exhaustion had snuck up
on her. Taking the e-mail message with her, she went
upstairs to lie down. She shut the door of the bedroom
behind her, kicked off her shoes, and walked over to the
dresser. The top was cluttered with bottles of hand lotion,
a few lumpy pots she'd thrown in a ceramics class when
she first came to D.C., a framed picture of her parents—
dressed up and looking almost happy—at her cousin's
wedding. Kate rubbed some ointment on her cheeks and
hands, then went over to the double bed and climbed under the covers. She would try to get some sleep now—an
hour or two, just enough to keep her going. Afterward,
she'd go on with her search. She'd check the closets, the
drawers, the attic. But now she would sleep.

Hermann, looking puzzled but grateful, hopped up and
curled over her legs. Sleeping on the bed was a luxury he
enjoyed only when Joel went away on business.

Kate dug her feet deeper under his warm mass. His
damp, woolly smell reassured her, like the smell of the
ratty hand-me-down blanket she'd carried around with her
until the age of five. For a second or two, she felt a wave
of something—fear? panic?—rising up inside her, but she
quickly deflected it. This was a trick of the mind she'd
learned as a cop. Sleep, she knew, was what she needed
now. Everything else could wait.

She put out the light and fell asleep within minutes.

In the dream, which arrived with a caffeine-fueled urgency, Joel was on fire. One minute he was standing across the kitchen from her, telling her something about radishes. She wondered why he wouldn't look her in the eye. He seemed nervous, uncertain. Then, suddenly, there was a muffled, rumpling sound—like a thick carpet being shaken. Fire dashed across the house, a bright explosion that blew her hair back but gave off no heat. Confused, she watched the cold flames licking the edges of the cabinets and counters. Why had she been afraid of this? she asked herself. There was no danger here. But then she saw Joel, his hair and arms in flames, turning away and running from the kitchen. She heard the sound of splintering glass, and realized that she'd knocked over an empty vase. Jagged pieces of it lay scattered across the linoleum. Where was Hermann? she wondered. She heard his whimpering, and worried that he'd been cut by the flying glass. Then she remembered Joel.

A part of her brain pulled her up from viscous sleep. The whimpering was real, not a dream, and, her waking mind working backward, so was the sound of breaking glass. Kate sat up in bed. Hermann was at the closed bedroom door, pawing at it and whining. "Quiet!" she hissed at him. Cowed by her tone, he settled down for just a second, but it was enough—the thud was unmistakable. Downstairs, she thought. The sound seemed to come from far below, probably the basement, two floors down. There was someone in the house.

She was on her feet instantly. She hurried to the door and grabbed Hermann's collar. "Quiet, it's okay," she said, pulling him away. She stood still for a second, listening. Another sound, sharper this time, like somebody knocking together two heavy metal boxes. It had to be Joel, she thought then. He was back. He had let himself in, was probably drunk and worried about explaining him-

self. She felt the fear drop from her like a robe. Kate
opened the door. Hermann, coming to life again, shot past
her and out into the hall. She was about to call out, to say
Joel's name, when she remembered the sound of breaking
glass. It stopped her in midstep. "Hermann!" she said in
a loud whisper, but he was already scrabbling down the
stairs to the first floor.

The sounds in the basement became louder and more
urgent. Hermann was barking now. She heard him skittering across the kitchen floor below, toward the basement
steps. Afraid more for him than for herself, she called
again and turned on the hallway lights. She thought of her
pistol—unloaded and unassembled—sitting in a box at
the bottom of her closet, but she knew there wouldn't be
time to put it together and load it.

She started down the stairs to the first floor. At the
bottom, she turned a corner and the kitchen came into
view, the open basement door. She saw a thin beam of
light playing across the dark space below.

Hermann was in the basement now, snarling. He
seemed to have the person in sight and was snapping at
him. Kate's eye went to the knife block on the counter.
She ran across the kitchen and grabbed the first knife that
came to hand—a stainless-steel cleaver. As she pulled it
out of the block, she heard a muffled thump downstairs,
then silence. "Hermann!" she shouted.

She bolted toward the basement door. When she got to
the head of the staircase, she heard a door swing shut,
more glass breaking. She hit the lights. Hermann stood
wobbling at the foot of the stairs below her. She rushed
down to him. He was bleeding from a cut under his left
ear. Across the room, the door to the outside stood half
open, the glass pane broken. Kate ran over to it and peered
out. Nothing. The burglar was already beyond the light
thrown by the house. For a second or two, she considered
going after him. But she was barefoot, and unarmed ex-

cept for the cleaver. Her foot, she noticed—as if from an
enormous height—was bleeding.

She turned back. Hermann, still looking stunned, was
staggering across the room. She went back to him and put
her arm around his blood-matted neck. The cut under his
ear looked minor, but she worried about a concussion. As
she held him, his eyes gradually came back into focus.
He shook his head twice, barked, and then looked at her.

"You okay?" she asked him.

He tried to pull away. But she wouldn't let him go.
Blood seeped from her left heel, smearing the carpet. "Oh
shit," she muttered. She let the cleaver drop to the floor,
then pulled the dog's body closer to her own and began
to weep.

3

Lt. Harry Grainger squinted at the blank computer screen. He pressed a few keys on the keyboard. "I get it. It doesn't work. So what?"

Kate stood beside his chair with her arms crossed. "It worked last night, Lieutenant—that's so what."

"You're saying the guy broke your computer."

"No, I'm saying the guy erased everything on the hard drive. The computer is physically okay, as far as I can tell. It's just that there's nothing on the disk—no programs, no files, nothing. Same for the laptop."

Lieutenant Grainger kept staring at the blank screen, shaking his head. He was about forty-five, tall, round-shouldered, and a few pounds overweight. There was a sickly blue tinge to the skin of his face and hands, as if he spent most of his time in a cave. And he didn't seem to have much of a sense of humor. Kate was glad that she'd taken the quote about LSD and computers off the monitor before the Lieutenant showed up.

"I'm not sure how he did it," Kate went on, "but I think

if you have a strong-enough magnet, you can wipe the thing clean in a second."

"Erase the contents with a magnet."

"Right."

"But nothing is missing, as far as you can tell."

"Information is missing, Lieutenant. The information on the two hard disks."

"Okay. Information is missing." Lieutenant Grainger frowned and pressed a few more keys. Kate could read the feelings playing across the man's razor-burned face: Frustration. Annoyance. Distrust of technology. He obviously wasn't thrilled to be on this case. A burglary with no tangible property missing. True, there was some evidence to work with—a broken window and a home office turned upside down. But she could tell that the Lieutenant considered last night's break-in something that wasn't really worth his time, just like a burned dog or a missing husband. Kate could practically see fumes of irritation in the air around his head.

She didn't like Lt. Harry Grainger. He wasn't at all like the uniformed patrol officer who'd responded to her 911 call last night—a young Latino with the whitest teeth Kate had ever seen. That cop had been friendly and sympathetic, writing down her testimony, asking intelligent questions, promising her a full investigation. He'd even taken a look at Hermann's head wound before he left.

But Grainger—one of only two detectives on the Lewisburg force, Kate knew—was another story. There was something about the Lieutenant's whole style, from the fake Rolex to the dyed, fussily cut hair, that she disliked. Even his black overcoat bothered her. It was too clean, too fashionable to belong to a good, hard-working cop. Maybe that's why she hadn't told him about the e-mail she'd carried with her to the bedroom the night before. She could just picture him reading it, looking up at her, and saying, "Okay. A note in code. So what?"

Lieutenant Grainger pushed himself back from the computer desk. His bogus Rolex clicked on the glass-topped desk. "Look, Mrs. Baker," he began.

"Ms. Theodorus-Baker," she said, just to annoy him.

She succeeded. "Look, Ms. *Theodorus*-Baker. I'm not sure we've really got ourselves a crime here."

"What do you mean, not sure? I grew up in Chicago, but I'm pretty damn sure that breaking and entering is a crime in Maryland, too."

He heaved a big, impatient sigh. "You want to know what I think, Ms. Theodorus-Baker?" he said. "My honest opinion? I think the guy who broke into your house last night wasn't any burglar. I think, frankly speaking, that it was *Mr.* Theodorus-Baker. Who knows, maybe he forgot his toothbrush or something when he walked out, and he was coming back last night to get it."

"Right. And he just happened to have a magnet with him to erase his computer drive?"

"Maybe this information you're talking about is information he doesn't want his wife to have."

"I spent hours looking through both hard disks last night, Lieutenant. There weren't any computer love letters, if that's what you mean."

"Whatever."

"And what about Saturday?" Hermann, hearing the edge in Kate's voice, got up from his rug in the corner. "Did my husband light his partner's dog on fire, too? To distract attention from his getaway?"

Lieutenant Grainger, looking pleased that he'd rattled her, lifted himself from the office chair. "Now I've offended you, Ms. Theodorus-Baker. That pains me."

Kate was tempted to throw him out then, but she held herself back. It was time for one of them to make peace. "Lieutenant," she said, "let's take a minute here, okay? It's pretty clear that we're off on the wrong foot together . . ." She stopped, looking at the perfectly brushed curve of hair around his ears. "But to tell you the truth, I don't give a fuck. You've got a job to do. You've got somebody lighting a dog on fire in my yard. You've got my husband missing. You've got somebody breaking into my house. Maybe you're right; maybe this is all some complicated escape plan of my husband and his secret lover. But maybe not. And if you're not willing to investigate it, I'll keep making calls until I find somebody who is. Are we clear on this?"

Lieutenant Grainger was staring at her, his eyes unreadable. Kate wondered if he even took in anything she'd said after the word "fuck." He'd probably never heard a Lewisburg woman curse before, and it probably just reinforced his impression of her as some shrill wife who couldn't hold on to her husband. Kate looked down at the Lieutenant's left hand. He wore a thick gold wedding band, inlaid with showy diamond chips. So there was at least one woman in the world who found Lieutenant Grainger bearable.

He began to reply when the phone rang upstairs. Kate was grateful for the excuse to leave. "Maybe you should just get your little Peter Policeman Fingerprint Kit and start working," she said. She turned. So much for making peace, she told herself as she quickly ran upstairs.

She caught the phone in the kitchen on the third ring. "Joel," she wished silently before she said hello. But it wasn't Joel.

"Kate? I just wanted you to know that I've got your cases covered through Wednesday." It was David Streib, Kate's supervisor at Child Services, the agency she worked for part-time. She had called him the day before to tell him about Joel, and David had been smart enough to spare her the formalities; he knew that what she wanted from him wasn't sympathy but action—finding coverage for the six kids she saw every week at Holbrook House, a residential treatment facility for juveniles in the District.

"If you need it, I can get the rest of the week lined up, too."

"Thanks, David. Let's wait and see."

"Still no word?" he asked.

Kate leaned back against the kitchen counter. She considered telling him about the break-in last night but decided against it. Added to everything else that had happened, it would make her seem pitiful, and needing sympathy was something she definitely didn't want to admit to. She'd even resisted calling her brothers to tell them about Joel's disappearance. The thought of them feeling sorry for her made Kate instantly defensive. Besides, she told herself, there was still time. Joel had been gone for less than two days. "Nothing yet," she said.

"Anything I can do . . ."

"David, three neighbors have already left casseroles on my doorstep. The whole neighborhood's in sympathy mode."

"It wasn't a casserole I was offering, necessarily. Something more like a shoulder to cry on?"

Kate's jaw stiffened. "What you've done already is what I really need." She took a deep breath and started winding the spiral phone cord around the burns on her wrists. "So," she went on, "what are you telling the kids? About why I can't come. Like they really care."

"The story is you have a bad case of flu. And they do care. Whether they show it or not."

"Sure they do, David." Then, irritated by her own attitude, she added, "Thanks for everything. I'll call if anything changes."

"Please do. I know you have a tendency to tough it out and handle everything yourself, but—"

"David," she interrupted. "Come on. Enough with the fatherly lectures, okay?"

She knew she was acting like a jerk. First with Lieutenant Grainger, and now with her boss.

"Good-bye," she said quickly, and hung up before she could make things worse.

She turned and started walking toward the basement door, but then she saw the bakery box on the counter. Inside was a pear tart, left over from the party on Saturday. She would cut a piece, she decided. She would put it on a nice china plate and carry it downstairs to Lieutenant Grainger—as a peace gesture.

But she didn't get that far. As she reached for the box, which her compulsive husband had closed tight with a thick rubber band, her body gave in to gravity. She slumped into a chair. Does a man who's leaving his wife bother to take care of leftovers? she asked herself. Does he leave without his clothes, his bankbooks, his goddamn laptop computer? Not unless he wants it to look like his exit wasn't planned in advance. But was Joel capable of pulling off that kind of deception? Was he a good-enough liar to fool everybody, even Kate?

She'd met him four years ago in a museum—the East Building of the National Gallery—where she'd gone to kill time between a dentist appointment and a ceramics class. This was about a year after she'd come east. She was living in a dark, yellow-walled, overheated apartment in Adams-Morgan, taking eight graduate credits at Catholic University, changing her haircut every two months as she tried to pound out some kind of rough fit between the person she'd been back home and the better person she wanted to become in D.C. She was tired, lonely, and still feeling out of place in her new territory. Even being in that museum was a self-conscious act. The Theodoruses weren't a museum-going family. They were cops. They watched television.

And so she'd found herself, at four o'clock on a Friday afternoon, wandering past the huge Klines, feeling dense and intimidated. Then a man showed up, appearing at her side and staying with her as she walked from room to room. She snuck a few quick glances at him. He looked about five or ten years older than she was—tall, thin, his hands pushed deep into the pockets of an unbuttoned gray overcoat. His maroon scarf and tie were both loose around his neck, giving him a careless, casual look that she liked. She could tell that he'd been watching her, too. She thought of stalkers, serial killers, good anonymous sex. In spite of herself, she didn't move away from him.

"You don't feel at home here," he said finally, stepping around into her line of sight.

His brown eyes were glassy—something that aroused her old street caution. She'd seen a lot of coke addicts with eyes like those.

"And that," she answered, "is a pretty rude thi..g to say to a stranger."

"True. You're right. I'm sorry." He held up his hands, surrendering. "But I'm not wrong, am I?"

She crossed her arms in front of her chest. "Maybe, maybe not."

He moved again until he was standing right in front of her. She caught his smell—of wool and aftershave and something medicinal. "Let me guess," he said. "A messy divorce, no children, and now a new life in a new city—a new life with plenty of museums, concerts, pottery classes—"

"Wrong," she said, interrupting him. "And fuck you." She turned and began walking away.

He caught up with her and planted himself in her path. His longish hair fell over his forehead in a way that seemed too youthful for his age. She had a quick impulse to hit him, to surprise him with a few of the martial-arts moves she'd learned back at the police academy. But she had to admit that a part of her was intrigued. The ones who persisted beyond "fuck you" were usually the good ones.

She let herself be talked into coffee. They went down-

stairs and sat in the museum café, surrounded by the echoing sounds of silverware, thick plates, and children. He
did most of the talking. One of her conditions for being
there was that he tell her about himself first, and, like most
men, he clearly had no problem with this. "Let's see," he
began, drumming the sides of his coffee mug with his
long fingers. "I guess you'd call me a businessman. I own
an importing company—carpets, furniture, tea, spices. All
from small, locally owned companies in the Third World.
It's one of the things we try to do—encourage small businesses in poor villages, mostly in places like Brazil and
Indonesia."

"It sounds very . . ." Kate stopped, looking for the right
word. What first came to mind was "left-wing," but what
she finally said was "selfless."

Joel laughed. "Nope, we're a business like any other
business," he said. "We don't pretend to be selfless."

"But it sounds like you have some kind of philosophy,
at least."

Joel seemed to think about this for a few seconds,
glancing over at the moving walkway carrying people into
the café. "Okay, yes," he said, bouncing his knees up and
down under the table. "We do have a philosophy, but it's
changed over the years. We were pretty unrealistic when
we first started."

"Who's we?"

"My partner, Don, and I. We went to New Mexico State
together, back in the late sixties, early seventies. That's
where we got the idea for the company: From the Rainforest Imports, Incorporated. Catchy, isn't it?"

Kate rolled her eyes. "Yeah, real catchy," she said. She
had to admit that she was starting to enjoy herself. There
was a confidence and intensity to Joel that attracted her.
Here was a man that her family would instantly mistrust.
Too smart, too sure of himself, too rich. But the way he
leaned forward, his hands and legs in constant motion,

made her wonder if he was on something. What would he say when he found out she used to be a cop? Would the attentiveness in his face drain away? Would he start to look nervous and then make some lame excuse to get away? She'd seen enough dopeheads in her day to be suspicious. During her six months with the Chicago North Sex Crimes Unit as a decoy prostitute she'd seen plenty of prosperous, good-looking men like Joel cruising the streets for drugs. The fact that they wore Italian suits and carried leather briefcases didn't mean that they weren't addicts. So she decided to keep her distance for the time being. When her turn came to talk, she told him mostly about her studies at Catholic, then a little about her work with ghetto teenagers, but she didn't tell him about her previous job. That information, she thought, could wait a while longer.

After the coffee ran out, they made a dinner date for the next Saturday. He offered to pick her up, but she told him she'd meet him at the restaurant. He gave her his number and his name: Joel Baker. It sounded like an alias. She decided not to give him her own number yet.

Kate was relieved—when Saturday came and she saw the little Italian trattoria in Cleveland Park—that Joel hadn't felt it necessary to take her to a really expensive restaurant. Her brothers always accused her of being contrary, of stubbornly refusing to be impressed by anything that was *supposed* to impress her, and Kate knew that they had a point. If Joel had taken her to some fancy Washington restaurant full of senators and cabinet members, she'd probably have written him off before she even sat down.

She was wearing a simple black dress, black stockings, no jewelry—exactly what she would have worn to a Greek funeral. She noticed that a few heads turned as she made her way across the dining room.

Joel got up when he saw her and gave her a quick kiss

on the cheek. His own cheek was warm and flushed. He was wearing a forest-green cotton shirt with a maroon wool tie and no jacket.

"You look great," she said, sitting down.

He seemed surprised. "I thought I was supposed to say that to you."

"Feel free."

He smiled. "Okay. Fine. You look great, too. Black is my favorite color."

"I never could get away with wearing it back home," she said, unfolding her napkin on her lap. "My brothers would always look at me and say, 'So who died?' "

"Brothers can be tough critics, I guess."

"Tell me about it."

They ordered, agreeing to share their pastas. Still worried about feeling too hopeful, Kate spent most of the meal looking for reasons not to like Joel, but she couldn't find nearly enough of them. He was more subdued tonight, easier and funnier, digging into his penne vodka as he told stories about his old dog, Hermann, who was living with his mother back in New Mexico. Kate felt her caution dissolve away as the meal and the conversation wore on. She usually disliked what most people called "charm" (her contrariness again), but Joel's seemed different to her, with no slickness or salesmanship about it. He wasn't like the men she'd gone with in Chicago—the sweet shy cops and dull, always-respectful neighborhood boys. For one thing, he didn't back down if he said something that struck her the wrong way. Once, when he dropped an offhand comment about the Nicaraguan woman who came in twice a week to clean house and do his laundry, she interrupted him. "Oh, is she one of those poor third-world businesses you like to help out?" she asked, teasing.

He didn't seem at all defensive. "I told you before," he said. "My philosophy has changed over the years. My hippie days are over. Now I like to have my jeans laundered once in a while."

It was a good answer, she thought, and later, when he asked her to come back to his place in Chevy Chase for a drink, she agreed without hesitation.

The house Joel lived in at the time was big but not huge, a white-brick colonial tucked away in one of the quiet lanes off Western Avenue. She'd been expecting something exotic in the decor—he was an importer, after all—but the furniture was heavy oak, Mission- and Shaker-simple, masculine and solid. There were dozens of antique maps on the walls, along with a few Japanese and Indonesian prints. Only the carpets seemed really extravagant. They were thick, Persian, and richly colored. She found herself staring, wanting to take off her shoes and sink her toes into the deep pile.

When he came up behind her and put one hand carefully on her right thigh, she was ready to fall over in relief.

They made love on the futon in the upstairs guest room. Kate liked his body—lean and tight, with amazingly little hair. She was used to sex with men who had to be reminded that there was a second person in bed with them, but Joel was always attentive, licking the silky insides of her thighs, tracing the curves of her ass with his fingertips, telling her how much he loved the way the plum color of her nipples faded away at the edges. She found his energy daunting, and there were times when she wished he would just slow down and let her enjoy one thing at a time. Eventually, she had to push him away and tell him to take a breather. "Oh," he said, looking embarrassed. He pulled a lock of hair away from his eyes. "Fine. We'll continue later." Then he gave her a kiss on her eyebrow scar, rolled over, and fell asleep.

About a half hour later, as he dozed, Kate slipped out of bed and went downstairs. She stood on the thick carpet in the dark living room, naked, her arms folded over her cold breasts. She was feeling tired and satisfied. A bay window, rimmed with bookcases, looked out on the small backyard. It was snowing, and she watched the flakes as they drifted down, burying the lawn and the Adirondack chairs on the deck. This was how it was snowing on the night of her father's funeral, the night she decided to leave Chicago, to end her career on the force and put her duties to the Theodorus family behind her. Snow marked an ending then; she connected it with her own sadness. But this snow made her feel hopeful. Is this it, she asked herself, watching the yard fill with white. Is this what's next? And do I deserve it?

Joel was behind her again, the heat of his groin against her cold ass, the pressure of his mouth on her neck. "I like to sneak up on people," he said.

She lifted her chin stiffly. He'd scared her. "I didn't tell you I was a cop," she said.

There was no break in his caresses. "I thought you said you worked with ghetto kids."

"That's what I do now, here. In Chicago I was a cop."

"Oh," he said. "Okay. That explains the foul mouth. You like doughnuts, too?"

She turned and grabbed him by the shoulders. The hair was in his eyes again. He was grinning down at her, looking boyish and seductive.

Maybe I'm wrong about the cocaine, she told herself. And if not, maybe I don't care.

"A cop, huh?" he went on, pulling her to his damp chest. "You wouldn't still have your handcuffs, would you?"

She bit him, harder than she meant to, and then they made love again on that gorgeous Persian rug.

"Excuse me?"

Kate nearly jumped out of the kitchen chair. Lieutenant Grainger was standing in the doorway to the basement, still wearing his black overcoat. Dangling from his hand were five or six plastic bags, some filled with pills, others with something dark and organic-looking. "Look at what I found," he said.

Kate got up and walked toward him, a sick feeling in her stomach.

"Seems there was a little space in the back of your husband's file cabinet," he continued, "filled with goodies." He shook the bags at her. "Maybe this is what your intruder was looking for. Who knows what these little capsules contain?"

"Don't get your hopes up, Lieutenant," Kate said, trying for confidence in her tone. "Have you ever heard of something called 'smart drugs'?"

"And what might they be?"

"Totally legal, for one thing. They're supposed to boost your brain power. Nootropics. You can buy them in Europe and Mexico and import them—legally—for your own personal use."

"Sorry, Ms. Baker, you're already beyond me."

"Yeah, I'm not surprised," Kate said, unable to stop herself. "They're drugs that aren't approved yet by the FDA for this kind of use, that's all. You can find some in every medicine cabinet in the house. Piracetam, vasopressin. It was something my husband was interested in."

"Maybe, maybe. But then I wonder why he hid these in particular." He tossed the bags onto the kitchen table. "And what about these two bags? Looks to me like magic mushrooms and peyote buttons. Which, unless this is a wigwam and your husband's last name is Big Rock by the River, *are* illegal. At least in Maryland they are."

Kate stared down at the plastic bags on the table. She could hear her husband's voice talking about "recreational botanicals." Was it such a huge step from pot and ginkgo to magic mushrooms? Joel was always curious, almost recklessly curious, taking things like antidepressants just to see what they would do. But when would he have used hallucinogens like peyote buttons, and so many of them? She was hardly ever gone from the house for more than a few hours at a time.

Kate didn't know what to say. She didn't know what to think. Joel, again, had ambushed her.

"Can I use your telephone, Ms. Baker? I think I'd like to get some people over here."

She nodded. Then, the implications of those bags now sinking in, she shook her head. "Hold on, Lieutenant. I'm formally withdrawing my consent to this search."

Lieutenant Grainger shook his head. "It's a little too late for that, isn't it?"

Kate moved toward the door to the basement.

Lieutenant Grainger stepped into her path. "I don't think you should go down there, Ms. Baker," he said.

Her hand went to her hair, to her earlobe. Again she found herself trying for a confidence she didn't feel. "We've got a probable-cause issue here, Lieutenant," she said. "This search is illegal."

"We'll just let a judge decide about that," he said, picking up the bags from the table. "In the meantime, I'd appreciate you staying in my sight for a while. Until the other officers show up." Lieutenant Grainger grinned happily as he reached for the kitchen telephone. "Maybe you could make us all some coffee."

4

On the day after he found the buried corpse, Evan Potter left school early. Passing his house without going in to drop off his books, he headed for the woods, straight toward the little egg-shaped pool under the oaks. He was starting to feel nervous. Gray clouds were moving in from the northwest. Evan worried that a hard rain would wash the leaves away from the corpse, making it easy for someone to find. He ran as fast as he could over the roots and rocks in his path, slipping twice in the mud and almost falling.

The hours since he'd left the body had been torture for him. Evan usually loved secrets—hoarding them like money, like extra power points in a computer game—but this secret was almost too huge to bear. At dinner the night before, he'd tried to make normal conversation with his mother and Aunt Rita, but the situation was just too weird. The two of them talked about firewood—where they would get the winter's supply. The man they bought from last year had given them unseasoned wood, and

Evan's mother wanted to call somebody else this time.
Both women seemed totally upset about this, as if it really
mattered, as if firewood could be worth even a minute's
thought at a time like this.

Afterward, Evan had left the table and gone to his
room, closing and locking the door behind him. He put
on the TV—an old "Bewitched" rerun—but couldn't
stand to watch it. He paced around the room at first, whispering. Then he lay on his bed and just stared at the ceiling, fingering the gold cross in his earlobe, thinking about
the body in the woods.

Finally, he'd turned his computer on. After logging on
to his Internet account, he connected to the Usenet newsgroup with the police photographs. He read through some
of the messages attached to the picture files: "Gang hit
10/14/92. allged Gambino fam. 4 mins at 28.8 but worth
it." "Female prostitute; Detroit; don't lose your lunch over
this one!" "2 for 1 gay new orleans. veryvery sick." He
thought about posting a picture of the headless corpse on
this same electronic bulletin board. It would be easy
enough to do: he'd just have to get his mother's camera,
photograph the body, and digitize the pictures on the
school's scanner when nobody was around. He wondered
what message he would write to go with the picture file.
Would he make it serious, or would he try to be cute, the
way so many people on Usenet were: "unidentified male,
franklin MD. look, ma, no hands (or head neither!!!)."

Thinking about this—this and a hundred other things
having to do with the corpse—Evan had stayed awake
until three A.M.

And now, racing through the woods after school, he
thought again about taking pictures of the body, posing it
straight and stiff on the stream bank. It would be no problem sneaking the camera out of the house, but how would
he get the film developed? Could he take film like that to
the Fotomat booth in the parking lot of the Giant?

Wouldn't the person who developed the pictures report him to the police?

The woods were already turning dark by the time Evan reached the pool. When he saw that the mound of leaves was exactly as he'd left it, he felt relieved. For now, he thought, God had spared him. The body was safe, and so was he.

Evan put his schoolbooks on a rock and got the gloves he'd left the day before. After pulling them on, he knelt and began clearing leaves away from the body. He worked quickly, uncovering the body with gentle brushes of his hands, like an archaeologist in a film sweeping rock dust off an old skeleton. When he'd cleared most of the leaves away, he stepped back, took off the gloves, and studied the corpse again.

Today it seemed less pale than before, the skin a strange yellow-green. Evan wondered what could have made the body turn that color, so different from his own light, freckled complexion. The color didn't seem natural, even for a dead, bloodless corpse. Evan started thinking about who this person could have been and how he'd ended up dumped in the woods. But the missing head made it hard to think of this body as a person who was once alive and breathing, walking around, buying cigarettes, watching TV. This man had obviously gotten into trouble. Evan wondered if he'd been a criminal—somebody who had become too powerful for the liking of his evil rivals, maybe—or an intruder who had slipped past the defenses of his enemies. He thought of Ice Assault, the computer game he played compulsively for hours every night. Had this man been like the Stone Warrior, wandering alone in the Frozen City, entering Arctic Hole or the Temple of Friga, fending off dozens of enemies attacking from every direction? Ice Assault was different from a lot of other games. You got no second life in the Ice World; when you died, you died. The wizards and

snow devils danced a victory jig over your body, celebrating your destruction. Would they cut off your hands
and head as souvenirs of their triumph? The idea seemed
reasonable to Evan, but you never knew what happened
after death in Ice Assault, because you were finished, paralyzed on the floor of the Silver Fortress or the P'torian
Glacier, with no one to mourn for you.

Thinking about Ice Assault made Evan nervous again,
and he looked around carefully, listening for movement
in the woods. Probably no one would be walking here on
such a cold day, but he couldn't be sure. Evan wondered
what kind of trouble he could be in if they found him
with the corpse. Would they think he had killed the person? Would they think that he was a pervert of some
kind?

He remembered the only other time he'd ever seen a
real dead body. It was at the wake for his grandmother,
his father's mother, when he was six years old. He remembered the strange, shiny-gold wallpaper of the funeral
home; the thick blue carpeting; the heavy, important look
of men in black suits smoking cigarettes in doorways.
Evan was dressed in a little suit himself. He was sitting
in the warmth of his mother's lap as she sat on a folding
chair, talking to relatives he'd never met before. The smell
of perfume was all around him. At the other end of the
long room was an open coffin. Inside lay his grandmother—or something that was supposed to be his grandmother. She wore a black dress, and her small white hands
were clasped together on her chest. Evan kept looking at
her, then turning away, then looking again. The face bothered him. It was like a bad wax version of his grandmother's face—too pale, too narrow and shriveled, as if
somebody had drained all of the juice from it.

Evan was the only child at the wake. Adults stood
around in the halls or in the long room with the coffin,
some crying, some smiling and looking brave. No one sat

in the first three rows of chairs in front of the coffin. Evan remembered wondering if it was because you could catch something from the corpse—a disease of the body or the mind. Maybe death was contagious. People would walk up to the coffin, kneel on the upholstered ledge in front of it, then quickly turn away.

That was before his father kissed it—before his own father kissed the dead body's lips. It happened just as they were leaving. The room had emptied out. The only people left were his parents, Aunt Rita and Uncle Dave, and some men who worked at the funeral home. They were all putting on their coats, his mother kneeling to zip Evan's coat up to his chin. Evan saw his father standing over the body with his head bowed. Then, incredibly, his father bent down and put his face into the open coffin. The sight stunned Evan. It was like watching a person eating rat poison, or turning a gun to his chest and firing. His father was sucking in the disease from that mouth. He was contaminating himself. He was killing himself.

A little while later, his father was dead. Dead to Evan, at least—gone forever. Everyone said that he'd just run away, that he was too upset to go on with the same life. But Evan knew that his father's leaving had something to do with that kiss.

He remembered getting up the morning after the funeral feeling scared and empty. It was a school day, and no one had come to wake him up. He padded out of his room and down into the living room. His aunt was there, which didn't make sense, since she and his uncle had left the day before, right after the service. But here she was again, looking pale, with a mouth as wrinkled and tight as his grandmother's.

"Where's Mom?" he said.

"She's not feeling so good today," his aunt said. She took his hand and led him to the couch. "Evan," she said, "Daddy has gone away."

He was too surprised and confused to say anything except, "Whose Daddy?"

His aunt's eyebrows wrinkled. "Your father," she answered. "He's gone away. At least for a while. I don't know. He won't be living here with you and your mom anymore."

"Where's Mom?" Evan said again, trying to start over.

"She's in her room. She doesn't—"

He was already up and running toward the stairs.

"Evan, leave her alone now," his aunt said from behind him. "She doesn't want to see anybody."

He took the stairs two at a time. His parents' bedroom was at the end of the hall, next to his own room. The door was shut. He ran up to it and knocked. When there was no answer, he knocked again, louder, and yelled, "Mom?"

"Not now," his mother's voice said, muffled by the door. "Later."

"Mom!"

"Later," she said.

Evan pictured her inside, sitting on the edge of the bed, twisting a tissue in her hand. Maybe she was dying, too. Maybe his father had kissed her and infected her with the disease of death. "Let me in!" he shouted then, rattling the doorknob.

"I can't, Evan," the voice said. "Go away now."

Trying not to cry, Evan fell to his knees in front of the locked door. His mother was dying. He had to save her. She needed him, but he couldn't get to her. He couldn't help.

And now, as he stood in front of the uncovered body in the woods, he was starting to feel helpless in exactly the same way. He had breathed the air of this corpse. He was infected, and now he would change, too, just as his mother had changed after his father left. Evan would turn into a different person—harder, colder. He would die in the same way she did.

Evan looked down at the corpse. Why had God made this happen to *him*, he asked himself. At first, it had seemed like an amazing stroke of luck, finding this thing, something hugely important that no one else knew about. But the body was more frightening to him today. He knew that this whole situation could get out of control. What would happen when the flesh started rotting? It would smell. Insects would get to it, maybe a dog or a raccoon or a coyote. He'd even heard of dead bodies exploding— it was something he'd read about in history class, in a book about the Great Plague. Some kind of gases filled the skin of the dead person like a balloon until it burst.

Evan realized then that it was raining. Drops were hitting the leaves around the corpse. The sound got steadily louder—not because the rain was getting harder but because it was turning into sleet. Evan pulled up the collar of his leather jacket, tucking his ponytail inside. It had gotten cold early this year. That's why his mother and aunt kept talking about firewood. "Coldest November in years," his mother kept muttering at the dinner table. "We'll have to spend a fortune on wood." How could he even think of telling this woman that he'd found a body in the woods? Would she even understand what he was saying? She'd probably think he was confused, that he got it wrong somehow. Evan could imagine her reaction: "He can't even tell what's real and what's on television now."

Evan began to cry. He sank to the ground, sitting back and feeling the cold and wet through the seat of his jeans.

He didn't cry for very long. After a minute or two, the panicky feeling passed. He wiped his nose on his sleeve, embarrassed. Crying was something he'd told himself he was going to give up. He was too old to cry. He was fourteen now.

Evan got to his feet again. He had made a decision. He picked up the work gloves, damp now from the freezing

rain, and put them on. Then he slowly began reburying
the headless body in leaves. He covered the middle first,
then the legs and feet, then the chest. As he worked, the
sleet kept rattling all around him. But just as he was covering up the thin, mutilated arms, silence moved in suddenly, like something sneaking up behind him. He looked
into the sky. The sleet had turned to snow, a damp swirling snow. For a second, he felt as if he were on a space-
ship, passing stars and solar systems at high speed. This
made him feel better. The snow was a sign of God's approval. It told him that his decision was right.

Evan hid the work gloves under the rock again. Then
he got to his feet and picked up his schoolbooks. Without
looking back at the mound of leaves, he headed home.

Nobody was in the house when he got back. Evan let
himself in the front door, put down the books, hung up
his jacket, and went to his room. He turned on the computer and paced around impatiently as it booted up. He
was not going to change his mind, he told himself. When
the computer was ready, he turned on the modem and
started working. Using a borrowed account and password
he'd picked up on one of the hacker bulletin boards, he
accessed the Usenet newsgroups. When he got to the
group with pictures of crime victims, he opened a message
window and started typing as fast as he could: "let's say
u walk in the woods and u find a dead body and u don't
tell about it for awhile. what if anything can they do to u
if they find out. and what should u do if u find it. it doesn't
have a head or hands and is yellow but not rotten yet. this
is a serious message not a joke."

He quickly closed the message and posted it, afraid he
might lose his nerve if he thought too long about what he
was doing. Then he sat back in his chair and watched the
screen. He knew that the message would be impossible to
trace, no matter what happened. The fake username he'd
used was registered to some private prep school in Indi-

ana. These people had pitiful security on their system. They had no idea that their accounts were accessible to anybody with the brains to find them.

After a few minutes, Evan shut off the computer and turned on the television. He was feeling better already. His mother would be home from work in an hour. He'd eat with her and his aunt, watch a little more television, and then come back to his room. By that time at least one person would have read the message and answered it. Somebody else would be thinking about his situation. Somebody else would give him an idea of what he should do.

For the second time in two days, Evan had to sit through an agonizing dinner conversation. His mother and aunt, sisters only two years apart in age, with the same red hair and sharp-nosed faces, were talking about Thanksgiving and the people they would ask over to dinner. Aunt Rita kept suggesting names, but Evan's mother found some reason not to invite every one of them—this person because she was a snob, that person because she couldn't talk about anything but her boyfriend's house in the mountains. Evan thought about last Thanksgiving, when his aunt Rita had invited two divorced women from her office. He remembered them all sitting around the dining room table, four women in their fifties and himself, giving thanks for a dinner of turkey and salad—no corn, no baked potatoes with sour cream, no cranberry sauce. One of the women had brought crumbcake. He remembered them all oohing and aahing over it, as if crumbcake could be a real dessert.

"I've got some homework to do," Evan said now, under his breath, as he got up from the table.

His mother eyed him. "You make sure it's homework and not just fooling around on the computer."

"Right," he said. He put his plate in the sink and ran up to his room.

There were already three answers to his posting. Evan clicked his mouse to open the first one: "This newsgroup is for binaries. If you have a picture of this body in the woods, post it. Otherwise nobody's interested. Stop screwing around A-HOLE!!!!"

"Dickhead," Evan said aloud. He moved to the second response in the thread: "If it doesn't have a head or hands, that means somebody doesn't want it to be ID'ed. Mob assassins do it all the time, crude but basic technique. But there are ways of ID'ing bodies w/o fingerprints or facial features. It's just that they take a long time and use technologies that most county and city crime labs can't afford. The feds can do it easy though. I've heard the FBI is working on a database that would let them match up blood/skin/hair DNA samples to a list of anybody who ever was arrested or ever applied for a gov't job, and come up with a match w/in hours. Hey, Big Brother is watching all the time. More than we know."

That was the end of the second message. The guy hadn't even tried to answer the question. It hadn't even sunk in that this was a real situation, that Evan was looking for help.

"Dickhead," he muttered again at the screen.

The third message was the shortest and worst: "what to do w/ yr corpse, man? i say make a nice soft place in the leeves lay down and let nature take its course!! PS: post pix here after."

Evan pushed himself away from the desk. He felt his face and ears getting hot. He should have known better than to expect anything, from anybody, anywhere. He threw himself down on his unmade bed. He grabbed his Walkman from the night table, put on the headphones, and turned on the tape he'd been listening to last—some stupid Nirvana-ripoff band he didn't really like. He jacked up the volume as high as he could stand. And then he just lay there, staring at the cracks in the ceiling, wondering what to do next.

He woke up at 2:49 A.M., sweating, even though his mother had turned down the heat as usual. The snow had stopped, and now there was a big white moon showing through the trees outside his window.

Evan got up, pulled on a pair of thick socks, and opened his door. The house was quiet. His mother and aunt had probably been in bed since ten.

He slipped out into the carpeted hallway. The moon-light from the window threw a crooked patch of light across the floor and halfway up the wall. Evan moved through the light to the stairs. He went down into the kitchen. Without turning on a light, he picked up the phone next to the cutting board and dialed 911. When he heard a voice answering at the other end, he said, very fast, without waiting for the voice to finish its sentence: "There's a dead body in the woods off Kings Mill Road. Back pretty far by a stream and covered with leaves." Then he hung up the phone.

Evan went over to the sink. He grabbed a glass from the drying rack and filled it from the tap. The water was cloudy with air, almost as white as milk. He drank it down. Then he put the glass into the sink, went upstairs, got back into bed, and lay awake until morning.

5

" 'Rohypnol, 50-milligram tablets, 22 count; Dilantin, 100-milligram capsules, 43 count; mushroom, Stropharia cubensis, 2.5 ounces; Zoloft'—at least that name I recognize—'50-milligram capsules, 19 count; unspecified MAO inhibitor, not available commercially in the U.S. . . . 5 ounces unspecified peyote cactus . . . GH-3 procaine . . . 2 ounces botanical substance, probably fungal, yet to be identified.' Not to mention Percodan, Thorazine, Ecstasy; oh, and 47 morning glory seeds—was Joel planning to do some gardening?"

Adrianna Davis let the police lab report flutter out of her hand and fall to her desktop. "That's only part of the list. I left out the dried insects and animal viscera from God knows where. What in the world was Joel up to?"

Kate sat across the lawyer's desk, feeling in some way responsible for the contents of the lab report. Adrianna, another college friend of Joel's, and for the last two years their personal lawyer, was not really Kate's own friend. There was something about the older woman that Kate

had never been able to warm to. Adrianna, in her mid-
forties, was almost too beautiful—her nose thin and
straight and perfect, her long black hair streaked with
gray, her skin perfect, its coppery tone hinting at her part-
Apache background. And she was a good lawyer—wit-
nessed by the fact that she'd managed to keep Kate out
of jail after the drugs were found in Joel's file cabinet.
But there was a sense of quiet superiority in Adrianna's
attitude that bothered Kate. Adrianna was aware of her
own power—as a woman, as a lesbian, as a person
smarter and better-looking than most of the people she
dealt with—and she sometimes used that power like a
club.

"Okay, let's assume that the drugs weren't Joel's," Kate
said. "Maybe whoever broke into the house planted them
there. To incriminate Joel."

Adrianna swiveled in her oversized leather chair.
"That's the argument we make, of course," she said. "But
the problem is that only a few things on this list are
Schedule One illegal. A lot of this is fully aboveboard
with a doctor's prescription. If you want to incriminate
somebody, you plant a couple rocks of crack in their underwear drawer. There'd be no reason to leave a whole
pharmacy of pills, and in quantities that fail to establish
an intent to distribute." She picked up the list again. "I
mean, look at some of this stuff: Thorazine—that's for
schizophrenics, I checked; it has no recreational value at
all, as far as I know."

The phone on her desk began warbling. The two
women just watched it until it stopped.

"But the mushrooms and Ecstasy alone are enough to
get him into big trouble," Adrianna added.

"We both know those drugs won't be usable in court."

Adrianna threw up her hands. "I'm not so sure. The
police were in Joel's office by your consent."

"The guy was there to search for clues to the break-in!"

"You're on the record as having consented to let that Lieutenant Whoever search the premises. The state's attorney can argue that the police had every right to go into that file cabinet, and that anything they found they can use."

Kate got up unsteadily from her chair. She went over to the office window and watched the traffic crawl past on Connecticut Avenue, four floors below. Across the street, a fat man in a purple jacket was waving his arms around, directing the installation of Christmas decorations in a store window. "I can't believe I let that happen."

Adrianna's leather chair creaked lushly. "Kate, your husband was—is—missing. Somebody broke into your house." There was a music to Adrianna's voice, a lilt that always sounded more Mexican than anything else. "You did what any reasonable person would do."

Kate came back to the chair. "He couldn't have been selling all of that. I can't see Joel pushing handfuls of Percodan as a sideline. It just doesn't make sense."

Adrianna took a deep breath. "I agree with you—that doesn't sound like Joel at all. But maybe he was just experimenting. That *does* sound like Joel." Her long fingers traced the edge of the lab report on her desk. "In college, he could lick toads with the best of them. Present company included." She pushed a few strands of hair behind her ear. Kate knew that Adrianna, Joel, and Don had lived together in a group house in Las Cruces during college. After graduation they'd all decided to move to D.C. and work for the soul of the nation. Now Adrianna was a lawyer in private practice and Joel and Don were businessmen—a pretty common result, in Kate's opinion, for a group of ex-hippies.

"I tell you," Adrianna went on, "it's a good thing we never got caught back then. You can imagine what a field day your lieutenant would have if he started digging up twenty-five-year-old arrest records on Joel *and* his lawyer."

Kate could only smile weakly. This line of conversation wasn't making her feel any better.

"Look, Kate," Adrianna said, leaning forward in her chair. "I think we have to be honest with each other. We both know that Joel is . . . well, an adventurous soul. He isn't one to worry too much about what's against the rules and what's not. It's something I think we both find attractive in him."

This last comment hung in the air, humming with significance. Kate knew for a fact that Adrianna and Joel had slept together at least once in college. It was one of the things that gave an edge to every conversation she had with Adrianna. But it had happened twenty-five years ago. Now Adrianna lived with another woman—a fifty-year-old nutritionist from Pakistan, as trim and smart and beautiful as Adrianna—and didn't seem interested in men anymore. But sometimes Kate wondered. And she was wondering again now—now that she had to wonder about anything and everything connected to Joel.

Adrianna folded her hands on the desk in front of her. "Let's go on the assumption that the drugs are his and that they have something to do with his disappearance."

Kate wasn't ready to let go on this point, but she agreed anyway. "Okay, if that's true," she said, "and Joel left the house knowing he was heading off somewhere, why wouldn't he take the drugs with him? Why would he leave them there to be found?"

"Good point." Adrianna picked up a pen and began scrawling notes on a legal pad. "Assuming he left the house thinking he was coming back, what could have happened while he was out?"

"Well, he could have made contact with somebody who convinced him to disappear. Or forced him to."

"But who?"

Kate was about to mention the e-mail she'd found on Joel's computer, but her instincts told her not to. The e-mail was still a piece of this whole mess that was hers alone, and she wasn't ready to give up that advantage yet.

Adrianna went on: "I bet your lieutenant has gotten the phone logs. And I bet there was an incoming or outgoing call right before Joel left the house." She wrote down a few more notes. "I'll look into it. In the meantime, I know this guy, a private investigator, who I think you should hire. He's good. He'll find Joel if anybody can."

"No," Kate said.

Adrianna obviously wasn't used to clients refusing her advice. Especially not female clients. "I'd recommend it," she said, looking put out. "As your attorney, I'd recommend it."

"And as the person paying you, I'm not taking the recommendation. Yet. I'll think about it."

Adrianna put her hands down flat on the desk. Kate could see she was offended. "In that case, how do you want me to proceed?"

"I don't know, see what else you can do to get the original search thrown out. Maybe you can make a case that I had no right to consent to a search of Joel's office since it wasn't a jointly inhabited part of the house."

Adrianna thought this over for a few seconds. "It won't work," she said finally. "The office was a crime scene. But I like the way you're thinking. I never had a cop as a client before."

"Ex-cop," Kate reminded her. "Anyway, see if you can at least get the potential charge knocked down to a misdemeanor possession. I don't want to have a felony charge hanging over him."

"I'll try my best."

Kate got up from the chair. "Oh, and thanks for keeping me out of jail."

Adrianna smiled. "My pleasure." Kate began to leave, but just as she was stepping away from the desk, Adrianna put her hand out. "There's something else to think about," she said. "I'd have to ask you this at a certain point, so I might as well do it now. Am I acting in all of this as your attorney or as Joel's?"

"You think it makes a difference?"

She nodded. "Depending on what's really happened here, it could make a big difference."

Kate avoided meeting Adrianna's stare. She knew this was a question she should answer for herself, the sooner the better. But she couldn't stand to think of separating her interests from Joel's. He was her husband. They *had* to be on the same side. "For right now, you're *our* lawyer," she said finally. "I count on you to let me know when that won't work anymore."

"Right." Adrianna walked her to the door. They hugged stiffly. Kate, thinking of Joel and Adrianna together in 1972, let go a little too quickly. "Take care of yourself," Adrianna said. "And call me anytime—if you hear anything, if you don't. I know what you must be going through."

"Yeah," Kate said doubtfully. "Thanks."

"One more thing," Adrianna went on. "Whether or not I can get those baggies excluded, I think the police will be taking a definite interest in where you go and what you do now. They don't get too much serious crime out in Lewisburg." She shrugged. "Just something to keep in mind."

"Right."

Kate left the office, now feeling the deep fatigue of her sleepless nights. She took the elevator to the lobby of Adrianna's building and pushed through the revolving doors to the street. It was a gray Wednesday afternoon, and the damp wind gusting down Connecticut Avenue was kicking up litter from the streets. Kate barely noticed.

Her white Volkswagen Jetta—which she'd bought used when she first came to D.C. and had stubbornly kept, even after Joel offered to buy her a new one—was parked around the corner, and she'd already walked a block past it before she realized her mistake. She backtracked and found the car. A parking ticket was flapping cheerfully under the left wiper. Kate grabbed the ticket, unlocked the car, and got in.

"Two ounces botanical substance, probably fungal, yet to be identified." Somehow those words were even scarier to her than the long list of drug company trademarks and Latin names. Joel was not stupid; he couldn't have been taking even a quarter of the substances in those bags, at least not on a regular basis. But then why were they there?

She put the key in the ignition, then sat back. There had been times when Joel admitted to her that he was on something other than the usual stuff he bought at the health food store. Depending on what new smart drug he was trying out, he would become more talkative, more energetic, more focused. Kate's feelings about these experiments were mixed to begin with—one part of her disapproved while another got a thrill at the thought of defying her conservative Greek-cop upbringing—but Joel could be very convincing in his arguments about consciousness and chemistry. Nature is far from perfect, he would say, so why not fiddle with the chemistry of the brain for a better result? How is it different from taking vitamins?

Kate shook her head, resisting this argument in her mind. How had she gone along so easily with Joel's drug-taking? Sure, it had always seemed harmless enough, even exciting sometimes. Whatever the cause—the placebo effect or a real chemical boost—the herbs and drugs did have an effect on their time together. Joel could often be impatient, frustrated by every sign that the rest of the world didn't think or move as fast as he did, but some of the pills he took seemed to mellow him. Even their sex improved with some of his chemical aids. There would be a deeper hunger to Joel's lovemaking, or a sharper edge of concentration. He would be moving constantly, his head between her legs, his cheek skimming the surface of her inner thighs. His hand would slide up her wet belly to her breast and her whole body would shudder in response. She'd bite her cheek, or grasp handfuls of his hair. Suddenly, his mouth would be on hers, tasting fishy and metallic. This is my own taste, she would think, and wonder why she didn't find it disgusting. Once, as she climaxed, her tongue felt one of her own pubic hairs between Joel's teeth. Instead of pushing her back, though, it shot her ahead. She shoved him over on his back, straddled him, and squeezed him between her legs so hard that she could feel the sharp points of his hips against her own thigh bones.

Her husband, she thought now as she fingered the key in the ignition, could always be counted on to surprise her. But she had to admit that this was exactly what drew her to him. Adrianna was right.

Kate thought of the strange line in Joel's e-mail: "It is said that the effect of eating too much lettuce is soporific." It sounded like a taunt to her now, some kind of flippant reference to his secret drug-taking—as if he'd been making fun of her all along, just as he'd been making fun of the neighbors by throwing the dog party. Maybe he despises us all, she thought.

"Stop it, stop it," Kate said aloud. She leaned forward and turned the ignition key. This kind of thinking, she knew, would only drive her crazy. The thing to do now was concentrate on how to find Joel.

She drove straight home. As she turned into the driveway, Elena ran out of the house to meet her, Hermann pulling her along by the leash. Kate rolled down the window. "Why aren't you at work?" she asked. Elena had a job at a local real estate office and always claimed to be the fifth-lowest-grossing agent in Hampton County.

"With my best friend practically in jail, I'm going to go to work?" Elena opened the car door. "I spent the afternoon at the bank, juggling my account balances. I thought I might have to bail you out."

Kate pulled herself out of the Jetta. "Don't sweat it," she said. "My beautiful lesbian lawyer took care of everything. Judges can't say no to beautiful lesbian lawyers."

"Wait, Adrianna is a lesbian?"

For the first time in days, Kate laughed. "Elena," she said, "who do you think that woman was, the one who came to dinner with her that night?"

"I had no idea. But now that you mention it . . ." Elena ran her hand through what she called her "chemically assisted" brown hair. "I feel so dense sometimes."

"You're not the only one," Kate said, slamming the car door.

Kate stopped to check Hermann's cut, which looked fine, then sent him ahead as she and Elena went inside. The house still showed traces of the police search. Lamp shades hung askew, books stood at different depths on the shelves, and there were scuff marks on the floors that looked like messages written in Greek.

"Oh, the man was here to do the annual maintenance on your furnace," Elena said as they hung their coats in the hallway closet. Kate was wearing a blue silk blouse and black skirt—meet-your-lawyer clothes—and felt overdressed standing next to Elena in her gray slacks and red turtleneck. "I came over when I saw him," Elena continued. "I told him you'd reschedule. When things got back to normal."

Normal. At that moment, the word seemed to Kate like an expression of faith. "You really said that: 'when things get back to normal'?" She hugged Elena awkwardly, embarrassing them both. "Thanks."

"I'll make some coffee," Elena said, slipping out of Kate's arms, "before you tell me that you're a beautiful lesbian, too."

Kate followed her to the kitchen, Hermann clicking along behind her. "Elena," she began then, "you read a lot in college, didn't you?"

"Tons. English Victorian poetry was my specialty. It comes in handy when I'm trying to sell one of those mansions over in Breakstone."

"Think you could help me find the source of a quotation?"

She turned with the ruby-colored kettle in her hand. "Maybe. It's been years. But try me."

Wanting to get the quotation word for word, Kate went to the bedroom and got the e-mail from her night table drawer. One of Grainger's men had been through the bedroom during the search but had apparently overlooked the printed message, which was tucked in with Kate's social work newsletters and photocopied journal articles. Coming back to the kitchen, Kate said, "Do you have any idea where this is from?" She read aloud: " 'It is said that the effect of eating too much lettuce is soporific.' "

Elena shook her head. "It sounds like someone British," she said. "But other than that I haven't got a clue. Why?"

Kate studied the printout in her hand for a few seconds. "Elena," she said, "can I ask you to do something really, really boring?"

Elena's brow wrinkled. "There's probably a good joke in there about life with my ex-husband, but I'll let it pass," she said. "Sure, what is it?"

"I want you to help me find that quotation—it's probably somewhere in Joel's books."

Elena seemed to think this was a joke at first. "There are a *lot* of books in this house, Kate."

"I'm guessing the quote will be underlined. Joel had a

thing about underlining in his books. But I could be wrong."

"Can I ask why you want to find this quote?"

Kate hesitated, then shook her head. "I really think the less I tell you the better. That way nobody can accuse you of withholding evidence."

The water was boiling. "Okay, sure," Elena said finally, turning off the burner under the kettle. "Of course I'll help."

They fixed their coffees and carried them down to Joel's office. Starting with the two bookcases next to Joel's desk, they began pulling books off the shelves and flipping through each one. Kate quickly realized how long this was going to take them. Some of the books had a passage or two underlined on every page. The search could take days.

Kate and Elena worked in silence for the first half hour or so, as intent on their work as two conscientious librarians. But eventually, out of boredom, they began reading passages aloud to each other. "Oh, listen to this," Elena said: " 'The tongue and penis are the North and South Poles for the male; the lips and labia majora, the Poles for the female.' That sounds dirty, though I'm not exactly sure." She looked up at Kate. "I had no idea that Joel was such a deep thinker."

"Most of this stuff is probably from college," Kate said. "He probably hasn't looked at it since then. Don't all smart college boys read philosophy and fill the margins with exclamation points?"

Kate pulled another book off the shelf. In spite of her comment, she really was troubled by some of what Joel had underlined in his readings. One book especially bothered her. It was full of marked passages about mushrooms and shamans and the use of tryptamine hallucinogens "to attain higher levels of consciousness." Kate happened to know that Joel had bought the book sometime in the last year.

Sighing, Kate took a step back and looked over the tightly packed bookshelves. The answer to Joel's disappearance, she felt, had to be here somewhere. She remembered what an instructor of hers used to say back at the academy in Chicago: "A house is full of coded messages to the smart investigator." Kate ran her hand over the spines of Joel's books. She read the titles: *After Many a Summer Dies the Swan, The Moral Animal, Internet Yellow Pages, White Man's Grave, The Old Left, The Way of Herbs*. She remembered Joel's habit of inspecting the books of people who had them over to dinner or for a party. He said he could find out more about people from ten minutes at their bookshelves than he could from ten hours at their dinner table. A house, Kate said again to herself, is full of coded messages.

Elena, sitting cross-legged on the floor, elbowed Kate's shin. "Hey," she said, "don't tell me you're giving up already."

"Okay, okay," Kate said. She looked at the title of the book in her hand: *Civilization and Its Discontents*. More fancy college stuff. Would Freud have said anything about the soporific effect of lettuce? She didn't think so, but she was determined to look through every single book. One thing she'd learned as a cop was to do something thoroughly the first time, since you may never get a second chance.

Kate opened the book, but then looked up. "Did you ever suspect Alan of anything?" she asked Elena. "I mean, the whole thing with Blondie or whatever." "Blondie" was how they always referred to the woman Elena's husband had married. Kate had already forgotten the woman's real name.

Elena thought about the question before answering. "Yes," she said at last, "I have to say I did." She put a finger in the book to keep her place. "It wasn't anything specific, but toward the end he just seemed too happy."

Elena reached for her mug of coffee. "It sounds strange, I know. But it's true. I remember our last vacation together. We were down at his mother's house on Sea Island. First time I'd ever left the girls alone for more than twelve hours. Every day we'd get up early and swim. Alan would bring his cellular phone with him. I can remember the sound of that damn thing tootling out on the sand. I told Alan that he was making himself ridiculous with that thing at the beach, but he just shrugged it off. He'd stand with his feet in the surf and the phone in his hand, and every time a wave broke he'd have to hold it over his head. Once, I said to him, 'What do you need that phone for anyway? You have a secret lover you have to keep tabs on?' He laughed and pressed a few more buttons. Something about the way he reacted worried me. 'Do you?' I asked. He looked at me. 'No, of course not.' So I said, 'Alan, put that thing down and tell me that you don't have a secret lover that you're calling.' He rolled his eyes, but he did put the thing down. 'No,' he said, making it sound like I was some annoying child or something. 'I don't have a secret lover that I'm calling. I have an office that I'm calling, an office where I have a job that pays for vacations like this, understood?' Then he picked up the phone and started punching buttons again. I didn't want to listen, so I got up from the blanket and went down to the water to look for shells. I felt stupid and suspicious and who knows what else. Then, three weeks later, I get the divorce papers."

"Shit," Kate said.

"Exactly. It wasn't his secret lover he was calling; it was his lawyer." Elena looked over at her. "But this isn't the kind of thing I should be telling you now."

"I asked for it."

"Anyway, that was Alan. Joel is different."

"Maybe, maybe not," Kate said, rubbing her fingertips along the cover of the Freud book. "It's scary, don't you think? Marriage, living with other people, how much you have to take on faith. You can't be suspicious all the time or else it'll never work. There's this kind of trust . . ." She didn't know how she wanted to finish the sentence, didn't really know what she believed about marriage. She'd waited long enough before starting on married life herself—she was already in her early thirties when Joel proposed—but she'd felt about as prepared for it as an eighteen-year-old. Growing up in that house full of men in Chicago had somehow turned her against the idea of marriage. She loved her father and brothers fiercely, but she'd seen too much of men at home to want to run out and find one of her own to move in with. For years, she'd felt satisfied with dates and occasional sex. Then Joel had come along—Joel, who was as different from her father and brothers as he could be.

"Back to work," she said finally, opening the Freud again.

She and Elena kept searching for another few hours, but they found nothing even close to the quotation in Joel's e-mail. Eventually, Kate decided she was asking too much of her friend. After thumbing through the third volume in some Trollope novel series, she shoved the book back onto the shelf and said, "Let's stop. My eyes are ready to fall out."

Elena looked relieved. "We'll continue tomorrow," she said, struggling to her feet. "So how about some dinner? We can drive into the District if you want. Georgetown maybe?"

"Thanks, but I'll just stay here tonight." Hermann lifted his head. He'd been there on the rug the whole time— sleeping, watching them for a while, then sleeping some more.

"You're sure?" Elena asked.

"Yeah, I'm sure. But thanks for helping with this. And for taking care of Hermann. And for everything else."

They went back upstairs. "Well," Elena said as she put on her coat. "Just remember that I'm right next door. If you want to watch a movie later. Or talk."

"I'll remember." Kate saw her to the door. Outside, the November night was dark and frosty. The clouds from the afternoon had started to clear, leaving patches of blacker sky speckled with stars. "Get home safe," Kate said as she opened the door. It was what they always said when one of them was heading out on the fifty-yard walk home—a throwaway joke that didn't seem so ridiculous anymore.

"I owe the girls a phone call anyway," Elena said. "Thanksgiving's coming up. I've got to browbeat them into coming home from school. 'Night."

Kate watched with the storm door open as her friend cut across the dark lawn, through the bushes separating the two properties, and up to her own door. She waited as Elena put her key in the door, pushed it open, and then waved a last goodnight. Kate waved back. The thought of Elena being nearby was surprisingly reassuring to her. She turned and was about to go back into the warmth of the house when she saw the car at the curb across the street— a brown Caprice. She remembered it. It was one of the Lewisburg Police Department's unmarked cars. Inside, barely recognizable in this light, sat Lieutenant Grainger, watching her.

Shivering, she quickly pulled the glass door shut and closed the heavy door behind it, turning both of the locks.

6

Desmond Ellis was in one of his difficult moods. The teenager slouched in the chair across the scarred oak table from Kate, one hand over his birthmark—a bright pink splotch that ran along the edge of his jaw, behind his ear, and down the left side of his otherwise smooth black neck. Kate wondered if his silence was meant to be a way of getting back at her for two missed appointments. Desmond wasn't buying her flu excuse. He'd reacted to it with a toss of the head and a snort, as if to say, "Sure. Right. Flu." Kate wondered what he would think of the real reason for her absence: your case worker couldn't make it because she was busy trying to keep herself out of jail on drug charges. Maybe he would open up to her a little if he heard the truth. Desmond, after all, wasn't exactly a stranger to trouble with the law. He was just fifteen years old but had already been picked up twice for narcotics possession and once for assault. His father was dead, his mother was addicted to coke, and his older brother had disappeared when Desmond was ten. Who wouldn't be silent and resentful with nothing ahead of him but a few more years in Holbrook House, a few more years of locked doors, overcooked vegetables, and nervous white women showing up twice a week to ask how he was doing?

Kate looked over his file. Desmond was the third kid she'd seen that day. It was Thursday, the day after her meeting with Adrianna, and Kate had decided to pick up her six cases again, though her motives weren't totally pure. Yes, she felt an obligation toward these kids—and she actually missed one or two of them—but she'd also hoped that seeing them would distract her from the disaster her own life had turned into. "It says here you missed some vocational classes this week, Des," she said. "Is that true?"

Desmond wouldn't lift his eyes from the table. His oversized white T-shirt was draped like a parachute over his shoulders.

"Is that true?" she asked again.

The attendant in the corner of the room—an overweight Latino man who had to be present at every meeting between Kate and Desmond—shifted on his chair.

"Yeah," Desmond said after a few seconds.

"Why'd you miss them?"

Desmond grinned, still looking down at the table. "I was sick," he said. "I had the flu."

Kate took a slow breath. Desmond was her most promising kid. Every once in a while, as they were playing cards or talking about television shows, she thought she saw in him a glimmering, a hint of trust. But it always took time to reach that point.

"You had the flu? What a coincidence."

He nodded, still covering the birthmark. "Real bad. Probably caught it from you."

Kate lifted an eyebrow, trying to let him know that she was in on the joke and was willing to play along for a while. But Desmond wasn't looking. "I bet your flu wasn't as bad as mine," she said.

Desmond lifted his eyes and stared at her. "Bet it was," he said. "Bet it was worse."

Kate knew she had him interested now. She sat back in her chair and thought for a few seconds. Pale yellow light was pouring through the mesh-covered windows. The attendant in the corner was looking out at the boarded-up building across the street. "Well, shit, I threw up all over my dog," she said. "Can you beat that?"

Desmond didn't answer. He looked toward the windows, pretending to be bored, but Kate knew that she'd gotten his attention—and the attendant's, too.

"Yeah, I couldn't help myself," she went on. "He was, you know, blocking the way to the bathroom. So I threw up all over him."

Silence. Desmond started playing with a little scrap of paper on the table, folding it over and over again. Kate wondered if she'd have to say more.

"What'd he do then?" the boy asked finally.

"Who? Hermann? He did what comes natural to dogs when they get wet."

Desmond looked up. "What?"

Kate smiled, grateful for the tiny victory. "He shook it all off. Sent the whole mess flying, all over the walls, all over me. It took me two hours to clean it up."

That grin was there again on Desmond's face. "Sure," he said.

The attendant shook his head, then put his face in his hands, rubbed his eyes, and yawned.

"That's how sick *I* was," Kate went on. "How sick were you? You throw up on anybody?"

Desmond seemed to think about the question for a few seconds. Kate watched him, hoping he'd go on and say *something*. All she asked for some days was a sentence, one single sentence that wasn't offered grudgingly. It was stupid, she knew, but sometimes she felt that just getting a kid like Desmond to talk openly about anything at all would help him.

He rearranged his long legs under the table. "Not that sick," he said, looking away.

Kate closed her eyes in frustration. For the hundredth time she wondered what good she was doing here. She remembered what some of her cop friends in Chicago thought of social workers. "Futility experts" was what Vic, her partner, used to call them. "Just another way to spend even more tax money on these kids." Kate looked over at Desmond, who was slumped again in his chair, folding the paper in his fingers. Maybe Vic was right. Was there really anything she could do to keep this boy out of jail? "Have you called your mother at all, Des?" she asked.

The dismissive snort again. He seemed to have perfected it in the six days since she'd last seen him.

Kate gave up. It was obvious that she wasn't going to get anywhere with him today. "Well, it looks like you've gotten over your flu, at least," she said. "So you can go to the next class, right? Right, Des? Remember the deal."

"Right," he said.

Kate wanted to make eye contact with him before she left. "I mean it. It's useful stuff. Besides, if you miss one more, they'll drop you a level. No more Friday movies. Okay?"

Desmond looked up at her with an expression he must have used on his mother. "Okay, I said. Leave me the fuck alone."

"Hey, Ellis," the attendant warned from his corner.

"It's all right," Kate said, getting up and gathering her papers. Remember the deal, she repeated silently. Desmond wasn't the only one with a deal to keep. Seeing him and the five other boys at Holbrook was part of her own deal. One of the things she'd promised herself when she came east was that she would do something for all those kids she'd arrested in her years as a patrol cop. She would try to talk sense into them instead of putting handcuffs on them. She would find a better, smarter way of keeping them off the streets. "I'll see you next week," she said.

The attendant got up from his chair and put a hand on Desmond's shoulder. The boy got to his feet, his body language almost a parody of cool. He threw the little folded-up piece of paper onto the table in front of her. "See you around," he said. Then the attendant, who was twice Desmond's size, led him out of the room.

Kate began putting files and papers into her bag. Maybe seeing her cases wasn't such a good idea after all. Maybe she had only enough strength to keep one hope alive at a time. Why can't everybody just obey the fucking law, she asked herself suddenly, tearing a manila folder as she shoved it angrily into the bag.

She left the conference room and walked down the dim hallway to the exit. Before leaving, she went into the front office to sign out. The receptionist—Jason Coombs, a sophomore at Howard who didn't look much older than the kids who lived at Holbrook House—nodded and said, "Busy day for you today."

"Yeah, but it's over," she said, signing her name.

"Not yet it isn't."

She glanced at him, not sure what he meant. Jason tilted his head toward the lobby windows. "Some gentlemen waiting to see you. Some gentlemen of the law enforcement persuasion."

Kate turned and looked through the glass. Two men— obviously cops though not in uniform—were standing in the lobby. One was tall, black, square-jawed, and in his thirties. His white partner—younger, stockier, with a thin, Clark Gable mustache—seemed to be telling him a story. He gestured wildly, making the loose belt of his gray overcoat swing back and forth like a horse's tail.

"Oh shit," Kate mumbled.

"Good luck," Jason said.

The two men turned as she opened the door to the lobby. "Mrs. Baker?" the black one asked.

She nodded, letting the door swing shut behind her. She crossed her arms, unconsciously taking the stance she'd seen so often as a cop—the defensive posture that women always took when there was a cop at the door, waiting to talk to them about their husbands and sons.

"I'm Detective Starks," the black one said. "And this is Detective Jerrold. Hampton County Police."

"Homicide Division," Jerrold added.

Kate felt suddenly dizzy. "Is it Joel?" she asked, short of breath.

The two men looked at each other. "What makes you think it's your husband, Mrs. Baker?"

She closed her eyes. "Tell me, damn it. Is it Joel?"

Detective Starks cleared his throat. "No, ma'am. It's not your husband."

A deep shudder ran through Kate's body. "Thank God," she said.

She opened her eyes. Detective Jerrold was studying her. "Well, Ray," he said to his partner, "that reaction looked pretty convincing to me. How'd it look to you?"

Kate felt something break inside her. Her arm shot out. The heel of her hand caught Detective Jerrold in the jaw, jerking his head back, sending him sprawling over onto a table covered with magazines.

"Oh Christ," Kate whispered to herself.

Detective Starks, staring at her in disbelief, pulled aside the overcoat and reached for the handcuffs on his belt.

"You seem determined to test my ability to keep you out of jail," Adrianna said when she walked into the holding cell at Hampton County Police headquarters. The metal-reinforced door slammed shut behind her. "Punching out an officer of the law is not an easy ticket to fix."

Kate looked up from the small cot in the corner. The cell was an awful place—nine-by-nine, fluorescent-lit, with nothing in it but the cot, a seatless chrome toilet, and a video camera mounted high on the far wall. "How did it go?" she asked.

Adrianna sat down next to her. "They agree not to press any battery charge," she said, "as long as you cooperate fully with the homicide investigation. Between you and me, I think Jerrold's partner thought he deserved to get hit."

Kate tried to smile. "He did," she said. Then, rubbing the half-healed burns on her left wrist, she asked, "So who's the corpse they're investigating?"

Adrianna turned a page of her legal pad. "Their best guess is that it's a man named Jin-Liang Lu, some biochemistry post-doc teaching at Johns Hopkins. But the ID isn't a hundred percent certain right now, for reasons they won't tell me yet."

"But what does this guy have to do with Joel?"

Adrianna sighed and got to her feet again. "You'll hear all of this from Starks in a few minutes," she said, stepping across the echoing cell. She turned. Her face was beautiful even in this light. "It seems Joel's business has been under surveillance by the feds for the past three months. It's a Customs Department investigation, but apparently some other agencies are interested—Fish and Wildlife, the FDA. Fortunately for Joel, the DEA has more important business for the moment."

"Fish and Wildlife?"

Adrianna shrugged. "There's some suspicion that the company has been importing zoological and botanical specimens from Asia and Latin America. Illegal things: endangered animals, rare plants."

"But why?"

"That's what they can't figure out." Adrianna's eyes

darted toward the video camera on the wall. "This morning they raided the Rainforest warehouse out in Northeast and impounded some evidence. It was plant matter mostly, and they say the quantities are small. They've got people trying to identify the stuff now, but none of it seems to be marijuana, poppy, or coca leaves."

"Plant matter?" Kate said. "What about Don? He could probably tell them more than I could. The business is half his."

Adrianna hesitated before saying: "Kate, Don's missing now, too. He disappeared early this morning."

Kate thought of Jeannette, Don's wife. Jeannette was not a strong person. She was probably out of her mind with worry.

As if reading Kate's thoughts, Adrianna said, "Jeannette's sisters are with her. And her kids are on their way home from college."

Kate nodded, feeling overwhelmed by all of these new developments. "And this biochemist? The one who got killed?"

"According to the feds, he was doing some kind of work for the company. But most of the relevant records are missing." Adrianna sat down next to her again. "Kate, the feds think this Chinese man might have been cooking up designer drugs for Joel and Don, possibly for sale on the street. Now he's dead. And Joel and Don are missing. They're being treated as suspects in the murder."

Detectives Jerrold and Starks showed up outside the holding cell. "Knock, knock," Jerrold shouted through the reinforced glass. Even at this distance, Kate could see the long, narrow bruise along the edge of his jaw.

A uniformed officer unlocked the door to the cell. The two detectives stepped in. "Everybody's ready, Counselor."

"I get to be present, of course," Adrianna said.

"We wouldn't dream of leaving you out, Counselor."

Jerrold stepped around her to Kate. "Shall we go, Mrs. Baker?"

Kate took a step back as he reached for her arm. "Detective," she said, "I know you won't believe this, but I'm sorry I hit you."

"I'm touched to hear it," he said, taking her elbow roughly. "Now come."

He led Kate out of the cell. In double file—Kate and Jerrold in front, Adrianna and Starks behind—they walked down a few hallways, through heavy metal doors with combination locks, and into a bright cinder block interrogation room. Several men—one of them Lieutenant Grainger, who looked pleased to see Kate in this situation—were standing around in front of a few folding chairs. In the middle of the room was a thick wooden table, scratched and scarred. It reminded Kate of the table in Holbrook House, but now she was the one who was supposed to sit behind it.

"By the way," Adrianna whispered as they moved toward the other side of the table, "I'm *your* lawyer now, not Joel's."

Kate sat down. Detective Starks, rolling his shirtsleeves up over his muscular forearms, pulled an extra chair over to the table for Adrianna. "Just about everybody here has met, I think. Mrs. Baker, this is Special Agent Foster of the Customs Department and Kurt Washington of Fish and Wildlife. Lieutenant Grainger of the Lewisburg Police you know." He sat down and opened a manila folder on the table in front of him. "This is quite a collection of law enforcement agents we've got here, Mrs. Baker. And who knows when the FBI or DEA will decide to get in on this."

"Detective Starks, am I a suspect?" Kate asked.

He stared at her, as if looking for some kind of sign in her face. Starks had vivid green eyes, the same shade as her own—unusual in a black man. "Not in the homicide, no," he said. "And according to these gentlemen, not in the federal case, either. As for the Lieutenant's possession case, your lawyer's doing her best to make that one a little problematic for us, too."

Lieutenant Grainger was staring at the floor, twisting the band of the gold watch on his wrist.

Adrianna spoke up. "I just want to remind everyone in the room, for the record, that my client is the legal spouse of Joel Baker—"

"And I just want to remind counsel," Detective Starks interrupted, "that your client will find herself slapped with a battery charge and who knows what else if she doesn't cooperate fully with this investigation."

"It's okay," Kate said. "I'm willing to tell you anything I can. I'm sure my husband is innocent."

Detective Starks nodded, his high, dark forehead glossy in the fluorescent light. "Then this should all go very smoothly." He shuffled through some of the papers in the file, as if unsure where to start. "Lieutenant Grainger tells us you were a uniformed officer with the Chicago PD some years ago."

"That's right."

He looked up. The green eyes again made her uncomfortable. "Good. Then I don't have to worry about upsetting you with these pictures." He began putting color enlargements on the table in front of her. "This body was found early yesterday," he said. "Though it took us until today to identify it. For obvious reasons."

Kate's jaw tightened as she looked down. The body in the picture was laid out on what looked like a bed of leaves. It was pale, streaked with black mud. And where the head and hands should have been, there was nothing at all.

"Okay," she said softly, closing her eyes and counting to three.

•   •   •

She needed sleep. Kate felt that she needed sleep more than anything else in the world right now. More than food, more than water, more than hope. Just sleep.

She stared up at the smoked-glass light fixture on the bedroom ceiling, waiting for the drug to take effect. She had taken Contac, with the tiny time pills. After getting back from the Hampton County Police headquarters, she'd ransacked the medicine cabinets for anything that would make her drowsy. But Lieutenant Grainger and his men had bagged and bottled everything remotely suspicious in the house—even the leftover alcohol from the dog party— and sent it off to the county crime lab. Kate was finally forced to call Elena, who had nothing to offer except Contac. It wasn't exactly the drug Kate had in mind—Ambien would have been more like it—but she'd swallowed one anyway. Cold remedies usually knocked her out within minutes.

But not this time. Kate lay in bed wide awake, her feet anchored under Hermann's warm belly. She tried a few breathing exercises to get rid of the nervous energy in her body, but the air in the room seemed too thick. It was damp and stale, like a sick person's breath.

"Joel," she said aloud, wanting to hear the name spoken in an ordinary, casual tone of voice. Then: "Joel, honey . . . as if he'd just walked into the room. "Joel, it's Thursday. Did you remember to take out . . . ?"

She turned over on her side. The image of the corpse in the pictures sprang to her mind—the thin, almost feminine body, so colorless and frail-looking, mutilated at the neck and wrists. There'd been no real reason for Detective Starks to show her the pictures, except maybe to shock her, to drive home the seriousness of Joel's situation. It worked. Kate had seen worse during her time as a cop: the body of a prostitute stabbed seventy-three times, throat cut, legs broken; a twelve-day-old gang hit, teeming with

flies and maggots. But those had been different somehow.
She had been different.

Kate thought of the teenaged boy who had found the
body. The police had been evasive about him, but Adrianna had read her some local newspaper accounts of the
story. The kid had found the body days earlier but kept
it a secret. Strange. Though maybe not so strange for a
fourteen-year-old. In her work, Kate had always found
that adolescents—adolescent boys especially—were like
another species of animal. They seemed to react to things
in all the wrong ways. If they got knocked around by their
fathers, they raped their baby-sitters. If they got humili-
ated at school, they tortured a pet rabbit. If a robbery
wasn't going right, instead of cutting their losses and running, they'd make everything worse by shooting somebody in the head.

Kate tossed again on the mattress, rousing Hermann,
who yawned, baring his loose black gums and stained
teeth.

Thinking about all of those screwed-up teenagers, about
the dozens of kids she used to put away when she was
working patrol with Chicago North, made her remember
how wrong it had felt being a cop. And yet she'd done
the job for almost four years, buttoning herself into the
uniform every day, strapping on the service revolver, the
belt with the pepper spray, the baton, the radio and flashlight. She'd always felt like a packhorse with all of that
around her waist. Not like a woman at all. During her last
year, when she sometimes worked as a decoy with the
Sex Crimes Unit, she would have to dress up in prostitute
clothes—clingy dresses, satin gym shorts, body stockings.
She actually liked that uniform better. At least it didn't
hide what she was. She even got a kind of thrill from
wearing the hooker clothes. She'd swing her hips at some
prospective john, finger a few buttons suggestively, and

feel an excitement that she could never tell anyone about, not even her closest friends.

Kate looked over at the clock beside her pillow. It was 2:24 A.M. Even with the Contac in her system, she wasn't going to get any sleep, at least not for a while. She got out of bed, went over to the closet, and pulled out some jeans and an old sweatshirt of Joel's that still smelled of his sweat. "Let's go for a walk," she said to Hermann.

The night was dry and chilly and full of stars. Kate clipped the leash to the dog's collar but then changed her mind and let him run free. Another law broken, she said quietly to herself. Fortunately, Lieutenant Grainger wasn't around at this time of night. In the three days since finding the drugs in Joel's office, he and his patrolmen had started spending lots of time outside Kate's house—making no effort to hide the fact that they were watching her—but it looked like the graveyard shift had better things to do tonight.

Kate pulled her coat tighter around her neck and then headed down the walk. There were no sidewalks in their neighborhood, and the edges of the streets were still piled with fallen leaves. The leaves crunched under her sneakers as she walked, while Hermann trudged beside her with calm enthusiasm.

Kate stopped for a second and looked down at a small pile of cigarette butts near the curb. This was where Lieutenant Grainger had sat in his car all evening, smoking, watching her house. She shook her head, remembering the sheer boredom of surveillance, the boredom of so much of her job as a cop. Her decision to join the force seemed incredible to her now, but it was what you did if you were a Theodorus, at least if you were a male Theodorus. Kate's father, a thirty-year veteran of the CPD, had been with the Organized Crime Unit for twenty-four years. Her oldest brother, Phil, was a detective in Sex Crimes North; Daniel was a hotel crimes specialist for Area Six Property

Crimes. When Kate's time came, she decided to follow the family example. Besides, joining up seemed like her only possible escape from the grind of that old row house on the South Side. If she didn't become a cop, she knew she'd be trapped in that house just the way her mother had been, lost to life, drowning in the needs of five men.

Her father had been opposed to the idea at first. He didn't think women should serve in uniform, especially not his own daughter, who had the house and the family to look after. But Kate was determined. She interviewed a dozen housekeepers until she found one who satisfied him—a balding Greek grandmother who knew how to make all his favorite dishes. The woman insisted on having Wednesdays off, though, and so on Wednesdays Kate was still expected to have the meal on the table when everybody came home. She remembered once, in her first year as a patrolwoman, chasing a coked-up pursesnatcher through back alleys and side streets near the Loop, finally tackling the kid against a Dumpster and breaking his nose. The chase got her adrenaline flowing, and she sailed through the rest of the morning on a kind of dazed high. It was only later, after starting on the paperwork late in the afternoon, that she remembered it was Wednesday. Her heart started pounding again. The image of her father and brothers sitting around an empty table scared her. And so she left the paperwork undone and hurried home, just in time to throw a chicken in the oven for dinner.

Kate shivered. She was ashamed of how she had acted today. She'd given in to her aggression, those old fight-or-flight emotions that she'd experienced almost daily while on patrol. This time, it was a cop she'd punched instead of a criminal, but the adrenaline rush had felt just as good.

She called out to Hermann and turned to go back to the house. As the two of them retraced their steps, Kate noticed a light on in Elena's house. Kate's first impulse was to walk past, to give her friend a call when she got back into the house and complain about insomnia, but her curiosity was too strong. She slipped through the bushes that separated Elena's house from the street. Elena was right there in front of her, framed by the window over the kitchen sink, and for a second Kate felt exposed. But then she realized that Elena wouldn't be able to see out into the dark. With the light above and behind her, she'd only be able to see her own reflection—her own face, her own kitchen, all in reverse.

Elena was washing dishes. From where she stood, Kate couldn't see the sink, but she could see Elena looking down, lifting a dripping dish every few seconds, letting it drip, and then moving it carefully to the drying rack. Lift, pause, move. Lift, pause, move. There seemed to be a tremendous sadness in this calm repetition, the sadness of a woman washing dishes in the middle of the night, a woman thrown over by a husband she'd given everything to—her youth, her trust. Watching her, Kate felt a pull at her throat. What a mystery marriage is, she thought—any marriage, every marriage. You try to make it good, but you never really know if you're succeeding. Elena had believed, all of those years, that she had a good marriage; Alan told her that he loved her; they'd raised two little girls together; they'd celebrated birthdays, anniversaries, and Christmases together. Every night, they brushed their teeth at the same sink, used the same toilet, and then slept in the same bed. Could anything be more intimate than that? And yet, as it turned out, there was never any real intimacy there. Elena's husband had left her, to share another woman's sink and toilet, to sleep in another woman's bed.

Kate turned and pushed back through the bushes. She walked quickly down the street to her own house. After letting herself and Hermann in, she closed the door and looked around the house as if it belonged to someone else—the oak-and-leather couch, the grandfather clock in the corner, the Persian rug that she had liked so much in Joel's house in Chevy Chase. It occurred to her that she had no idea how her life would turn out now. Would she be alone for the rest of her life? Would she ever have children? Kate had resisted the idea of children for so long, having acted as mother to four brothers back in Chicago. But lately, seeing young mothers—women ten years younger than Kate—pushing carriages and strollers along the streets of D.C., she'd started feeling envious. But now—what would happen now? This time next year, would she even be living in this house? Would she still be married to Joel? Would he be alive? Would she?

"It must be the cold medicine," she said aloud, hanging up her coat in the closet. Then she turned to Hermann and said, "I'm going downstairs to look through more books. Want to come?"

Hermann padded across the living room to his beanbag in the corner. He plopped down in it, sending a few beans skittering across the wood floor.

"You split a seam," Kate said. She scooped up the beans from the floor and carried them over to his bed. "Okay, move."

With a groan, Hermann got up from the beanbag. Kate knelt and turned the thing over. More beans spilled out of the broken seam, and then something else—something silver, which made a soft metallic sound as it fell. Kate picked it up. It was the key to a safe-deposit box.

Confused, Kate stared at the thin piece of metal in her palm. She and Joel shared a safe-deposit box at a bank in town, but she had both keys for that one in her own file cabinet. This must be for another box, one she didn't know about.

Kate closed her fist on the key and stood up. She felt a sudden lightening of her spirits. A secret safe-deposit box was at least a clue to work with; it was the beginning of a path that could be followed. Finally, after days of just reacting to events, she could actually *do* something to find her husband.

PART TWO

7

"Okay, go ahead." Elena stood in Kate and Joel's bedroom in her white cotton underwear, holding out a pair of green paisley slacks. "If you tell me how loose they are, I'll never speak to you again."

"Yeah, right," Kate said, taking the slacks from her friend. Kate was also standing in her underwear—a racier maroon satin. "I'll be lucky if I can squeeze into these things."

"Well, you certainly know what to say to a girl, don't you."

It was nine o'clock on Friday morning. Kate had called Elena early and asked her to come over right away in her most noticeable casual outfit. Elena had agreed, showing up at the front door ten minutes later in the paisley slacks, a red wool turtleneck, a green cashmere overcoat with fur collar, and a green wool hat. Before letting her in, Kate made sure that Lieutenant Grainger, sitting in his Caprice up the street, had gotten a good look at her.

Now the two women were trading clothes. Kate slipped

into the paisley slacks and zipped them up over her narrow hips. "A perfect fit. I'm serious."

Elena took Kate's black jeans off the bed. "So, logically speaking, yours should fit me, too." She sat on the edge of the bed and pulled on Kate's jeans. She struggled for a while, and the zipper got caught once or twice, but she finally managed to get into them. "Well," she said breathlessly, "so much for logic."

"Just hand over the turtleneck."

Elena started pulling the sweater over her head. "Now, I know there's probably some sensible reason we're doing this," she said, the static electricity crackling.

Kate had already taken off her canary-yellow, cowl-necked top. She took the red sweater from Elena. "Remember what I told you. The less you know, the less trouble you can get into. All I can say is that it's an errand I want to run without the Lieutenant tagging along," she said. She put on Elena's sweater. "How do I look?"

Elena frowned. "A lot better than I do in those pants," she said. "But if you really want to look like me, you'd better keep my hat on. The hair would be a dead give-away."

Kate nodded. "Your car keys?" she asked.

"In the pocket of the coat." Elena took the green cashmere overcoat from the chair and helped Kate into it. "What do I do while I'm waiting?"

"Stay away from the windows. And let the machine answer the phone." She took Elena's wool hat and began stuffing her hair into it. "With any luck, I'll be back in an hour. Now don't show yourself when we open the door."

"Right." Elena followed Kate through the house to the front door. "Good luck with whatever it is," she said. "And take care of those pants, okay?"

Kate opened the door and slipped out. She forced herself to move slowly and casually, like any neighbor head-

ing back home after a short visit. At first, she was tempted
to look toward the street, where Lieutenant Grainger was
sitting in his car, but she knew that her face might be
recognizable. Using Elena's usual shortcut, she angled
across her own lawn, passed through a wide gap in the
bushes, and then climbed the stairs to Elena's front porch.
She let herself in with the key, closed the door behind
her, and began counting. When she reached five hundred,
she pulled the door open again, left the house, locked the
door behind her, and headed toward the driveway, where
Elena's blue Toyota Corolla sat waiting. Kate got in,
keeping her face turned away from the street. She started
the car, pulled out of the driveway, and started down the
road away from Lieutenant Grainger's car. He didn't follow. So far so good.

She drove into town. Her plan was to visit the two
banks in downtown Lewisburg. She would say that her
husband was away on business—in Dubai—and that he'd
asked her to get some documents from the box and fax
them to him. Kate knew that, as Joel's legal spouse, she
should be able to get access to the box, even if her name
wasn't on the registration. The only problem would be
explaining her mistake if the first bank wasn't the one
with Joel's box. And, of course, it was possible that neither local bank was the right one. If the key opened a box
somewhere in downtown Washington, Kate would have
no hope of finding it.

There was no box registered to Joel Baker at the first
bank, so Kate was forced to fall back on her lame story
about the international phone lines going down in the middle of the call from Dubai, before Joel could give her all
the information she needed. The bank officer, a stocky
black woman with tiny delicate ears, looked dubious
about this explanation (not to mention Kate's outfit). Feeling the heat in her face, Kate excused herself quickly and
left.

At the second bank, she had better luck. "You're right, Mrs. Baker, your husband's box *is* available to you," said Mr. Jeb Fagles, a short, balding man who had called her "young lady" when she walked in. "We'd prefer, of course, to have something from him in writing, but, well, a pretty woman like you. It's not likely you're a bank robber, is it." Kate was tempted to steal the old guy's wallet out of spite, but she just smiled and followed him back to the vault. He unlocked the barred door, took her key, and opened a small box halfway down the line at about chest level. Handing the box to her, he said, "Any booth will do, Mrs. Baker. Just give a yell when you're done."

"Thanks," she said, taking the box from his hands. She went into one of the booths opposite the vault and closed the door. The box rattled as she put it down on the veneer countertop. Kate eyed the thing for a few seconds, bracing herself, then opened it.

The box was empty except for a single small book. Kate picked it up. It was a children's book—*Tales of Peter Rabbit* by Beatrix Potter—and couldn't have been much bigger than three inches square. Kate was totally confused. She opened the book and flipped through the miniature pages. The type was large, and the text was interrupted every few pages by beautiful little illustrations. Then, about three-quarters of the way through the book, at the beginning of the third tale, she saw an underlined passage: "It is said that the effect of eating too much lettuce is 'soporific.' " It was the quotation from Joel's e-mail.

Kate put the little book into the pocket of Elena's paisley slacks, closed the box, and left the little booth. "I'm done, Mr. Fagles," she said.

"Please, call me Jeb," he said as he got up from his desk and took the box from her. "Get everything you needed?" He slid the box back into place, locked it, and handed back her key.

"I did, thanks. Jeb."

"Anytime I can be of service." He gestured for her to go ahead of him back into the main part of the bank. Just as she was leaving the vault, she saw a familiar figure pushing through the glass doors across the main room— Lieutenant Grainger, looking nervous and out of breath.

"Oh wait," Kate said, spinning around, colliding with Mr. Fagles. "I think I left something in the booth." She edged past him, went back into the little booth, and closed the door behind her. She had no idea how Grainger could possibly have found her, and for a second even wondered if Elena had betrayed her. She took the tiny book from her pocket. She had no choice but to brazen it out. Acting quickly, she unzipped the green paisley pants and slipped the book into her satin underwear. Then she zipped up again. Thank God Elena's slacks really were a size too large for her. Finally, smoothing the pants down over her thighs, she stepped out of the booth and began walking as naturally as possible across the lobby of the bank. She was halfway to the glass doors when the Lieutenant intercepted her.

"Wait up, there, Ms. Theodorus-Baker," he said. Sweat was beading on his forehead despite the cold. "We just got a report from Citizens Bank. About some woman trying to get access to a safe-deposit box registered to Joel Baker? Somehow I thought it might be you." He looked down at what she was wearing. "Cute pants. Seems to me I've seen them somewhere else today."

"I didn't think that sharing clothes with a neighbor was against the law in Maryland."

"Nah, it isn't. But withholding evidence in a homicide investigation *is*."

"Withholding evidence?"

"Did you find anything in your husband's box?"

"Lieutenant," she said, crossing her arms. "Are you planning another illegal search? You want to exclude any more evidence than you've already excluded?"

"Are you giving me permission to search you?"

"Wouldn't you love *that*," she said. "No, Lieutenant, I'm not consenting to anything today. Though I'm glad to see you've read the Fourth Amendment since our last talk." She began to push past him, but he grabbed her arm.

"Hold on a minute," he said.

Kate glared at him.

"Nobody else thinks you're involved in this thing. They all buy the deceived wife crap. But I'm a pretty good judge of character, Mrs. Baker." He squeezed her arm tighter. "In fact, I'm a damn good judge of character, and I have some other ideas about you. A lot of ideas."

Kate didn't answer. She pulled her arm free, turned, and pushed through the glass doors, trying to ignore the pounding in her ears.

She read *Tales of Peter Rabbit* that night after dinner. It didn't take very much time—the little book was just 122 pages long, with about fifty words on each page—but reading it left Kate feeling as confused as ever. There was nothing in the book (which she hadn't read since she was a child) that she could connect to Joel's disappearance. The only underlined passage was the sentence about the soporific effects of lettuce, which might conceivably have something to do with drugs, but she had no idea what it could really mean. Did Peter Rabbit represent Joel in some way? Did Mr. McGregor, the owner of the garden where Peter trespassed, stand for someone else, a supplier that Joel was swindling, maybe?

"Oh, come on," Kate muttered aloud, feeling ridiculous. She remembered her English class from college, where there was a lot of talk about symbolic figures and subtexts.

That course—Survey of the Novel in English—was a requirement; she was majoring in sociology and criminal justice, going to lectures at night while working patrol during the day. She wanted to be a detective, and so she'd decided to study for a pretty serious degree, something that would impress the chief. Naturally, her brothers had given her a hard time about it. "Hey, Katie," Phil had said to her once. "If you make lieutenant before I do, I'm turning in my badge." He was teasing her, as usual, but she knew that he really was worried.

She still hadn't called to tell Phil or her other brothers about Joel's disappearance. She'd convinced herself that it would do no good for them to know. Sure, they would be sympathetic; one of them might even fly out to stay with her. But Kate knew that there'd be an enormous "I told you so" hanging over every act of sympathy, every offer of help. "We knew you'd get hurt with this guy," Phil would say. "This is what happens when you leave behind the place where you belong."

Kate stirred in the armchair. Just the thought of being back in Chicago made her feel claustrophobic. No, she told herself, she belonged here. She loved Joel. She had known this as early as the second time she was with him, when they met at that Italian restaurant and later went to his house in Chevy Chase. Five months after that night, they were already married. At the time, her brothers—especially Phil, whose jealous protectiveness was always a problem—had seemed to think that this romance was a little suspicious. Here she was, running away from Chicago, starting over in a new place, studying for a job not known for its high salaries and stability, when a rich, good-looking man comes up to her in a museum one day and saves her. Kate was honest enough with herself to see how they might think the worst of her. But she'd asked herself the hard question long before her brothers did: would she have fallen for Joel so fast if he'd been a poor man unable to give her the security she needed to reinvent her life?

The answer she'd come to was a definite yes. Being with Joel was exciting from the very beginning. He wasn't the usual bland, pleasant date she knew from her Chicago days. In fact, he seemed to thrive on conflict. "What makes you think you're doing any good for these kids you counsel?" he asked her one night over dinner, a few months after their first date. "Aren't you just playing the government's game, getting these kids out on the street again so they can get killed and stop draining tax revenues?" Coming from anyone else, this question would have seemed like an attack, but Joel meant it as a challenge. And she accepted the challenge. They had argued for hours that night, drinking two bottles of red wine between them. By midnight, she was more firmly convinced than ever of the value of the work she was doing. But she'd been forced to clear up a lot of her thinking to get to that point. She'd been forced to *earn* the sense of satisfaction she felt.

The morning after that argument—a breezy May morning, complete with birdsong and the lazy buzz of distant lawnmowers—they'd made love, both of them still feeling the emotions of their disagreement. Afterward, Joel had looked over at her and said, "Give me one good reason why we shouldn't get married today."

She couldn't think of one, aside from the matter of the blood test, but Joel claimed they could easily get around it. And so they'd found a willing Justice of the Peace later that day, a woman named Sarah something-or-other, who'd taken Kate aside to make sure that this marriage was really what she wanted. Kate said that it was, and promised the woman that she was not pregnant or acting against her will. After the ceremony, Sarah kissed them both warmly and gave them directions to the nearest interesting restaurant—a cheap Thai place in Gaithersburg—

where Joel and Kate shared a wedding feast of squid in garlic sauce, mee krob, and Sing-ha beer.

"So, we did it," Joel said suddenly, after they finished their dinner.

"What? Got married? You make it sound like we just climbed a mountain or something."

He shrugged. "I told myself in college that I'd never get married. I remember announcing to Don once that I'd 'never feel the need to get official ratification for a commitment.' "

"What made you change your mind?"

"You, for one thing," he said, pouring her more beer. "And twenty years of living. I also used to say that I'd never be caught dead in a place like Chevy Chase, and here I am—house, car, the whole deal, right down to the illegal Peruvians mowing my lawn every week."

"You grew up," she said.

"Well, I grew older, at least," he answered, signaling the waiter.

Their families were surprised and annoyed about their sudden elopement, so they made ceremonial visits, first to Kate's brothers, then to Joel's ailing mother. In Chicago, Kate's brothers gave them an informal reception at a neighborhood restaurant called Man of La Mancha, the kind of Spanish place where the waiters wore tuxedoes and the seafood was always overcooked. At the end of the meal, each brother made an awkward little speech, tender and full of bad jokes, with lots of mock warnings to Joel about how he'd have the entire Chicago PD on his tail if he ever did their little Katie wrong. Kate sat at the head of the table, her heart swimming in affection and embarrassment. She wondered what Joel was thinking about all of this. A few times she wanted to apologize to him for the sheer corniness of the evening. But she was afraid that if she *did* apologize, and if Joel seemed to think there was really something to apologize for, she would

have hit him. But Joel turned out to be a good sport about
the whole thing, and even got up after dessert to make an
awkward little speech of his own (including a lame joke
about Kate's having had to use her pepper spray only
twice during their courtship). The rest of the evening went
pretty well, and as they were saying good-night to everybody, her brother Phil had whispered to her, "Okay, I
admit it, he's not a jerk. Happy?"

Visiting Joel's mother, Helen, in New Mexico was another matter. She lived with her dog, Hermann, and a paid
companion in a big house in the mountains east of Alamogordo, not far from the Jicarilla Apache reservation. It
was the house that Joel had grown up in, a huge tree-
shaded pile of brick and timber that seemed to have no
relation at all to those southwestern clichés of adobe, Nav-
ajo rugs, and cactus that Kate had expected. Joel's mother,
a trim little woman with agate-gray eyes and a long,
deeply lined face, seemed unable to take Kate in somehow, as if the fact that her son had a wife was too ridiculous to believe. Fortunately, Hermann had seemed more
receptive.

They'd stayed for just a few days, eating breakfast and
dinner with Helen but spending little time with her otherwise. Instead, Joel showed her around. He drove her to
a racetrack in Ruidoso, and then to a luxury mountain
resort run by the Apache tribe, where they ate a terrible
lunch in the dining room overlooking a slate-blue lake
surrounded by pines. Kate told him that this kind of scen-
ery was not the way she imagined New Mexico, that she
had been expecting an entire state of flat desert and tum-
bleweed. He listened, and then, the next day, showed her
that New Mexico, too. He borrowed his mother's old Cad-
illac and took her west, driving down from the mountains
into the vast, empty Tularosa Basin. There was a road
heading straight north from Alamogordo, and Joel dem-
onstrated how he used to drive it as a teenager. He jacked

up the volume of some Mexican station on the radio, floored the gas pedal, and yelled at the top of his lungs while hot desert air blasted through the windows. When the speedometer hit ninety-five, Kate put her hand on his forearm and said, "Okay, okay, I get the idea." She couldn't believe how ugly the landscape was—scraped and scoured, and so different from the steep pine forests just a few miles east. But Joel seemed to love it. "There's nothing in your way out here!" he shouted to her over the engine noise. "Nothing to stop you any way you turn!"

That night, the night before their trip back to Maryland, they ate with his mother and went to bed early. But sometime after midnight, Kate felt Joel's lips on her ear. She snapped awake. There was no moon yet, and the room where they slept—his old bedroom, the walls plastered with Jefferson Airplane posters—was dark. "Come with me," he whispered to her. "Get dressed, and I'll meet you down at the car." Then he was gone.

Feeling strangely excited, Kate dressed, went down the stairs as quietly as she could, and slipped outside. The night air was crisp and full of strange smells. She found Joel in the rented Jeep, with the motor running and the lights off. She climbed in. There was a bottle of spring water on the seat between them. "I want to show you something," he said.

He eased the car out of the driveway. A hundred yards down the road, he turned on the lights and picked up speed. Kate recognized where they were heading: down into the basin again, into the desert. "Here," he said, handing her a little capsule. "Take this."

She hesitated.

"It's an herb," he said. "Trust me. Take it and then go back to sleep. We won't be there for a while."

She decided to put herself in his hands. She quickly swallowed the mystery herb, washing it down with a sip of spring water. What if it's arsenic? she asked herself, and then laughed at her own stupid recklessness.

"Good," Joel said. He slipped a tape into the player—
some kind of American Indian music, full of low-pitched
chants and soft, steady drumbeats. "Go back to sleep and
I'll wake you again when it's time."

At that moment it seemed like the thing she most
wanted to do—to fall asleep while her husband drove
through the desert night, and then to wake up someplace
new and unknown. Without another word, Kate closed her
eyes. Eventually, between the chanting and the slow rock-
ing motion of the Jeep, she began to doze. And when Joel
woke her an hour or two later, she felt refreshed, as if
she'd slept an entire night.

She leaned forward and rubbed the blood back into the
arm she had slept on. They were sitting in the dark again,
in the middle of an unpaved road, under a ceiling of blue-
white stars. "We have to be quiet," he whispered. "Just
follow me."

They got out of the Jeep, Kate feeling slightly woozy.
She wanted to ask Joel what kind of herb he'd given her,
but somehow her mouth didn't work right. She just
watched as Joel took a little penlight out of his pocket
and used it to light the way up a rocky path. Kate's eyes
had adjusted to the dark by now, but since the moon
hadn't risen yet, she could sense the buildings around her
only as patches of blankness against the starry purple sky.
She held Joel's hand as they rounded the corners of dusty
buildings and passed through a metal livestock gate—
something she'd never seen before, and that seemed bizarre and confusing in the night. Finally, he led her
through a doorway and into the damp, scented air of a
barn.

Inside, Kate had an overwhelming feeling of life all
around her—of warmth and breath. "Follow me, slowly,"
Joel whispered. He inched forward, still leading her by
the hand. And suddenly, they were in it, surrounded by

the humidity of living things, moving around them. Kate felt scared at first—where had Joel brought her? She felt small heads butting gently against her thighs, a rough tongue on her wrist, the pressure of damp bodies on every side. She thought they were children at first, and almost shouted out. But of course they were sheep, newly shorn and mostly half awake. She heard a few soft cries around her as the herd shifted uneasily, making room. "Touch them," Joel whispered. "Close your eyes, put your hands out, and just walk through them." His hand was gone, and for a second she felt panicky, her mind too fuzzy to get a grip on the situation. But gradually, feeling the warmth of the animals, she understood. There was something communal in this movement all around her, something sexual and unsettling, but somehow innocent. She let the restless animals press against her, and put her hands on their warm, soft bodies. She wanted to cry.

"Isn't it amazing?" a voice whispered in her ear. It startled her. Somehow Joel had worked his way behind her. "We'd better go before they really wake up."

He took her hand in the darkness and led her again through the shifting bodies, out of the barn. They went back through the gate to the car. By this time, the moon was just creeping over the mountains, and she could see her husband's face beside her, the farm buildings in the distance, the high ridge of mountains behind, all with stunning clarity. Joel was smiling at her. "Saturday night in southern New Mexico," he said. "This was something I used to do when I was growing up. I almost got myself shot once or twice."

They climbed into the Jeep, back to reality again, quiet.

"There's a real presence there, don't you think?" he asked her then. "Animals have this weird power. It's like a radiance. Something we smart primates lost way back along the evolutionary trail."

She nodded. What he said was true. If someone had

told her beforehand that she would be taken in the middle
of the night into a barn full of sleeping sheep, and that
there would be a kind of transcendent feeling in the experience, she would have laughed. But that's exactly what
it was, a kind of magic. She turned. Her tongue was still
sluggish, and her mind clouded, but she managed to make
a wry comment: "So that's . . . what you were doing when
the other, you know, boys in the class were getting drunk
at girlie bars?"

"More or less." He started the Jeep. "Though I went to
my share of girlie bars, too."

It was still dark when they arrived back at the house.
They slipped in as quietly as they could, then undressed
and got into bed. Joel fell asleep right away, but Kate lay
awake until sunrise. She kept thinking of something that
Joel's mother had said at dinner the night before, when
telling Kate about Joel's old habit of trespassing on the
neighbors' property. "No," Helen had said, "Joel doesn't
have much respect for fences, that's for sure." Somehow,
the sentence stayed with Kate. She found herself thinking
about it that night, as he lay asleep beside her, the smell
of sheep still clinging to him.

And now, three years later, as she sat in her living room
with the children's book in her hand, she was thinking
again about Helen's comment. A disrespect for fences was
something that Joel and Peter Rabbit had in common.
Kate wondered if it was this that had gotten Joel into
trouble.

Kate put the book aside and got up from the chair. She
had to stop feeling helpless. She had to *do* something.
The safe-deposit box had seemed like a start, but it had
turned out to be useless. Tomorrow she would have to
begin the real legwork—the meat-and-potatoes stuff that
Starks and Jerrold had probably done days ago. For start-
ers, she'd go to Joel's office in the city and talk to Velma,
the secretary who had been with Joel's company for over

ten years. And as long as she was playing cop again, she might as well head up to Johns Hopkins and ask around about the dead Chinese chemist, Jin-Liang Lu. She'd probably be followed by the Lewisburg Police all the way, but what could they do to prevent her from talking to people?

Kate went to the kitchen, Hermann tagging along at her heels, and grabbed the pad and pen near the phone. She wrote down: "1: Velma; 2: Lu (Hopkins)" on the top sheet. As she thought about these names, the phone above the counter rang, giving her a start. She had learned by now to beat down the instant hope that every phone call was from Joel, but it was almost ten o'clock now, too late for a social call. "Hello?" she said cautiously when she picked up the phone.

There was a three-second silence. Then a male voice: "Hello, is Joel Baker there?"

Every muscle in Kate's body tensed. "No, he's not. Can I take a message?"

Another pause. "Where is he?" The voice was strange. It sounded like a boy's voice—deep but immature.

"Who is this?" Kate asked.

"Is this the wife?"

Kate's first thought was that this might be a business connection of Joel's, someone who hadn't heard about the disappearance. But the voice didn't sound like that of a supplier or a customer. She wasn't sure *what* it sounded like.

"Yes," she said. "I'm Joel's wife. Can I take a message?"

"Do you think he really did it?"

This time she was the one who paused. "Did what?"

"Killed that guy in the woods."

This is a crank call, Kate told herself. The discovery of the body had made the local news. Adrianna had told her that Joel's name was mentioned several times—identified as "a local businessman, now missing, being sought for questioning." This was probably some kid who had looked up Joel's name in the Hampton County phone book—

"I found him," the voice said then.

It felt like a blow to her head. Kate closed her eyes and whispered, "What?"

"I found him. I was the person who found the body in the woods."

The misunderstanding was brief, but it left Kate shaken. "Him" meant the body of the Chinese chemist. The caller must be the teenager Adrianna had told her about.

"Do you really think your husband did that?" the boy went on. "I mean, cut off the head like that?"

"What's your name?" Kate asked.

"I don't think your husband could've done that. It doesn't make sense. Only an animal could have done something like that."

"What's your name? Why are you calling me?"

"I'm sorry to bother you," the boy said then, in a different tone of voice. "I was just thinking about it. I'm the one who found him. I just wanted to call."

"Can you tell me your name? Mine is Kate. So you tell me yours."

"I shouldn't have called, maybe."

"Wait!" she shouted. "Don't hang up!" But the boy was already off the line.

Kate slowly put down the phone, her hands feeling shaky and useless. Hermann was looking at her oddly. "It's okay," she told him. She wondered if the call could really have come from the boy who found the body. The detectives from the county police had claimed that he wasn't relevant to the investigation. But could he possibly have seen something that the police didn't want her to know about? She remembered the exact words the boy had used: "I don't think your husband could've done that.

It doesn't make sense." How would he have an opinion like that? Why had he called?

"Only an animal could have done something like that." Something like what? Decapitation, she guessed, but could he have meant something else? She knew she should talk to the boy. Her years as a cop had taught her that you don't pass up any possible source of information. He could at least tell her about the burial site, give her some idea of whether it was a professional job. Bodies buried by pros aren't usually uncovered within days.

Kate picked up the phone again and dialed Adrianna's number. It rang six times before she picked up. "Adrianna? It's Kate. I'm sorry to call you at home."

"Is everything all right?"

"Fine," Kate said. "I was just wondering about that kid who found the body. What was his name?"

"The kid? Ethan something-or-other. Why?"

Kate hesitated. She should have thought of some excuse before calling. "Can you find out his name for me?"

"Kate," Adrianna said, "you're not thinking of talking to this kid, are you? I mean, what could he possibly tell you?"

"I just want his name. For my own reasons."

Adrianna put on her lawyer voice. "I think it would be very counterproductive at this point for you to talk to this kid. Besides, I get the impression that he's half wacko."

"Adrianna, there are plenty of ways I could find out the name. You can make it hard for me, or you can make it easy for me."

There was another long silence before Adrianna said, "Hold on a minute. My notes are in the bedroom."

Kate heard the phone being put down, then a different female voice in the background asking a question. This was probably Farida, the woman Adrianna lived with. Kate heard Adrianna say "Kate Baker," then a few other words she couldn't make out. Listening to this murmured

conversation, Kate wondered about Adrianna and her
"partner." Was their marriage any different because they
were both women? Did they know each other any better,
any more deeply, than she knew Joel or Elena knew Alan?

Adrianna was back on the phone in less than a minute.
"Evan, not Ethan," she said. "Last name Potter. Lives way
out in the woods in Franklin. Now, can you kindly tell
your lawyer what you intend to do with this information?"

Evan Potter, Kate said to herself. Maybe a long-lost
descendant of Beatrix. "Nothing," she said finally. "Probably nothing. But knowing the name helps. I don't know
why."

"Are you still not interested in hiring that private investigator I told you about?"

"Not yet. Good-night. And thanks."

Kate put down the phone. She grabbed the pen and pad
again and brought them over to the kitchen table. Under
the names of Velma and Lu she wrote: "3: Evan Potter
(Franklin)."

She looked over her list, repeating the names silently
to herself. These were all long shots, she knew. But they
were at least three leads to follow, three people to talk to.
It was enough to give her a little hope.

8

He liked the sound of her voice. Somehow he'd known he would. The wife of a suspected murderer, the wife of someone who might actually have cut off another person's head, would have to have an interesting voice. It didn't sound high and false, like his aunt's or his mother's when they were talking to somebody they didn't know. This voice was real—a little hoarse, a little tired.

And a little scared, Evan thought, tossing on his bed. There was definitely fear in that voice on the phone, and he himself had put it there. Talking to Evan had made her feel afraid, and this pleased him.

Evan leaned back against the pillows. He was feeling worn out, as if he'd been through a huge test at school. For three days, they'd kept him home. People had come to the house—police in uniform, detectives, doctors, people who "just wanted to talk." He didn't know what they all wanted from him. He'd told them everything he knew, everything he saw, but somehow it wasn't enough. What they couldn't seem to get over was that he'd waited so

long to report the body, that he'd dug it up and then re-
buried it. Was that weird? Sure it was weird, but he'd
done it and now it was over. People do weird things sometimes. Was everybody supposed to be perfect every second of the day? Besides, he *did* report the body finally.
But now these cops and doctors wouldn't leave him alone
about it.

Evan grabbed the remote and turned on the television.
He channel-surfed for a while until settling on some National Geographic show about otters. He watched it for a
few minutes—watched the otters opening mussels by
smashing them with rocks—but then hit the Off button.

Kate Baker. He couldn't get the name out of his head.
Maybe he would call her again sometime. She sounded
nice. She had asked Evan his name, had seemed interested
in him. They could be friends. When her husband was off
in jail for murder, maybe he and Kate Baker could do
things together—go to the movies or go shopping or
walking. He could show her the place in the woods where
he'd found the body, and some of the other places he liked
to go.

Kate Baker. He'd heard the detectives talking about her
the day before. This was after they'd identified the body
and decided that Evan wasn't involved. The detectives
named Starks and Jerrold had taken him over to the crime
scene for a last look. There were still people crawling all
over the site. The body was gone by this time, but the
technicians, who wore thick red parkas with "Crime Scene
Team" written on the back, were sifting through every
inch of dirt for yards around. When Evan and the two
detectives showed up, one of the technicians started teasing Jerrold about something—being punched by a woman
earlier that day. Evan figured out eventually that it was
Kate Baker they were talking about. One of the men
called her "a fox."

So Evan knew that Kate Baker was pretty. Probably a

lot prettier than his mother and aunt. Prettier and younger. "The way I like my women," he said aloud, enjoying the sound of the words. He tried for Jerrold's cocky tone: "I've always liked them pretty and young."

Feeling embarrassed now, Evan picked up the remote and turned on the television again. The otters were still knocking mussel shells together, making little high-pitched squeaks. Like women do when you fuck them, Evan said to himself. He liked the sound of these words, too. "When you fuck them," he said aloud. He laughed, but then felt another flush of embarrassment. His mother had strict rules about cursing. Once, she'd heard him say "shit" and sent him to his room for the rest of the night, with no TV and no computer. "You're turning into a stranger right before my eyes," she had yelled as he marched up the stairs. "A stranger in my own house."

Evan shoved another pillow behind his neck and leaned back. His mother was mad at him, he knew. The day before, she had driven him to the Community Mental Health Center in Hammond for an evaluation. It was something that the police psychologist had arranged after his talk with Evan. It would just be a checkup, Detective Starks had told them. Just some testing so he could write it all up in his reports and be done with it.

They'd gone after lunch. Evan sat next to his mother in the car during the ride, silently absorbing the rays of anger coming off her body. A couple of times he felt her looking over at him, her eyes burning into the side of his cheek. Then she would sigh and drag her hand through her short red hair. When they pulled into the parking lot crammed with cars, Evan felt instantly on edge. The tan brick hugeness of the building, the people moving in and out through the glass doors, the sun reflecting off the car hoods in the asphalt lot—it all seemed ominous to him. And when he followed his mother into the lobby, he was hit with a whiff of chlorine and soap that seemed to drain the life out of his body, leaving only a burning, empty feeling.

"Looks like they could use some paint," his mother muttered to him, with a look on her face that made it seem like the whole place was his fault.

They had to wait an hour to see someone—an hour of sitting in a room full of broken toys and odd children, listening to his mother leafing impatiently through magazines. By the time they called Evan, he was feeling scared and panicky, and seeing the tiny, white-walled examination room only made things worse. It was crammed with electronic equipment, including three desktop computers that Evan could see were total dinosaurs. He couldn't believe the dot-matrix printer, a small cream-colored thing that looked like it was held together with electrician's tape. What kind of place is this, he asked himself as he sat down on the little folding chair across from the observation mirror. These are the people who are supposed to judge *me*?

A man in his twenties came in—tall, with a ponytail, glasses, and a beard, wearing a gray cardigan sweater. He said his name was Mr. Glynn, asked Evan how he was doing, and then pulled a few packs of cards and some cardboard sheets from two boxes he was carrying. He tried to keep the pictures turned away, but Evan got a look at a couple of them. They were ink blots, some all black, some black and red, some other colors. Evan sat up straighter in the chair when he saw them. He'd seen ink blots like this on television shows, but never thought that people actually used them in real life. A Rorschach test. He even knew the name. The test was supposed to drag out a person's secrets, without the person realizing it or being able to stop it from happening. Evan knew then that he would have to be careful.

The man named Glynn talked to him for a while, trying to get him to relax. Then, sitting across the table, he began showing some cards with dots and designs on them. He asked Evan to copy the designs onto a sheet of paper. Then he took away the cards and paper and asked Evan to draw the same things again from memory. This was easy, and Evan thought he was doing all right. After fifteen minutes or so, Mr. Glynn changed seats, moving next to Evan, and started showing him some pictures—pictures of people who looked like they came from old movies. Then he asked Evan to make up stories about these people. This part Evan found harder, but he did his best. He made up one story about a boy who couldn't play the violin, another about some doctors cutting open a sick man, and another about a farm boy who forgot that his mother was supposed to pick him up at school.

After a few more questions, Mr. Glynn brought out the Rorschach sheets. He showed them to Evan one by one, and asked him what each of them looked like—an all-black one first, then some black-and-red ones, then more all-black ones, and finally the colorful ones. In the beginning, Evan tried to say that the ink blots didn't remind him of anything, that they just reminded him of ink blots, but Mr. Glynn told him to take his time. Everybody, he said, could see something in the ink blots. Evan finally had to make things up: a bat with broken wings, a bear with bloody jaws, a squashed moth—anything to get the man to move on to the next sheet. After each answer Evan gave, Mr. Glynn would stop to write in a little notebook on the table in front of him. Evan wanted to see what he was writing, but couldn't figure out a way to do it. Mr. Glynn pulled the notebook closer to himself, as if he knew every one of Evan's thoughts, even this one.

After a long hour of testing, Mr. Glynn got up and put away the cards. Somebody else, he told Evan, would be in to see him now: Dr. Spoon. As Mr. Glynn was leaving, Evan wanted to ask how he'd done on the Rorschach test—had he passed or failed?—but Mr. Glynn was already out the door.

Dr. Spoon, who came in after another fifteen minutes, turned out to be Dr. Jennifer Spoon, a wide-hipped woman with a helmet of graying black hair and a lot of eye makeup. She seemed distracted as she came in, banging her stuffed leather briefcase around, but the minute she looked at Evan she seemed to shift gears, to slow down and focus on him. "Evan," she said, as if giving him the answer to a question. "I'm Dr. Spoon, and I'd like to talk with you for a bit. Okay?"

Evan felt that same burning, empty feeling in his chest. "Okay."

She sat across from him, scraped the chair forward, and folded her hands on the desk. "I heard about your adventure in the woods . . . ," she began, smiling at him, her eyes goggling through her thick glasses.

Their talk lasted over an hour. Dr. Spoon asked him about all kinds of things, including his sleeping habits, energy level, and appetite. She also wanted to know about his father. Evan told her the truth—that he hadn't seen his father in years, that his mother got checks from him every month but no letters, and that the only thing he knew about his father these days was his address in White Springs, Oregon.

Dr. Spoon pushed him for details about his family life. Evan tried to answer her questions as honestly as he could: Yes, his parents had argued a lot when he was little, but no, they'd never hit him or touched him in any way. Yes, he guessed he loved his mother and aunt. No, he couldn't really say that he loved his father anymore, or ever had. No, he'd never heard voices, or thought about killing himself or anyone else. No, he didn't think about what was going to happen to him when he grew up. And no, he didn't really care.

When they finished, Dr. Spoon let him go back to his

mother in the waiting room. Evan thought he'd done okay. He thought he'd passed. His mother was called into the office then and was gone for another half hour. Meanwhile, Evan sat and tried to read a magazine article about decorating your house with dried flowers. When she finally came out again, she was scowling. "Come on," she said.

Evan threw the magazine aside and followed his mother out of the waiting room, through the cool, squeaky-floored lobby, and into the parking lot. They got into the car without another word. Evan's mother started the engine, then turned to him. "You knew you could have come to me if you had any problems. If you didn't feel right. You knew that."

Evan realized then that he hadn't passed. He'd said the wrong things to the bearded man, and then to the goggle-eyed woman. "What'd they tell you?"

"They went to a lot of trouble to score your tests right away," Evan's mother said. She reached for her bag and pulled out a little slip of paper, a prescription. "You'll have to take some medication. And she wants you to see her once a week, for a few months at least."

Evan thought about the word "medication." Pills, she meant. He would be taking pills—to cure himself of his sickness. "What kind of medication?"

"Prozac," she said, reading off the prescription. "The current cure for everything, I guess." She looked over at him. For a second, there was a kind of softening in her face. "It's an antidepressant, Evan. Two bucks a pill, but it's supposed to make you feel better. Less sad."

Evan knew what Prozac was. Jeannie, one of the girls in his class, was taking it, and she would sometimes give her pill to some boys from the high school. But Jeannie was a lot worse off than Evan was. She was seriously weird. There was a story going around that she'd even tried to kill herself once—she'd slit her wrists in a bubble bath while listening to The Cure.

Evan turned and stared out the side window at the car next to them. Am I sad? he wondered.

"Aunt Rita and I will have to work something out to drive you here every Wednesday," his mother went on. "Dr. Spoon's last appointment of the day is four o'clock."

Am I sad? Evan asked himself again. Was "sad" the word for what he felt? It didn't seem right. Bored, heavy, always tired, but sad? Then, to his total disgust, Evan felt tears in his eyes, blurring the image of the cars in the lot.

Are you sad? he asked for a third time. He looked down at his cold-chapped hands.

His mother shifted into gear and pulled out of the parking lot. As she pushed a lever on the dashboard, filling the car with foul-smelling air, Evan realized that there was only one answer to the question that fit, only one that made any sense at all: yes, he was sad. Whatever he had been before, now he was sad.

The next night, a few hours after his call to Kate Baker, Evan sat in front of his computer in the dark. It was late, but he had a headache and couldn't sleep. He was playing game after game of Ice Assault—with the sound turned off so he wouldn't wake his mother or aunt—and was doing incredibly well. Twice he had reached the thirteenth level, the Prison of Dendriox. The second time, he'd even managed to put together all three pieces of the flame bazooka, and he was killing demons at an awesome rate. Finally, at about four A.M., he reached the Vortex, where the Princess Artemis of Xantor was held captive. He'd never gotten this far before. He didn't even know what happened when the princess was freed. Was the game over? Would he have to fight his way out again? Would a second population of wizards and demons be released from the depths to stop him?

The princess was visible now, beyond the pillars of frozen mercury. Moving the mouse, Evan edged toward her. But just as he entered the cell, something materialized in front of him. It was a demon—huge and powerful. Clicking as fast as he could, Evan threw every ounce of firepower he had at the demon, but the thing barely seemed to flinch. It pointed a finger at him, and then there was a silent red flash, and an explosion that filled the screen. When the fog cleared, Evan knew that he was down, that the Stone Warrior was toast. He was lying paralyzed at the feet of the enormous demon. Through its legs, he could see the Princess Artemis in mourning.

Then a message was spelled out in purple letters across the screen. "You're lunch meat, Stone Warrior! Better luck next century . . . if you're man enough to try again."

Pulling at the gold cross in his earlobe, Evan hit the escape button and exited the program. There would be time to save the princess, he knew. It didn't have to be today.

He got up and went over to his bureau. He picked up the container of Prozac they'd gotten from the drugstore the day before and opened it. It was half full of little green and yellow capsules. He'd taken the first one that morning, washing it down with apple juice. Evan tried to sense the chemicals washing through his body now, creeping into his brain, fixing what needed to be fixed.

Evan put the cap back on the container. He would go to sleep now, he decided, putting the pills aside. Tomorrow was Saturday; his mother would let him sleep late.

He went over to the window and closed the venetian blinds to shut out the moonlight. Then he climbed into bed and pulled the quilt over himself. The clock next to his bed read 4:13. Still a couple of hours until dawn.

Evan turned over onto his stomach. He would call Kate Baker again, he decided. Maybe not tomorrow, but he definitely would call her. Because he now realized that

this was their fate, this was why he had found the body
in the first place—in order to meet Kate Baker. It was the
hidden meaning in all of the events so far. It was the plan
that God had in mind.

Evan buried his face deep in the pillows. "This is your
fate, Stone Warrior," he said aloud, into the warm mass
of feathers, making his voice hum loudly in his head.

9

Kate got up early on the day after the call from Evan Potter. She had people to see, so she dressed up—teal silk blouse, simple black skirt, black hose, her most comfortable flats. She wound her hair into a French braid and even put on a little mascara, as if she were going to a job interview. "Not too bad," she said to herself, checking the whole effect in the full-length mirror in the bedroom.

At a little before nine, leaving Hermann alone with full dishes of Iams and water, she pulled on her black suede fringed jacket (another remnant, like the rusty white Jetta, of her life pre-Joel) and left the house. It was a damp, chilly morning, the branches of the cedars white with frost. Jingling her keys as she crossed the slippery lawn, Kate noticed that the unmarked police car across the street, a fixture on the block by now, had a different cop inside today, a young black man with a mustache. Kind of cute, Kate thought—cute in that old bashful-cop way. She watched him watch her as she got into the Jetta. They started their engines at the same time. Kate let the defroster run for a few minutes, then pulled into the street and drove away, the unmarked car right behind her.

It took about forty minutes to get to the offices of From the Rainforest Imports. It was a Saturday, but Kate was certain that Velma would be at the office, keeping the business together while her two bosses were missing. The single-story prefab building, which sat between a clothing warehouse and a PEPCO substation, was part of a decaying industrial park near the National Arboretum. Kate parked in the small, almost-empty lot and headed toward the dark-glass entrance. The sun was out now, glimmering off the hoods of the cars. Kate noticed that the unmarked car had stopped on the street just beyond stretch of yellowing lawn.

Velma Sampson, a fleshy but stylish strawberry blond in her fifties, was on the phone when Kate walked into the front office. Velma had been with Joel and Don's company since the mid-1980s, and was now considered indispensable by both of them. She handled the company's books, processed orders and invoices, and spent hours every day telephoning and faxing suppliers on five continents. If anyone besides Joel and Don knew what was going on, it would be Velma. But Kate knew that getting information from her wouldn't be easy. Velma was fiercely loyal, and would probably try to keep Joel's secrets to herself.

Velma, wearing a rose-colored dress that somehow didn't clash with her hair color, was frowning as she spoke into the phone. "Next week, George," she drawled in her soft Tennessee accent. She saw Kate and waved. "We have a fax promising delivery by next week. Don't worry so much, you old lady."

Kate waved back and then wandered around the office while Velma kept trying to reassure the customer. Kate didn't visit Joel's office very often, but whenever she came she was impressed all over again by the Japanese prints on the walls. They seemed nicer and more elegant than the ones at home—something that had always annoyed her.

"Absolutely," Velma went on. "You'll be the very first to know, sweetie. You have my word. 'Bye." She hung up the phone, hit the No-Disturb button, and then came around the desk. "Hello, Kate," she said. They hugged and touched cheeks awkwardly. They'd talked on the phone since Joel's disappearance, but this was the first time they'd seen each other in person.

"How are you holding up?" Kate asked.

"Oh, you know me. Iron Velma. But how about you?" Velma held her at arm's length for a second. "Holding up?"

Kate shrugged. "I'm trying." She nodded toward the phone. "Was that a nervous customer?"

Velma rolled her eyes. "He'd be a lot more nervous if he knew the whole truth. I'm not telling them diddly, Kate. I don't know what else I can do. Some of them have heard, from the TV news and all, but the ones who don't know I'm not telling. Maybe you think that's not right . . ."

"No," Kate said. "I think that's absolutely the best choice, for now."

Velma smiled, looking grateful. A button was blinking on her phone, but Kate could see Velma make a conscious decision to let the voice-mail system answer it. "You heard about the police action here, I guess. They had a search warrant, some mean old dogs, the whole works. It was like a circus out in the warehouse."

Kate nodded. She was trying to decide how to begin. There were several possible ways of approaching Velma, and she wondered which of them Detective Starks had used. Intimidation, she guessed, and it had probably backfired. A better way, Kate thought, would be to play on Velma's loyalty to Joel, to make it seem that telling every-

thing she knew would be in Joel's best interest. But Kate
had no idea how to begin.

Finally, as Velma turned with a steaming cup of coffee
in her hand, Kate decided just to wing it and try honesty,
the cop's last resort. "Velma," she said, taking the coffee
and sitting in the leather director's chair across from her,
"I don't know what to think about all of this."

Velma sat, too, falling a little heavily into her chair.
"Neither do I, honey. Neither do I."

Kate looked down into her cup and said, "I was hoping
we could maybe help each other figure it out. Tell each
other what we know."

She saw right away that she'd moved to the point too
fast. Velma stiffened, and her eyes seemed to cloak over.
"I told those police goons everything I know, Kate, which
isn't much."

Kate reached out and—half-genuinely, half-cynically—
put her hand on Velma's. "I'm not the police," she said.
"I'm Joel's wife."

This seemed to have an effect. Velma turned her hand
over, squeezed Kate's, and then leaned back in the chair.
"I really don't know what to say. Sure, I had my suspicions that something was going on, and I knew that there
was probably stuff in some of those rooms back there that
wasn't exactly kosher." She looked straight at Kate. "I
trust that husband of yours. He's been good to me. If he
did something and it's against the law, well, it's probably
the law that's wrong." She looked away then. "I know for
sure that he didn't have anything to do with that body in
the woods, no matter what the police think."

Kate murmured in agreement. At least someone else—
someone whose judgment she regarded as sound—agreed
with her on that point. But could both of them be wrong?
"Was there anybody you saw, or anybody you heard Joel
or Don talking to, who could have something to do with
that?"

"I'll tell you exactly what I told those detectives." Velma sat forward in her chair. "I remember seeing a young Chinese man here twice, once to see Joel and Don and once to see Joel alone. The first time, there was somebody with him, a man, looked like an ex-hippie—long hair, big nose, Vandyke beard. Kinda pitiful-looking, really. I'd guess he was in his forties, and you could tell that he was used to people following his orders. A real big shot. He had money behind him. You can always tell."

"Was he wearing a brown overcoat?" Kate asked. A shot in the dark.

Velma thought for a second and then shook her head. "No, it was a long gray coat. Cashmere, something expensive. I remember thinking that he looked like a bum who'd found somebody's fancy overcoat."

"Did you hear him say anything?"

"No. Joel just hustled him and the Chinese man into his office, without introducing them, which wasn't usual. Joel seemed a little put out that they were here, in the office. He didn't like the surprise, I think."

"So he wasn't expecting them?"

"That's what it looked like to me. I know Joel's moods. I could see it in how he pushed them into the office. He liked the Chinese man, but the hippie was a pain in the rear, somebody he had to, you know, handle—the way you handle a rich customer."

"You think Joel and the Chinese man were friendly?"

"Like I told you, honey. It looked like there was definitely some kind of understanding between them."

Kate took a slow sip of coffee. She trusted Velma's instincts about Joel completely. Velma probably knew him better than anyone else did. Working closely with him over the past decade, she'd probably learned to read every tone of Joel's voice, to interpret every gesture. Velma was divorced. Her one child, a son, lived in Seattle now. She probably had nothing else to devote herself to besides this

job. Is she in love with Joel? Kate asked herself suddenly.
Are they involved in all of this together? Kate shook her
head, trying to get rid of the thought. The pressure was
starting to make her paranoid. She looked down at her
fingernails. She'd been biting them—a habit she thought
she'd broken long ago. "And you told the police all of
this?" Kate asked finally.

Velma nodded. "And lots more. They asked about
every customer we have—names, addresses, orders."

Kate hesitated before saying, carefully, "And is there
anything you didn't tell the police?"

One beat too many passed before Velma said, firmly,
"They were here for hours, honey. I told them everything
but my shoe size."

Kate got up from the director's chair and took her coffee over to one of the prints on the wall. The framed
picture showed a man and what looked like his courtesan,
standing on a bridge half-hidden by willows, the woman's
robe slipping from a thin white shoulder. In the lower
right-hand corner was an animal—a highly stylized dog
or cat—staring straight out toward Kate.

She turned. "Velma, I don't know how to make you
trust me. I think Joel is in danger. I know you want to
protect him. I do, too, but the only way I can do that is
to find out what happened to him. That's why I need your
help." She came back to the desk and stood directly in
front of Velma again. "Is there anything you know, anything at all, that could help us figure out what was going
on here?"

Velma was playing with a pencil, turning it in her fingers.

"Please," Kate whispered.

Velma cleared her throat and said, "He asked me to
keep some documents for him." She looked over at the
telephone. "He bought a safe to keep in my basement at
home, and he put some documents in it. He told me that

nobody else would know anything about those documents."

Kate sat again and tried to force Velma to look at her. "What kind of documents?" she asked.

"I never saw them. They were in some expandable file. He'd show up at my house every few weeks and throw some more in or take some away."

"And are they still there?"

Velma shrugged her shoulders. "I assume so, honey. But I haven't checked."

"You haven't opened the safe since Joel's been gone?"

"He never told me the combination. It wasn't that he didn't trust me with it. He just didn't want me more involved than I had to be."

"But you know the combination?"

"I told you, it wasn't that he didn't trust me. He opened it a couple times while I was there."

"And you saw the numbers he dialed."

Velma grimaced. "I thought I should know the combination in case he lost it or something. But I have never opened that safe. Not once."

Kate stood up again. A safe-deposit box, now a safe. Her husband's secrets. She wondered what the safe could contain—under-the-table account books, lists of suppliers, more Beatrix Potter? She looked at Velma again. "You have no idea at all what those papers could be?"

Velma threw up her hands. "Oh, Kate, what can I say? Something was going on, some business that maybe even Don didn't know about. And any business makes documents—financial records, whatever. I guess that's what's in that old safe." She looked at Kate then. "Joel is a good man," she said. "Not a saint, thank God, but a good man. I know that. And you should, too."

Kate nodded. "I do," she said, wishing it true.

Kate stared at the Japanese print for a few seconds,

wondering how to go on. "Velma," she said finally, "I'd
like to see those papers."

Velma shrugged again. "All right, honey," she said.
"But just you. Not the police. Come over tonight after I'm
through here. I'll open the safe."

Kate remembered the police tail. She'd shaken it once,
and would have to shake it again. "Let me call you. I'm
not sure exactly where I'll be."

They both stood up. The buttons on Velma's telephone
had been blinking throughout their talk. By now, Velma
probably had a backlog of suppliers to put off, customers
to reassure.

Velma seemed listless now, as she came around the
desk again to say good-bye. "I just hope I'm doing the
right thing here," she said.

"We are," Kate said, as she hugged Velma with all the
warmth she could manage.

After leaving the Rainforest offices, Kate got back onto
the Beltway and almost immediately ran into bumper-to-
bumper traffic. Sighing, she looked out over a broken
plain of car roofs gleaming in the low wintry sun. Although she was usually as impatient in traffic as a man,
she didn't mind so much right now, since Lieutenant
Grainger, two cars back, was just as stuck as she was.
Apparently, the younger cop had called his superior on
the radio while Kate was inside with Velma, and now the
Lieutenant himself was picking up the tail. Every once in
a while Kate could get a distant glimpse of his scowling
face in her rearview mirror.

Kate saw an opening in the next lane and started to
shoot for it, but a green Isuzu Trooper beat her to it. She
hit her horn, and let out another huge sigh.

Poor Lieutenant Grainger. What would Kate's brothers
think—what would her *father* have thought—about the
way she was treating the three detectives involved in her

husband's case? Everything people said about the tribal-
ism of cops—the intense loyalties, the clannishness—was
absolutely true, as Kate knew better than almost anyone.
She'd seen her brothers' automatic solidarity with the cop
on the six o'clock news, the one from Chicago South or
Evanston or Oak Park who'd shot the proverbial unarmed
honor student in the back alley. They didn't have to hear
the evidence—to them, the cop was justified, even if he'd
made a mistake. She remembered the motto her brothers
used to recite: "Better to be judged by twelve than carried
by six."

These were the people she grew up with. How could
she not like cops? Her brothers aside, the nicest men she
knew were cops—patrolmen, beat cops, detectives. They
would do anything for you, would literally lay down their
lives for you. At least if you were one of the good guys.
Back in Chicago, Kate had been as good as they come—a
cop from a family of cops. Kate Theodorus was in the
tribe, she was *okay*. But now that she was Kate Baker,
everything was different. She'd gone over the line to the
other side. Her father would probably have been ashamed
of her.

Traffic began to move ahead, the tight lock of cars
shifting and loosening. Kate could see the flashing lights
of a police car up ahead. An accident, probably—although
traffic on the Beltway never seemed to need a reason-to-
be. After a minute, the black Volvo in front of her pulled
into the middle lane, freeing her. Kate saw the cause of
the delay then, and her stomach clenched. Two mutilated
deer—big tawny bucks—lay sprawled across the right-
most lane. Their big, muscular bodies were twisted into
wild poses, the necks obviously broken, the white chest
of one torn open and trailing a weirdly elegant smear of
entrails. Kate got a glimpse of the cloudy, staring eye of
the animal. She shuddered and looked away. A blue Taurus—the car that had hit the deer—was stopped at an

angle, half on the shoulder and half on the yellow grass. Its two front doors were open, making it look like a huge fallen bird. An old woman stood on the shoulder, listening to but not hearing what two uniformed patrolmen were telling her, her hand wrapped tight against her wrinkled mouth.

Kate changed lanes and drove past the scene as quickly as she could. If there was some kind of omen in what she just saw, she didn't want to think about it.

"Okay," she said aloud when she'd finally regained her composure, a few miles later. She found Lieutenant Grainger in the mirror again. She knew that a single cop couldn't keep a tail on somebody indefinitely if that somebody didn't want to be tailed. And she knew that the Lieutenant probably wouldn't call for backup if she started trying to shake him. His surveillance of her had to have a very low priority in the homicide case. But Kate had no idea how she would get rid of him.

When they reached the next exit, she quickly pulled off. She checked her mirror hopefully, but Lieutenant Grainger had managed to follow and was right behind her. At the end of the ramp, she turned left, then immediately right into an Exxon station. She parked in a spot next to the air hose and waited while Lieutenant Grainger's car began to make the turn behind her. It occurred to her that she might try to get him turned around on some side streets. D.C. was full of narrow alleys. Her Jetta could probably maneuver through them more easily than his clunky Caprice could. But just as he was turning into the station, the Lieutenant swerved sharply back onto the street, his tires squealing. He gunned the engine and then sped off down the road.

Kate got out of the car, confused. Had he gotten an emergency call, she wondered. Had the county cops found something related to Joel's case? Or was it an entirely unrelated call?

Feeling oddly abandoned, Kate climbed back into the Jetta. She backed up and then pulled slowly into the street again. There was no sign of the Lieutenant's car. Another unexplained disappearance, she said to herself, and then realized that what she felt was disappointment. She'd actually been looking forward to losing the tail. A part of her had been anticipating the excitement, the defiance, the adrenaline rush. "That's sick," she said aloud, thinking again about her father.

Sighing, she turned into traffic and drove north toward the entrance to I-95, direction Baltimore.

10

Kate got to Johns Hopkins at four in the afternoon. After parking in the visitors' lot, she walked across a patchy lawn to the nearest public building, found a campus directory, and looked up the name of Jin-Liang Lu. He was there with three other Lus—Joan, Harry, and Li-Mei. The directory gave Jin's office address in the New Engineering Building and his telephone extension. Kate found a campus phone, punched in the dead man's number, and got his voice mail, which no one had bothered to change yet: "Hi," said the recorded voice in a clipped Chinese accent. "This is Jin Lu. I guess I'm somewhere else right now, so please leave a message at the pleasant tone." Kate wondered if there was some way she could retrieve his messages. She pressed the star key. "Please enter your pass code," said a synthesized female voice. On a whim, she pressed a few three-digit numbers. After giving the same polite rejection three times—"I'm sorry, I did not get your pass code, please try again."—the voice turned icy: "Call back when you can remember your pass code. Good-bye."

Kate hung up. She located the New Engineering Building on a campus map and then wandered across campus until she found it—a modern brick building attached to an older one on the quad. She went in through the unlocked doors and searched the deserted hallways of the first two floors, hurrying over the gray-and-black linoleum tiles, passing paper-choked bulletin boards and closed office doors covered with signs saying: BIOHAZARD, RADIATION HAZARD, CANCER SUSPECT AGENT. In one open room stood a tangle of gleaming equipment that Kate couldn't even begin to understand. Finally, past another bulletin board marked BIOMEDICAL ENGINEERING NEWS, she found Jin's office, the door standing wide open. It was a group office—a long, narrow space crammed with four wooden desks, three of them overflowing with papers, books, and journals. Beside the fourth desk was an ancient gray machine that looked to Kate like some kind of spectrograph. A fly-specked Chinese scroll painting of bamboo hung above it, along with a bumper sticker: BIOCHEMISTS MAKE BETTER LOVERS.

Kate stepped into the office. The uncluttered desk would have been Lu's; the police had probably taken every scrap of paper from it as evidence days ago. After checking the door, Kate pulled the desk chair out, sat, and started opening drawers. All of them were empty—just a few paper clips and loose ball bearings rolling around in them. Then she pulled out both extension shelves. The one on the left was clean, but the one on the right had a few things written on it, pen marks etched into the soft wood—some Chinese characters, a little drawing of a cat, and then a name and date: Julia—12/5. Kate took out her notebook. She began trying to copy the Chinese characters but found it hard to get them right. Finally, she ripped out a blank sheet, lined it up over the characters, and started shading the paper with the edge of her pencil. The characters slowly appeared on the page like a gravestone rubbing.

"Can I help you?" Kate looked up. A young Asian was standing in the doorway—a chubby, smooth-cheeked man who looked scarcely out of his teens. He was wearing blue jeans and a green polo shirt, and was staring down at the sheet of paper she'd been working on.

Kate shrugged self-consciously. "It's kind of a souvenir, I guess," she said, thinking fast. "It's all I have to remember him by."

"You knew Jin?" he asked, in an accent that struck Kate as pure California.

Kate nodded. Impulsively, she said, "I gave him some English lessons. A long time ago."

The young man stared at her, his round face giving nothing away. "He spoke pretty well," he said. "You must be a good teacher. I'm John Feng."

Kate shook his hand. "Kate," she said. "Kate Theodorus. Did you know Jin well?"

"Nope. Just moved into this office two weeks before he disappeared."

"You hear all this they've been saying about him? Everything he was involved in?"

"I heard a little. The cops think he was cooking up designer drugs or something, right?"

Kate shrugged. Either John Feng was a great actor, or he really didn't know anything about his office-mate's activities. "I'm looking for Julia," she said then.

"Julia Tao?" he asked.

Kate nodded.

"Sorry. Haven't seen her. I think she's back, though."

"Back?"

"From home. She took some time off after . . . you know, after they found Jin. Must have been hell for her. They were supposed to go to Saint Martin for her birthday."

Kate looked down at her paper. "December fifth?"

"Sometime around then."

Kate got up from the chair. "Well, thanks. Sorry to come into your office when nobody was here. But I was away when they found him."

"Hey, it's okay. And if you see Julia, tell her again how sorry I am."

"I will," Kate said, going out the door. Then she came right back in. "Can I ask you something else?" she asked. "Can you tell me what these characters mean?"

"Oh Jesus," John said, giving her a huge smile. "I can try, but my Chinese sucks." He took the paper from her and stared at it for a few moments in silence. "Weird," he said finally. "Something like 'Cabbage'—no: 'Too much cabbage makes you sleepy.' " He looked up. "I don't know, maybe it's one of those old Chinese proverbs. Who knows what it means?"

Kate took back the sheet of paper. She remembered the line from Beatrix Potter.

"Well, thanks anyway," she said. " 'Bye."

Kate quickly left the building. She folded the paper into the pocket of her suede jacket and crossed the quad to the first building she'd gone into. She found the campus phone again and looked up Julia Tao in the directory. Her name was there, too, with a telephone number off-campus. Kate moved to the pay phone, fed it a quarter, and dialed.

A girl picked up after four rings. "Hello?"

"Hi, is Julia there, please?"

"Sorry, not till tonight. Can I ask who's calling?"

"Kate," Kate said, in a voice as carefree as she could manage. Then she added quickly: "You have any idea where she is?"

"Probably Eisenhower. She usually studies down in the carrels on B-level."

"Okay, thanks," Kate said and hung up. She searched the campus map on the bulletin board until she found it—

Eisenhower Library. It was just a short walk away.

She hurried out into the cold air again. Night was already falling, the sky turning a deep winter blue. Students were walking briskly along the paths, carrying books and knapsacks, calling out to friends and classmates. A scholarly-looking man with a salt-and-pepper beard inched by on a mountain bike, formally begging her pardon as he passed. College. In the last few years, Kate had been feeling strong regrets that she'd never gone away to school, to a serious college. Her brothers had all been to Warren Community College at night while working day patrol, and she had done the same thing. Only recently— only since meeting Joel, really—had she let herself admit that she'd been much too smart for Warren Community, that she should have gone to Northwestern or Chicago. Or Johns Hopkins, she thought, looking around.

The smell was what she noticed the minute she walked into Eisenhower Library. It was faint in the entrance hall of the building, and one flight down in the bright, open mezzanine, where she had no trouble signing in with the guard as a guest user. But once Kate got down to B-level and started wandering the stacks, the smell became stronger, and she found herself breathing it in with a pleasure that she couldn't explain at first. This was a good smell, a combination of dust and paste, plaster and old books. It brought back images she hadn't thought about in years—of gray-painted school walls, a cavelike lunchroom full of echoes, the tight freshness of a brand-new spiral notebook. The smell even brought to mind a certain ruby-colored dress, velour, with spaghetti straps—not a nice-girl dress, her mother had called it—which at the time had seemed to Kate the most desirable thing in the world.

The third Asian student Kate talked to on B-level turned out to be the one she was looking for. The girl was poring over a textbook at one of the wooden carrels set off at one end of the floor. When Kate asked if her name was Julia Tao, she looked up suddenly, surprised. She was pretty, with a small nose and a wide, thin-lipped mouth. Twenty or twenty-one, Kate guessed. Probably an undergraduate. "Yes," the girl said. "Why?"

Kate lowered her voice to avoid being overheard. "I'd like to talk to you about Jin," she said.

Julia's face seemed to sag. She looked down at her book again. "I've talked to so many of you people about Jin."

"You haven't spoken to me," Kate said softly. "My name is Kate Baker. The police think my husband is the one who killed Jin."

Julia turned from her book and stared at Kate for a few seconds. Kate sank to a crouch beside the chair. "They're wrong," she said. "I think Jin and my husband were friends. Maybe good friends."

Julia put a slip of paper into the book she was reading. "Let's go someplace," she said.

As she stood up, Kate noticed the title of the textbook: *The Foundations of Literary Criticism*. She followed Julia across the room and into the stacks.

Julia stopped when they reached a quiet place. She crossed her arms, then uncrossed them. "So your husband was Joel Baker?"

Kate nodded, thinking: Is. My husband *is* Joel Baker. "Did you ever meet him?" she asked.

"I never heard his name until the police mentioned it." She put a hand out and grabbed the edge of one of the bookshelves, as if she needed to steady herself. Kate noticed that she wasn't wearing an engagement ring. "Do you have something to show me who you are? Some ID?"

Kate opened her shoulder bag and rooted around until she found her wallet. She showed Julia her Maryland driver's license.

Julia looked at it carefully, then nodded, apparently deciding that Kate was to be trusted. "They told me that Jin and your husband were working together on something. Synthetic drugs or something?"

"You probably know more about it than I do. The police don't tell me much, since my husband's their prime suspect."

"Well, I don't understand much about Jin's work. Biomedical Engineering. That was his field."

"Did you know Jin long?"

Julia shrugged, looking glassy-eyed. "We've been seeing each other about a year and a half. We met at this Asian student social. He was kind of out of place around here. From Taipei. Most of the Chinese students here are either from the mainland or were born here." She stopped, then, near tears, she added, "We were supposed to go on vacation next month."

Kate wanted to touch her, but she wasn't sure how Julia would react. "Did you have any idea what Jin and my husband were doing?"

"Jin always said he was doing some research on the side for Squibb. I never asked any more about it."

"And *was* he working for Squibb?"

"The police say no. They say he was working for your husband's company. That they were manufacturing illegal drugs." Julia's eyes locked onto Kate's. "I had no idea," she said. "He kept it all from me. Did you know anything?"

Caught off guard, Kate shook her head quickly. "No," she whispered, "I didn't know anything, either." We're all the same, she said to herself—Julia Tao, Velma, Elena, me.

"Did you ever see Jin with a man," Kate went on. "A man with a beard and long hair?"

Julia thought for a few seconds before saying no.

"Did you ever see him with anybody you didn't know? Anybody who could have been involved in this thing?"

Julia shook her head. "The police asked the same question. But I really don't remember anybody. Really."

"How about friends? Can you tell me about Jin's friends?"

"All I can give you is the same information I gave the police," she said. She started listing names, which Kate wrote down on a piece of scrap paper.

As Julia was talking, Kate became aware of a figure moving slowly on the other side of the shelves to her right. It was a male, she knew—his black jeans were visible above the books on one shelf, his faded blue T-shirt higher up—and probably a student. She'd been sensing his presence for a minute or two now and hoped that he'd go away. But the student didn't leave. And as her conversation with Julia went on, Kate edged forward to get a glimpse of his face through the stacks.

"And that's about all the people I can . . ." Julia said, her voice finally giving way. She looked away. "They're all still alive, and Jin's dead."

Kate moved another few inches to the left, and the face came into view: a patch of beard, a corner of horn-rimmed eyeglasses, an eye staring straight at her.

"Are you looking for us?" Kate asked aloud.

The head jerked away. Kate heard the student moving down toward the end of the stacks.

Kate put a hand out and touched Julia's arm to apologize for the interruption. "Are you looking for us?" Kate asked again, walking toward the end of the stacks.

The student began running.

Kate pulled the bag off her shoulder and threw it back toward Julia. "Could you look after that a second?" she asked. Then she took off after the student.

He'd already turned a corner somewhere, and Kate wasn't sure in which direction. She moved quickly down the stacks, checking each row. A few people looked up at her as she passed, but none of them was the one she'd seen. Then she heard the screech of a rubber sole against linoleum, and she sprinted down a stretch of shiny floor toward the sound, catching a glimpse of him just as he was disappearing around a corner. Kate set off after him, the fringe on her jacket flying.

She came out of the dark stacks into a narrow, bright area full of metal study carrels and chairs. The student was already on the far side, pushing past anyone who stood in his way. Kate ran through the study carrels, kicking books aside as she ran. "Security!" she shouted. "Out of the way, please!" A crowd of young men in sweatpants parted ahead of her. She reached a long corridor. He was already halfway down it, sprinting, his arms pumping. Kate followed. She gained on him, but then he turned into a stairwell, the wooden door smashing back against the wall. By the time Kate reached the door, he was gone, either upstairs or down. She stopped and listened, straining to separate the noise she needed from the hollow roar of the cinder block stairwell. Hearing nothing useful, she took a chance and headed down. The door on C-level was just swinging shut as she reached it. She pulled it open and ran straight into a huge blond girl, almost knocking her over.

"You see somebody running?" Kate shouted at her. The girl nodded, as if in shock, and pointed. "Thanks." Kate ran. She rounded a corner, then another, and there he was again, going through another door. Kate sprinted up to it. It was a men's room—as if that would stop her. She pushed her way in through one door, then another. Two students—neither one the man she was looking for— stood at the sinks, washing their hands, but in her peripheral vision, she saw the door of one of the stalls swinging shut. Kate reached it just before it closed. She stiff-armed it open again, throwing the bearded student hard into the cinder block wall behind the toilet. She grabbed his arm, twisted it behind his back, and pushed him against the wall.

"What's going on?" One of the guys from the sinks was behind them now. "What the hell is this?"

Her heart racing, Kate shouted as loudly as she could: "Baltimore Police. Get out!" There was no movement behind her, so she screamed: *"Get the fuck out, NOW!!"*

She heard both students behind her scrambling for the door.

Kate held the bearded student pinned against the wall for a few seconds while she tried to catch her breath. There was a curved smear of blood on the yellow cinder blocks—from the student's nose, which now dripped quietly, the drops spattering on the white porcelain of the toilet. Oh Christ, Kate said to herself. What the hell am I doing? This kid was just eavesdropping. He was probably a friend of Julia's making sure she was okay.

But there was no way she could back down now. "I want to know who you are and what the hell you know about Jin-Liang Lu," Kate said to him, trying not to let any of her sudden doubt leak into her voice.

The student seemed to be crying now, his cheek still pinned against the wall. "I don't know what you're talking about," he said.

"You were listening, and then you ran. You sure as hell know what I'm talking about."

They were both still panting, like two animals after the chase, in the quiet pause before one of them ate the other.

"Where's your badge?" the student asked after a second.

"What?"

"Your badge. If you're a Baltimore cop, show your badge." She cranked up on his arm, squeezing a little moan from him. She was hurting him now, but it felt good. "I'm not a cop," she said finally. "Does that make you feel safer?" Kate knew that if she pretended to be working for the police, or for the people who had killed Lu, the student would probably just clam up or scream. "I'm the wife," she went on, "the wife of the guy who was working with Lu, and I don't want my husband to end up dead in the woods like him, okay? So I need to know what you know about Lu—and if you say you don't know anything, I'll break your arm, I swear to you."

She let him think about that for a few seconds. Two more drops of blood fell from the student's nose, hitting the water in the bowl this time, sinking to the bottom in a trail of pink. Kate noticed then that she had put a big run in the leg of her black hose.

"I'll tell you what I know," the student said at last. "But let go of my arm first."

Slowly, Kate released his arm and stood back, bracing herself for a punch. But this kid obviously wasn't going to hit her. They were about the same size, but Kate had learned in her cop days how to be intimidating. The kid was scared, and ashamed of being scared. "Here," she said. She unrolled a foot of toilet paper and handed it to him. "Wipe your nose."

He took the paper and began dabbing at his upper lip. "So you're the wife of the guy they've been asking about," he said. Then, "You beat up on your husband like this?"

"I'm beginning to think I should have," Kate muttered. She stepped out of the stall, walked over to the first door leading out into the hall, and twisted the lock closed. "What's your name, first of all?" she asked, turning back. When he didn't answer, she pushed him and then whispered, with as much threat in her voice as possible, "Look, I'm not a cop, and nothing you say to me will get back to the cops, if that's what you're worried about. But I've got a personal involvement here, and I need to know what Lu was doing, and if I don't hear it from you, I swear to you—"

"Okay, okay," he said. "I believe you."

"Good." She crossed her arms. "So, who are you?"

"Ken," he said. "Ken Wilkerson. Jin and I are both TAs in the biochem department."

"Fine. So what was going on?"

He paused again. "This is just between me and you, right?"

"I promise you. Now come on."

Ken took a deep breath, then began: "Jin didn't tell me much, but I know that it wasn't, like, anything really heavy. I mean, no cocaine derivatives or PCP or anything like that. The people he was working for were into more exotic stuff, a lot of it organic—animal hormones, amino acid derivatives."

He hesitated again. Kate moved closer to him. "Come on," she whispered.

Ken looked down at the bloodstained toilet paper in his hand. "Jin came to me. This was, I don't know, about a year ago. They'd hit a couple of promising leads, he said, and now they needed somebody to help."

"And you were that somebody."

"Or one of the somebodies, at least. And not with anything serious. I mean, I really wouldn't have gotten involved if it was seriously illegal."

"Right, right. So what did he give you to work on?"

Ken looked away, uncomfortable. "Let's just say that the compound was something the federal government wouldn't have approved of."

"Tell me."

He sighed. "Dichloredrine. I guess you'd call it an excitant, related to the amphetamines."

"Excitant? So you were manufacturing this stuff?"

"No. Hell. Fooling around with the molecule is more like it. You make a little change in this chain, add a little planar ring there, see what happens. It's what the big drug companies do when they're looking for a new drug. Take one that works okay and fool around with it until you find a form that works better."

"I don't understand," Kate said, feeling frustrated. "What does that mean?"

"Well, usually the idea is to minimize toxicity, so you can up the recommended dosage without killing the patient. But sometimes you get lucky and make the molecule a lot more active biologically. Organic molecules are like that. You make a little change, and it might do something very interesting—make you see God, kill cancer cells, whatever. Then you've got a billion-dollar molecule on your hands."

Someone pushed on the locked door of the men's room, then began knocking. Kate stared at Ken in warning. "Say 'out of order,' " she told him.

"Out of order!" Ken shouted at the door.

"Shit," said the voice outside. Then it was gone.

Kate turned back to him. "Who paid you to do this?"

"Jin paid me. Some guy down in D.C. was paying him, probably your husband. But he wouldn't tell me any more."

"But what was the point? What were they after?"

"I don't know exactly. I was just doing bench chemistry. Jin gave me, like, specific problems to solve—making structural changes in the molecule. He never let me in on the big picture. But I get the feeling Jin thought he had the makings of a new smart drug here—a real one, I mean, instead of this nootropic and amino acid crap."

"And was all of this going on here, on campus?"

"Are you kidding? Jin had a basic setup in the basement of his house, and that's where I worked. I hear the cops have ripped that one up pretty bad. But a lot of Jin's work had to be done somewhere else. Somewhere with enough room for lab animals and high-powered equipment."

Kate realized that this lab, if it truly existed, could be anywhere within three hundred miles. "Was there anyone else involved that you know of? Anyone on campus?"

Ken shook his head. "Not anybody I heard about. Jin was pretty secretive about the whole thing, but there had to be at least a couple molecular biologists and biomedical guys working on these things. Over at the med school, maybe. Like somebody doing the modeling and structural analysis? I'm a biochemist, but Jin did some stuff with people in the pharmacology department over there."

Kate thought this over for a few seconds. "But how does work like this end up getting somebody killed?" she asked.

"Believe me, if I knew it could get my head chopped off, I wouldn't have gotten involved." He dabbed a few more times at his nose, but the bleeding had stopped. "All I can think is that Jin made trouble somewhere along the line. Maybe they wanted him to work on harder drugs all of a sudden—who knows? He was kind of an idealistic guy."

"What do you mean, idealistic?"

"He had, like, strong opinions. There were things he would do and things he wouldn't, and it didn't matter to him if they were illegal or not." Ken cleared his throat before going on, more quietly. "When he came to me with this work, I was a little . . . you know. I mean, this molecule was dicey. Illegal, basically. But Jin gave me this spiel about the big difference between illegal and immoral. He went on about how nothing could be more immoral than making cigarettes, but making something useful and safe like THC was illegal. Thanks to the FDA and all those people."

"And you agree with him?"

Ken put his hands up. "I could live with dichloredrine. It's really just like an animal hormone, or a better version of caffeine or something. Nobody's going to die from it. Besides, I needed the money."

Someone began banging hard on the locked bathroom

door. "Open up!" a voice shouted. "Campus security!"

Kate was running out of time. She leaned toward Ken and said, "Quick, what's your telephone number?" When he hesitated, she hissed, "I could look it up, damn it!"

He gave her the number.

"Okay. You know not to tell anybody else about the work you were doing?"

She could see the confidence coming back to his face. "Lady," he said, "I'm not stupid. I wouldn't have told you if you didn't break my fucking face first."

She reached up and touched his already swelling nose. "Sorry about that. Just some animal hormones of my own coming back."

She walked over to the door, turned the lock, and pulled open the door. Outside stood a wiry old black man in a campus security uniform. Kate smiled at him. "We worked it out, Officer," she said. "I don't want to press charges. It was just a misunderstanding, but I'm fine."

The man looked at her warily, an interpretation taking shape in his mind. "You sure?"

"He didn't touch me, really. We're friends. No charges."

She eased past him out of the men's room, turned into the stairwell, and, before the security man could say anything else, calmly climbed the library stairs to get her shoulder bag.

11

Kate reached Franklin at about seven-thirty—already the dead of night at this time of year. She drove the Jetta through the quiet streets of the town, slowly passing the dimly lit facades of the municipal building, the auto parts store, the twenty-four-hour deli that now seemed to be closed. The only business open was the Franklin Diner, a perfect little aluminum-sided diner that might have come right out of a book of fifties Americana. Kate had been living in the D.C. area for four years, but she'd never come this far out into the Maryland exurbs. She couldn't believe how rural it was—how isolated and dark—less than fifty minutes from Dupont Circle. Franklin wasn't a poor town, but it wasn't one of those quaintly rustic rich towns like Lewisburg, either. It was just a working town in the woods. And the woods around it were real, not like the tamed parks of the nearer suburbs. These were woods you could bury a body in.

Kate pulled into an empty parking lot and turned on the overhead light. She opened her Hampton County atlas and found the road she was looking for—Evan Potter's road. She had gotten his address from the phone book. She'd have to drive north out of town on Main Street, then go left after a mile or so. Kings Mill Road. The Potters lived at number 26.

Kate put the atlas aside, turned off the light, and pulled the Jetta back onto the street. Seven-thirty on a Saturday night was probably not the most considerate time to make a surprise visit, Kate realized, but she didn't have much choice. She assumed that the boy would be out during the day, and she didn't want to call ahead and let him know she was coming. She thought it would be a good idea to put him a little off balance—exactly what he'd done to her on the telephone last night.

The streetlights petered out as she left town and headed north. A few cars passed her on the road, one of them forgetting to dim its brights and nearly sending Kate's Jetta off the side of the road. She cursed aloud, recovered, and then almost drove right past the turnoff for Kings Mill Road. But she saw the little road sign in the bushes at the last minute. She signaled—stupidly, since nobody was around to see it—then made the turn onto a narrow asphalt road.

She passed a few brightly lit houses—brutal little pockets of halogen light in the darkness—and strained to read the numbers on the roadside mailboxes. The road curved, and her headlights picked out the sloped roof of a half-collapsed shed, then a stone cairn marking the entrance to some brand-new development. She rounded another corner and came face-to-face with the red, reflective eyes of a doe crossing the road. Kate stopped and watched the animal pass. It stopped, too, at the edge of Kate's headlights. The two of them stared at each other blankly for a second, locking eyes, until the doe turned and bolted away into the brush.

At the mailbox for number 26, Kate pulled into a gravel

driveway behind two almost identical red Honda Civics. The house, which stood above and to the right of the long driveway, seemed to be in good shape—a white colonial surrounded by well-trimmed bushes and trees. There was a second-floor deck in back, with a wooden stairway to the ground. At the foot of the stairs was a large pile of firewood. Somehow, Kate had expected Evan's house to be different, less neat and prosperous. "Something more white-trashy," she admitted aloud. She sat in the car for a few more seconds before smoothing her skirt down over her legs, taking a deep breath, and getting out.

She shivered as she walked up the concrete path to the front door. The small porch seemed tidy and freshly swept, although up close she could see that the house was a little more worn than she first thought. A button beside the door was illuminated, reminding her of the eyes of the doe she had just seen. The button went dark when she pressed it. Kate heard its muffled ring deep inside the house.

After a few seconds, the door was pulled open by a trim, red-haired woman—about fifty, Kate guessed—with a narrow, pale face deeply lined around the eyes and mouth. The woman gave Kate a guarded smile. "Yes?"

"Are you Mrs. Potter?" she asked. "Evan's mother?"

"Yes," the woman answered, her posture stiffening.

"I was hoping to talk to your son for a minute or two."

"And who are you?"

"Elena Theodorus," she said. "I'm from the Teen Crisis Center." Then she added: "In Gaithersburg"—as if this would make the claim more believable.

The woman shook her head firmly. "Not now," she said.

"Mrs. Potter. I think it will help your son to talk to somebody."

This comment seemed to spark anger in Mrs. Potter's eyes. "Talk? He's been talking to you people for days.

It's time to leave the kid alone now." She started closing the door.

"Mrs. Potter," Kate said again, and had to stop herself from planting her foot in front of the door. "I know how you must feel."

The door stopped moving. "Mrs. Theodorus," the woman said. "Do you have a teenage son?"

The question caught Kate by surprise. "No, but—"

"Then I don't know how you can say something like that."

Kate couldn't think of any reply. The door swung shut in her face.

She stood there for a few seconds, watching the vapor of her breath rise and then slowly sink to her feet. "Shit," she said finally. She turned away and started down the walk toward the car. This was her first serious misstep of the day. She had gotten everyone else to talk to her—and talk to her honestly, she thought. Until now.

She opened the door of the Jetta and got in. "Stupid," she muttered to herself.

Kate had just turned the key and was about to pull back into the street when somebody knocked sharply on her window, startling her. It took her a second to catch her breath. A teenager stood outside the car, wearing a ghostly-looking white T-shirt. He had dark red hair, short on the sides, with an anemic little ponytail in back. In his left earlobe was a tiny gold cross—the kind the little Hispanic girls used to wear back in Chicago.

Kate rolled down her window. "Hi," she said.

"Hey," he answered. He was staring at her so hard that Kate wondered if she was supposed to recognize him. "You're not from any crisis center," he said.

This was Evan, she realized suddenly, annoyed at her own denseness. "No, I'm not."

"I bet you're Kate, that guy's wife. I recognized your voice when you were talking to my mom."

"You're right," she said. "Does your mother know you're out here?"

"I came down the back," he said. "She thinks I'm in my room, prob'ly."

Kate found the way Evan was staring at her unnerving. The boy seemed to be studying her. "I want to talk to you, Evan," she said. "About the body you found."

He stopped staring and looked off into the dark woods behind the house. After a long pause, he turned back. "Okay."

"You want to get in for a minute? You must be cold."

"Sure." He ran around the front of the car, the headlights glaring against his black jeans as he passed. Then he got into the passenger seat beside her and pulled the door shut. "You're pretty," he said, fingering the cross in his ear. "I knew you'd be pretty when I talked to you."

Kate nodded, taking this in, wondering if she should be worried. "Why did you call me last night?" she asked.

Evan shrugged. He cleared his throat self-consciously, then rearranged his gangly legs in front of him. He was such an awkward presence beside her—so alien and uncomfortable, as if that deer on the road had climbed into the car with her.

When Evan didn't answer, Kate tried a different approach. "You said you didn't think my husband could have . . . you know, killed the man you found. Why did you say that?"

Evan inhaled sharply, as if about to speak, but then just shrugged again.

"Evan," Kate said, shifting in the seat to face him more fully. "The reason I'm asking is because I don't think my husband killed that man, either. That's why I'm here. I want to find out as much about this whole thing as I can."

Kate watched him as he seemed to think about this for a few seconds. She guessed his age at fourteen or fifteen—not an easy age for boys, she knew. An age when a lot of them died—from drugs, from guns, from suicide. A dangerous age.

"Come on," Kate said softly, "I know the police and other people have been all over you since this happened. I've been going through the same thing. But this is different. I'm not the police." Something occurred to her then—her tack, her line. "In fact," she said, "the cops are looking for me right now. They think I was involved along with my husband." She touched his arm. "I'm trusting you not to tell them I was here to see you, okay?"

This seemed to have the effect Kate had hoped for. Evan was looking at her now, still fingering the earring. "So you think I should tell you what I didn't tell the police?" he asked.

Kate tried not to look too eager when she heard this. What could this boy have seen? And why wouldn't he have told it to the police? "If there's something you didn't tell them," she said, "you can tell it to me and it would never get back to them. I promise you."

Evan turned away from her and looked out at the flood-lit woodpile. "There's a diner in town," he said. "We could go there and talk."

"What about your mother? What if she goes to your room to look for you?"

"I go for walks," he said. "She knows I go out in the woods when I feel like it. Even late at night."

Kate nodded. She was wondering if this boy could really know something important. There was only one way to find out.

"Okay," she said finally. She put the Jetta in reverse and backed it slowly out of the driveway. "You direct me back to town."

She was older than he'd thought she would be, older, taller, but even prettier. She had green eyes that looked like they could hypnotize you. And long, braided dark hair, which also surprised him. For some reason he'd thought she would be blond. She sounded blond, like one of those hoarse blond women who smoke cigarettes in old movies. But Evan wasn't disappointed. It was better—*she* was better—than he'd imagined. Different, but better.

It was Fate again, he decided, as he sat in the warm front seat of the car. He'd been calling her telephone number all day, getting the message machine, listening to her voice say the same sentence over and over again: "No one can get the phone right now, so please leave a message." And now here she was, Kate Baker, sitting in a car next to him. It had to be Fate.

Evan leaned back against the headrest. There was a good smell in the car, something coming off her clothes that wasn't really sweat and wasn't really perfume. She was wearing a black suede jacket with fringe, and a black skirt and black stockings, one leg with a rip from the ankle straight up along the inside of her calf to her knee. He thought again of the legs of the deer in his dream, the legs of the body in the woods, the kind of smoothness that seemed hard not to touch.

Evan knew then that he wanted to stay in that car with Kate Baker for as long as he could. He couldn't stand the thought of this drive being over, of going back alone to his room, so he knew he'd have to be careful of what he said to her. She was a little scared of him—he could see it in her eyes—and that was good. But he didn't want her to be too scared. He would have to play this just right.

She asked him questions, only some of which he answered. She seemed to think he knew something important about the body, something secret. He wondered if he should tell her about the missing head and hands. But she probably knew all about that. It was on the news, and in the papers. Evan worried that if he said something about the head and hands, pretending it was a big secret, she would realize that he didn't have anything to tell her that

she didn't already know. She'd go away. She'd forget
about him and tell him not to call her again.

So Evan decided to fake it. He'd have to pretend he
knew something. "So you think I should tell you what I
didn't tell the police?" he asked her. It wasn't a lie, exactly, but it hinted at something that wasn't true. And
when he saw the expression that his question put on her
face, he knew that he had done it right. She was his. For
at least a little while, Kate Baker would be in his power.

He got her to take him to the diner in town. Like a
date, he thought; they were going out to dinner together.
As they drove down Kings Mill Road toward town, she
kept asking him questions, mostly about his family and
friends. Then she asked him what grade he was in, what
subjects he was taking, and what his favorites were. These
questions were safer. Evan knew how to answer them in
a way that adults liked to hear them answered. So he told
her about his computer classes, mostly, and about American history, which was really the only other subject he
could even stand.

The diner was almost deserted. There was one family
in a booth in the back, two or three couples at the tables,
and a few lone men at the counter, drinking coffee. Everybody looked up as Evan and Kate came in. As they
crossed the room, Evan noticed one man staring hard at
Kate, watching her in a sexual way that made Evan feel
angry but proud at the same time. He wondered what the
man was thinking. He wondered if the man could possibly
believe that Evan was Kate's boyfriend.

They slid into a booth near the back of the diner, away
from most of the other customers. Kate asked, "Are you
hungry?" He nodded, even though he wasn't. But he knew
he should order something, maybe something that would
take a while to cook. Whether he ate it or not wouldn't
matter.

The waitress came up to them with two menus and a

pot of coffee. It was Natalie, somebody his mother and aunt knew, and when Evan saw her, his shoulders tensed up. She looked at Kate and then at Evan. "Your mother know you're here?" she asked, handing him a menu.

Evan didn't know what to say. He just stared stupidly at the menu in his hand.

"I'm his caseworker," Kate said then, keeping her voice low. "It's okay. We just want to talk a little bit, somewhere away from the house." She lifted her eyebrows at Natalie. "It's sometimes easier to talk about things when you're away from the house," she said, as if giving some kind of warning.

This seemed to work. Natalie turned over Kate's coffee mug and filled it. "You want something to drink, Ev?" she asked.

"A Coke."

"I'll bring you the kind with no caffeine," Natalie said. "Then I'll be back to take your order."

When she had gone back into the kitchen, Kate asked, "Will she tell your mother?"

Evan shrugged. He thought she might, but he didn't want Kate to know that, so he said, "Prob'ly not. They're not friends. Just people who know each other."

"Good." Kate picked up her coffee and took a sip. Then she looked at him through the rising steam. "So what do you have to tell me?"

Evan put his hand out and touched the fork in front of him. He looked down at the napkin in his lap, then at Kate's waiting face, then at his napkin again. This was going to be hard, he thought. Like a game, when you get to the most advanced levels. He would have to think about strategy, timing, maneuvers. It was going to be hard.

The boy was in bad shape. Kate could see that right away. Given what he'd told her about his life—a fourteen-year-old boy living with his middle-aged mother and aunt, no father in sight—it didn't really surprise her. Especially after getting a look at the mother. Not a lot of warmth there, Kate thought.

Evan was staring down at his napkin now, avoiding her eye in a way that reminded Kate of the kids she counseled. They all had the same inconsistent eye contact, the same sour expression, the same passive-aggressive tendency to shrug as an answer to a direct question—the textbook symptoms. Who could be surprised when kids like these screwed up? When they went out and made friends with corpses or knocked over old ladies for their social security checks or started peddling crack to kids even younger than themselves? But this was the kind of thing that she was supposed to fix. With modern counseling techniques. Two hours of attention a week to make up for fourteen years of neglect.

Kate looked more closely at the boy sitting across from her. He was a good-looking kid, probably smart enough to do well in school if he felt like it. But here he was, in trouble with the police at age fourteen. She wondered if the kid was in therapy. Or if he was on any drugs, recreational or medicinal.

Kate could tell that Evan was attracted to her. It was something else he shared with the boys at Holbrook House—this early, half-formed sexual feeling. She thought of a certain fourteen-year-old Latino boy she'd seen at Holbrook who flirted with her blatantly during their weekly appointment. Kate had flirted right back—a questionable strategy, maybe, but she didn't see any other way to get through to the kid. And so they'd played little games of sexual innuendo during their appointments. One or two of the attendants had even talked to the director about her. But Kate really believed she was getting through to this kid. She thought she was making progress. Then he disappeared from the facility one night and later got picked up on sexual assault charges. He'd raped and robbed a thirty-three-year-old woman in the projects. The news had kept Kate awake for three nights in a row, sorting through her feelings of guilt and inadequacy and fear.

Kate took a sip of the hot, bitter coffee. No, she told herself, this is not something to think about now.

The waitress came back to take their order. Kate asked for an English muffin; Evan said he wanted a Spanish omelet. The waitress scribbled the order on her pad and then stalked off toward the kitchen.

Kate resettled herself on the maroon vinyl and leaned across the table toward Evan. "Can you tell me everything from the beginning? Exactly what you saw and did?"

He looked up at her with a faint smile. "The way I told it to the police?"

"The way it really happened." She waited, then, sighing, took off her suede jacket and folded it on the bench next to her. "Evan," she said. "Please."

Evan shrugged and looked away toward the family in the back of the diner. "I found it after school last Monday," he began.

Kate listened as the boy told the whole story. He stopped often, and Kate had to prompt him, asking questions, using little tricks to get him to say more, the way she did with her cases at Holbrook House. Evan seemed distracted. He kept looking over her shoulder toward the back of the diner. And once the food arrived, he had the omelet to occupy him. When he finally got to something like the end of the story, Kate started asking for more details. "Let's go back a little. Was there anything about the burial place that seemed unusual? Any shovel marks, footprints, or anything like that?"

Evan stared at her for a few seconds, as if about to say something, then shook his head.

Kate finally lost patience. "I'm tired of playing around, Evan. What was it you didn't tell the police?"

She waited as he swallowed a bite of omelet and took

a sip of Coke. "I didn't tell them," he said, "about what I found."

"What you found?"

"A couple feet from the place where the body was. Down in the leaves, like somebody dropped it."

Kate eyed the boy carefully. It was very unlikely that the person who buried the body had dropped something. As an ex-cop, she knew that such flukes were rare in real life. But maybe, just maybe, with the struggle of moving a dead weight through the woods, it had happened.

Kate pushed her coffee cup to the side. "What did you find?" she asked Evan.

The boy swallowed another mouthful of omelet. He seemed to decide something then, to come to the end of a train of thought. "I've got it with me," he said finally.

Kate watched as he reached into the front right pocket of his jeans.

Evan had run out of ideas. He had stalled as long as he could, putting all sorts of pauses into his story. But Kate kept pushing him. She kept forcing him to say more, to be more specific, to come up with answers.

And then there was that family in the back, all blonds— father, mother, two boys (about five and eight, he guessed) with thick glasses. They kept distracting him, pulling at his thoughts. The parents had their backs to him, but he could see them moving their hands, pointing and signaling. The two kids watched them like a show on television.

"What did you find?" Kate asked him.

The idea came to him suddenly. A key. He had a few in his pocket—the front- and back-door keys to his house, his computer key, and the key to the filing cabinet where he kept all the printouts he didn't want his mother to find. He could say that he'd found one of them. It was something, at least—something to keep her interested.

He leaned to the side and reached into his pocket. "Here," he said. He brought out his chrome key ring and twisted off the little filing cabinet key. He placed it on the table and put his hand over it. "It's mine," he said. "I found it and I want it back. Okay?"

She nodded, staring at his hand.

He delayed for a while, pleased at her hungry interest. Then he lifted his hand and pushed the key over to her side of the table.

She looked at it for a few seconds before picking it up. He watched as she turned it over in her long fingers. "Looks like the key to a desk or file cabinet," she said.

Evan shrugged. "I guess."

"And you found this next to the body?"

"About four, five feet away. But it wasn't buried. It was just laying there."

"On top of the ground that was dug up to bury the body?"

He nodded.

"In that case, there'd be a decent chance that the person who buried the body was the one who dropped it." She turned the key over a few more times. Then a look of doubt crossed her face. Evan worried that she didn't believe him. If she found out he was lying, she would never believe him again. "You're sure you found this there?"

"Yeah, I'm sure," he said, wishing now that he could take back the key and try something else. "But it could be that somebody else dropped it, I guess."

Kate stared at him, as if trying to see into his head. "You never know," she said finally, closing her fist on the key. "I'll take this for a little while, if that's okay. But you'll get it back. I promise." She grabbed her suede jacket off the seat and slid the key into one of the pockets. "Okay, anything else?"

Evan put his fork down. He was disappointed in her reaction to the key, and now he had no idea what else he could say to keep things going. He pushed his plate away and looked around the room. The father of the blond family in the back was standing now, pressing his fingers against his forearm. The little boys were squinting at him. "They're deaf," Evan said aloud then, just realizing this.

"What?" Kate twisted around to look. "Oh right." She turned back to him. Somehow Evan felt that even this was a letdown to her. Just a deaf family. What else is new?

"Let me pay for your coffee," he said then, even though he knew he had no money with him.

Kate smiled at him, like a mother smiling at a clever five year old. "Thanks," she said, "but you're *my* guest." Then, as if to make him feel even worse, she lifted her hand to signal for the check.

They drove back to Evan's house in silence, the croon of the Jetta's heater the only sound in the car. Kate was trying to put together everything she'd found out that day, but she kept being distracted by Evan's gloomy face flashing white in the headlights of other cars. He was obviously feeling depressed, slouching in the passenger seat, staring out at the road ahead of them. Any sense she'd had of this boy as a threat was gone now. He was a hurt, messed-up kid, that was all. Kate wondered if she'd somehow raised his expectations more than she realized. Maybe he was waiting for something in return for the key, some sign of gratitude or friendship or special trust. But she didn't know what to offer him.

She stopped the car at the side of the road just before his driveway. "Hey," she said. "Thanks for talking to me. And for the key. It'll be our secret, okay?"

He didn't move.

The next sentence came out of her mouth before she could really stop it. "You can call me again, if you feel like it. You know the number."

He glanced up at her, his expression brightening. "I

could send you e-mail, too," he said. "What's your e-mail address?"

Kate threw her hands up. "I'm one of those computer idiots," she said. "My husband did—*does*—have an e-mail address, but not me." Then she remembered what he'd told her earlier about his computer lab at school. "So you're pretty good on the computer? I mean, you know how to hack and do all that fancy stuff?"

"It's pretty easy," he said, "if you know what to do."

Kate thought for a second before saying: "Could you hack into somebody's e-mail if you had their address?"

Evan sat up straighter in the seat. "It depends," he said. "If they picked a good password, it would be hard. But most people pick totally obvious ones, like their birthdays or their middle names or something like that. Even if they don't, there are these programs that can throw every word and number combination at somebody's account until one of them works. And there are other ways, too."

Kate was nodding. This was the longest series of sentences Evan had put together all evening.

"Even if you get in," he went on, "there might not be any stored mail on the host server. I mean, some people download all their mail onto their personal machines, and connecting with their personal machines is kind of impossible—"

Kate put her hand out to stop him. "There's something you could do that would really help me," she said. She grabbed her bag and rummaged through it until she came across a photocopy of the e-mail she'd found the night after Joel's disappearance. "Here's a message I got off my husband's computer. One of his addresses is on it. You think there's any way you could get into it?"

Evan took the paper from her. She turned on the overhead light while he read it. "The Well," he said. He looked up at her. "Your husband's on the Well. Cool."

Kate wasn't surprised that Joel would have picked a

cool Internet address. "What do you think?"

"I could try," Evan said. His mood seemed to have lifted. "I could work on it a couple days and get back to you when I have something."

"That would be great. But listen. Don't do anything that could get you into trouble. And don't tell anybody about this, not even your mother, okay?"

Evan laughed—a strange, awkward sound. "Yeah, like she'd be the first person I'd tell."

"Good." Kate put her hand on the boy's bony shoulder. "I appreciate it."

Evan cleared his throat and then slowly got out of the car. "Thanks for the omelet," he said. "And don't lose the key, okay?"

"I promise."

He slammed the door shut and started off toward the house.

Kate watched as Evan ran up the driveway, silhouetted by the headlights. She wasn't sure about what she'd just done. Had she made matters better with Evan? Or had she just sunk to a new low of cynicism? "This is highly unethical," she told herself aloud, trying not to think of what her boss at Child Services would say.

She waited until Evan had disappeared around the corner of the house. Then she turned down the heat, shifted into first, and drove off.

Evan didn't even notice the cold when he got out of the car. He ran up the driveway, climbed the back steps of the deck, and let himself into his room again. It was still early. He could hear the television going downstairs, his mother and aunt talking to each other during a commercial. They had no idea that he'd been gone. Evan smiled. Turning to his computer, he sat down and spread the photocopy of the e-mail beside the keyboard. He would start right away. With any luck, he might even have the husband's password by morning.

12

About a half hour after she dropped Evan at his house, Kate pulled into the parking lot of a dark strip mall near Rockville. She had one more lead to follow up on before going home to bed. By now, Velma Sampson would have opened the safe she'd told Kate about that morning. A simple phone call would tell Kate what was in it.

Kate found a pay phone at the end of the strip mall, just outside a Japanese grocery store. She parked beside it, scrounged around until she found a quarter, and got out. The night had turned colder, raw and damp, and the sky seemed to hang low over her head.

She pushed the quarter into the slot and punched Velma's number. It rang four times before someone picked up.

"Velma?" Kate said breathlessly. "It's Kate."

"I know," Velma replied.

"You got the safe open?"

Velma didn't answer for a few seconds. Traffic passing on the road behind Kate made it hard to hear. She pressed a fingertip into her ear and leaned in closer to the phone.

"Did you—"

"I opened it," Velma said. "And it's just what we thought, honey. Financial records, invoices, inventory lists. But it sure isn't From the Rainforest inventory. And some of the pages are in a kind of code."

"A code?"

"Bunches of numbers."

Kate remembered the e-mails she had seen on Joel's hard disk before it was erased. A few of them had contained lines and lines of numbers.

"There's something else, too," Velma said.

"What?"

"A videotape was in there. No label."

"You look at it yet?"

Velma hesitated again. "Not yet. I decided it would be better if we saw it together. Misery loves company, you know."

Kate thought about this for a second, shifting the phone from one ear to the other. She watched as a red Miata pulled into the lot and stopped at the ATM halfway down the strip mall. A tall, young, gray-suited Asian man got out and began searching his wallet for a bank card. Kate watched him, thinking: "Jin-Liang Lu." She turned, shaking the notion out of her head.

"When can you come over?" Velma asked.

Kate forced herself to concentrate. "What time is it?" she asked.

"About nine-thirty."

She would have to go over tonight. If she didn't, she'd lose another night's sleep. "If it's all right with you I'll come over now."

Velma seemed to sigh in relief. "I'll be here."

Kate hung up the phone. By now, the Asian man had found his card and was punching numbers into the ATM. He had left the Miata running, and its exhaust pipe was spewing luminous gray smoke. She could hear something like punk rock music pouring out of the car's speakers.

The man turned and caught her looking at him. He seemed suspicious at first, but then, apparently deciding that Kate wasn't about to rob him, he smiled. His face was beautiful, perfect. "Do I know you?" he asked.

Kate shook her head, feeling embarrassed. "Sorry," she said. "I was just thinking about something."

His smile widened. "Thinking about introducing yourself?"

Oh God, she thought, a dead man is flirting with me. "No," she said. "Sorry." And she hurried back to the Jetta, fumbling for her keys.

Velma Sampson lived in a small Tudor just off Wisconsin Avenue near the National Cathedral. There was no driveway or garage, so Kate found a curb space down the street and then walked back. The house and yard looked neat and well groomed, even in the late fall. Velma had been widowed shortly before she took the job at From the Rainforest, and her husband had apparently left her fairly well off. According to Joel, she worked more for distraction than for money.

Velma opened the front door before Kate had a chance to ring the bell. She was still wearing the rose-colored dress from work, though she'd changed out of high heels into black slippers. "Kate," she said matter-of-factly, letting her in. "I almost thought you'd stood me up, honey."

"I was farther away than I thought when I called." She looked around. Velma's house was clean, the furniture simple and spare, the art on the walls nondescript. The whole place seemed to smell of vanilla. After spending so much of the past three years in the elaborate, fussily decorated houses of their Lewisburg neighbors, Kate felt instantly at home here.

Velma took her coat. "Everything from the safe is on

the dining room table. I've been through most of it already." Then, as if remembering her manners, "Can I get you anything? Coffee, juice, bourbon?"

"Bourbon," Kate said.

"I know the feeling," Velma assured her. "There's some Wild Turkey in the kitchen cabinet."

"Good."

Kate went into the dining room while Velma got the drinks. On the plain rosewood table was an accordion file, a few ledger books, and a videotape in an unmarked box. Kate hung her shoulder bag on a chair and sat down.

"The file contains invoices, mostly," Velma said from the kitchen. "Some of them are normal, some are kinda hard to make out."

Kate reached into the file and brought out a handful of documents. There were curly faxes and e-mail printouts, along with some spreadsheets and order forms, all with the letters "BP" printed in large type at the top. Kate quickly scanned the sheets, but couldn't find any sign of what was being bought and sold. Where item descriptions should have been, there were just numbers, like those in the e-mails she'd seen.

"They were careful," Velma said, coming into the dining room with two small glasses of bourbon. "I've looked through about three-quarters of the papers, and I can't see a single place where the item descriptions make any sense. It's all in code."

Kate took the glass from her. The bourbon seemed to glow in the light from the chandelier. "Cheers," she said, and took a sip.

Velma pulled up a chair beside her. "It's a pretty consistent code," she said. "Four numbers, the first one usually much larger than the others." She shuffled through the papers. "Looking at the quantities and prices, I'd say we're dealing here either with drugs or precious metals. Look at this."

Kate calculated quickly in her head. "Too expensive for marijuana, too cheap for cocaine."

Velma looked at her wearily. "So you think it really is drugs?"

"Of some kind or other." She thought of the plastic bags in Joel's file cabinet, and of her conversation in the men's room at Johns Hopkins. "What about the ledger books?" she asked.

Velma reached across the table and slid one of the books in front of her. "A lot's in this damn code here, too." She opened the book and leafed though a few pages. "I could be wrong, but some of the ... oh hell, what do I call it? Merchandise? Some of it looks like it was sold at cost."

"At cost?"

"Depending on what it is. Some of the stuff, like this here—where the first number is 113?—that has no markup at all. Other things have a huge markup."

Kate looked more closely at the ledger. "So is there a profit here? From what you can tell?"

"I can't say. But there are these huge outgoing payments to the same column every month. Here, look." Velma pointed to a column on the far right, labeled with another four-number code. "Unless I'm way off, that's *not* a payment to suppliers."

"Payment to who then?"

"My guess would be investors."

Kate stared at her. "Investors? You mean like stockholders? For a drug operation?"

"You're just guessing that it's a drug operation, honey," Velma said. "And besides, it doesn't have to be anything formal like stockholders. Just people who put money in and get a share of the business. Limited partners, like."

"Except if something goes wrong, you go after people with a hit man instead of a lawyer." Kate flipped through a few more pages of the ledger. "Did you find any names or addresses anywhere?"

"Not in what I've looked through so far. They're being real smart about this. Real careful."

Kate swallowed another mouthful of bourbon. "Maybe the video will tell us something," she said.

"Let's see."

They got up from the table. Velma picked up the tape and carried it to the den like something very fragile. "I hardly ever use this damn thing," Velma said, pointing her chin at the VCR on the lower shelf of the TV cart. The LCD was flashing the wrong time. Velma crouched, her knees cracking loudly. She slipped the tape into the slot and turned on the television above. "Have a seat," she said, as if about to show Kate the video from her most recent vacation.

Kate sank into the futon across from the television. Velma came over and sat beside her. "Here goes," Kate said.

There were a few seconds of static, then some wild flickering. Finally, the static melted away, leaving a view of a landscape. The image was black-and-white, washed out, obviously old. Kate could barely make out the picture—a flat desert basin, cut in half by an absolutely straight road. "Is there a contrast knob on the TV?" Kate asked.

"Probably." Velma leaned over and switched off the lamp, throwing the room into darkness.

"Better," Kate said. The image on the screen wobbled and cut to another desert scene—a stretch of sage and mesquite trees, backed by a sharp, high ridge of mountains. "New Mexico," Kate said. "Those are the Organ Mountains, near Las Cruces." She turned to Velma. "Looks like an old super-eight movie or something, transferred to video."

Another cut—to a young man in hiking boots, cutoff

jeans, and a backpack, filmed from behind. He was climb-
ing a rocky trail, between mesquite and scrub pines. The
person holding the camera was following him up. At one
point, the figure ahead turned, showing his young, bearded
face, strangely familiar.

"Oh jeez, that's Don," Velma said.

The recognition clicked in Kate's mind as soon as
Velma said the name. It was Don, looking like a classic
young hippie. He flashed his middle finger at the camera,
then turned and climbed higher up the trail.

"This must be back when they were at college—seventy
or seventy-one. Joel and Don lived together, in some kind
of group house in Las Cruces."

Velma nodded, her eyes fixed on the screen. "I've
heard. Don told me once it was supposed to be an all-
vegetarian house, but Joel kept bringing home pork chops,
just to aggravate people."

"Sounds about right," Kate muttered.

The tape showed a few more scenes in the mountains:
Don standing on top of a big boulder covered with Indian
petroglyphs; a pan of the main ridge of the Organ Mountains; Don sitting on the hood of an old Chevy Impala at
the trailhead, drinking beer. Then the tape cut to a shot
of downtown Las Cruces, the streets full of old cars—
Ramblers and finned Cadillacs and Volkswagen Bugs.
The camera moved along the street until it came to a
ramshackle, one-story cinder block building with dark,
plate-glass windows. A rickety neon sign hung over the
entrance: Julio's. Two men came out of the painted-glass
door: a small, middle-aged, Mexican-looking man in an
apron, and then a taller, lanky, bearded hippie—Joel, at
twenty or so. He seemed to be joking with the older man,
pointing at the camera, calling it closer. The Mexican,
looking pleased but embarrassed, pushed him away, then
waved at the camera. Finally, he turned and walked back
into the restaurant.

"He looks so young," Velma whispered.

Kate murmured in agreement. The sight of her husband on the screen—or else the Wild Turkey—was making her stomach churn. God, how she missed him.

The camera switched to what seemed to be a party. People milled around the back patio of a single-story house, holding beer bottles and glasses. Joel stood at a little hibachi set up on the bed of an old pickup, turning what looked like huge chile peppers on the grill. There were scenes of people dancing, others of people sitting around a table smoking from a bong. Then the film switched to what looked like a garage. Don and Joel had their arms around each other and seemed to be singing. The camera bobbled for a second—it was being set down on something. Then the cameraman came out from behind it and joined them. He was a shorter, lighter-haired man with smooth, blunt features. He had a small goatee and long hair that fell in greasy strings around his shoulders. Kate could feel Velma's body tensing beside her. "That's him," Velma said.

Kate looked over at her. "Who?"

"The one who was in the office that time. With Joel and the Chinese man."

"Are you sure?"

"Positive. It's that grin, honey. He had the same smug grin."

Kate looked back at the screen. Smug was exactly the word for the man's grin. He had his arm around Joel now and was making the three of them sway. Kate tried to make out the writing on the man's T-shirt, but his arm was blocking it. Finally, he pulled the arm away and she could read the message: Perfect Drugs Make a Perfect World.

Kate realized now that this, whatever it was, had been going on since college. It had been going on when Joel introduced himself to her in the National Gallery that af-

ternoon; it had been going on when they first slept together, when they first moved in together in Lewisburg,
when they got married. It was a part of her husband the
whole time, hidden from her. She'd never known this man
in the least.

"Kate?" Velma said softly.

Kate turned her head. "What?"

"It's over."

She meant the video. There was white noise coming
from the television now, restless static on the screen.

Velma struggled up from the futon and turned off the
television. "The sixties," she said.

Kate stayed where she was, finding it hard to move
right then. "Did Joel or Don ever mention anyone from
college?" she asked Velma. "Any name that might be this
guy with the smug grin?"

Velma had started shaking her head even before Kate
finished the question. "I've been racking my brain for
days to remember things like that," she said. She fingered
the gold chain around her neck. Then, just now thinking
of it, she said, "Adrianna."

"Right." Kate got up from the futon. Adrianna, who'd
lived in that house in Las Cruces with Joel and Don,
would know who the man was. "Can I take it to her?"

Velma hesitated, apparently still worried about betray-
ing Joel's trust. After a few seconds, though, she agreed.
"Go ahead."

"And you have a little copier here, right? Can you make
copies of some pages from the safe? Just a few samples?"

"It'll take a minute for the old thing to warm up," she
said. "It's in the office—the spare bedroom."

"Good. I'll pick out some pages."

Velma went down the hall while Kate took the video
from the VCR and hurried back to the dining room. She
pulled a few pages from the accordion file—a couple of
e-mails, three invoices, a page or two of spreadsheets. It

seemed clear to her now that the video had to be related
to the business, that the third man at the end was a partner
in whatever was going on. If she could find that man, she
might be able to find Joel. Kate picked up her glass from
the rosewood table and drank down the rest of the bourbon. Then she gathered up the pages and carried them
back to the office.

Velma was standing in the dark, her back to the doorway, the humming machine open in front of her. She was
idly pressing the Copy button, making the bar of harsh
light pass back and forth under the empty glass, the shadows of her arms and head sweeping across the dark walls
with military precision. Kate stopped in the doorway. "Is
it ready?" she asked.

Velma turned. Her eyes were glassy and her mouth was
a hard, straight line. "Goddamn him," she muttered to
Kate. "And goddamn me for trusting that man."

Kate just stood there, her hands full of papers, the whis-
key burning in her stomach. She could think of nothing
to say or do except nod.

Kate got back to the house after midnight. Hermann met
her at the door, looking hungry and resentful. She'd left
the dog door unlatched downstairs, so he'd been able to
go out, but she'd forgotten to put the lights on timers, so
poor Hermann had been moving around in the dark for
hours. "Sorry," she said as she took off her suede jacket
and tossed it onto the couch. She felt a little put out. Why
hadn't Elena come to feed Hermann when she saw that
Kate wasn't home by dinnertime? Then Kate remembered
the reason—Elena was at her sister's in Virginia for a day
or two, celebrating the sister's fiftieth birthday. "I'm taking advantage," she said aloud. She reminded herself that
life for everybody else, even for Elena, was going along
normally. Birthdays were being celebrated, gutters were
being cleaned, shirts were being dropped off at the dry

cleaner's. Kate wondered if she'd ever again have the luxury of worrying about something like an overdue library
book.

In the kitchen, she filled Hermann's food and water
bowls, then checked the mail and phone messages. Nothing important: a postcard of Barbados from her youngest
brother, a message from her boss, David, saying that he'd
found coverage for her at Holbrook House for another
week if she needed it again. There were also three hang-
ups on the answering machine—Lieutenant Grainger,
Kate guessed, trying to find out if she was home. There'd
been no unmarked car waiting for her tonight, and Kate
thought the Lieutenant might have given up on the idea
of tailing her. She remembered how he'd sped away from
her that morning. What could have called him away so
suddenly? Was there some development in the case that
they weren't going to tell her about?

Kate sat in a kitchen chair and watched Hermann eat.
She was hungry herself—she hadn't eaten anything all
day except for a hot dog in Baltimore and that English
muffin at the Franklin diner—but she wasn't up to the
effort of looking for something in the refrigerator. She
kicked off her shoes, peeled off the black hose (which
were in tatters now), and sat back, breathing deeply. Her
head ached—a pulsing just above the eyes, which she'd
first noticed when watching the flickery video at Velma's.
Aspirin, she thought.

She dragged herself up to let Hermann out the back
door. Then she went into the dining room to get the little
aspirin bottle she carried in her bag. As usual, it was buried deep under the keys, gloves, wallet, lipsticks, and
other junk crammed inside. She started pulling things out
onto the table in frustration.

The first thing to tumble out was the little children's
book—*Tales of Peter Rabbit*. Kate pushed it aside, but
then stopped. "It is said that the effect of eating too much

lettuce is soporific." Kate felt a snap of insight. The code, the book. That was where Peter Rabbit fit in.

She picked up the book and ran back to the living room. She took a few of the photocopies from her bag and sat down. As Velma had pointed out, the code was made up of various series of four numbers, the first higher than the others, but none higher than 120 or so. Kate quickly turned to the last marked page of the little book; it was page 122.

This was it, the key text. She suddenly understood the code. Each group of four numbers in the notebook must correspond to the location of a letter in the book: page number, line number, word number, and letter number. So any message could be easily encoded or decoded, one letter at a time. This kind of book code was primitive and time-consuming, but it had Joel's stamp on it—Joel, the high-tech junkie who always complained about premature obituaries for ink and paper. And the code was definitely effective. It was impossible to break if you didn't know or have the right book, since any letter could be represented in lots of different ways: a different "E" on a different page for every "E" in the message.

Kate chose an invoice and started decoding. The first series under the Item column was: 114-11-1-1. Page 114, line 11, first word, first letter. It was a D. She moved on. It took her a minute or two to complete the word—Dexedrine—but Kate had guessed it long before she was finished. Dexedrine was a narcolepsy treatment, available by prescription only, a Schedule II drug on the federal list. It was an amphetamine, a kind of speed that was popular in the neighborhoods she used to patrol back in Chicago.

Kate threw down the book and papers. This was it, she thought: hard evidence, no more speculation and guesswork. Here was definite proof that Joel was a felon. "Your husband," she said aloud, "is a drug pusher."

Kate felt a sudden urge to give up, to turn everything

she'd found over to Detective Starks or even Lieutenant
Grainger and let them handle it. "You were right, Lieu-
tenant," she imagined saying. "He's no good, he's slime.
Put him in jail and throw away the key."

But the impulse passed. After a few minutes, Kate
pulled herself up from the armchair. Grabbing the book
and the papers Velma had copied, she found a legal pad
and then sat down again at the dining table. She had work
to do.

It was on an invoice—the fifth sheet she worked on—
that she came across the address. She'd found a long series of numbers in the place on the page where she
guessed the delivery address would be, and so began de-
ciphering carefully: Page 78, line 4, word 4, letter 1—
that was a "P." Page 35, line 11, word 1, letter 2 was an
"O." P.O., as in P.O. Box. Kate pulled her chair closer to
the table. She kept at it until she had the full address:

P.O. Box 29
Karlstadt
PA
17201

She read and reread the address she'd written on the legal
pad. A box number wasn't as good as a street address,
but it was something.

Kate sat back in the chair. It was late, and she knew
she would need to be fresh for the morning. She got up
and went to the back door to let Hermann in. Then she
made her way upstairs to the bedroom, turning out lights
as she went. Her bed looked powerfully inviting. She took
off her skirt and blouse and crawled under the covers in
her underwear. Hermann, looking happier after being outside, hopped up beside her. She gave him a rough scratch
behind the ears and then put out the bedside lamp.

But she couldn't fall asleep. Moonlight was streaming

through the half-closed venetian blinds, falling across the
bedspread in pale, thin slices. Kate passed her hand
through the stripes of light, replaying the scenes of the
day in her mind. She was troubled by a keen uneasiness—
something beyond her anxiety about Joel, beyond her
sense of betrayal. Kate reached out to touch Hermann's
warm flank. Today she had manipulated people who
trusted her. She'd beat up a poor graduate student, and
she'd even used a boy's sexual interest to get information
from him. All because she wanted to believe that her husband was a victim, not a criminal, because she wanted to
prove to herself that her marriage was a marriage, not a
sham.

Kate rolled over and pulled the blanket up to her neck.
Her husband, she told herself again, was a criminal. And
to find him, she was turning into a criminal herself. She
was deceiving people, using her friends, withholding evidence from the police. "You're a felon," she said aloud,
wondering how, despite her good intentions, her new, better life in the east had come to this.

13

"That's Duncan."

Kate and Adrianna Davis were watching the old video. Kate sat on the cotton couch in Adrianna's office; Adrianna was beside her, staring at the screen of an elaborate VCR/TV that Adrianna had borrowed from another lawyer in the practice. The machine was sitting on a black steel cart in the middle of the room, its cords stretched tight to reach the outlet. Though it was Sunday afternoon, there were plenty of people in the office, hurrying through the halls with files and briefcases, looking busy and self-important.

"Duncan?" Kate asked.

"Duncan Lloyd. He lived with us in the group house for a while. Back in the fall of seventy or seventy-one. Then he dropped out and went to Mexico. I remember getting postcards about his adventures in the mountains with the Indians."

"Tell me about him."

Adrianna sighed. Her hair was pulled back into a tight

ponytail streaked with gray. "It would be better if you
told me what this is all about, Kate. It's impossible for
me to represent you if I don't know what the hell you've
found out."

Kate picked up the remote and stopped the tape. "I'll
tell you when I know more," she said.

Adrianna stared at her for a long few seconds in the
fuzzy light from the television. Finally, she blinked and
looked away. "Fine," she said. She got up from the couch,
walked over to the television, and turned it off. "Duncan
comes from the Lloyd family of Albuquerque. The Lloyd
Department Store Lloyds?"

Kate gave a small nod. It was a famous name.

"More money than God, but you wouldn't know it
looking at Duncan. He's the family rebel. At least he was
back then. Though he never went so far as to disinherit
himself."

"And he lived with all of you for a while?"

Adrianna hit the light switch by the door. The fluorescents blinked twice, then lit. She crossed the room again
and opened the venetian blinds. "Duncan had a room in
the house on Alameda for at least a few months, though
a lot of us couldn't stand him. He was a little crazy, really.
Always high, always making speeches. He and Joel and
Don would sometimes hike up into the Organ Mountains
to drink tequila and eat peyote buttons under the stars.
They'd come back three or four days later with dirty
clothes and bloodshot eyes, saying they hadn't slept since
they left."

Kate listened, twisting a little gold bracelet on her left
wrist. Her memories of that era were dim at best. She
remembered her father and brothers at the dinner table,
talking disgustedly about long-haired drug addicts who
camped out on the beach and in the city parks.

Adrianna pushed the television cart back toward the
wall. "He was supposed to come with us, actually. When

Don and Joel and I and a couple of the other housemates came out to Washington after graduation. He and Don were supposed to get jobs at the ACLU, but he never got around to it. Not that Don did, either."

"Do you know what happened to him?" Kate asked.

"Last I heard he'd taken some of his trust money and started a venture capital firm."

"Oh right. That whole thing."

"No, it's not what you think. At least from what I heard. He was raising funds for small pharmaceutical and biotech startups, businesses that would cultivate supply lines from small co-ops and communes in Mexico and South America. Like what Rainforest was in the beginning—very counterculture, very progressive, very Duncan. He had these ideas about basing biomedical research on the knowledge of traditional shamans and herbalists. Developed lots of good contacts down there. In fact, when I was helping Don and Joel set up the partnership for Rainforest, we thought about getting Duncan to come in as a limited partner."

"What happened?"

"It was one of Duncan's 'intervals.' He used to disappear for months on end. In Mexico, Peru, Brazil. Nobody knew where he was at the time."

"And when was the last time you heard anything about him?"

"Oh, five years at least. Until now I hadn't even thought about him for ages." She turned. "But I guess he's back, since you're showing me this tape. Back, and involved in all of this."

Kate said nothing, still twisting the bracelet.

"Kate," Adrianna went on, after a pause. "I think we have to be realistic. If somebody wanted to set up a pipeline for cocaine or marijuana or whatever, there'd be no better person than Duncan. And no better cover than a company like From the Rainforest."

"I know," Kate answered softly.

"I should tell you that the DEA has gotten involved in the case. They've got arrest warrants in the works for both Joel and Don."

"Shit."

"Yes. With all due respect to the Hampton County Police, this puts a different complexion on things. If the feds decide this is top priority . . ."

"Do you have any idea if they're close? Either the feds or the county police?"

Adrianna shook her head. "All I've heard is that everybody's cooperating. The homicide is still a separate investigation, but they're all sharing information."

Kate walked over to the VCR, ejected the tape, and put it into her bag.

"Since you haven't told me where or how you found that tape," Adrianna said then, "I have no way of judging whether it's evidence or not, right?"

"Right." Kate came over and stood directly in front of Adrianna. They were about the same height, though Adrianna always seemed smaller to Kate. "You'll keep your ears open?" Kate asked.

"There's really no reason you have to be alone in this, Kate. I'm perfectly capable of looking after my own professional ethics, if you wanted to tell me what's going on."

"I'll think about it," Kate answered. "And thanks."

Kate left the office and took the elevator to the lobby. As she pushed through the glass doors that led to the street, she saw Detectives Starks and Jerrold standing outside, looking cold and shabby under a dishwater sky. Kate groaned.

"Mrs. Baker," Jerrold said, stepping up to her. "Visiting your lawyer, I see. And on a Sunday."

"Yeah," Kate said, trying to keep the hostility out of

her voice. "You tend to visit your lawyer a lot when people accuse your husband of murder."

"I wouldn't know," Jerrold said. "Never being in the situation myself."

Starks put his hand on his partner's shoulder. "Mrs. Baker," he said, "we'd like to talk to you for a few minutes."

Kate took a slow breath, thinking of the videotape in her shoulder bag. "All right," she said. "Talk away."

"We might be more comfortable inside somewhere."

Kate looked across the street. Kramerbooks was just down the block, with its café in the back. "We can get some coffee over there. I read something about their Kahlúa-walnut pie. Is that okay with you?"

Starks nodded, watching her carefully.

"Kahlúa-walnut pie," Jerrold said then, pressing a hand to his chest like a man in love.

They crossed Connecticut and went into the bookstore. It was busy for a Sunday, with dozens of browsers standing around the tables and shelves. Kate led the two detectives through the crowded science section to the café. They found seats at one of the marble-topped tables near the windows and ordered three black coffees.

Starks, looking more comfortable now, shifted his legs under the table and started talking, raising his voice over the clatter of cups and silverware. "You'll recall, Mrs. Baker, that we had a deal. No battery charge in exchange for your full cooperation in the investigation. Now we hear from Lieutenant Grainger that you've been very busy in the past two days. In fact, he thinks you maybe found one or two things that would be of interest to us."

Kate fought the impulse to pull her shoulder bag closer to her body.

"We did finally get the paperwork to have that safe-deposit box opened. Nothing, as you know. But Lieutenant Grainger thinks you took something out of it."

Kate still said nothing. The waiter came with their coffees. She grabbed hers and pressed the hot cup tightly
between her palms.

Starks stirred some sugar into his cup. "How's that jaw
of yours, Dennis?" he asked.

Jerrold made a show of rubbing his cheek. "Still hurts.
I might just have to push that battery rap after all."

"Mrs. Baker," Starks went on, "we can put you in handcuffs right now and carry you out of this coffee shop or
bookstore or whatever the hell it is, in front of all these
people, unless you give us some sign of cooperation here.
We want to know, first, what you found in your husband's
safe-deposit box, and second, where you went yesterday
after Lieutenant Grainger left you." Starks picked up his
spoon again and tapped it on the tabletop. "We also want
your consent to search your bag right now."

Kate tried to pass off her sudden panic as anger. "This
is coercion, Detective. Sheer, fucking coercion."

The two men stared at her and said nothing. Jerrold
reached into a pocket of his overcoat and brought out a
pair of handcuffs. He tossed them onto the table, making
a loud, metallic clank.

Kate looked down at her hands. She would have to give
them something. She was making too much progress to
risk getting thrown in jail again. Besides, if they arrested
her on the battery charge, the contents of her bag would
automatically be catalogued. Any evidence found in it
would be legally admissible, so they'd get the video and
e-mails anyway.

"I found a tape," she said quietly. Starks and Jerrold
exchanged a quick look. "A videotape and a few pages
of documents. I have them with me." She put her bag up
on the table and took out the videotape first, then the few
pages Velma had copied the night before. Fortunately, out
of sheer paranoia, she'd tucked the scrap of paper with

the decoded address into her bra that morning. "I can't make sense out of any of it."

Starks looked over the pages while Jerrold took the video. "What's on the tape?" he asked.

"Old home movies, it looks like," Kate said. "My husband and some of his friends from college, back in the early seventies. He and Don Fordham were undergraduates together at New Mexico State."

At the mention of Don's name, the two detectives exchanged another quick glance.

"We'll have a look at it," Jerrold said. "Tonight. Right after Homer Simpson."

Starks was still flipping through the pages. "These are all the documents you have, just these?"

Kate nodded, not wanting to offer any more information than she had to. If the detectives assumed that she found the tape and documents in the safe-deposit box, that was their problem.

Starks handed the pages to Jerrold. "Some kind of code, looks like," he said. He turned back to her. "And what about yesterday?" he asked. "You visited your husband's office. You find out anything there?"

"His secretary said she'd told you everything she knew."

Starks was staring at her, trying to judge her honesty. "And after Lieutenant Grainger left you?"

"I drove up to Johns Hopkins to talk with Jin-Liang Lu's girlfriend. She told me the same thing—that you'd been there before me and got all the information she had to give."

"And that's it?"

"That's it. After talking to her, I drove over to Great Falls Park in Potomac and had myself a good cry. Satisfied?"

Detective Starks was still watching her closely, tracing

the rim of his coffee cup with an index finger. "I do have one more question, though, Mrs. Baker."

"Okay, fire away."

"I want to know why you're doing this. Why won't you let us handle this investigation?"

"We're hurt that you don't seem to trust us," Jerrold added.

Kate ignored the sarcasm. She sat back in her chair and crossed her arms. "I like to find things out for myself, Detective. I used to be a cop, too, you know."

"Oh right, we've checked out that angle. Lieutenant Grainger thought you might have had some trouble with the Chicago PD, some special reason you left. He couldn't find anything, though—no dismissal, no ethics violations." He leaned toward her. "So why did you leave?"

Careful now, Kate said to herself. "I didn't like the uniform," she said. "It made me look fat."

Starks cleared his throat, obviously annoyed with her. "Mind if we have a look in your bag now?" he said.

Kate had been hoping that they wouldn't go through with that part. "Yeah, I mind," she said, pushing the bag over, "and my lawyer and the ACLU and the Supreme Court would probably mind, too. Not that you care."

Jerrold took her bag and started pulling out the contents. Starks was still watching her. Kate stared back at him for a few seconds, into those light green eyes, but she couldn't help glancing nervously at what Jerrold was doing. The little Peter Rabbit book was in her bag, but she hoped that it would seem innocent enough to pass. She watched as Jerrold found it and took it out of the bag. He flipped through a few pages, turned it over, and then tossed it aside along with her car keys and her mirror. "Looks like nothing else," Jerrold said, pulling out the last few crumpled tissues and running his fingers along the inside seams of the bag.

"Okay," Starks said. Jerrold began stuffing everything back into the bag.

"I'll do that," Kate said, reaching for her things. "It's not a duffel, Detective."

"Could've fooled me."

Starks took out his wallet and signaled to the waiter. He paid for the coffees while Kate gathered up the book and everything else that Jerrold had taken out of her bag. "We'll probably be coming to you with questions about this material after we've had a look," Starks said, nodding toward the videotape and the photocopies. "But I want to say one thing to you, Mrs. Baker. We can't stop you from conducting your own investigation into this thing, and tell you the truth, I'm not sure I'd want to anyway, seeing as you've turned up a thing or two that might be useful. But if we find out that you're withholding any more evidence, anywhere along the line, now or in the future, we're going to push that battery charge. Understood?"

Relief was flooding through her, otherwise Kate would have done something other than nod meekly. "You'll let me know if you manage to decode those pages, right?" she asked then.

Starks laughed. "Right," he said. "We'll call you the minute we break the code."

The three of them got up and walked through the bookstore out to Connecticut Avenue again. The cold seemed even worse now, after the coffee. A cloud of exhaust vapor from an idling car crept along the sidewalk like a seaside fog. Kate and the two detectives walked north for a block or two in silence. At R Street, Kate stopped and said, "I'm parked this way."

Jerrold smiled. "We know."

"By the way," Starks said. "There's something else we should tell you."

Kate recognized the falsely casual tone and braced herself. The wind tore at her cheeks and ears.

"Don Fordham's been found," Starks went on. "In his car in the long-term lot at BWI Airport. That was what pulled the Lieutenant away from you yesterday." He took a pair of black leather gloves from his pocket and began pulling them over his pale-palmed hands. "Swallowed a thirty-eight semiautomatic in the front seat. No note, nothing. You wouldn't know anything about that, would you?"

Kate shook her head, feeling broadsided again, as if Don's death was some kind of punishment for her lies of a few minutes earlier. Suddenly, she imagined what this scene must look like from above: two detectives telling a woman on the street that somebody she knew was dead. I could sit down, Kate thought then. I could sit down now on the cold pavement and not move for days.

"Well, it wants to look like suicide," Starks said, "but we're not assuming anything. Could be another homicide. In which case, you'd better keep it in mind." He stared straight at her. "Bodies tend to accumulate in cases like this. And it's usually the less guilty people that turn up dead. Remember that next time you decide to keep something from us. It's not a smart policy."

Kate walked. She walked for two hours through downtown Washington, noticing but not caring about the cold. She walked from one end of the Mall to the other, dodging strollers and tourists, trying to calm herself. She knew she had to get her feelings under control; she had to keep a lid on her fear, and on the anger she now felt—at Joel, at the police, at everyone responsible for bringing this hell down on top of her.

Don Fordham was dead. Her husband's friend and partner. Another of her husband's friends and partners. Kate knew that Don's death would just make the police more certain about Joel. The detectives, jumping to the obvious conclusions, would be reinterviewing all of the employees at From the Rainforest. They'd be asking the standard questions: Were there tensions in the partnership? Disagreements? Arguments? Did either of them ever threaten the other? Kate had no idea what kind of answers they'd get. Things had never been very easy between Joel and Don. Although they'd been friends for most of their lives, they disagreed all the time about business. Joel always claimed that Don had lost the original vision of the partnership, that he'd forgotten their goal of dealing only with small farms and startup businesses in the developing world. Don, for his part, accused Joel of taking chances on too many shaky deals. It was Don who pushed for the incorporation of the business four years earlier. He said he wanted to limit his own personal liability, in case one of Joel's unilateral decisions (which were allowable under their first partnership agreement) came back to haunt them. But Kate was sure that they had remained friends through it all—old friends, good friends, with the strength of their shared history behind them.

After reaching the Hirshhorn Museum, Kate went down the steps to the public sculpture garden. She walked past the Calders and Rodins, thinking of something Joel had said to her once about Don. They were on a beach somewhere at night, in midwinter. "Don's problem," Joel had told her, "is that making money has become his main goal in the business."

"Oh, so you're *not* interested in making money?" she had asked, always ready to tease him on this topic. "I wish the hell you had told me that before we got married."

Joel had laughed. "Money can buy freedom or it can buy enslavement. That's what I've learned since getting out of college. I have no objection to money that buys freedom."

Thinking about this now, Kate shuddered. Had Joel been giving her some kind of advance warning that night? Had he been telling her that he was going to buy his freedom from her someday? She remembered then where he'd made the remark. It was at Don and Jeannette's beach house on the Delaware shore, just a week or two before Christmas, less than a year ago. It was a strange time to go to the beach, but Don and Jeannette had convinced them to come just for a weekend. Jeannette always claimed that the shore was extraordinary in winter: deserted, dramatic, and great for the dogs, who could run up and down the empty sand all day without much supervision.

That weekend, Kate remembered, was the only time she felt completely comfortable in Don and Jeannette's company. The four of them would split up into various pairs to walk the dogs, go to the supermarket, cook. To her surprise, Kate found that she really enjoyed talking to Don. He was more thoughtful than she'd ever imagined him, more philosophical. She recalled trudging up the beach with him early on the Saturday morning, while Hermann and Pearlie romped around them. She and Don were both wearing heavy winter coats and sneakers, and the sand sprayed out in front of them with each step they took. He talked nonstop for a good hour, telling her things about himself she'd never heard before: how he and his brothers had grown up poor and motherless in Albuquerque in the late fifties; how his father had to work two jobs to swing his costs at NMSU; how his father nearly had a heart attack when Don was almost thrown out for being caught at a biology lecture with three joints in his pocket. Listening to this, Kate wondered if Don felt the same awkwardness she did in their current circumstances, being married to somebody from an environment of money and education and privilege. Did he also feel that need to prove himself, to be smarter, work harder, and show himself worthy? Probably not. He was a man, for one thing, and married to Jeannette, who was nobody's idea of a challenge. A thought had come to Kate then: did Don marry Jeannette just for her money? She turned away from him and looked out at the ocean, trying to push the question from her mind.

That night they ate lobsters for dinner—lobsters and spinach salad and some strange combination of Gorgonzola, hummus, and pita bread that Don had dreamed up. The four of them sat around the oak table in the dining room for hours, drinking vodka tonics and white Burgundy, listening to old Jo Stafford and Ella Fitzgerald tapes, laughing, arguing, telling bad jokes. Joel passed around capsules containing his latest discovery: Ma Huang, an ancient Chinese herb that was supposed to counteract the depressive effects of alcohol. They each tried one, even Jeannette. And the herb really seemed to work. Kate drank four glasses of wine and never once had her usual urge to fall asleep on a couch with a warm dog wrapped around her feet.

Around ten or eleven, Kate and Joel got up from the dinner table, put on their coats, and carried their mugs of coffee out to the beach. The sky had clouded over by this time, blotting out the moon, but they could still see the dark ocean in front of them, wrinkled by whitecaps and veined with dark strands of seaweed.

"Isn't this great here?" Kate asked, wrapping her fingers around the mug. Her dark hair hung loose and strands of it were floating in the gentle breeze.

"I'm cold as hell, actually," Joel said.

Kate laughed. "Me, too."

When they finished their coffees, they put the mugs down in the sand and just walked and talked for a long time—about Don and Jeannette, about the business. It was then that Joel made his comment about Don's main goal being to make money.

A few minutes after that, Kate asked, "Why do you think Don married Jeannette?"

Joel stopped walking. "The timing of your question

makes it pretty obvious that *you* think he married her for money."

"No," Kate said quickly. "It's just that they don't seem so . . . I don't know—well paired."

"Are we well paired?" he asked after a few seconds.

"Fuck yes."

"And that's why you married me?"

She hesitated, not wanting to meet his eye. "I don't know why I married you. No, wait, I do know. I married you because I fell in love with you. But I don't know why I fell in love with you."

"Oh, right. Semantics."

"Well, why did you marry me?"

He smiled. "I guess I don't know, either. Ex-cop turned liberal do-gooder, thinks she's tougher than she really is, but generally adorable. What's not to fall in love with?" He stooped to pick up a piece of driftwood and then started walking again. "To answer your other question: I'm not really sure why Don married her. But I do know that most of the capital for his share in the business came from her family. We wouldn't have been able to start without her help. So maybe he did marry her for money."

Kate shook her head, thinking of everything she knew about Don, everything he had told her during their walk. "I'll never get it about you ex-hippies and your relationship to money."

He laughed. "You're right," he said. "It's complicated. Almost as complicated as the relationship of you ex-blue-collar types to money."

The comment stung her more than Joel probably realized. "Well," she said after a second, "Don's an ex-hippie *and* an ex-blue-collar type. As complicated as they come."

Joel pulled the collar of his coat tighter. "Everyone's out to better their lot in life," he said. "That's what being alive is all about. You take the hand you're dealt and you try to make it better."

"Is that Joel Baker's Draw-Poker Theory of Life?"

He looked at her. "Hey, baby," he said. "Marrying you was like filling an inside straight."

Feeling very happy suddenly, she pushed him over into a sand dune.

Remembering all of this—now, as she sat in the sculpture garden—Kate was suddenly overcome by a deep, ragged feeling of loss. Only eleven months had passed, and now Joel was gone, Don was dead, and she was certain that no time in her life would ever again be as happy as that weekend at the beach.

Kate got up from the chair. The chill of the wrought-iron had seeped through her coat and skirt to her skin. She shivered. It was time to go home.

She was back at the house an hour later. As soon as she walked in the door she noticed something was wrong. The lighting was strange—not as bright as it should have been. At first she thought the bulb on one of the timer-controlled lamps must have burned out. But when Hermann came shuffling up to meet her at the door, she knew something else had happened.

"What's going on?" she asked him, crouching just inside the door to look at Hermann's eyes. They seemed glassy and unfocused. She felt a limpness in his shoulders. "Did you eat something bad?" She got to her feet and was about to check his food and water when she caught sight of a glowing blue rectangle in the living room. It was a computer screen. An open laptop—Joel's PowerBook from his downstairs office—sat on the coffee table in front of the armchair, its power source plugged into the wall outlet, a phone line running from the back into the phone jack near the bookcase.

She understood then what had happened: Hermann had been drugged. Someone had been in the house while she was gone.

14

Kate crossed the room to the laptop on the coffee table. She could see that the computer was on, although the screen was partially dimmed. Hanging from the front of the keyboard was what looked like a yellow Post-it.

Kate stopped and quickly scanned the room. Nothing else had been disturbed, as far as she could tell. But someone had been there—someone who had thought in advance about Hermann and how to keep him out of the way. She leaned forward and ripped the Post-it off the keyboard. A message was written on it in blue felt-tip, the handwriting unfamiliar: "Press Return on the keyboard when you arrive—nothing else please, or you won't get me."

"What?" she said aloud. She sat down in the armchair in front of the laptop. She touched the trackball and the little screen sprang to full brightness. Kate looked over what was on the screen. The machine was running what looked like a communications program, something just recently loaded onto the hard drive, since the laptop, like

Joel's desktop, had been scraped clean during the burglary. There was a small window open, with a masked command at the top. The cursor was blinking at the end of the command line.

Kate knew just enough about computers to have an idea of what was going on. If she hit Return, the internal modem would dial up a number—another person's computer or an Internet server—and put her into direct contact with somebody. Somebody who could be anywhere in the world by now.

She hesitated before following the instructions on the Post-it, wondering if there was some way of tracing the contact she was about to make. Maybe, but if so, it certainly wasn't in her power to do it.

She pressed the Return key. The computer's modem made its soft musical noises, calling up whatever number it was programmed to call, and then connected. It took another few seconds for the masked command to run. Kate watched the screen anxiously. It read: "[Trying to connect to your party's talk daemon]."

"Whatever the hell that means," Kate muttered.

Another message: "[Connection established.]" Then: "[Switching . . .]" Suddenly, a new window opened, with two lines at the top:

STUBBORN SPOUSE has joined the chat.

DR FEELGOOD has joined the chat.

As she looked on, another message appeared in the window, in the blank field below:

DF: finally, you're there. I was getting worried.

Kate leaned back in the armchair, still confused. Was this the man who'd been in her house? A quick thought passed through her mind: could this be Joel?

Another message appeared:

DF: just type normally. hit return when you want to
     send what you've typed. surely any wife of Joel
     Baker must know how to chat on-line.

Kate leaned forward and began typing. She hit the Return
key, and the question she had typed appeared on the
screen:

SS: Who are you?

There was only a short delay before the answer appeared
right below her question:

DF: excellent. we are in business.

DF: isn't this laptop thing a nice touch? old technology
     by now, but so much nicer than a gun to yr head
     and a lot of tough talk. don't you think?

SS: Who are you?

DF: its not important. whats important is what I have
     to tell you.

SS: Why did you drug my dog? Why were you here?

DF: just wanted to open a line of communication. the
     dog is fine BTW. a dose of Librium derivative.
     harmless.

SS: Where are you?

DF: I could be anywhere, couldnt I. down the block,
     other side of the world.

She paused, then typed carefully:

SS: Is my husband alive?

DF: I admire your perfect punctuation and orthogra-
     phy, by the way, even under pressure!

SS: I want to know if my husband is alive.

DF: would you stop looking for him if I said no?

SS: Maybe. If I believed you.

DF: and if I said yes he's alive, but he doesn't want to be found???

SS: Are you saying that?

DF: Im not saying either one. Im just saying Ud better stop putting yr nose into places it doesnt belong.

SS: Is that what happened to Don Fordham?

Twenty or thirty long seconds passed.

DF: Don was stupid. he lacked the vision required for our purposes.

SS: So you killed him.

DF: killed him? I thought he committed suicide. ;-)

SS: And so did Jin-Liang Lu??

DF: U realize that even if U got me to say that I killed one or both of these people, there wld never be any way of determining who is making the admission. *I* is a problematic concept out here, ma'am.

SS: I know who you are.

DF: I am dr feelgood.

SS: You are Duncan Lloyd.

There was a long pause.

DF: not a screenname Im familiar with.

SS: I could go to the police with the name. I haven't yet but I could.

DF: I wouldnt. it would just confuse them even more.

SS: But you are Duncan Lloyd.

DF: I M someone w/ the power to kill U at any time.

Kate didn't answer. She didn't know how to feel about a threat like this—so abstract, coming from a phantom on the other end of a wire.

After another minute or so, the conversation went on:

DF: U were at johnshopkins yesterday. I wld really recommend U not do things like that in future.

SS: You make me want to go back now. Maybe I missed something if you're so worried about it.

DF: J's girlfriend is a waste of time.

SS: I found that out. But she's not the only person at Johns Hopkins.

Kate was working on instinct now, unsure how much to provoke this man, how much to reveal to him. This conversation was clearly not designed just to warn her off. Duncan Lloyd wanted to find out how much she knew. And now Kate wasn't sure if she should give him the impression that she knew more or less than she really did.

DF: people can die from talking to U. U can die from talking to them too. the subject of your husband is like a disease.

SS: Joel can probably tell you how I react to that kind of threat. I'm supposed to be afraid of some guy who won't even face me? Who has to use little technology tricks to protect himself?

"Shit," Kate muttered to herself. This was a dangerous tack, but she didn't know how else to go on.

DF: ;-) !!!!!!!!!! they taught U well in police acad, sweety. clearly U want to escalate. fine by me.

next time it could be strychnine in the dogs water.
or in his masters chardonnay. hasta luego.

She was losing him. She typed faster:

    SS: wait

There was an agonizing pause before he answered:

    DF: U rang???
    SS: Is Joel alive?

She waited for the answer, but it didn't come. She typed
again:

    SS: Is Joel alive?

She waited thirty seconds, then a minute. She thought now
that she would have to get an answer—a simple three- or
two-letter word, yes or no. But would it be the truth, whatever it was? Duncan, or whoever she was talking to, must
have been weighing his options, deciding his strategy.
"Come on, come on," Kate said, staring at the screen.
    The computer gave out a sour little beep, and then a
note appeared on the screen:

    DR FEELGOOD has left the chat.

"Shit!" Kate shouted aloud as she jumped out of the armchair, sending Hermann skittering backward across the
room. She'd played him wrong. She'd been in direct contact with the one man who could tell her what all of this
was about, the one man who could tell her what had happened to her husband, and she'd let him get away.
    She looked back at the little blue screen glowing on
the coffee table. There must be some way of tracing the

communication, she thought. Was anything on the Internet really untraceable? "Evan," she said aloud. She could take the laptop over to him—keeping the computer on and the program open. Maybe he could find a way to get some information out of it.

She started toward the phone, then stopped. What if his mother or aunt answered? Her eye went back to the computer screen. She could e-mail him, if she knew how. Why hadn't she paid more attention to this stuff when Joel tried to teach her? No, she'd have to use the telephone. She'd have to get past the mother.

Kate found Evan's number and dialed it on the kitchen phone. Her hopes fell when she heard the female voice saying, "Hello?"

"Hi, can I speak to Evan, please?"

After a short pause, the woman, who must have been Evan's mother, said, "Who's calling?"

"Kate Drummond," Kate said, as naturally as she could. "I'm from Panic Software. An Evan Potter called us about a bug in one of our programs."

"My son the computer genius," Mrs. Potter said. "Just a minute."

Kate heard the phone being put down, some footsteps, then a call in the distance: "Evan! Telephone!"

The footsteps came back. Kate heard Mrs. Potter picking up the phone again. A second later, another extension was picked up. "Hullo?" It was Evan's voice—thin, uncertain.

"Yes," Kate said. She knew that Mrs. Potter was still on the line. "Evan Potter? This is Kate Drummond from Panic Software. You called about a problem with our Internet software program, and we were just following up."

Silence. Kate could barely keep herself from yelling: Figure it out, Einstein!!

"Kate Drummond?" Evan asked.

"Yes. From Panic Software," she answered, emphasizing the word "panic."

Another silence. Then: "Oh right. The e-mail thing."

Kate nearly dropped the phone in relief. "Exactly."

She heard the tiny click of Mrs. Potter hanging up. "Evan?"

"I was about to call you," he said. "In an hour I was gonna call you."

"You found something?"

"Yeah."

Kate squeezed the phone cord in her fist. "How can we get together? You think I can sneak in by the deck door?"

"They're leaving," he said. "When my aunt finishes the dishes, they're going into D.C. for a play. They do it once a month, with some lady friends."

"Great. So if I get there at, I don't know, eight?"

"They'll be gone, definitely."

"Okay, I'll see you then. I have something else for you to try, too." She was pacing around the kitchen now, stretching the cord to its limit. "So you got into Joel's e-mail?"

"I got into something else. I'll tell you when you get here."

"Okay."

Then, just as she was about to hang up, she heard him say: "I'm good at this."

"What?" she asked.

"I'm good at this stuff. I can do it for you, whatever you need."

Kate thought suddenly of Desmond Ellis, her case at Holbrook House, and the glimmerings she got from him. "I know you're good at this, Evan," she said, taking the time to mean it. "I'm really grateful for your help."

"Um, okay," he said. "See you later."

Kate hung up. Hermann came up to her then and stuck his muzzle into her hand. "Oh God, I'm sorry." She sank to a crouch and looked him in the eyes. "Here you are, sick, and I'm ignoring you. First Joel is gone, and now you must be wondering about me."

The dog whimpered a few times, then yawned. "You lay down and rest," Kate said, feeling dishonest, and then ridiculous for feeling dishonest with a dog. "I have to go out again, but I'll be back in a few minutes. I promise."

Hermann stared at her.

"I promise," she said again, resisting the impulse to cross her fingers behind his head.

She got to Evan's at 8:15. She parked opposite the house, then ran across the road and up the icy walk with Joel's open laptop in her arms. The telephone cord and power source cord trailed behind her like a tail.

Evan opened the door. "Hi," he said. He was wearing a black T-shirt and clean black jeans. It looked as if he'd combed his little red ponytail for the occasion.

"Evan," she said. "I brought this laptop, and I want to plug it in before the battery runs down."

"In my room." He took the laptop carefully, as if taking a baby from her arms. The screen, which had dimmed automatically to save power, lit up again as the computer changed hands. "PowerBook 165. Ancient history," he said.

"Do you have any idea when your mother's coming back?" Kate asked.

"Late," Evan said. He went ahead of her through the dark house, the blue light from the laptop throwing shadows like candlelight. Kate could barely make out the dim forms of furniture around the living room. "Over this way," Evan said impatiently. He'd already started up the staircase toward the lights on the second floor.

His room was a mess. There were piles of magazines in the corners, open CD cases strewn on the floor, and a big fantasy poster on the wall of a huge-muscled warrior bristling with high-tech weaponry. On the desk across from the bed was a new-looking computer with a large color screen. Evan seemed eager to start. He put the laptop down on the bed, plugged in the power pack, and then sat down at the desk. "I'll look at that later," he said.

"So, you did or didn't get into my husband's e-mail?" Kate asked.

"Not yet," he said, seeming annoyed. "He must've picked a smart password. My program hasn't been able to get it yet."

"What did you find, then?"

"Let me get on the Web a minute," he answered, moving the computer's mouse. Kate stood behind him, watching the screen. "You probably want to sit," he added.

She moved some T-shirts off a wooden chair and dragged it over to the computer. Evan was staring at the big screen, leaning forward. It looked as if the thing was trying to suck him in. "You'll hurt your eyes," Kate said.

Evan didn't seem to hear her. He slid the mouse around a black pad with the phrase "Dark Forces 2" spelled out in big letters. He was clicking furiously, his eyes never leaving the screen. "The sender's e-mail address on that message you gave me was on a domain called 'bioper.com.' I couldn't get that guy's password, either, but when I was checking out the bioper site on the Web, I found something," he said. "It's buried real deep, if you don't know the URL."

Kate nodded, hoping she'd catch on as they went along.

"Here we go." Evan clicked one more time and then sat back. A little icon spun in a corner of the screen for a few seconds before a black square appeared, slowly turning into a picture—two rabbits standing on either side of a logo: Bio-Perfection Inc. "Welcome to Bio-Perfection" said a prerecorded sound clip.

Text started appearing under the logo. A title came first:

"Better Living Through Biochemistry." Then some text: "BioPerfection is your independent source for information about safe, nonaddictive substances to improve your health, lifestyle, and mindstyle. Some of these substances are classified as 'controlled' in the outside world; some are not. Some are natural; others are engineered in the lab. What they all share is an ability to change you and your life—for the better. Because many of these substances have been made illegal, unavailable without prescription, and/or prohibitively expensive by the misguided intervention of the FDA, the AMA, government law enforcement agencies, and the pharmaceutical industry, it has become necessary to provide this service. We at BioPerfection give you the information you need to access the medicines, recreationals, and enhancers that these organizations want to withhold from you."

There was another image below that, of a cartoon bonsai tree, and then more text: "NOTE: BioPerfection is devoted to the enhancement of life on Earth, not to self-destruction. Thus, we do not offer information on PCP, addictive barbiturates, nitrites and other inhalants, addictive opiates, tobacco, free-base preparations of cocaine, and any other substances whose harm, in our opinion, outweighs their benefits. Please click on one of the icons below."

"Okay," Kate said, scooting her chair closer to the screen.

Evan scrolled down to a row of seven colorful buttons that seemed to be pulsating on the screen. "Check out the applets," he said. Each of the dancing buttons had a label: Performance Enhancers; Experience Enhancers; Prescription and Traditional Medicines; Experimental Derivatives; Our Philosophy; BioPerfection FAQ; and Cornucopia.

"Click on Experience Enhancers," Kate said.

Evan moved the mouse and clicked. The screen went

blank again, except for the program's toolbar and the little spinning icon. After a few seconds, more text and icons appeared against a psychedelic background, another title, "Experience Enhancers," and under it some bulleted headings, each underlined:

- <u>Designer Hallucinogens</u>

- <u>Cacti and Dissociatives</u>

- <u>Mushrooms</u>

- <u>Safe Opiates</u>

- <u>Experience-Enhancing Herbs</u>

- <u>Antidepressants</u>

- <u>Other Mood Modifiers</u>

Kate read down the list. Just about everything in those categories would probably be on the DEA's list of controlled substances. "Okay, can you go back again and click on Performance Enhancers?"

Evan did as she asked. After another few seconds, a new page appeared on the screen:

PERFORMANCE ENHANCERS

- <u>Amphetamine Derivatives</u>

- <u>Safe Steroid Derivatives</u>

- <u>Nootropics</u>

- <u>Other Smart Drugs</u>

- <u>Coffee and Tea</u>

- <u>Performance-Enhancing Herbs</u>

- <u>Vitamins and Minerals</u>

"So what happens if you click on one of the underlined words?" Kate asked.

"You go a page deeper. You get, like, information on everything—dosages and side effects and stuff like that. You can even download little videos and sound files about some of the drugs."

Kate stared at the screen for a few more seconds before saying: "Go back again and click on Our Philosophy."

Evan looked pleased at her interest. After a few more seconds, another page appeared—an illustration of a balding Greek philosopher holding a scroll:

OUR PHILOSOPHY

BioPerfection is your one-stop connection to the world of biochemical life enhancement, providing you with the tools you need to help build a better self and a better society—tools that the DEA, FDA, AMA, FBI, GOP, and other maintenance organizations of the dominator culture would like to keep from you. Bio-Perfection believes profoundly in the freedom of body, information, and spirit, and in the ability of technology to ensure and expand those freedoms. We do not recognize the authority of entities like the Food and Drug Administration to make pronouncements on the efficacy, safety, or desirability of the various means of consciousness engineering now available to us in the form of physio- and psychoactive substances, both natural and human-made. Using the tools rapidly becoming available to us through advances in biochemistry, molecular biology, gene therapy, and biotechnology— and made widely available in the informational free market represented by the ascendance of unhindered digital internationalism—we foresee the emergence of a better, freer world community, in which individual responsibility takes the place of external centralized

authority in the governance of life. Thus, our motto:
Perfect Drugs Make a Perfect World.

Kate remembered the video in Velma's safe as she read
the last sentence. "Perfect Drugs Make a Perfect World"
was the phrase on Duncan Lloyd's T-shirt.

"Okay," she said aloud, more to herself than to Evan,
"but this isn't really breaking any law, right? I mean, information like this isn't illegal in itself. It's free speech."

Evan smiled, barely able to hide his delight. "Just wait,"
he said, moving the mouse again. "You should see the
on-line shopping mall first."

He made his way back to the home page and then
clicked on the pulsating button labeled Cornucopia. "This
page you need a password for, otherwise you don't get
in. But my blasting program got this one, after like a
thousand tries." He let go of the mouse and typed in a
few letters, so fast that Kate couldn't tell what he had
typed.

"What was the password?" she asked.

" 'Soporific,' " he said, pronouncing it soap-errific.

Kate felt a tingling in her hands and feet. The little
Beatrix Potter book was still in her bag.

"It's a stupid password, just one word, but the security
gets tighter when you get deeper in," he said. Then, "Here
it is." The computer played a short sound clip of trumpets
as the page appeared:

WELCOME TO BIOPERFECTION'S
PHARMACEUTICAL SHOPPING MALL!

BioPerfection is not just an information clearinghouse.
Our aim is to become a full-fledged underground drug
company, operating over the Internet in defiance of the
FDA, DEA, the US Patent Office, and the profit-
oriented "legitimate" pharmaceutical industry. While

we are still growing, we already offer a full array of
life-enhancing, lifesaving substances by <u>mail</u>, <u>over-
night courier service</u>, or, for items of a more sensitive
nature (i.e., controlled substances on Schedules I and
II), <u>private delivery</u>. Our products are affordable, high
quality, and, if used as instructed, safe. However,
BioPerfection assumes no responsibility for any physical harm or legal problems incurred through the ordering or use of the products listed below. Please read
the full <u>DISCLAIMER</u> before ordering. Any access
beyond this page is allowed only under the conditions
outlined in the full disclaimer. <u>Continue</u>.

"I can't believe this," Kate muttered. "Go on."
Evan clicked on the word "Continue" to reach the next
page.

ELECTRONIC ORDER FORM

Please note that all business conducted with Bio-
Perfection is, for obvious reasons, cash only. <u>Ordering
Instructions</u>—in particular, encryption instructions—
must be strictly followed. Since a certain amount of
mutual trust is required for these transactions, you may
wish to keep your first order small. However, the fact
that you are in possession of the password allowing
access to this page means that you understand and
sympathize with <u>BioPerfection's mission</u>, and have an-
ecdotal evidence of our good faith. Like any business,
BioPerfection relies on the word of mouth of satisfied
customers for its survival.

Following this was an order form, consisting of a long
list of substances, along with prices and quantities.
"The ordering is where it gets weird," Evan said.
"That's where the tighter security stuff shows up."

Kate got up and started pacing around the cluttered room. It made sense to her that the shopping mall would be relatively easy to get into. BioPerfection would naturally want its offerings to be available to as many potential customers as possible. A simple password, one that could be spread by word of mouth, would make the page accessible to people in the know, but would stop a casual surfer from stumbling on it by accident. They would obviously need more security than a password, though. "Show me," she said finally, sitting down again.

Evan clicked on the Ordering Instructions hypertext. What appeared next was a long paragraph swimming in acronyms like "PGP" and "RSA." It told the orderer to get something called a public encryption key on a bulletin board service and use it on the completed order form. She skimmed over the details and then focused on the second paragraph:

> BioPerfection reserves the right to refuse any orders it regards as suspect, including obvious attempts at infiltration by unsympathetic persons or organizations. We will make every attempt to have your order delivered within seven business days of receipt of payment. However, supplies of many of the products we offer are necessarily erratic, so we rely on your faith and patience. Until the Revolution, we've all got to be just a little bit careful.

Evan looked over at her, apparently satisfied with the effect of his discovery. "Anyway," he said, "I got the encryption key and made an order. Just to try it out."

"You what?" Kate said.

"I e-mailed them an order, just to see what would happen."

"Order for what?"

"Prozac. It was in the Prescription and Traditional Medicines section." He kept his eyes on the screen. "It was the first thing I thought of. A kid I know at school takes it."

Kate shook her head, trying not to think about the fact that she'd more or less encouraged a teenager to order drugs illegally. "And what happened?"

"Well, along with my order form, I had to send them an encryption key that I had the decryption code for. It's pretty complicated," he said. "But I got back an encrypted e-mail in a couple hours. Here's what it said." He brought up the decoded version on the screen:

Thank You, Warrior@gmk.net, For Your Order!

Your recent order for:
    Fluoxetine ("Prozac") 20
    20 mg Capsules
    10 × 28 Count Pkg.
    Price: $200
has been received and provisionally accepted. PLEASE NOTE: The substance you have ordered is fluoxetine, NOT (strictly speaking) Prozac, which is a proprietary name belonging to the Eli Lilly Company of Indianapolis, Indiana. However, the substance you will receive is exactly the same in chemical structure as Prozac. The only difference is the little name on the capsule—and the price tag. Since BioPerfection operates outside the inflated patent-and-profit structure of the "legitimate" pharmaceutical industry, we can offer you the very same substance at a substantially reduced price.

Payment Instructions: Please send: $200, IN CASH ONLY, to the address below (NB: FedEx will not deliver to a post office box). Your order, along with complete documentation, will be delivered to you via: COMMERCIAL OVERNIGHT DELIVERY SERVICE within five business days of payment. Remember, this address is confidential!!!

Under this was the very same P.O. box address that Kate had found in the document from Velma's safe. "Can you print out that page?" she asked.

Evan hit a button on his keyboard, sending the printer into action.

Kate leaned back in the wooden chair. She knew that it was time to follow up, that her next step should be to go to that town in Pennsylvania. She unbuttoned her blouse and took the scrap of paper from her bra. "Do you have an atlas?" she asked Evan.

Evan nodded, looking amazed at what she had just done. "I've got one on a CD," he said, then began rummaging around on his desk.

"I'd rather have good old ink and paper."

Evan laughed. He got up and pulled a Rand McNally atlas from the bookshelf. Kate took it and looked up Karlstadt in the index. She found the town on the Pennsylvania map, in the south-central part of the state, a few miles south of Interstate 70 in the Allegheny Mountains. It looked like a middle-sized town, surrounded by mountains and state forest, within a few hours' drive of Johns Hopkins. A nice quiet place for a company to make illegal drugs. Or for a person to hide from the world. She closed the atlas. Was Joel there right now?

She realized suddenly that she had to pee. "Can I use the bathroom?" she asked Evan.

"End of the hall on the left," he said.

Kate slipped out of the room and found the bathroom. Things were starting to make a kind of sense to her. The documents they'd found in Velma's safe must have some-

thing to do with BioPerfection's business. And the drugs
that the police found at the Rainforest warehouse must be
part of the organization's inventory. So was this what had
taken Joel away from her? But where was the connection
between BioPerfection and the mutilated corpse of Jin-
Liang Lu? There was more here. Something must have
gone wrong somewhere along the line, and now she knew
where to go to find out what it was.

Kate finished up in the bathroom, threw some cold water on her face, and went back to the bedroom. Evan,
looking a little sheepish, was still sitting in front of the
huge computer screen, clawing nervously at his ponytail.

"Okay, Evan," she said, pulling her chair up close
again. "Surf to your heart's content. I want to read everything you can dig up about these people."

15

The husband was winning. As much as he tried to convince himself otherwise, Evan was eventually forced to admit it: Joel Baker was beating him.

In the first hour or two after Kate left, Evan felt great. He'd started to show her what he could do. She'd sat next to him, her body throwing off heat like a radiator, and they'd explored the website together. She took notes on a legal pad while he controlled the mouse, opening up this hidden world for her. Once or twice she squeezed his forearm in excitement, and Evan felt instantly energized: he was powerful; he was unstoppable; he was the Stone Warrior.

But now that sense of triumph was draining away. Yes, he'd found the Web page for her. Yes, he'd gotten past the site's defenses and had shown her what the husband was up to. But Joel Baker was still winning. He was still hiding from Evan, laughing at him. The main task that Kate had given Evan was still unaccomplished.

He couldn't get into the guy's e-mail. He'd connected

to the Well, tried a few obvious passwords, then started
bombarding it with passwords from his dictionary CD.
But Joel Baker was too smart for that to work. He'd
picked a smart password—probably something with numbers and symbols in it. Meanwhile, the Well cut Evan off
after every few attempts to sign in. He eventually had to
set up multiple telnet sessions, each of them trying passwords, but even that took forever.

At one point, Evan considered planting a password-
capturing program. He'd read about them on the hacker
bulletin boards—little planted programs that would come
between the caller and the system, asking the caller to
enter the password once, then again. The first time the
password was captured for the hacker; the second time
the password let the caller into the system normally. It
was a pretty interesting idea, Evan thought. But although
he knew how to write the code for a program like that,
he had no idea how to plant it on the Well, let alone do
it without being found out.

He was in over his head. He had to admit that to himself. Some of the hackers he read about could patch into
phone systems, rerouting calls and switching numbers
around to cover their tracks. They could get into Unix and
VMS machines at credit agencies and pick up credit card
numbers, then erase all evidence that they'd been there.
Those guys could probably get into the husband's e-mail
with no sweat at all. They'd slice through his defenses
with programs available only on the private bulletin
boards. They'd have no problem releasing the husband's
secrets like birds from a cage.

But Evan couldn't do any of that. He wasn't powerful
enough. He was just a fraud, an impostor, a lamer.

This wasn't the way he wanted it to turn out. Kate
Baker was supposed to come to him for help, with an
impossible task, and he was supposed to accomplish it—
by fighting his way in, penetrating deeper and deeper into

the enemy's defenses, and then finally saving her and earning her undying gratitude.

And now she'd given him a new challenge, this laptop on his desk. Evan was expected to do something to it, to make it spill all of its secrets. She was counting on him.

Evan stared at the open PowerBook on his desk. He was almost afraid to touch it, afraid that whatever information it held would evaporate the second he put his fingers on the keyboard. There were so many ways to hide on the Internet, with remailers, looping, network weaving. How would he ever work his way through all of that to find the guy he was looking for?

It was supposed to be better than this. *He* was supposed to be better than this.

Evan opened the drawer of his desk. Inside was the address he'd gotten from Kate's scrap of paper. She'd left it in the atlas when she went to the bathroom, and Evan had snuck a look at it: P.O. Box 29, Karlstadt, PA. It was the same address as the one in the BioPerfection e-mail. The fact that she'd found it somewhere else made Evan sure that she was going to go there to try to find her husband.

He turned the paper over. On the back was the other information he'd taken from her bag while she was in the bathroom. Her Visa number, American Express number, ATM, driver's license, medical card numbers. He'd just been writing down her Hampton County library card number when she flushed the toilet.

Evan had no idea what he would do with this information. He wouldn't cheat her, of course, though he now had that power. He could call up Eddie Bauer or PC Mall or even Victoria's Secret and buy whatever he wanted. He could order her a silk nightgown and have it delivered right to her house. She'd probably think it came from him, the husband. But then she'd read the card: Best wishes,

Evan. Joel Baker, if he ever found out about it, would probably freak.

Evan looked over at the little gray laptop. Somewhere on that hard drive was the telephone number that the communications program had been commanded to call. Evan would have to find it.

He went to his bureau and opened the top drawer. Inside, under his balled-up socks, was a diskette. It contained a couple of utility programs that he'd downloaded one night when, by incredible good luck, he'd managed to worm his way onto one of the heavy-duty hacker boards. The programs were probably illegal, which is why he hid the diskette. But now he needed them. He would use them to beat Joel Baker. They would be his secret weapon.

He carried the diskette over to the laptop on his desk. He figured he had a few hours. Kate wouldn't leave for Pennsylvania until tomorrow at the earliest. He might be able to find something by then. There was still a chance that he could save the day.

Kate got home by ten. Hermann, looking fully recovered from his canine Mickey Finn, met her at the door. Kate took off her suede jacket, threw it onto a chair, and listened to the messages on her answering machine—two from Jeannette's sister about the funeral for Don and one from Adrianna telling her that it really was time to hire that private investigator. Kate ignored all three messages and headed straight upstairs. She had to pack.

In the bedroom, Kate slid open the closet door and knelt to pull a red metal box out from under a pile of scarves. She carried it over to the bed and took the lid off. The smoky scent of oil rose from the box. Inside was her pistol, a Sig Sauer 9 millimeter, wrapped in an oiled cloth. The gun had been in this box for years. She took it out once every six months to clean it and check it over, usually when Joel was at work. He never liked seeing her handle the gun. It bothered him, he said, that she felt the need to keep it. He made her store the thing unloaded and partially disassembled in the metal box in the closet. She'd always gone along with this, even though she knew that having a disassembled, unloaded firearm in the house was like having nothing at all.

Kate lifted the Sig and carefully reassembled the barrel. It was always strange to feel this hunk of metal in her hands again. The weight of the Sig was a physical reminder of something she tried hard to forget: an earlier Kate, a proto-Kate, a discontinued model. But now, as she snapped in a neat, new, eight-round clip, she wondered how much things had really changed. Here she was again, loading up, giving herself the power to do harm.

She'd never fired a pistol at another human being—the Sig or any other firearm. Even during her time in uniform, she'd never used the Smith & Wesson revolver that was constantly on her hip, except on the practice range. So many people, when they hear of a cop who quit, automatically assume that the cop must have killed or maimed someone, but Kate had never had that excuse, thank God. She'd killed only in her thoughts, when some pimp or drug dealer proved to her just how low the human species could sink. But Kate knew that the only difference between someone who killed in her thoughts and a real killer was opportunity and equipment. And as a cop she'd always had too much of both.

Kate got up from the edge of the bed and put the Sig on her bureau. She had to start packing. How long would she be gone? she wondered. Two days? A week? It seemed a ridiculous thing to think about right then, but she had to know how many bras she should pack, how many pairs of slacks. She opened the top drawer of her bureau and looked down at the tangle of white, black, and red underwear. She hadn't done laundry in weeks, but

there seemed to be plenty left to choose from. She went
back to the closet then and pulled a black canvas duffel
from the top shelf. She decided she would just keep putting clothes in until it was full. That way, she wouldn't
have to decide how long she'd be gone.

As she opened the duffel on the bed and began to pack,
it occurred to her that she would have to rent a car for
the trip. Even though the police seemed to have dropped
their tail, she knew she couldn't use the Jetta. After she'd
been missing for a while, the police would definitely put
her license plate into the FBI's computer. If she got pulled
over for any reason, the stopping officer would routinely
run her plate number. And that would be the end. She'd
be found. She thought about asking to borrow Elena's car,
but the police would eventually figure that out, too, especially after the clothing switch she'd tried a few days
ago. No, she would have to leave the Jetta in the garage,
get Elena to drive her down to Hammond, and rent something—something rugged and sturdy but not too conspic-
uous.

Poor Elena, Kate thought as she stuffed a pair of black
jeans into the duffel. Elena would have to look after Hermann again. And what about Evan? What if he actually
managed to get something out of the laptop? Should she
wait a few days and give him a chance to work it out? It
seemed important to him.

She looked around the bedroom, to see if there was
anything else she should pack. Lipstick? Earrings? Ha.

She walked over to the bureau and picked up the Sig.
Would this thing protect her, she wondered. Was she
crazy to put herself in this kind of danger? Maybe so, but
there was a part of her—the cop part—that had learned
to push aside physical fear. Don't start doubting now, she
said. This is something you have to do.

Kate pulled the clip out of the pistol again and put it in her pocket. Then she stuffed the Sig into the duffel, deep down in the folds of a gray turtleneck sweater.

It was time to head out into the woods.

PART THREE

16

The tires of the rented Jeep Cherokee crunched to a stop in the gravel parking lot of the Big Creek Motel. Kate turned off the engine, sat for a second, and then climbed out. A pale wintry sun sat low over the pines, throwing long, blurred shadows across the gravel. Kate breathed deeply. The air tasted good up here, she thought. Cold and smoky and crisp. Mountain air.

Kate stretched as she looked over the miserable single-story motel—its line of blue doors opening onto the parking lot, the grimy heating/air-conditioning units sticking through the stucco walls, the rust-colored curtains closed over each window. There were only a few other vehicles in the lot—muddy 4-by-4s, mostly, and one ancient, low-slung Plymouth station wagon that was probably abandoned.

Kate zipped her suede jacket up to her neck. Now that she really looked at the place, she wondered if even Kate Drummond, the fictional divorcée from Baltimore hiding out from her abusive ex-husband, would stay in a motel like this. Not that it mattered. The desk clerk, a tidy little man with a waxed mustache, seemed to accept her cover story—and her cash for the room—with an air of total boredom. In fact, she probably didn't need to tell him any story at all. He wasn't the least bit curious about her *or* her reason for checking into the motel alone for three days. Whatever happened to small-town nosiness, Kate wondered, reaching back into the Jeep to get her duffel.

Room 4 was just as depressing as she expected—spacious but flimsy, the air reeking of ammonia and other people's luggage. There was a double bed, a thirteen-inch television bolted to the wall, and an imitation-wood bureau. A plastic ice bucket stood on a counter outside the bathroom, along with three plastic glasses wrapped in cellophane and a squat foam pitcher without a cover. The room's harvest-gold carpeting, most worn near the metal double-locking door, was covered with a series of cigarette burns that reminded Kate of hieroglyphics.

After closing the door behind her, she hauled her duffel into a corner and collapsed onto the soft bed. It had been a long drive, north from Frederick to Gettysburg, then northwest on small roads that seemed to get narrower and rougher the farther she traveled. Karlstadt itself was a gray little town crisscrossed by strips of dirty snow and mud. Its downtown area consisted primarily of a Wendy's, a Dairy Queen, a few strip malls, and three or four stoplights. And the whole town was surrounded by miles of state forest.

On the way to the motel, Kate had stopped at the post office. It was a one-story orange-brick building, sharing a parking lot with a deli, a five-and-ten, a video rental place, and a pizzeria. Fortunately, the mailboxes were located in a little entrance foyer, visible from the parking lot. She'd gotten a look at number 29. It was one of the bigger boxes, at about shoulder height. She'd stood on her toes to peer inside the tiny window, but the box was empty.

Kate's plan was to stake out the post office. She'd just wait in the parking lot until somebody came to collect the mail from Box 29. It could take days or even a week of constant watching (the foyer was open from six in the morning to seven at night), but it was the only way of proceeding that she could think of. To pass the time, she'd brought along some sociology books she was supposed to have read while getting her master's—George Herbert Meade, Erving Goffman—as well as a couple of Dorothy Sayers novels.

Kate roused herself from the bed and went into the bathroom. The toilet, wrapped with one of those "Sanitized For Your Protection" strips, actually did look clean. She turned on the faucet and splashed her face with cold, fizzing water.

She had been up since five. After waking to the squeal of her alarm, she'd eaten a quick breakfast, walked Hermann, and satisfied herself that Lieutenant Grainger hadn't started watching the house again. Then, at six, she'd taken Hermann over to Elena's house. Elena was already dressed and ready to take Kate to the rental car agency in Hammond. They drove over in near silence, then said good-bye on the street. "Here," Kate said, handing Elena a manila envelope. "It's a ten-page account of everything I know about all this. Open it only if you have to."

"Oh Kate," Elena moaned, struggling to hold back tears.

"Come on, stop. I promise you, I'll be here again in a week to take that back from you."

Now, as she reached for the thin motel towel, Kate thought again about this promise. Where would she really be in a week, she wondered. She rubbed her face dry and then stared at her reflection in the mirror. It occurred to her that she was doing exactly what Joel had done. She was disappearing without any explanation, leaving every-

body—Velma, Evan, even Adrianna—with no idea what
had happened. What will they think, Kate asked herself.
Will they decide that Joel and I are in this mess together?
A husband-and-wife crime team? Maybe. And yet Kate
wasn't involved, no matter what it looked like from the
outside. Could the same thing be true about Joel?

She sat down on the closed toilet lid and looked at her
watch. It was almost two in the afternoon. There would
be no point in staking out the post office today, since the
mail had apparently been collected already. But there were
still a good three hours of daylight left and Kate didn't
want to waste them. She wondered if it would be worth-
while asking questions around town. If there was an illegal drug lab somewhere out in these mountains, a few
of the locals might have their suspicions. Or maybe somebody had seen Jin around town—a young Chinese man
would probably stick out in a small white-bread town like
this. But she knew she could ruin her chances if she
started poking around too noticeably. Better to start
slowly, quietly. She'd just drive around and follow some
of the roads leading out of town into the wooded mountains, checking names on mailboxes. Maybe she'd get
lucky and there'd be one marked "Lloyd."

Kate got up and stared at herself in the mirror again.
"Oh shit, you're scared," she said aloud. She pulled her
hair back and looked at her drawn face, the dark semicir-
cles under her eyes. "You're old and tired and scared,"
she said. "But you're my only hope."

Nobody was home when Evan called the Bakers' number
at seven in the morning. He heard the machine answer,
listened to the outgoing message, then hung up.

Later, he told himself. Maybe she was in the shower.

Not that he knew what he'd tell her if she answered.
He'd been up all night working on the laptop, with no
luck at all. He'd been able to find the telephone number

that the computer was programmed to call—he recognized it as the local number of a well-known Internet access provider—but the fields for user ID and password in the settings file were blank. The way the program was set up, that information would have to be entered manually every time the application was used. So the guy had probably typed in a one-line macro containing the ID and password, along with the talk command and the guy's own e-mail address, before Kate had come home the night before. Once Kate pressed the Return key, all of that information was entered; then it was gone forever—bam—electrons disappearing into air.

He called Kate again at 7:30. He listened to the phone ring four times, then heard the voice, *her* voice: 'No one can get to the phone right now . . .''

He hung up again. He knew now that she was gone. She hadn't even waited to hear from him.

"Evan!" his mother called from downstairs. "Aunt Rita left some oatmeal for you on the stove! I have to go!"

"Okay," he shouted back.

"Don't dawdle! The bus won't wait for you!"

"Okay!"

"And don't forget to take that pill!"

Evan heard the front door slam. He listened to his mother's steps as she went down the walk, started the car, and then pulled out of the driveway.

He checked his watch: 7:43. He'd try once more at 8:00.

As the minutes passed, though, Evan felt himself getting angrier. Kate didn't really want his help, he could see that now. He was just a kid to her, no real help. He was nobody.

He got up from the bed and walked to the bathroom down the hall. He took the little white cup from the holder and filled it with water. Balancing carefully, he carried the cup back to his room. He let himself out through the

glass sliders onto the deck. The morning was cold, the
long grass at the edge of the woods furry with thick frost.
Evan was still dressed in the T-shirt and sweatpants he
always slept in. He felt the chill in his bare feet and arms,
but tried not to let it bother him.

Fuck her, he said to himself.

He set down the water and planted his bare feet on the
cold, damp planks. He touched his toes fifteen times,
holding the position on the last bend for five seconds as
the tendons stretched in his legs. He straightened up and
let his lungs fill with cold air. Sinking to the push-up
position, he then did twenty quick, perfect push-ups.
Holding the position again, he breathed steadily and
deeply—three times—and then began a set of slower
pushups. Finally, his muscles gave out. He lay facedown
on the deck for a while, letting the wet seep into his
clothes.

Fuck her, he said again, silently.

He got to his feet, walked to the edge of the deck, and
sat down, his back against a post of the wooden railing.
He took a sip of the water he'd left there. The ache in his
muscles felt good, like a deep burn.

A big red truck was passing on the road in front of the
house, struggling up the hill. Just as it passed the driveway, its chrome side mirror caught the low sun, reflecting
a flash of light at Evan. He thought of himself in a photograph: Evan sitting on the deck, alone, pitiful. The
driveway started wobbling then. Evan put his thumb and
forefinger up to the inside corners of his eyes and
squeezed.

He thought of something his mother had said a few
days after the police came to their door that Saturday
morning. She and Evan had been arguing at the dinner
table, and at one point he just walked out of the kitchen,
up the stairs, and into his room. He slammed the door,
but then came out again right away to go to the bathroom.

He heard his mother and aunt talking. "He's becoming a closed book to me," he heard his mother say. "Just like his damn father."

Evan began staring at his feet now, at the ridiculously bony ankles and long, skinny feet. It was the cold, he told himself; cold weather always made his eyes water. He wasn't really crying.

He got up quickly and went back into the house. He would try Kate Baker's number one more time. Just once more.

If no one answered, he knew exactly where to find her.

Kate got back to the motel room after dark. She'd been driving around all afternoon, scoping out the town, following roads until she came either to the next town or to the end of the pavement. There were a lot of houses far out in the woods—some modern and well kept, others run-down—but none seemed especially suspicious. Then, at six, she'd gone to the Wendy's for dinner. She figured there was no way that Joel or anyone he knew would be found eating at a Wendy's.

Kate let herself into the room and turned on the light. She double-locked the door behind her, sliding the end of the chain into the slot. Then she stepped over to the television and turned it on. A lurid face appeared on the screen—a man with a perfect haircut, his skin the color of a pink grapefruit's flesh. He stood to one side of a map covered with big white snowflakes. A storm was on its way. "Great," she said aloud. At least she'd packed for bad weather.

She took off her fringed suede jacket and hung it over the chair, making the Sig in the right-hand pocket clatter against the metal leg. One magazine for the gun was in the left-hand pocket, another in the glove compartment of the Jeep—sixteen rounds in all.

She climbed onto the bed and watched television with

the sound off. The newscast had moved on to sports—
some footage from a basketball game. Kate watched for
a few minutes, hugging a pillow to her chest. Joel had
always tried to get her interested in basketball, with no
success. He was a fanatic himself. It was one of the few
things he had in common with her brothers. She remembered one Christmas in Chicago. Joel and her brothers sat
in Phil's living room, getting excited over some Bulls
game. She came out of the kitchen, where she'd been
helping her sister-in-law with the dishes, and saw the men
crowding around the set, yelling. It had made her happy—
seeing her husband and her brothers together like this,
laughing and drinking beer. Somehow it reassured her that
she was a whole, united person, instead of someone with
two entirely different lives.

Closing her eyes, Kate wondered what her brothers
would think of her now, going after Joel with a Sig in
her jacket pocket. Would they approve? Not a chance, she
decided. They'd probably tell her to stay home and let the
professionals handle it. They'd never taken Kate seriously
as a cop, just as they'd never taken her seriously as anything else. Brothers.

Kate opened her eyes and got up from the bed. Someone knocked just as she was reaching to turn off the TV.
Kate literally jumped, stumbling against the edge of the
bed. She grabbed for her jacket and reached into the
pocket for the Sig.

Another knock. "Who is it?" she asked.

There was a short pause; then she heard a small voice
muffled by the door: "Evan."

For a second, Kate couldn't place the name. "What?"
she asked aloud. She put the gun back in the pocket and
walked over to the door. She unlocked it quickly—the
chain making a loud rattle—and pulled it open. The boy
was standing outside in a thin leather jacket and black
jeans, a grimy backpack slung over one narrow shoulder.

"Jesus Christ," Kate said. She just stared at him for a few seconds. Then she stepped back. "Get in here," she said.

Evan came into the room slowly, hunching his shoulders as if he had to duck to get through the doorway.

"I cannot believe this," Kate went on, as Evan slipped the backpack off his shoulder and put it on the floor. "You got the address from that e-mail, didn't you. You knew I would come here."

His little ponytail bounced as he nodded. "I figured you would."

"And how did you get here?"

He shrugged. "Hitched."

"You hitchhiked all the way here?"

"I got one ride, like, all the way from Frederick to Gettysburg. After that it was easy."

"But how did you find the motel?"

Evan seemed pleased at his own cleverness. "There are three motels in this town, and this is the only one with a Maryland rent-a-car parked in front."

Kate closed her eyes for a second before asking, "Does your mother know you're here?"

He laughed and shook his head.

"Listen to me." Kate grabbed Evan's chin and made him look her in the face. They were almost the same height, though Kate probably outweighed him by five or ten pounds. She noticed a few pimples high up on the boy's cheeks, near his temples. "Do you know how much trouble you can make for me? Do you have any idea?"

He licked his lips. "I can help you," he said.

Kate stopped, an explanation just now hitting her. "Did you find something? Did you find something important on the computer?"

She could see the deep disappointment on the boy's face. He hadn't found a thing.

"Okay," she said, going over to the television and turning it off. "Fine. You have to go back home, that's all. I have to get you home somehow."

"No," he said.

"What do you mean, no? Of course you're going home."

His jaw stiffened. "If you make me go, I'll tell the police where you are."

That stopped her. Kate crossed her arms in front of her chest. Looking at his face, she couldn't tell for sure if Evan would actually do something like that.

"Of course you're going home," she said again.

He poked the backpack with the toe of his black high-top sneaker. "I don't think so."

What could she do? He had given her no choice. "Well, at the very least we'll call to let your mother know you're safe."

"No way. She knows I'm safe. I left a note. I swear."

Kate felt a surge of rage toward the boy. For a second, she had an impulse to slap him. As if her job wasn't hard enough before, now she had to baby-sit this pouting adolescent. "Oh Christ," she said finally, turning away.

"It's the right thing," he said. "Really."

She turned back to him and looked over his clothes—the thin leather jacket, the T-shirt and jeans. "Is that the warmest jacket you have with you?"

Evan shrugged. He seemed to realize that he'd made it past a hurdle. "I guess," he said.

"There's an Army-Navy store in town," Kate said. "We can get you a heavy sweater or something tomorrow. It's supposed to get cold."

"I like cold."

"Yeah, I'm sure you do," she said. "But I don't have time to nurse a goddamn teenager with pneumonia." It was clear now that Kate would have to let the boy stay with her—at least for a day or two. He could watch the post office with her. Then, if anything developed, she could leave him at the motel, just sneak out while he was sleeping. "I'll have to get you a room," she said then. She grabbed her bag and counted the cash she had left. It was enough. "Look, from now on, you're my son, okay? And we're hiding out from Dad together."

"Nobody will believe I'm your son," he told her. "Tell them I'm your brother. Or maybe your boyfriend."

"Yeah, right," Kate said. But it was true that Evan looked too old to be her son. She would tell the clerk that he was her nephew. Not that the clerk would care.

Kate grabbed her jacket, shielding it with her body so that Evan wouldn't notice the heavy weight in the pocket. "I'll try to get you the room next door. Wait here."

She slipped out the door and pulled it nearly shut.

As her steps faded into the distance, Evan started looking around the room. The television display showed the time in red digits: 7:22. By now, his mother and aunt would have read his note telling them that he was going away for a few days. They'd be calling the parents of some kids in his class, then Mr. Palitori, the adviser of the computer club, then the police. They'd all start looking for him, checking the diner in town, the malls on the highway. Maybe they'd think the murderer got him. They'd probably go to the same place in the woods to see if his body was there now, headless and handless. Or maybe they would think that Evan himself was the murderer after all, and that now he'd escaped from under their noses.

Smiling at these thoughts, he picked up his knapsack and untied the flap. He still had the laptop Kate had brought over. Before leaving the house that morning, he'd loaded some of his own software onto it—a couple of utilities and communications programs, a few games. Aside from the computer, all he'd packed were a few extra pairs of socks and underwear, two shirts, a second pair of black jeans, a Game Boy, a hairbrush, and a toothbrush. He couldn't think of anything else he would need.

He took out the hairbrush. He loosened his ponytail from the rubber band and pulled the brush through his fine red hair. Then, checking himself in the bathroom mirror, he redid the rubber band. He looked carefully at his face. The zits were annoying but not too noticeable. He looked okay, actually.

He went back into the main room and stuck the brush into his knapsack. He was feeling hopeful again. He had gotten this far, so who knew what could happen next?

Kate got back a few minutes later with another key. "We're set," she said, closing the door behind her. She held out the key, dangling from a green, diamond-shaped tag. "You're in number five next door."

"Okay," he said, taking the key. "You still have the key I gave *you*?"

"The little file cabinet key? Yeah, I do." Kate tried to rub the cold air out of the sleeves of her jacket. "It's a long shot, but I'm hoping there's a file cabinet somewhere in this town that fits that key."

"So what's the plan?" Evan asked.

"No elaborate plan, so don't get your hopes up. I was just going to watch the post office box. See who comes to pick up the mail."

"Then follow them?"

"Maybe."

Evan pointed to his knapsack. "I brought the laptop so I could keep trying to get into your husband's e-mail."

"Good," she said. She thought this might be one way of keeping Evan occupied.

"It's not easy," Evan went on. "He was tricky about picking a password."

"Yeah, I'm sure he was," Kate said as she took her jacket off. It felt light in her hands now. On her way back from the motel office, she'd stopped and locked the gun into the glove compartment of the Jeep. "Joel is a tricky guy. Too tricky for his own good."

"If he picked a one- or two-word password, I would've gotten in by now. But I'll keep going."

"Good."

Kate looked over at the boy sitting stiffly on the bed across from her. If she'd had a baby at twenty, then it really would be about Evan's age right now. You're getting old, she told herself. Old and childless. "You have dinner?" she asked him.

He shrugged again. "I was trying to save my money."

Would having a son of her own be this frustrating, she wondered. "There's a pizza place a few minutes down the road," she said. She got up and grabbed her key. "I'll buy you a slice and a Coke. Come on."

A light snow was falling by the time they got back to the Big Creek Motel. They climbed out of the black Jeep and stood for a few seconds under the spotlights, watching the flakes spiral down.

"I wonder where the big creek is," Kate said. "The one they named this place after."

Evan just shook his head.

She glanced over at him in the shadowy light. He had said barely a word at the pizzeria. She'd watched as he calmly and systematically worked his way through four slices of anchovy with extra cheese. What does this boy want, she wondered. What is he really here for? He obviously had a strong desire to please her, or at least to prove something to her. But what? And why? This was one way in which Evan was totally different from her kids at Holbrook House. Most of them pretended not to care what she thought of them; some really didn't care. She wondered again if Evan was in therapy. Should she ask him? Or would the question just make him close up and turn sullen again?

"The post office opens at six," Kate said finally, glad to see the end of this long day. "Let's shoot to leave here at five-thirty. We can pick up doughnuts and coffee somewhere and head right over."

"Okay," he answered. Wet snowflakes were clinging to his eyebrows and hair, making him look like some kind of strange elf.

"I'll knock on your door at five to wake you up. But it's important that we both get some sleep. Okay?"

"Right."

"Okay. Good-night."

" 'Night."

She watched as he unlocked the door to Room 5, flipped on the light, and closed the door behind him. Then she let herself into her own room. The electric unit under the window was puffing away, filling the room with stifling heat. She quickly undressed. She washed her face and brushed her teeth, then set her alarm clock. She thought about watching television for a few minutes to occupy her mind, but she was worried that the noise would bother Evan next door. So she crawled into bed, rechecked the alarm clock, and switched off the light.

She'd just turned onto her side when the phone rang, its shrill warble tearing the silence. She panicked for a second, but then realized who it must be. She picked up the receiver. "Hello?"

"It's Evan," he said. "I just forgot to tell you that I'm going to repay you when we get back. For meals and everything. I have money at home."

She waited a second before responding. "Fine. It's a deal."

"Okay. See you tomorrow."

"See you tomorrow." She hung up the phone, then lay back on the thin pillow and listened to the croon of the heater for a few minutes. She knew she would have to find some way of isolating Evan, some way of protecting him, and of letting his mother know that he was all right. But it would be dangerous to make contact with the woman. The police would probably be tapping the Potters' telephone. They would have to assume that there was some connection between Kate's disappearance and Evan's.

Kate turned over again on the soft mattress, resenting the fact that she was supposed to worry about the feelings of some woman she'd met only once, a woman who'd slammed a door in her face. Is this a test? she wondered. Was this God's way of showing her just how self-obsessed a person she'd become?

She turned again, trying to put the question out of her mind, and punched the pillow to shape it to her head.

17

"How's the coffee?"

"Good."

"Warming you up?"

"Yeah."

Silence.

"Sweet enough for you? Because there's a couple extra sugars in the bag."

"It's okay."

"How about milk? This is pretty strong. I think there's an extra milk in there."

Pause. "There's an extra?"

"Extra milk? Yeah. Here."

Kate handed Evan the white paper bag. He reached in and rooted around until he found the little plastic container.

"Thanks."

Kate watched him open the container and swirl the milk into his cup. "Are you sure you drink coffee?" she asked.

"What do you mean, am I sure?"

"I mean, are you sure you really drink coffee. Or is introducing you to caffeine something else to add to my list of sins?"

"Shit no," he said. "I drink coffee all the time."

"Decaf?"

"And regular sometimes. If I feel like it."

Kate sighed and stared out the side window of the Jeep. Evan was lying, probably. As far as she knew, fourteen-year-olds didn't drink coffee—except maybe in places like Spain and Brazil. She couldn't remember when she herself had started. "Well, eat the chocolate doughnut in there, too, okay?" she said. "Because if you don't, I probably will, and I don't want to."

"Okay." Evan reached into the bag.

"And don't say shit when you're in my car."

Kate glanced over at the entrance to the Karlstadt Post Office. It was still dark out—6:20 A.M.—but the parking lot seemed to glow faint blue from the thin covering of snow that had fallen during the night.

"Okay?" Kate said then.

No answer. Kate sighed again. It was going to be another long day. When they'd arrived at the post office just before six, three or four people in parkas and boots were already standing outside the glass door, waiting to get to their boxes. She and Evan had watched as someone from inside came to the door, unlocked it, and let the people in. But none of them headed toward Box 29.

"Anyway," Evan went on, after swallowing a mouthful of the doughnut, "I've done a lot worse drugs than caffeine."

Kate turned and tried to catch his eye. "Like what?" she asked. "Marijuana?"

"Yeah."

"You've smoked marijuana? And you're fourteen?"

He laughed, his fingers raking through his ponytail. "Yeah. Of course."

"What else?"

He shrugged. "Oh, other things."

"Be specific."

"Well," he said. He pulled down the sleeves of his leather jacket. "Like poppers, for instance."

"Poppers?" Kate almost shouted. "Shit, Evan, don't you know that stuff destroys your brain cells? It can make you stupid for life!"

"Okay, okay, I only did it once or twice."

"Glue? What about glue? Or aerosols? Do you do that stuff?"

"No. Not anymore. Really."

Kate blew the air out of her lungs. "Poppers . . . Jesus."

"It's not like it's unusual." He put the rest of the dough-nut back into the bag. "And don't say shit when you're in your car," he added.

"Right," Kate said then. "You're right."

They sat for a few seconds in silence, watching the door. There was a lot of foot traffic going in and out, but nobody had touched Box 29 yet.

"Besides," Evan said, "from the looks of that website, your husband was, like, doing a lot more drugs than pot and poppers."

"Yeah, and look at the trouble he's in now," she answered, a little too primly. "Let that be a lesson to you."

He grunted and took a long sip of his coffee. Kate watched him carefully, wondering what it must be like to be in his head, in his body. She'd barely had time for her own adolescence. Too busy with housework, cooking, and covering for her mother.

"Evan," she said to him.

"What?"

"I really think you should call your mother."

He stared at her. "What are you, crazy? No way."

"I mean it, Evan. She'll be worried sick. She'll think you've been kidnapped or something."

"No she won't."

"Yes she will. Believe me, I know. Better than most people."

"She won't," he said. "She's not like that. And besides, I told you, I left a note."

"Saying what?"

Evan shrugged, making the leather of his jacket creak. "Just that I was going away for a few days. To think about things. And that she shouldn't worry."

"That she shouldn't *worry*?"

"I figured with a note like that, the police wouldn't do a big thing to find me. At least not for a couple days, since they wouldn't think that somebody kidnapped me. They'd think I just ran away."

That was smart, Kate told herself. A smart move. Evan was a pretty clever kid. She wondered then if that was a good thing or a bad thing for her. She eyed him for a few seconds—the sharp nose, the pimply cheeks with their faint red fuzz. Bad, she decided. It was probably a bad thing for her.

Evan reached down into his knapsack and brought out his Game Boy. He turned it on and began playing, filling the Jeep with odd little beeps and chimes. Kate watched him, impressed by his easy expertise. "You're pretty good at that," she said after a while.

"Yeah," he said, without taking his eyes off the screen. "I am."

Kate watched him for a few more minutes, turning every now and then to check the entrance to the post office. She was surprised at how busy the place was. People came and went almost continually, collecting mail, dropping off packages. She was sure that no one would notice the Jeep standing in the parking lot all day, especially now that there was a kid sitting in the front seat.

The sky behind the strip mall began to turn violet, then

an increasingly lighter shade of blue. Dawn. It was beautiful.

Evan was still concentrating on his Game Boy. "Hey," Kate said.

"What."

"Put that thing away and talk to me."

"In a minute," he said. "Let me just get to the end of this level."

She waited while he finished, the Game Boy in his hand emitting a long series of noises that seemed to become more and more celebratory.

"Yeah?" he said finally.

"I was just wondering . . ." She stopped, then decided to risk it. "I was wondering why you didn't report the body right away."

"Shit," he said, looking away. "Everybody's favorite subject."

"I'm just curious. I mean, you knew it would get you in trouble, right? So why did you do it?" Kate realized that this was probably a useless question. Just as useless as the direct questions she sometimes asked the boys at Holbrook House. Why did you shoot your ten-year-old friend with his father's gun? Why did you hit your grandmother with your baseball bat? Were there any real answers to questions like that?

"Because it was interesting."

"Interesting?"

He seemed to become impatient with her. "Yeah, interesting. Besides, the guy wasn't going anywhere. If I didn't find him, he'd prob'ly still be there."

"In what way, though, was it interesting?" she went on, pressing him.

Evan squirmed. "I don't know," he said. "It was like having this secret. This big secret that nobody could give you any shit . . . any *crap* about." He turned and glanced out the window, looking embarrassed. "You know what I mean? There was something special in my life. Something really important. Finally."

Kate thought about this answer. Was this far beyond normal for a boy of Evan's age, she wondered, to think of a headless corpse as something special? How would she react if she saw something like this in the file of one of her Holbrook cases?

"So did you find the key the first day?" she asked. "Or was it after you dug the body up again?"

"No," Evan said, clearly uncomfortable. "Come on, I went through the story three, four times already with seventeen different people. I don't want to talk about it, okay?"

"Okay," Kate said. She put her gloved hands on the steering wheel and squeezed. "So what do you want to talk about, then?"

"Why do we have to talk about anything?"

"This is a stakeout, Evan. When I was a cop, I had friends who did a lot of these, and one thing they always said is that you talk to your partner during stakeouts. Otherwise you fall asleep and miss your quarry."

Evan laughed. "I can't picture you as a cop," he said. "I heard the black detective talking about that, but I couldn't picture it."

"Well, I was a cop. A good one, too, I think."

"You ever shoot anybody?"

That question again. Kate closed her eyes and pressed the bridge of her nose with her fingers. "No," she said. "I never shot anybody."

"You ever come close?"

It was starting to get cold, so she leaned forward and started the Jeep, turning the heat up. Kate knew she would be turning the engine on and off all day. "Close enough," she said.

"So why'd you quit?"

"For one thing, so I would never have to answer yes

when people ask me if I ever shot anybody." She took her gloves off and put her hand out to test the air coming from the vents. "But it's a good question," she went on. "Let's just say that maybe I didn't want to keep being a cop because it was what I was supposed to be. I mean, it was what you did in my family. You became a cop, end of story. And so that's what I started out doing. But after a while I said no, I didn't want to do what I was supposed to do. I made a choice."

"And what do you do now?"

"Well, I do social work. Basically, I tell kids who are supposed to become criminals that they can say no, too." Kate leaned back, feeling strangely satisfied with this answer.

"But you still have the gun from when you were a cop," he said.

"What do you mean?"

"The gun in your pocket. Is that from your cop days?"

Kate felt her cheeks flushing red with irritation.

"Come on," he said. "It clunks every time you move."

"No," she said at last. "No, all the Chicago PD would trust me with was an old Smith & Wesson revolver."

"What's the one you have now?"

"A pistol, semiautomatic. It's called a Sig Sauer. Made in Germany."

"Can I see it?"

"Evan."

"Come on. You can unload it first."

"It *is* unloaded," she said. "And I'll show it to you when we get back to the motel. Somebody could see it here. That's all we'd need."

"Okay," he said, turning to look out the window. "Later."

They spent the next few hours in the Jeep, talking occasionally, drinking coffee and eating English muffins from the deli in the strip mall. Kate tried reading the so-

ciology books she'd brought, but between the sounds of
Evan's Game Boy and the need to look up every minute
to check the foyer, she couldn't concentrate. So she read
a few chapters of Dorothy Sayers. Then she read the local
paper, looking first for information about the area that
might be useful, but finally resorting to the crossword,
"Dear Abby," and even the horoscope. Kate and Joel were
both Geminis, and their horoscope for the day was not
very encouraging: "Avoid conflict with loved ones. That
pet project should probably wait for a more propitious
moment. Meet objections calmly, with confidence. Taurus, Capricorn persons play a role." Kate turned to Evan
after reading this. "What sign are you?"

"Leo," he said.

Kate checked his horoscope: "This is no time for mistakes, miscalculations. The moment for action is now. Be-
ware the interference of Sagittarius, but welcome the
advice of Taurus."

Still no one came to open Box 29. After an early reconnaissance walk, Evan had told her that there was some
mail in the box. She wondered how many of the letters
contained cash—payment for six ounces of peyote buttons, a gross of Ecstasy, a year's supply of Darvon. She
was sure that the BioPerfection people wouldn't leave
mail like this for days at a time.

Traffic at the post office dropped off during the mid-
morning hours, then picked up again at noon. Kate and
Evan watched carefully as businesspeople on their lunch
hours got their mail. Everyone was busy, in a rush. Nobody even seemed to notice them in the Jeep.

It was getting colder. The sun had come out at around
ten to melt the snow, laying down sheets of painful brightness on the asphalt, but now it was clouding over again.
Kate could tell that Evan, who climbed out of the Jeep
numerous times to stretch his legs, was getting uncomfortable. He would shiver every time he got back in, and

then try to warm his hands in his armpits. Finally, at about three, when the post office traffic had thinned out again, Kate decided to show him some mercy.

"Hey," she said. "Let's get that sweater I promised you."

"What about the mailbox?"

"Nobody's going to come at this time of day. We'll take a chance."

Evan looked up at her, his forehead crinkling hopefully. "Can I drive?"

"Oh, you can drive, too? A boy of many talents."

"Our neighbor in Franklin taught me. He has a Ford Explorer, even nicer than this." he said. "So, can I?"

Kate shook her head. "Another time maybe," she said, starting up the Jeep.

They left the parking lot and drove through the wet streets of town, trying to find the Army-Navy store Kate had seen the day before. She finally located it on a street behind an A&P. The store looked like a relic from the forties—its fly-specked windows filled with outdated mannequins dressed in plaids and khakis. One of the mannequins wore a floppy hat with trout flies stuck into the brim.

Kate parked at the curb in front of the store. "This should be right up your alley," she said. "Believe it or not, there was a time when grunge was only for poor people."

They got out of the Jeep and went into the store. A sleigh bell nailed to the door tinkled as they entered. Kate and Evan looked around. There were racks of gray and green jackets, tables covered with navy blue pants, and a whole wall of hunting boots. In the back was a cloudy glass display counter containing Swiss Army knives, compasses, cigarette lighters, sunglasses, and fishing gear.

"Here are the sweaters over here," Kate said, leading

Evan toward a bin piled high with rag-wool pullovers.
"What size are you, small?"

"Medium, maybe. I like things big."

Kate rummaged through the sweaters for a minute or
two. "Here, try this." She held up a gray pullover against
his chest. Evan, looking mortified, turned his head away.
"Looks right. Want to try it on?"

He shrugged out of his leather jacket and took the
sweater from her.

"You're wise to prepare yourself, my love."

Kate and Evan both turned. The person who'd spoken
had appeared from a back room. It was a woman, tiny but
broad, with gray hair and black-rimmed half-glasses that
hung from a chain around her neck. She stood behind the
glass counter, smiling broadly. "More snow's coming."

"That's what I told him," Kate said. Then, turning to
Evan, she said, "Try it on. See how it fits."

Evan pulled the sweater roughly over his head, messing
his hair and snagging the collar on the rubber band holding his ponytail. Kate helped him free it.

"I can do it myself," he said testily. He reared back
when she reached out to fix his hair.

"Looks like a good fit to me, my love," said the woman,
peering through her glasses.

"What do you think?" Kate asked him.

"It's fine," he said. "Let's get it and go."

"Here, I'll snip-snip-snip the tags off and you can wear
it right now," the woman said, coming around the counter
with scissors.

Evan stood there, stony-faced, as the two women fussed
over him, Kate rearranging the sweater over his narrow
shoulders, the saleswoman cutting off labels and price
tags. After a few seconds of this, he just pushed them
both aside and headed for the door.

"Evan!" Kate said sternly.

He pulled open the door, whipping the sleigh bell, and went out to the street.

"They're so moody at this age," the woman said to Kate, wrinkling her nose.

Evan was sitting slump-shouldered in his seat when Kate got back to the Jeep. She climbed in on the driver's side and tossed his leather jacket into his lap. "Here," she said. "You forgot this."

He wouldn't even look at her.

Kate started the Jeep. A few flakes of snow had spattered the windshield, so she turned on the wipers. The blades swept across the glass with a loud, rubbery sound that seemed almost lewd. She put the Jeep in gear and pulled out into the street. "So what was that all about?" she asked.

Evan didn't answer at first, but just stared out the window at the passing stores. Kate was about to ask the question again when he spoke up. "You're not my mother," he said.

Kate pulled the Jeep to a stop at the curb. "Look," she said, "there's one or two things we have to get straight. I didn't ask you to come here, God knows, but now that you're here, you're my responsibility. No, I'm not your mother, but you're fourteen years old, Evan, and I'm thirty-six, got it? I'm letting you stay with me because I have no choice. But let's be clear on this. If I did have a choice, you'd be on a bus back to Maryland right now. This is a dangerous thing I'm doing here."

"I came to help you!"

Kate started to answer, but then thought better of it. How about some sensitivity, my love, she said to herself. Never argue with them at this age. You can only lose.

"You should get a divorce," he said then.

Kate was stunned for a few seconds. "What?" she said.

"You should get a divorce." He turned and looked at her. "You should have the papers with you, and when we find him tomorrow or whatever, you should hand him the papers and say, 'There, I'm leaving you, you're not leaving me, so fuck off.' "

Kate was so thrown by these words that she didn't know how to answer. Somehow the job of finding Joel had pushed everything else out of her mind. But now Evan's comment brought her doubts roaring back. Had Joel ever felt anything for her at all? Or had their marriage been a sham from the very beginning, just some kind of cover for the life he really cared about? "If I want marital advice from you, I'll ask for it," she said finally. "In the meantime, just put on your seat belt and keep quiet. I mean it."

She leaned forward to shift back into first, but something happened to her then. It was as if all resolve left her suddenly, as if the recklessness of this entire scheme became glaringly obvious. "Shit," she said aloud, falling back against the seat. "What am I doing?"

Evan turned to her. He seemed worried by her sudden change of tone. "What do you mean?"

"This is crazy. This is totally crazy. The thing to do right now is to take you home and then go right to the police with this box number. You're just a baby. What have I been thinking?"

Evan shifted uncomfortably in his seat. This was apparently not the effect he'd been looking for with his comment. "No," he said.

"Yes," she answered. "Yes, of course. What kind of jerk am I, following my husband out to his secret hideout like this? I'll just get us both shot."

"No," Evan said again.

Kate put the Jeep into gear. "I'm taking us back to the motel right now to pick up our stuff. The police can handle this." She revved the engine and tried to turn back into the street, but Evan reached out and grabbed the wheel. "Stop it!" she said, and the two of them struggled ridiculously for a few seconds. Kate's foot slipped and the Jeep lurched forward, the right front tire slamming into the curb with such force that both of them were thrown forward against the dash. Kate's foot found the brake just in time to stop the Jeep from mounting the sidewalk and hitting a mailbox.

"Damn it, Evan!" she yelled. His hands still gripped the steering wheel. Kate was amazed at how strong he was.

"You can't go back," he said. "This is the right thing. We're doing it. We can't stop now."

"Evan, no, it's crazy, can't you see?"

"It's not crazy. You're just getting scared."

"No, I'm getting smart."

He still wouldn't let go of the wheel. "Listen," he said. "We can do it. I promise you that I won't get hurt."

"It's over," she said.

"You'll never know if you leave now. You'll never know anything. You'll just be some little wife with a husband who left her."

Again, Kate felt broadsided by the boy. Her grip on the wheel weakened. Evan took her wrists then and pulled her hands away from the wheel as if he were pulling a vine from a tree branch.

"We can show him," Evan said then, in a softer voice. "We can both show him."

Kate sat there with her hands in her lap, the boy's spidery fingers still grasping her wrists. The episode—the attack of doubt, or panic, or whatever—was past now, disappearing as suddenly as it had come. "Okay," she said. She looked over into Evan's pimply face. "Okay. God forgive me this stupidity, but okay."

He seemed satisfied. He let go of her wrists then and sat back in his seat. "Fine," he said.

Kate took a deep breath. "Fine." She cleared her throat awkwardly. Then she reached out again for the gear shift.

They drove back to the post office in gloomy silence.

After her momentary failure of nerve, Kate now felt a dull heaviness in her chest. Evan's presence was becoming more and more disturbing to her. She knew that when the time came, she would have to ditch him, get him out of the way, keep him from distracting her. It wouldn't be easy—she could see that all too well now—but it would be absolutely necessary.

She pulled back into the parking lot, into the same space they had left earlier. Less than a half hour had passed. Kate turned off the engine and looked over at Evan, who was staring out the window. "Hey," she said in a forgiving tone, "You want some more coffee? My treat."

"Holy shit," he said.

Kate followed his gaze. He was staring straight at a figure in the foyer of the post office. It was a man—bearded, wearing a navy down coat—and he was peering into the open door of box number 29.

18

"Okay, get out," Kate said nervously, her eyes fixed on the man in the foyer.

Evan shook his head. "No way."

"Come on, Evan. Just get out. I'll pick you up here later. Or take a cab back to the motel."

He didn't move. Kate could sense his thin body tightening beside her. He was digging in.

The man pulled some mail from the box and shoved it into a gray canvas pouch. He took one last look into the box and then closed it, twisting the key in the lock.

"Evan, listen to me. This isn't a game. These guys have killed two people already."

"Fuck you. I'm not getting out of the car."

Kate turned and stared at the boy. Choose your battles, she told herself. Right now, she just wanted to see where this man took the mail. She wouldn't actually do anything risky until later. And a Jeep containing a woman and a kid wouldn't be very suspicious on the streets of a town like Karlstadt. "You owe me one," she said finally.

Evan nodded toward the windshield, looking satisfied.

The man was crossing the parking lot now, glancing around casually but carefully. He was big, overweight, and red-faced, with a shiny bald spot on the top of his head. They watched as he climbed into a mud-spattered sky-blue pickup.

"Okay," Kate said, starting the engine. "Let's see your best imitation of a kid being taken to his guitar lesson."

The blue pickup pulled out of the parking space, swung right, and then made a left onto the main drag. Kate waited for a few seconds, then followed. She wished suddenly that the rented Jeep didn't look so new and clean. She should have driven it off-road for an hour or two yesterday, to give it that grimy, workaday look of every other vehicle in Karlstadt.

Kate kept the blue pickup in sight as they drove through the small downtown. They passed the A&P again, then headed out in the direction of the Big Creek Motel. The pickup made a right just before the end of the commercial district. Kate followed. But when the pickup made another right, she pulled to the curb and stopped. The man was being careful. She wondered if he'd spotted the black Jeep with Maryland plates or if he was just taking normal precautions.

"What's the matter?" Evan asked. "We're gonna lose him."

Kate shook her head. "I know what I'm doing," she said. She counted to five, then pulled back into the street and made the right. The blue pickup was gone already. Kate guessed that it had made another right at the next corner. Checking her mirrors, she pulled a quick U-turn and drove fast a few blocks the other way, looking down each street to see if the pickup was running parallel to her. When she didn't see it, she made a left. She sped up to the next street and braked at the stop sign.

"There!" Evan said, pointing in the direction of the post

office. Two blocks down, the pickup was stopped at one of the town's few traffic lights, looking nondescript and entirely innocent.

"Thanks," Kate said. She made a left and started tailing him again, two cars back this time.

The pickup followed the main road straight past the post office and out of town. Kate took this to mean that the man's suspicions, if he had any, were gone. He was at ease now. He was heading straight home.

Evan wiped his nose with the sleeve of his new sweater. "Good," he said.

Kate hung back as far as she dared while they drove beyond the gas stations, empty garages, and tired old houses on the edge of town. The road climbed as it entered the patchwork state forest, curving first right, then, more steeply, left. They passed some of the side roads Kate had explored the day before, each one marked with a cluster of beat-up mailboxes.

After a few minutes, one of the cars between the Jeep and the pickup turned off. Kate worried about coming too close, but she didn't want to lose the pickup. Just as she came around one of the road's long curves, she saw the pickup turning onto a side road. She sped up slightly. She was about to make the turn herself when she changed her mind and drove past the intersection. It was the right choice; as they passed, they could see that the pickup had made a quick stop a few yards after the turnoff.

Kate continued around the next bend and then pulled off to the shoulder.

"Shit," Evan said. "They teach you this kind of thing in cop school?"

She watched her side mirror as the car behind them passed. "It's called police academy, first of all," she said. "And no, that was just common sense. Bad guys have to be very alert, if they want to stay bad guys for long. Remember that."

She pressed the accelerator and made a wide U-turn,
spraying gravel from the shoulder. As they passed the
turnoff again, she slowed. The pickup was gone now, the
driver having satisfied himself that no one was following,
so she quickly made another U-turn and came back.
"Here's where we have to keep our eyes peeled," she said,
making the turn. "Check down every driveway on your
side and tell me if you see it. I'll check my side."

They drove along the narrow road for a few hundred
yards, passing big chalet-style houses—expensive but
rustic-looking—tucked away in the woods. They'd been
driving only a minute before Kate said, "There." The sky-
blue pickup was parked in the driveway of one of the
bigger chalets, pulled up beside a tarp-covered woodpile.
The driver wasn't visible, but Kate decided to pass the
driveway without slowing down. Just as they were going
by, she caught sight of a little sign on the front lawn. It
spelled out the name "McGregor" in small, reflective letters.

Kate took note of the location and kept driving. "We've
found it," she said, as much to herself as to Evan. "We've
found Mr. McGregor's garden."

"Who?" Evan asked.

"It's from a book," Kate told him, rubbing her bottom
lip. "Another little joke of my husband and his friends."

Evan was afraid. It was the last thing he would admit to
anyone, especially to Kate. But that night, as they ate
dinner at the Wendy's on the edge of town, he had to
admit it to himself. He knew that the people in the redwood chalet were probably the same ones who had killed
and buried the man in the woods. He knew that they
would be a powerful enemy. And every time he thought
about going into the lair of this enemy, he got a sick,
empty feeling in the pit of his stomach. Butterflies.
Worms. Whatever. He was scared.

He and Kate sat under the white fluorescent lights. They were surrounded by empty plastic tables and chairs. Their dinners sat on paper wrappers in front of them.

"Six A.M.," Kate said then, breaking the silence. "While it's still dark, but not too long before dawn. That's the best time."

Evan nodded and wiped his mouth with a napkin. Control, he told himself. It would be like preparing for any other battle. You gather your weapons. You plan your assault. You conquer your fear.

"Because if there's any illegal chemistry going on in there," Kate continued, "it probably happens after midnight. Drug chemists are like jazz musicians—they like to work at night."

"How many bullets do you have for that gun?" he asked, too loudly.

Kate looked around the dining room. She seemed to be worried that someone might have heard. "The gun is for safety only. I won't be firing a single round, Evan."

"You don't know that for sure," he answered. "You don't know what's in that house." He thought back to the other night, when he reached the final level in Ice Assault. Even fully armed, he wasn't prepared for that last demon, the one that stood guard over the Princess Artemis. You were never fully prepared for anything if you were just physically ready. You had to be mentally ready, too.

"The fact that we don't know what's in there," Kate said impatiently, "is exactly why I should go alone. Evan, this is my fight, not yours." She tried to connect with his wandering gaze. "Won't you please just wait for me at the motel?"

Evan shook his head. To wait at the motel would be to admit defeat before the battle, and there was nothing she could say to make him agree to it. Evan knew the power he held over her now. He knew that all he had to do to get his way was threaten to call the police and tell them where he was. Evan looked down at his hamburger. She was his now. In his hands. He would be able to show her what he could do.

Evan reached for a french fry, then, changing his mind, put it back in the bag. Control, he repeated silently. This was his only chance. Something had to happen between them. He had to show Kate that he was worthy, that he could save her.

"You're not eating," Kate said, taking another french fry from the bag between them.

"I'm not hungry."

"You have to eat."

Evan shook his head.

He would fast, he told himself. He would fast like a warrior before battle. No more fries tonight, and no doughnuts tomorrow.

"I am the Stone Warrior," he said aloud, smiling at her lack of comprehension, pushing the food away with his hand.

Kate was afraid. She was afraid for herself, afraid for Evan, afraid for Joel. But she'd already given in once to her fear—in the Jeep with Evan, after his scene in the Army-Navy store—and she was determined not to do it again.

After dinner, she and Evan drove back to the motel. They watched a couple of television shows in Kate's room, then talked about the plan for tomorrow. Trying for a casual tone, Kate said she would knock on Evan's door at 5:30 in the morning, to give him enough time to take a shower and get dressed. When he was ready, they would go to the deli for coffee and doughnuts and then drive out to the house in the woods.

"Get some sleep," Kate said as she held the door open for Evan. "We need to be one hundred percent tomorrow."

He nodded and walked out into the cold night air.

"Good-night," she said as he unlocked the door to his room.

"Knock loud," he said. "I'm a heavy sleeper."

Kate stood in the doorway, listening as Evan shut the door and slid the chain into the slot. She peered out into the night sky—milky, starless, and cold. Getting ready to snow.

After a minute, she closed her own door and locked it. She quickly undressed, showered, and got into her pajamas. Then she took the little travel alarm off the night table and set it for 4 A.M.

She smiled at the thought of her deception. There'd be no 5:30 shower for Evan tomorrow, no stop at the deli for doughnuts. She'd leave the motel, quietly and alone, at 4:30. Without a wake-up call, Evan would probably sleep until at least eight or nine.

With any luck she might even be back by then.

Evan shut the door behind him and locked it. He walked over to the television on the wall and turned it on with the volume down. There was a hospital show playing; two doctors in blue scrubs were yelling at each other in a bright hallway. Evan sat on the edge of the bed and watched for a minute or two. Then he lay back, pulling the pillows out from under the bedspread.

He felt for the keys to the Jeep in his front right pocket. He'd taken them out of Kate's bag earlier, when she was in the bathroom brushing her teeth, while he was supposed to be watching a "Mr. Ed" rerun on television.

Evan wet his lips, thinking of her face when she found out what he had done. He was proud of himself. Maybe the fear was good, he thought. Maybe it was the thing that kept him sharp.

Shivering from the cold, he got up and headed to the bathroom to brush his teeth.

•   •   •

"Okay, let's make a deal," Kate said, rubbing her cheeks with her cold, stiff fingers as they sat in the Jeep's front seat. It was 5:45 A.M. They were parked in front of the twenty-four-hour deli, drinking coffee. Kate had looked for the keys for a full twenty minutes that morning—ransacking her bag, taking up the mattress, searching under the bureau—before realizing that Evan had taken them. Resisting the urge to beat the little jerk senseless, she'd calmly gone over to his room and knocked. Evan had come to the door looking rumpled and half-asleep. "I was right, wasn't I," he'd said to her. "You were gonna go without me." She'd answered with nothing more than: "Just get dressed and let's go."

"What kind of deal?" Evan asked her now, in the dark Jeep.

"We stop lying to each other from now on. No lies, no tricks. Okay?"

Evan didn't answer for a few seconds. He hugged himself in the predawn chill and finally nodded.

"Good," Kate said. She wondered how she would ever explain this to a judge. I tried everything to keep him out of it, Your Honor. I did my best. But the kid was just too damned smart.

She looked over at Evan, studying his sharp features, his gangly arms and legs. She could just imagine what a judge would make of this situation. He'd probably decide that she'd seduced the boy to get him to come along with her. Hell, why not, she thought, pinching the rim of the foam cup. How out of character would it be, given how she'd used him up to now? How much worse would it be than what she'd already done to this boy? "If you get hurt," she said then, "I'm going to be in so much goddamn trouble."

"I won't get hurt. I'll be careful."

"Yeah, right." She reached forward and turned the heat up. "I'm going to tell you how you can help me most.

And you have to promise to follow the plan, okay?"

"Maybe. As long as it's not another trick."

"No more tricks. Look, we drive up and park by the side of the road. There are enough houses up there so it won't be noticeable if we park fifty yards or so down. You stay with the Jeep while I go in and look around."

He looked as if he were about to object, so she added, "Don't worry, I'll leave you the ignition key, assuming you really can drive. But if I don't come out of that house, I need somebody outside to know where I am. Here." She handed him a card with Detective Starks's phone number. "If I don't come out of that house in an hour and a half, you drive back to town, find the nearest phone, and call this number. Don't come looking for me. It's no good two of us getting caught. Okay?"

Evan seemed to consider this for a while. "Okay," he said finally.

"Fantastic. I'm thrilled." She put her cup into the holder and shifted the Jeep into first. "There should be enough coffee and doughnuts in the bag to hold you if you get hungry."

"I'm fasting," he said, but Kate, too nervous now to bother, decided to let the comment pass.

They drove in silence through the sleeping town of Karlstadt, past the post office strip mall and out into the mountains. It took them ten minutes to reach the turnoff. Kate steered the Jeep up the smaller road and stopped a little distance before the redwood chalet.

"Okay. Your main job now is not to be noticed. If you see headlights coming up or down the road, get on the floor and don't come up till they pass. Got it?"

"Yeah."

"Okay, it's five fifty-seven by my watch. If I'm not back by seven-thirty, you just start this thing up, drive to town, and don't look back." She stopped then. "You really do know how to drive a stick, right?"

She could see the anger in his face. "I can probably drive this thing better than you," he said.

"Okay, okay. I didn't mean to offend your manhood." Kate handed him the keys. "Thanks," she said.

His eyebrows went up. He didn't seem to know what she was thanking him for.

"Thanks for not letting me run away yesterday." She put her hand out to him. He looked at it for a second before putting the keys down and shaking it awkwardly, as if they were closing a business negotiation. "All right," Kate said. "Wish me luck. And remember: seven-thirty. No sooner. The police are just a last resort."

She got out of the Jeep and closed the door, giving Evan a thumbs-up through the window. Then she ran across the road and began to make her way along the frost-tipped weeds on the far shoulder. The night sky was overcast, but there was enough light for her to find her way. She was dressed for cold—a thick gray turtleneck under a puffy black down jacket, jeans lined with flannel, thin black leather gloves, black wool hat, and insulated hiking boots. The Sig was in the right pocket of the jacket, loaded now, with the extra magazine clattering softly against the flashlight in the other pocket.

She reached the break in the underbrush where the driveway met the road. She glanced back. The Jeep was already invisible around a curve in the road. There were other vehicles parked along the shoulder—not many, but enough to make the Jeep seem unremarkable. Evan, she hoped, would be safe.

Kate patted the bulk of the Sig in her jacket pocket. Then, moving slowly, she turned in and started up the edge of the driveway.

The chalet-style house stood in front of her like a dark monument. No lights were on inside, but there was a single floodlight hanging over the attached garage. It was aimed directly down, creating a pool of light on the asphalt. As she'd hoped, the pickup was gone, meaning that whoever drove it didn't live there. Kate walked just beyond the perimeter of light, angling her way closer to the house.

She reached the corner of the garage and stopped for a second, safe in the shadows. There was no way she could know for sure if somebody was inside. Even if this house was what she suspected it was—a lab, a place of business—there still could be someone inside. And there would probably be an alarm system. If so, she might have to settle for a quick look around the outside.

The wind picked up suddenly, rolling some brittle leaves over the ground. It was getting cold. Kate shivered and zipped the down jacket higher around her neck.

She took the Sig out of her pocket and slowly began walking around the outside of the house. The first window she passed looked in on the garage. Light from the flood streamed around the loose-fitting garage door, so Kate could see inside fairly well. There was a car parked to one side of the two-car garage, covered with a green tarp. She could see no sign of an alarm system on the window frame.

She moved on toward the back of the house. The next window she passed was the kitchen window. She could just make out a half dozen coffee cups on the counter, standing between a large coffeemaker and a microwave. She checked the edges of the window frame. Her hopes fell. Up near the top of the sash was a little box made of beige plastic. It was part of a circuit alarm system, a type she recognized. If the window opened, the electrical circuit would be broken. This would set off a delayed alarm unless the right code was punched into the system keyboard, which was probably located near the front door.

She rounded the corner to the back of the house. A couple of the windows here were blocked by venetian blinds, closed tight. These windows were also wired. Kate cursed silently. Down at ground level were two other windows, painted black, but these were too small for anything but a cat to crawl through. Kate took a few steps back onto the lawn. The second-floor windows were probably not wired. But how could she reach them?

She delayed answering that question and continued her circle around the house. The far side of the chalet had no windows at all, except for one tiny one up near the top, just under the steeply pitched roof. Probably an attic window, with no possible access.

Finally, she came around to the front of the house. She slipped into the narrow space between the rhododendrons and the foundation. More windows here, more blinds, more wires. Frustrated, she slipped out again. The garage seemed to be her best bet.

Wanting to avoid the floodlight in front, she made her way back around the house and returned to the garage window. Standing with her back to the pane, she waited for the wind. When a gust blew up, scattering leaves noisily, she closed her eyes and slammed her down-padded elbow into the bottom pane of the window. The glass shattered and fell to the cement floor of the garage inside. Remembering the break-in at her own house, Kate felt oddly avenged.

She waited, listening for any disturbance, any movement in the house caused by the sound of breaking glass. Nothing. She reached her gloved hand through the broken pane and unlatched the lock, then slid the window up. Not much room, she thought, but enough. She climbed head-first into the open window, bringing her legs in after her. She eased herself to the ground, her boots crackling the glass at her feet. The garage smelled like wet sawdust and motor oil. She took the flashlight out of her pocket, turned it on, and checked the dark corners of the garage. There were some metal drums in one corner, the kind of container used for storing bulk chemicals. She crossed the garage and read one of the labels: Bromobenzene. It meant nothing to her.

The door to the main house was on the other side of the shrouded car. She moved slowly toward it, then stopped. She sank to a crouch and lifted the tarp to get a look at the car. The recognition hit her with an almost physical force, leaving her breathless. The car under the tarp was a black Saab wagon. The license plate number was familiar. It was Joel's car.

Kate found herself sitting on the cold floor of the garage, the dampness seeping into the seat of her jeans. Think, she told herself, think. Did this mean that Joel was here? Not necessarily. It would be stupid to let this car be seen. The plate number and description were on the FBI computer. Naturally, they would tuck the Saab away somewhere, whether Joel was with them or not. Whether he had come voluntarily or by force. Whether he was alive or dead.

Kate got to her feet. Whatever hesitation or doubt she'd felt earlier was gone now. She was determined to follow this to the end.

There was a window in the door from the garage to the main house, covered with a small venetian blind. Using the flashlight, Kate checked the edges of the window frame, but she couldn't see any alarm mechanism. The door itself could possibly be alarmed, but there was no way she could know for sure from this side. She decided to take a chance. Before she could think too carefully about what she was doing, she turned her back to the door and hit one of the small panes with her elbow. Again, the sound of glass falling to the floor seemed painfully loud, but there was no sudden jangling of alarm bells. Kate reached through the broken pane as far as she could, jostling the blinds as she felt around the edge of the door for a beige box. She couldn't feel any, so she unlocked the deadbolt and turned the doorknob from the other side. The door opened. She was in.

She stepped into the dark kitchen. She closed the door behind her and made sure that there was no alarm device on the frame. Then she moved deeper into the room, the gun in one hand, the flashlight in the other.

There were two doorways leading from the kitchen— one down a flight of stairs to the basement, the other into the rest of the house. She decided to check out the basement first, since that was probably where the lab was. In her pocket was the key Evan had given her a few days earlier. If her luck was good, it might just fit some file cabinet down there.

Kate eased herself down the basement steps. There was a pungent smell down here—sulfurous, dank. She played the light around the pitch-black space. The beam picked out lab tables and various chemical apparatuses around the room, creating spiky shadows on the far walls as she moved. She counted four separate lab stations. A notebook was open on one of them. She began walking over to look at it.

The sound from above—a shrill, unbelievably loud ringing—set her bones and teeth resonating. The whole house seemed to be shaking. An alarm. She had set off an alarm.

"Oh shit," she said aloud. She looked around. There was no exit down here. She'd have to go back upstairs. She raced toward the stairway and climbed the steps three at a time. The front door, she thought. It would be the easiest, fastest way out. She ran through the kitchen and out the other doorway just as the sound of the alarm stopped. She froze midstep. A light went on overhead, and there, next to the front door, next to the alarm control box, was a man with a gun.

It was her husband, Joel, aiming a pistol at her.

Kate realized that her own pistol was in her hand, leveled at her husband's chest.

19

Joel was the first to lower his arm. He seemed about to say something but then held back, shaking his head in disbelief.

Kate held the gun level. This was Joel, she told herself. Joel in a pair of navy sweatpants and a V-necked T-shirt, Joel with three days of stubble on his chin. Her husband, Joel.

Kate felt a weird falling sensation in her chest. Something she'd wanted so badly had suddenly been pushed into her hands. She'd found what she was looking for. But somehow she felt that whatever happened next could only hurt her.

She lowered the gun.

Joel stepped toward her slowly and put his arms around her. "Kate," he said, his voice flat and hopeless.

His familiar smell, of sweat and medicine, washed over her. I could cry right now, she told herself, and it would be okay; it would be an acceptable reaction. But the tears didn't come. All she could say was "Why?"

He pulled back and looked at her. "I can't answer that question," he said. He must have noticed the sudden look of worry in her eyes—her brain's return to the immediate situation—because he shook his head and added, "There's no one else here. They don't come until late morning."

She nodded, and wiped an eye with the cloth cuff of her down jacket. Joel pulled her to his chest again. He began kissing her, gently at first, on top of her head. The emptiness Kate felt was confusing and frightening her, and when Joel kept kissing her, covering her eyes and cheeks and mouth, she pushed him away. "I need to sit down," she said.

Joel looked away. She couldn't tell if he was hurt or embarrassed. "Kitchen," he said.

They moved awkwardly into the next room. Once inside the kitchen, Kate sank into one of the wooden chairs and put the Sig down on the table. Joel left his pistol on the counter and sat across from her. He touched her cheek. "You amaze me," he said. "I had no idea . . ."

Kate set her jaw and looked straight into his face. "You have to tell me something, before anything else. You have to tell me that you didn't kill Don and the chemist."

Joel shook his head. "Not me," he said softly. "Though I guess I have no right being surprised that you have to ask." He got up then and went to the counter. He pulled out the glass pot of the coffeemaker and started filling it at the sink.

"A note," she said, looking down at her hands. "A phone call, anything. Just to let me know you were alive."

He turned with the full pot. "I couldn't. For a lot of reasons." His voice trailed off. He seemed to be at a loss about what to do next. Kate wondered if he felt as shocked and disoriented as she did. "I hear you've had a computer chat with Duncan," he said then. "I should warn you. The man is out of control. Don didn't believe that; he relied on twenty-six years of friendship. That's why he's dead now." Joel stared at her for a few seconds, the lines deep around his eyes, and said, "I'd rather not put myself in the same situation."

Kate didn't answer. She knew she had questions, dozens of questions, but none came to her just then. The pounding in her ears seemed to keep them from taking shape in her mind. Slow down, she told herself. Think.

"I'll make coffee," Joel said.

Evan sat in the driver's seat of the Jeep, his hands clenched in his lap. The engine was running. He'd heard the alarm—everybody in the neighborhood must have heard the alarm—and now he didn't know what to do. Kate must have made a mistake, must have touched something. But where was she now? He kept expecting to see her bursting from the underbrush. He wondered if he should pull up closer to the driveway. It might save her a few seconds in her escape. But what if she ran here through the woods? She would come out at the spot where the Jeep should be and not find it there, not find *him* there. No, it was better to wait where she'd left him.

But where *was* she? At least three or four minutes had gone by since the alarm. Had Kate found a way to turn it off? Or had somebody caught her in the house? He had no way of knowing. Wouldn't there have been shots fired if she'd been caught? Probably. But even if the house was empty and she'd found a way to turn off the alarm, shouldn't she be leaving now? Someone must have heard. One of the neighbors could have called the police.

Evan put his hands on the steering wheel. He thought of the key—of the bogus key he'd given her that night in the diner. Why hadn't he explained to her about it, how he'd just made up the story about finding it near the body? They had agreed: no lies, no tricks. Was this his fault? Did she set off the alarm by trying to stick the fucking key in a lock somewhere in the house?

He stared at the curve in the road ahead, willing Kate's form to appear there, running toward him.

If she doesn't come in sixty seconds, he told himself, I'll drive straight into town, park at the nearest strip mall, and call that cop.

He remembered then what she'd made him agree to. An hour and a half—no more, no less. What if she did just turn the alarm off? What if she was finding things, important evidence, clues? He'd screw her up if he called the detectives. He'd ruin everything.

Evan squeezed the steering wheel tighter. One thing he knew for sure: he could not sit still in that Jeep any longer. He would have to see what happened to her. He would just go and look at the house from a distance. If there were no lights on, no sign of anyone being up and around, he'd assume that she'd turned the alarm off herself. He would go back to the Jeep and wait. Then she'd come back to him whenever, and never know that he'd disobeyed her directions.

Evan turned off the engine. It was obvious now that she wouldn't be running back to the Jeep with some bad guy four steps behind her. She was in that house for a while, no matter what the reason. "Fuck it," he said aloud. He zipped up the leather jacket over his new sweater, pocketed the keys, and got out of the Jeep.

He would be careful, he told himself. Careful and smart. She would have nothing to blame him for.

Sitting at the kitchen table, Kate watched her husband go through the familiar routine of coffee-making—shaking out the new filter, opening the can, spooning the coffee into the plastic cone. The questions were finally taking shape in her mind. "Did you know," she asked, "when you left the house that night? That you weren't coming back?" Somehow, it seemed the most important question to her now.

He pressed the Brew button on the coffeemaker. "No," he said. "We had a prearranged plan: the pay phone at the Safeway. We didn't want to risk calls to the house. I was supposed to go there whenever there was a signal."

Kate felt sick at the image that came to her mind: Don's Labrador in flames. "The signal that night was Pearlie?"

Joel nodded. "The usual signal was some innocuous e-mail, but Duncan apparently wanted to make a point. Don was already dragging his feet by that time. Duncan thought he was losing control of the situation, so he decided to put the fear of God into both of us."

A faint shudder passed through Kate's shoulders. "So what happened at the Safeway?"

"Duncan's guy was there," Joel said. "Paolo, the guy in the brown overcoat you saw, or almost saw. He was waiting for me at the pay phone. He got into the car and told me that they had killed Jin, and that Don and I had to disappear. He wouldn't take no for an answer."

"But why?" she asked. "Why did they kill Jin?"

"I'm getting to that," Joel said.

Kate watched him turn away and busy himself at the counter. His shoulders moved smoothly under the T-shirt. She could almost imagine that he was making breakfast for them back in Lewisburg on a normal Sunday morning. Three-egg omelets with smoked salmon and onions. Orange juice. Something boring by Mozart on the radio.

"I assume Jin died because of something with that BioPerfection business on the Web," she said.

Joel stopped what he was doing and turned back toward her, looking surprised. "You found that?"

"I had help," she answered, thinking suddenly of Evan in the car, and worrying.

"Do the police know about the website?"

"I don't know. I don't think so. But they have an e-mail now that might lead them in the right direction.

The way it led me, though it was really the stuff in
Velma's safe that did it."

"Do they know about Velma's safe?"

Kate shook her head. "Not from me, at least."

This seemed to give Joel some reassurance. The tension
in his face disappeared. "Anyway, if they don't have the
Beatrix Potter book, they couldn't do much with the contents of the safe." He smiled at her oddly, an echo of
something she'd once found so attractive in him. "Low-
tech encryption. I told Duncan it would be safer for internal communications. Too many smart-ass hackers out
there these days—"

"Joel," Kate said, interrupting him. "What is this all
about? What the fuck do you think you're doing?"

He looked hurt, as if she'd just asked him the one question he most hoped to avoid. "It's a project, Kate. Something that's been going on for a long time, from long
before I even met you."

"But what *is* this project? Joel, I feel totally confused.
You've got to have some idea of what I've been going
through."

He seemed to grant this point, but looked uncertain
about how to start. "It was Duncan's idea, to begin with,"
he said, sitting across from her and taking her hand. "He
had investors lined up abroad—small pharmaceutical organizations in Brazil and the Netherlands. They were
looking for access to American research expertise and
American markets, but they didn't want to deal with
American puritanism—the FDA and the whole business
about good drugs and bad drugs."

"Right. The dominator culture and all that. I've read
the mission statement on the Web. But you can't tell me
you believe all of that."

"The mission statement was Duncan's rhetoric—over-
blown, a little crazy. Tell you the truth, even I'm not sure
how much of it he really believes."

"But what about you, Joel? What are *you* doing in all of this? That's what I can't understand."

The question seemed to make him angry. "What do you want me to say, Kate? Are you looking for some sign of higher purpose here? Will it make you feel better if I tell you that half of all profits from controlled substances is put toward research, on the kind of drugs the pharmaceutical industry can't or won't do? Does that make this whole thing more acceptable to you?"

"Yes," she said. Then, "No. I don't know. I just want to know how you could be involved in all of this without telling me." She put her cold-scorched hands flat on the tabletop. "Joel, we're normal people, you and me. I *know* you're not some closet fanatic, or some half-assed revolutionary disguised as a middle-class guy to keep the feds away. We're a normal married couple—that isn't just a fantasy of mine."

Joel was shaking his head. He got up from the table again and walked to the counter. "I don't know if we're normal or abnormal," he said. "But I can't tell you how many times this project has kept me going. How much I've fed off the energy of this thing. No matter how frustrating the rest of my life got—the same routines, the same responsibilities—there was always this other thing, this amazing secret."

"But you kept me completely out of it!"

"Yes, I did. That's the nature of a secret, Kate."

Kate felt angry now. He wasn't even sorry for what he'd done to her. "I married you, Joel," she said. "I deserved all of you."

"Don't, Kate," he said. "Next you're going to tell me that I had all of you, and I don't think I can listen to that. You can't believe that you haven't had your own secrets, that there aren't huge parts of yourself that you've kept entirely private."

She was about to answer, but then the falling sensation

in her chest returned. She felt as if some sort of trap door had just opened at her feet. The door was swinging creakily back and forth, and she couldn't bring herself to look down.

It took her a few seconds to recover. "Nobody," she said carefully, "has died because of my secrets, whatever they may be."

The coffee was finished brewing. Joel took two mugs from the cabinet and filled them. He seemed unsure of how to respond to Kate's last comment. "Jin was working on a special project," he said then, turning his back to her. "We had about fifteen small research efforts going, in the U.S. and in Holland—analogs of common drugs, better versions of patented molecules, derivatives of traditional medicines. Ever hear of something called 'bromolide mesylate'?"

Kate shook her head. "No," she added, when she realized he wasn't looking at her. She felt relieved now to be talking about something else, something not directly about themselves.

Joel brought the mugs of coffee over to the table. "It's a dopamine receptor agonist. Comes from rye ergot. It's used as a treatment for Parkinson's disease, but it's also being tested experimentally for other things. Jin was researching analogs of the molecule. He thought it might work out as a smart drug."

Something seemed to snap into place in Kate's mind. "So he found a billion-dollar molecule."

"What?"

"Nothing. Just something somebody said to me a while back."

"What he did find was a version of the molecule that interrupted the D2 dopamine pathway."

"Come on, Joel. English."

"It means he made a big step toward a cure for cocaine addiction, Kate. Something that satisfies the craving *and* eliminates withdrawal. And not just of cocaine and crack. Possibly a whole slew of addictions. Anything that involves the same dopamine pathway." Joel came over and crouched in front of her chair. "Kate, this was the most exciting thing that ever happened to me. Can you understand that, at least? Here we were, this tiny Internet-based organization, and we made this huge discovery, all because we didn't play by the drug-company rules. Duncan and Don and Jin and a couple dozen grad students across the country and me. We made it happen, while the whole pharmaceutical and medical community was slogging around in FDA red tape."

"So what happened? How did Jin end up in the woods?"

Joel got to his feet. He was obviously uncomfortable with this subject. "Jin's molecule was a test of everybody's idealism," he said, walking away from her. "Jin wanted to go public with the research right away. It wasn't a cure, tied up in a neat ribbon, but it was important—too important to keep to ourselves, he said. He wanted to publish his findings, public domain, no patent."

"Which would be in line with Duncan's mission, right?"

Joel shook his head. "Duncan wanted to keep the research to ourselves until we had a product. Something solid. He told us that we had to remain true to the 'financial realism' of our mission, that we should follow the same procedure as with any other beneficial drug find. The money you make from Discovery One pays for Discovery Two. But Jin didn't buy it. He hid his notes and results, and wouldn't tell anyone where, and then he threatened to go public with them no matter what Duncan said."

Kate sat still, trying to connect all of this with the life she'd had just two weeks earlier. Here, then, was the explanation of Joel's sleepless nights, of those distracted moments at the dinner table, of the sudden bursts of anger.

Her life in Maryland had never been what she thought it was.

"Duncan went to Amsterdam and São Paulo in late October," Joel went on, "to consult with the investors. When he came back, he gave Jin an ultimatum. Jin came back with a threat. He said he'd written a program that would post his results automatically on the Web on a certain date. No matter what Duncan did to him, the results would eventually go public. Jin thought it would buy him some time. He knew that he'd be dead if he posted the results right away."

"So Duncan killed him anyway, knowing that?"

"Something went wrong. Paolo got carried away—or that's what Duncan says, at least. And so now Duncan's got somebody trying to find out where Jin stashed the results and the program. He thinks he's almost there."

"You should have turned yourself in at that point, Joel," Kate said. "You could have made a deal. Now you're an accomplice to a murder-one homicide."

"Kate," he answered, "that's the decision Don made. And Don is dead now."

She looked down into her coffee mug. Was this true? Could she accept this explanation? She took another sip of coffee. It was just the way Joel knew she liked it— strong and sweet and black.

"Besides, I happen to agree with Jin," Joel went on. "I don't want Duncan to find those files. And if I turn myself in now, there's nothing I can do to stop him from finding them and heading off Jin's program."

She looked up at Joel, her head strangely heavy. "But how are you going to stop him?"

"I have plans."

"Joel," she said, "if what you've told me is the truth, I still think your smartest move is to go back to Maryland with me—now, this morning. We're both in deep shit, but . . ." Kate stopped to organize her thoughts, but they seemed to be running away from her. What was she trying to say?

"I'm sorry, Kate. But I've got to be very careful in this situation."

Joel got up from the chair across from her. She followed him with her eyes—or tried to, but something was wrong with her. She had trouble focusing. Everything seemed to move in slow-motion spurts, like an old film. "You bastard," she said groggily, but it was somebody else's voice, somebody far away.

She reached out and picked up the Sig. It was unbelievably heavy. She tried to level it at the floating figure of her husband. "Bastard," her voice said.

His enormous hand came out and took the gun from her. "The alarm," he said. "It's programmed to notify Duncan's cell phone. He'll be here any minute. I'm sorry, but I've got to play this just right." He touched her cheek. "Trust me, Kate. Please."

There was nothing in the world she could do except close her eyes and sleep.

Evan stood by the broken garage window, peering in. The door to the kitchen was open, and he could just make out Kate's leg—the hiking boot looking heavy and masculine on her foot. It was hard to hear what was happening. He could make out the words when the wind died down, but the smallest breeze would block everything out.

He had to remind himself to breathe quietly, slowly.

He had seen the lights when he got to the driveway. The light in the kitchen and the driveway flood were the only ones burning. He wondered what that could mean. Could Kate have turned those lights on? Would she be that ballsy, that confident?

He crept up the side of the driveway, keeping in the shadows as much as he could. He saw the broken window of the garage and knew that this was probably the way she'd gotten into the house. Had breaking the window set off the alarm? If so, why hadn't she just taken off?

It was when he reached the broken window that he heard voices inside. One was Kate's voice, the other that of a man.

Evan strained forward to hear as much as he could. The man seemed to be doing most of the talking. Evan heard something about idealism, and something about posting results on the Web. Then the wind gusted for a few seconds and he heard nothing. By the time the wind died down, Kate was talking. She was trying to convince the man to turn himself in. Evan realized then that the man was her husband. She had found him.

What happened next confused Evan. Kate's voice seemed to change, to thicken and slow down. She called her husband a bastard. Then she seemed to faint, although he couldn't be sure. Her leg went slack; the foot splayed out. He heard the husband say, "I'm sorry," and walk over toward the table. He saw the man's sweatpants and T-shirt, his feet.

The husband started doing something then. It took Evan a few seconds to figure out what. There was a phone on the wall near the table, and the man had picked up the receiver and dialed. "It's me," he said. "You're on your way over?"

There was a pause, then he went on:"You're not going to believe this. It was Kate."

Another pause. "I got her to drink something. We had all of those sedatives in the cabinet . . . She got into Velma's safe. There must have been something there . . ."

Another gust of wind clawed at the collar of Evan's jacket, covering the next part of the conversation. Evan wanted to scream in frustration. When he could finally hear again, the husband's voice seemed louder: "Listen to me. Nothing happens to her. She's my wife, Duncan . . . I could have let her go, right? So I'm telling you now, if anything happens to her, I'm going to kill you, Duncan. I mean it . . . Yeah, I know you're on a cell phone, but I don't care. If Kate gets hurt, you and Paolo are both dead. You understand me?"

Evan's ear scraped against a shard of glass in the broken window. He almost gasped in pain.

"Okay, then," the husband said. "I'll see you in a few minutes."

Evan heard the phone being put down. He pulled away from the window and sank to a crouch under it. He thought of the husband's last sentence. It meant that the other guy was on his way over. He would see the Jeep. He would see Evan hanging around the garage.

Evan scrambled toward the bushes. His fear came back then: the husband had drugged his own fucking wife. Evan got to his feet. He knew that he had to get out of there. He began to run.

20

Geometry. A wash of marine blue light. It was interesting, how the bright rectangle seemed to do the hula before her eyes. She wondered what it was supposed to be: an aquarium? a television? the portal to Heaven? Kate giggled. She remembered somebody talking about a portal to Heaven once. It was a cop, he'd been shot in the chest by some manic-depressive Cuban pimp who thought he was seeing God. Came close to dying in surgery, Kate recalled. Danny something. Afterward, he was telling them the story from his hospital bed—Kate and her partner, Vic, and some of the other cops on the detail. "There was, like, this glowing doorway," Dannysomething said, looking serious, "and a beautiful woman was standing on the other side, waving to me, saying, 'Come in, come in!' " Vic and the others were nodding politely, stealing looks at each other that said, "Oh Christ." But then Dannysomething cracked a smile, he couldn't keep up the act, and they all practically collapsed with relief.

So maybe, Kate thought now, this blue rectangle was

her portal to Heaven, hovering out there in the darkness.
Maybe somebody was waving her toward it. Maybe she
was dying.

This last thought jolted as it hit a different level of
consciousness. Kate became aware that her head was loll-
ing to one side, then caught herself, snapping her neck
straight. She was sitting up—her hands bound behind her,
her shoulders flexed forward uncomfortably. She closed
her eyes hard and opened them again. Consciousness was
rushing back to her in waves now, each one clearer and
fuller than the one before. She was sitting in a hard
wooden chair. Her hands were cuffed behind her, with the
kind of disposable plastic cuffs cops used when making
mass arrests. The strip connecting the cuffs was laced
through the slats of the chair back. Her feet were bound,
too, by another set of cuffs that were wound around the
wooden dowel between the chair's front legs.

Another memory surfaced: Joel had drugged her. Her
husband had put something into the coffee while his back
was to her. The bastard had betrayed her.

Kate tried to stretch the aching muscles in her neck.
The blue rectangle. It was a screen. A computer sat on a
table ten feet across the room, the monitor facing her.

It was only then that she noticed the smell—a damp,
musky reek. Animal smells. She turned her head. There
were cages piled all over the room. She could make out
small white forms moving inside. They were mice, hun-
dreds of them. In one corner of the room stood a few
larger cages. Kate nearly cried out when she noticed eyes
looking at her from the shadows. The eyes were full of
intelligence and sadness. They were the eyes of a chimp.
It sat on the floor of its cage, grasping the bars with
strangely elegant, long-fingered hands, and just stared at
her.

She realized then that she must be in a different building. She'd been taken away from the chalet while she was

unconscious, probably to a more isolated place. But where was Joel?

Kate heard movement in the other direction. She turned her head in what seemed like slow motion, the pain in her neck intense. There was a man standing at a table, his back to her, busy with some bottles. He moved in and out of her sight behind another stack of mouse cages.

"Remember to do the dogs again at nine or nine-thirty," said a low, resonant voice—the voice of someone farther away, invisible to Kate. She quickly closed her eyes, let her head fall to one side, and listened.

"Shit, it's after eight already. I don't want to leave until I've talked to her." There was a pause, then the voice went on: "He must have given her enough to stun a horse."

"Why don't we just shoot her up with some Cat?" asked the man fooling with the bottles. "Wake her up quick enough."

The first man laughed. "It's an idea, but I'd rather not have her thinking *too* clearly."

Kate heard steps coming in her direction. Hands grabbed her head roughly, and then fingers pried open the lids of her left eye. Just before she forced her eye out of focus, she recognized the man staring into her face. She remembered him from the video—an older and puffier version of Duncan Lloyd, with the same bulbous nose and tight ponytail. "Nice try, Mrs. Baker," he said, "but faking unconsciousness is really a tough trick to pull off. How long have you been awake?"

"Where's Joel?" she asked. Her mouth was sluggish and her throat felt parched.

Duncan put his hands up, as if in surrender. "Hey, I don't want to get in the middle of a marital spat. Drugging you was his idea." He took a few steps, circling her, before he went on. "You're probably a little pissed at your spouse right now, but really, you shouldn't be too hard on him. He's been making very persuasive arguments that you should be kept alive and unhurt."

Kate licked her lips. They felt thick and wormy, like something not part of herself. "Tell him I'm eternally grateful," she said.

"Of course," Duncan went on, smiling, "Joel made equally persuasive arguments that Don should be kept alive, too. But that wasn't feasible." He stopped circling and stared down at her. "Your husband, Mrs. Baker, has a tendency to lose sight of the big picture. He's a philosophical dilettante. I told him that in college and it's as true today as it was then."

Duncan stuck his hands into his coat pockets. He was wearing a green canvas coat over a checked shirt, jeans, and high-top black gumboots. Without the ponytail, he'd have looked just like everyone else in the town of Karlstadt. "I depend on Joel, though. And you *are* his wife. You see my position."

"Look, I don't care about you or your little mail-order business, if that's what you're worried about. I came here to find my husband. I found him. Now it doesn't matter to me what happens to him or the rest of you." Kate looked away from him, unsure of how much she really meant this last part. She kept thinking of something Joel had said just before she lost consciousness, about "playing this just right." Did Joel really have a plan? she wondered. Or was that just another lie?

Two vertical lines appeared between Duncan's thick eyebrows. "I hope that's true, Mrs. Baker. I don't like killing people. But sentiment and revolutionary political movements don't mix, as I never tire of telling your husband."

"Oh right. You're the revolutionary with a dream of making the world safe for downtrodden dope addicts."

Duncan made a sound that could have been laughter. "Joel told me you'd found the Web page, and that you'd

even gotten the password to the shopping mall. Pretty re-
sourceful, ma'am. Even the feds haven't gotten that far
yet."

"They'll be very entertained when they do," Kate said.
She knew it probably wasn't wise to antagonize this man,
but she found it hard to hold back. It seemed like the only
way to keep her fear in check. "Especially by that crackpot mission statement."

Duncan sighed, as if at a child who hadn't met his
expectations. "I'll never understand you people," he said.
"Anyone who foresees a world at all different from the
safe, desperate one you've built around yourselves in suburban America is automatically a crackpot. Just because
we don't play by your rules."

"I've seen the rules you play by. Sudden death."

The man across the room laughed aloud. Duncan shot
him an annoyed look and then turned back to her. "Do
you have any idea, Mrs. Baker, what a fucking unique
moment of history you're living in?" He shook his head,
answering his own question. "No, of course you don't.
You're too busy trying to save the world with old-
fashioned good works, aren't you." He moved closer to
her. "I mean this talking cure you give to adolescent thugs
in the ghetto—raising their self-esteem, whatever. You
people can't even program your VCRs, but you pretend
to know how to keep sociological basket cases from rap-
ing and robbing the middle class." He took a big red hand-
kerchief from his pocket and rubbed his nose with it. "I
know all about social work."

"BioPerfection has a better plan, I guess. Like making
airdrops of Prozac on every ghetto in the country?"

Duncan made a face, as if really considering the sug-
gestion. "Not a bad idea, actually. I'll bring it up at the
next board meeting." He pulled a wooden chair over from
one of the lab tables and set it in front of her. "Mrs.
Baker," he said, sitting down, "I honestly want you to

understand what we're trying to accomplish here. You're
like so many intelligent people in the world right now:
engaged, well-meaning. But you're totally in the dark
about what's happening all around you. You want vision?
How's this: the millennium, ma'am. It's coming, and it's
coming right at a crucial turning point, just at the time
when technology is working itself loose from the old centralized power structures." He scooted his chair closer to
her. "Think of it," he went on. "In the year 2000 any two-
bit hacker on the Net can put together as much computing
power as the fucking Defense Department. Small investors with computers can get access to as much market
information as Salomon Brothers. And an organization
like BioPerfection can design drugs as easily as Merck
can—and a lot cheaper, too, since we don't have to worry
about the FDA approval process."

Kate turned her head away again. She hated this kind
of talk. A part of her rebelled against it, was intimidated
by it, recognized it as college-boy crap. "So what?" she
said lamely. "I'm supposed to be impressed?"

"Yes. Yes, you are, Mrs. Baker—Kate. It was little
BioPerfection that discovered the molecule to cure crack
addiction. Merck didn't. Glaxo didn't. Eli Lilly didn't.
And do you know why? Because Merck and Glaxo and
Eli Lilly aren't interested. They're too big. The FDA has
made the process of bringing drugs to market so expensive that now the big players in the industry won't even
look at any drug they can't patent and sell to a huge market with promising demographics." Duncan reached out
and took her chin between his rough fingers. He turned
her head back so that she was facing him again. "It's the
same story all over again. Big government and big industry deny addicts the tools to control their own illness, just
as they deny everybody else the tools to enhance their
lives and reach their goals."

His touch had revved up her anger again. "Those tools

being amphetamines and Ecstasy and bootleg antidepressants and everything else your organization can provide."

Duncan got up from the chair. A wave of tiny movement seemed to sweep through the cages around the room. "Consciousness engineering," he said. "More vision, Kate: in ten or twenty years, we'll have the ability to fine-tune our experience in ways we can only imagine now. Today's drugs are stone axes compared to the tools we'll be able to make in the future. We as individuals will be able to reengineer ourselves, remake ourselves into whatever we want. Need more ambition? We'll have a molecule for it. Want to be more outgoing? To feel more fulfilled? To be a kinder person? We'll be able to make you a fucking Mother Teresa if that's what you want. And that is *true* power: the power of complete self-determination. Of technological self-perfection."

"Right," Kate said. "And meanwhile you make a fortune selling this perfection."

Duncan's eyes widened. "Of course, of course!" He ran his fingers nervously through the thick hair of his ponytail, reminding her suddenly of Evan. "This is the concept Lu had trouble with, too. But you're all using old paradigms. We're not living in 1968 anymore. We've learned a thing or two." He picked up the chair and carried it back to the lab table. "Listen, I could go on about this for hours—it's actually my favorite topic in the world—but I don't have the time right now. All I can say to you is that I'm an entrepreneur, an entrepreneur in the great American tradition. I've learned what others have in the past two decades: the only way to improve the world is to align self-interest with the public good. Yes, I'm here to make money. The people I represent want to make money, too. So did Henry Ford, Alexander Graham Bell, and Guglielmo Marconi. But they worked in a different age. They let their technologies be monopolized."

"As far as I know," Kate said, "Henry Ford didn't kill

off his employees when they disagreed with him."

Duncan, looking disappointed again, turned and seemed to address the mice in their cages. "Mrs. Baker," he said, clearly annoyed, "Jin-Liang Lu and Don Fordham were my friends. Joel is my friend, and you are my friend's wife." He turned and faced her again. "But any results made under the auspices of BioPerfection belong to the company. Our investors need to see progress. If we gave away our first big discovery, what message would that send? They'd cut us off. BioPerfection would die before it's had a chance. And I will just not let that happen to my baby, Mrs. Baker." He rubbed his pale hands together then, a nervous look in his bloodshot eyes. "Which is why," he went on, "which is why I have to decide just how much of a threat you are to the survival of my business. Care to help me out on this?"

Kate was taken off guard. Would she really have to argue for her life? "I told you, I don't care about your business. I'm not a cop anymore."

"I wish I could believe that. I'd like nothing better than to let you go back to your nice house in Maryland and forget we ever met. Really, I would."

A cellular phone bleated somewhere across the room. The other man—Paolo, she guessed—got up from the computer keyboard and pulled the phone out of a knapsack. "Duncan," he said after a few seconds.

Duncan turned from Kate.

"Trouble," Paolo told him.

Duncan crossed the room and took the phone. Kate watched him. She saw the anger color his face as he carried the phone to the far corner of the room, out of sight beyond the mouse cages.

She remembered Evan then. If he had done everything right, he would be waiting safely back at the motel right now. The police would be on their way. After weeks of dodging the police—hiding things from them, lying to them, wishing they would disappear—she now wanted them more than anything in the world. The police were the good guys. How had she forgotten that?

Duncan came back around the row of cages with the phone in his hand. "They've found a boy hanging around outside the other house," he said. "You know anything about that?"

By an intense effort of mind, Kate managed to hide her alarm and disappointment. When had Evan been caught, she wondered. Had he had a chance to call Detective Starks? She'd been unconscious for at least a few hours— it was long past the 7:30 deadline. "A boy?" she said.

Duncan seemed to be looking right through her. "Shit," he muttered finally. "Keep him till I get there," he said into the phone. He flipped it closed. "I hope this is just some nosy neighborhood kid. For his sake and for yours."

He zipped his coat up. "I'm going back to the house for a little while," he said to Paolo, turning away from her. "Give her some water and something to eat if she's hungry. But don't take off the cuffs. Spoon-feed her if you have to."

Duncan grabbed a green corduroy hunting cap off the counter, a ridiculous-looking thing with leather earflaps. "We'll continue this later," he said. He took one last look at her before pulling open the door and disappearing into the brightness outside.

The fear was like a wire, a hot wire running from his throat to his groin, scorching his insides. Evan closed his eyes to control his nausea. The man had a gun—the husband, Joel. Evan recognized him from his picture on the news reports. The other man, the one at the computer, probably had a gun, too. What would they do to him? Would they kill him? Would they cut off his head and hands and bury him in the woods?

They'd put him in a tiny room in the basement. It was

dark inside, with just a thin outline of light around the
plywood door. The space was cramped and dank and
chilly, smelling of oil from the big tank standing in one
corner. It was like a tomb, he thought, like the Dungeon
of D'Acqor on Level 8, where the Stone Warrior always
had to rebuild his supply of Health points and search for
the secret portal. Evan opened his eyes. He was tired of
standing, but to sit would mean coming into contact with
the cold cement floor. It was the kind of basement where
insects lived—roaches and millipedes and spiders. Evan
tried to slow his breathing and think of other things.

He should have stayed at the motel, as Kate had told
him to do. He should have called that detective. He'd been
so stupid. He'd made stupid, stupid mistakes.

Evan closed his eyes again. How had things gotten so
out of control? He'd started out okay, following the plan.
After hearing the husband on the phone, he'd run back to
the Jeep, started it up, and, grinding the gears and stalling
the whole way, he'd driven it back to town. Traveling
through the dark streets just before sunrise, he passed the
post office, then the Army-Navy store and the Christian
Light Bookstore and The Gun Hut. He felt totally exposed
behind the wheel, but the streets of Karlstadt were quiet,
the whole town dead. Only the snowplows seemed to be
up and around, like huge metal animals at the side of the
road, their roof lights spinning as they waited for the snow
to start.

The sky was just turning pale when he reached the Big
Creek Motel. He turned off the engine and sat there for a
few minutes, trying to be calm and rational, trying to decide what to do. Kate had made a point of telling him that
the police were just a last resort. So would she want him
to call them now? The guy in the house was her husband;
he was the one she was looking for, the one she was trying
to protect from the cops all of this time. Maybe Kate was
hoping, right at this second, that Evan would be smart

enough *not* to call the detective. Maybe Kate was counting on him to figure it out, to realize that the plan was in effect only if she got caught by someone else, by the guy she thought was the murderer.

But it was the husband who drugged her. It was the husband who called somebody and told them she was there.

Evan stared at the line of blue doors in front of him. He would have to decide soon. It was almost 7:30.

A newspaper sat on the lid of a Dumpster in a corner of the parking lot. One of its edges was lifting and falling in the wind, waving to catch his attention. He decided to let the newspaper tell him what to do. He would get the paper, open it at random, and the first word he saw—the very first thing that caught his eye—would be the sign he was looking for.

Breathing carefully, Evan climbed out of the Jeep and crossed the slushy parking lot. He grabbed the paper off the Dumpster lid and quickly turned to the center spread, without stopping to think. "Wedding" was what his eye saw first. It was in an ad for a local caterer: "Your Wedding Is Too Important to Trust to Just Anyone. Let Us Help." Evan tried to figure out the meaning of this message. Did it mean that he should call for help after all? "Let Us Help" could be interpreted that way. Or did the fact that the very first word he saw was "Wedding," and that the wedding was "Important," mean that he should trust the husband, that Kate still wouldn't want the husband to get caught, even though he'd drugged her?

Frustrated, Evan turned to another page. "Having Trouble Getting Approved for a Mortgage?" He thought about this for a while, then flipped another page. A headline: "Karlstadt Developer Files Suit."

"Fuck," Evan said aloud, stuffing the newspaper into the Dumpster. He shoved his hands into his pockets and walked toward the door of his room. He let himself in with the key and went straight to the phone. After a few seconds, he punched in the number Kate had given him and then lay back on the spongy bed.

It rang three times before a woman answered. "Detective Starks's line."

Evan sat up. "Um, is he there?"

"Not until eight. Would you like to be connected to his voice mail?"

Evan hesitated before saying, "Yeah, okay."

He heard a few clicks, and then a familiar male voice: "Hello, this is Detective Raymond Starks. I'm sorry I can't take your call now . . ."

The beep was sounding just as Evan put down the phone. He had to be sure of what he was doing. After all, the husband had threatened the person on the phone. He'd said that he would kill people if they hurt Kate. Didn't that mean he was still on her side?

Evan made a decision then: he would go back to the house and have a look before calling the detective. Just a reconnaissance flight, to see what was happening. The other guy, the guy on the cell phone, would be at the house by now. Maybe Kate would be awake again. She might be tied up somewhere, in a separate room, and Evan could help her escape by cutting her ropes with his Swiss Army knife and leading her to safety through a window.

This idea began to appeal to him more and more, and so he drove back to the redwood chalet. He parked in the very same place as before, and walked to the house by the very same route. He noticed that there was a car in the driveway now—an old Mazda 323, not what you'd expect a rich drug dealer to drive. Pushing the thought aside, he slipped around the rhododendrons and stepped up to the broken garage window. The door to the kitchen was closed now. He thought he'd have to go around back and look in the windows.

That's when the rag-wool glove appeared on his shoulder, gripping it hard and tight.

It was the man from the blue pickup—the big, bearded one they'd seen at the post office. Evan almost fainted.

The man took Evan around back and into the kitchen. He sat him down at the table and began to ask questions: what his name was, what he was doing there, where he lived. Evan wouldn't answer at first. He could barely work up the courage to lift his head. Was this the man who'd mutilated the corpse in the woods?

"Tell me your name, damn it!" the man said, losing patience.

Evan realized he had to say something. "Mark," he whispered. "Mark Williams." It was the name of a classmate, somebody he didn't like.

The bearded man nodded. "And where do you live?"

"A couple houses down. I was walking my dog."

"What dog? I didn't see a dog."

"He ran off," Evan went on, feeling a little more confident now. "He ran into your yard. I was looking for him."

"What's the dog's name?"

Evan thought a second too long before saying "King."

It was no good. The man stared at him suspiciously. He knew that Evan was lying.

The man took Evan downstairs. There were two others down there—a scruffy, long-haired guy in jeans and three shirts, sitting at a computer, and the husband, Joel Baker, with the same streaky brown hair and square chin from TV.

"Who the hell is that?" the husband said when he saw Evan.

"I found him on my way out. Looking in the windows."

The husband put his head in his hands. "Jesus Christ," he said.

"Listen, I've got to go. You think you guys can deal with this?"

"I guess we'll have to." The husband came over and took Evan's arm. "What's your name?" he asked, almost gently.

"He says his name is Mark and he lives in one of the houses down the road, but I have my doubts."

"He see anything?"

The bearded man just shrugged. "Your call."

The husband looked into Evan's face, but Evan wouldn't meet his eye. "I don't have time for this," the husband moaned, to nobody in particular. Then, "Listen, Mark. We've got some important police work going on here, and it's supposed to be top secret. I don't know what you've seen, but it's important that . . . oh screw it," he said, as if he couldn't keep up the act. "Listen, I'm going to put you in a room for a while. Just wait patiently, okay? We've got a lot going on right now."

Evan didn't answer. He just kept looking at the floor, at the tops of his cold, wet sneakers.

"Okay, go," the husband said to the bearded man. "But call Duncan first. Tell him about this."

The man nodded and headed back upstairs. Mumbling to himself, the husband led Evan across the basement, past some complicated electrical equipment, and put him into the little room with the oil tank. "I'll get you a light in a minute," he said. Then he closed the plywood door and locked it from the outside with a hook.

But the husband had never gotten the light. The computer guy had called him over to look at something, and then he'd gone upstairs to make a telephone call. Evan had been left in the dark.

And that was where he still was, a half hour later, trying not to lose what little his stomach contained.

Control, Evan said to himself in the darkness. He was trying to think of his situation as part of an episode of Ice

Assault. It seemed to be helping a little. Conquer your fear, he chanted silently. Gather your weapons.

Evan moved closer to the door. The husband and the man at the computer were talking again. If Evan put his ear to the crack between the plywood door and the cement wall, he could just make out what they were saying— something about a password, about breaking into somebody's files. Evan held his breath and listened closely.

There was a loud banging overhead, a shout, and then the sound of heavy boots coming down the basement stairs. Evan shot away from the door. He went to the opposite corner of the small space and sank to his knees, his chest pounding. Prepare, he told himself.

"Where is he?" someone said outside.

A few seconds later, he heard the hook being undone. The door swung open and light poured into the dark space, blinding him. He put his arms up to block the glare.

"Come on out here," the man said.

Evan didn't move.

The man walked in, grabbed his arm, and pulled him roughly to his feet. He dragged Evan out into the light. It was a stocky man in a green coat and boots, half-bald with a ponytail, like a record producer. "Who are you, boy? What the fuck you doing outside my windows?" He pushed Evan hard against the cinder block wall, knocking the breath from his lungs. "You know I could shoot your balls off as a trespasser, you know that?"

"Easy, Duncan," the husband said, taking a step toward them. "We don't know who he is."

The man, Duncan, ignored him. He stared at Evan for a few long seconds. Evan could see the big pores in his nose, the eyes veined with red.

"I told the other guy already," Evan answered. "My name is Mark and I live down the street."

"Which house?"

Evan tried not to stammer. Conquer your fear, he told

himself. "The green one on the other side."

Duncan stared at him for a few more seconds. "And so what the fuck were you doing outside my windows?"

Evan swallowed. An idea occurred to him, an excuse for being there. "I heard that you could get pot here. That somebody here was dealing."

"What the fuck?" Duncan shouted. He turned and shot a quick look at the husband, then raked his fingers through his hair and turned back. "Where did you hear this, you little shit?"

"At school. A kid there I know." Evan cleared his throat. "He said there were rumors."

The man moved his ugly face closer. Evan could smell his minty breath. "Give me the name of the kid," he whispered. "Spell it out for me. I want to know what other little shit is spreading rumors about me."

"His name is Ray," Evan said, breathing steadily now. "Ray Black. R-A-Y . . ."

Duncan turned away, his face red with anger, before Evan could finish.

And there it was—the unprotected weapon, a gun in the waistband of the man's jeans.

Evan recognized his chance. He could save her now. He could save Kate, save himself. In a second, the fear inside him ripened, reshaped itself into motion. He was the Stone Warrior. He was the Stone Warrior. His moment was now.

Evan lunged at the figure moving away from him, his hand reaching for the weapon.

He regretted the move instantly. Time seemed to jump, and he found himself on the cement, his head ringing, his knees and palms burning. He was confused for a second. What happened to the gun? Blood seeped into his mouth from his lower lip, the metallic taste sickening. He felt a hand on his arm, pulling him to his feet.

"What the fuck you think you are?" Duncan hissed at

him. "James Bond? You think you're fucking Rambo, boy?" He pushed Evan hard against the wall, whipping his head back against the cinder blocks. The pain shot sparks of light all around the room.

"This is stupid, Duncan," the husband said. "He's a kid."

Everything was falling. The sparks started swirling around his head. Suddenly, the gun was there, at Evan's throat. Somebody shouted. Evan tried to talk, but the gun paralyzed him.

"You think you're some kind of fucking Rambo?" Duncan said again.

Evan felt himself being pulled back deeper into his own body. He knew now that everything was lost. He stared into Duncan's face, into his bloodshot eyes, and realized that he didn't care what happened anymore. If the man killed him or if he didn't, it wouldn't make any difference.

Duncan pressed the barrel deeper into the soft skin of Evan's neck. "I swear to you, I will pull this trigger," he whispered.

Evan couldn't move his mouth to speak. Ice was crystallizing all around him. It was encasing him in a clear, cold, invisible skin.

Duncan pulled away. Loose suddenly, Evan nearly fell to the floor. "I hate this shit," Duncan said. He took a few paces, then spun around and came back. He grabbed Evan's arm and pushed him back into the dark room. Then he slammed the plywood door shut, throwing the room into total blackness.

Moving stiffly, Evan felt his way along the wall in the darkness. He found the little space beside the oil tank. He sat down on the cold cement and put his hands on his knees.

It was better this way, he thought. It was easier. The ice. The invisibility.

"This whole thing is falling apart around my fucking

feet." It was Duncan's voice, muffled by the door, trailing off. "Next we'll have the whole fucking PTA showing up at our door."

In the darkness, Evan closed his eyes. He leaned his head back until it rested against the hard wall. It was a good feeling, he thought, this cold, this calm. The ice kept packing in tighter around his arms and chest. It was like a kind of armor.

"I'm dying here, gentlemen," Duncan was saying. "I'm dying."

Evan breathed. Nothing could touch him now.

Nothing could hurt him.

Game over.

21

She watched the man giving injections to the mice. He worked systematically. First, he measured out some white powder into a dish. He put the dish on a tripod, moved the tripod over a lit Bunsen burner, and stirred with a glass rod until the powder liquefied. Then he took a syringe and filled it with some of the liquid. With the syringe in one hand, he grabbed a tagged mouse from the cage with the other. He held the mouse's tiny head wedged between his fingers and the tabletop, then injected it with the clear liquid. He put the tagged mouse back in the cage and grabbed another, repeating the process.

"They teach you that in bad-guy school?" Kate asked, breaking a long silence. She remembered Evan's comment about "cop school."

He didn't answer for a few seconds. When he finished injecting another mouse, he said, quietly, "Funny lady."

Kate flexed her shoulders to stretch her aching arm muscles. The plastic cuffs were starting to cut circulation to her hands and feet. "Paolo, right?" she said. "I didn't think hired guns did this kind of work."

He smiled, without looking at her. "Yeah, well, the guy in charge of this experiment had a little accident. Maybe you heard."

"Oh, right." Kate rubbed her fingertips together behind her back. "I guess you were the guy who did him, right?"

Paolo didn't even look in her direction.

"What's it like to kill a man and then cut off his head?"

Paolo sniffed. "Not as much fun as killing a woman and cutting off her head."

Kate tried not to let the remark get to her. This man was scary. So quiet and focused. "So what are you on? Speed? Coke?" Still no answer. "You believe in this cause, too? Better dope makes a better world?"

"I do my job." Then, grinning, he added, "I get paid for doing what I love."

Kate watched the man more closely, wondering how dangerous he really could be. He didn't look too imposing physically—five-six or -seven, chunky, with balding hair cut short. But there was an intensity to every one of his movements that worried Kate. She'd seen men smaller than this get the better of three strapping cops when the drug was strong enough.

"What's that you're injecting them with?" she asked.

No answer.

"Some kind of smart drug? You turning those little guys into rodent Einsteins?"

"Funny lady," he said again. He reached into the cage for another mouse. "Shit," he said then. He dropped the animal onto the tabletop—it had nipped his thumb—and then quickly grabbed it again by its tail. He spun the mouse and cracked its head against the edge of the marble table, killing it.

"So much for science," Kate muttered.

Paolo turned and looked at her for the first time. He

carried the mouse over to her and held its misshapen white body in front of her face. Then he reached into his pocket and brought out a blue cigarette lighter. He lit it and touched the flame to the mouse's head. The fine white hairs singed instantly, curling and blackening. "Look familiar?" he said, and dropped the mouse into her lap. She let out a yelp and tried to jump back, but the cuffs didn't allow her much movement. The mouse fell to the floor with a tiny thud and then just lay there at her feet, reeking of charred hair.

"You sick fucker," Kate said.

Paolo just showed his perfect white teeth and turned back to his work.

Recovering gradually, Kate tried to clear her mind of everything except how to escape from this man. She looked around the room. She couldn't be sure from where she sat, but the room seemed to be part of one of those cheap prefab houses common in poor rural areas, one step up from a trailer. Judging from the mud on the doormat and the quiet outside, the house was probably on some dirt road in the woods—an illegal lab pretending to be somebody's hunting cabin. Where were the nearest ears to hear a scream? she wondered. It was worth a try.

"Help me!" she shouted, as loudly as she could.

She got no response from Paolo, but some dogs—two, she guessed, chained or fenced outside—began to bark wildly.

"Don't upset the dogs or I'll have to sedate you," Paolo said finally, when he'd finished another mouse.

"Pretty cool about the whole thing, aren't you. I guess we must be pretty far from the next house."

He chuckled. "There isn't any next house. Nothing around you but woods, most of it state land, so you can save your breath."

She looked over at the monkey in the large cage. It seemed sick, huddled in a corner of the cage, surrounded

by the squashed remnants of its food. Its eyes looked
bright yellow. "Hey," Kate said, "how about you take
these cuffs off my ankles? You can keep the ones on my
wrists if you have to, but my feet are starting to get
numb."

"Sorry," he said.

"Oh right. I guess a little guy like you can't take any
chances."

Paolo made a show of yawning. "You're real crafty,
lady, but why don't you just shut up now? You're boring
me."

Kate cursed silently. The man wasn't going to be pro-
voked into doing anything stupid. She'd have to try something else.

The dogs were still barking outside. Paolo looked at his
watch. "Shit," he said. He put the mouse he was working
on back into the cage and pulled the tripod away from the
Bunsen burner. Then he grabbed his canvas coat from a
chair in the corner. Kate watched him carefully, not sure
what was going to happen. He went over to a cabinet near
the door and pulled out a leather case. It looked like a
toiletries case, only bigger. Then he walked over to the
door and pulled it open. Kate saw trees, a bicycle, a
muddy road showing through snow. "Okay, I'm coming,"
Paolo muttered. He pulled the door half shut.

Kate moved without thinking. She leaned her upper
body forward, straining against the straps of the cuffs,
shifting her weight onto the soles of her feet. Her ankles
were bound just loosely enough to let her take tiny steps,
like someone trying to walk with her pants around her
ankles. Dragging the chair, she crept as quietly as she
could toward the lab table, concentrating too hard on her
target to let the cutting at her ankles and wrists distract
her. She reached the edge of the lab table and sat back,
letting the four legs of the chair settle back onto the floor.
The rubber tubing that led from the gas jet to the lit Bun-

sen burner snaked across the tabletop. She leaned forward
and hooked her chin around it. Then she slowly dragged
the tubing toward the edge of the table. The Bunsen
burner followed, like a toy on a string. She got a loop of
tubing between her chin and her shoulder and maneuvered
it carefully until the burner was right at the edge of the
table. She knew that the flame would be too high to reach
with her wrists unless she knocked the burner horizontal.
She tried to do this by twisting the tube with her chin,
but she ended up knocking the whole burner to the floor.
"Fuck," she whispered aloud. But the flame didn't go out.
It just burned there on the floor, scorching the linoleum.
She shimmied the chair closer to the burner, until she
could grab it with her feet. She got the base of it between
her boots and carefully tilted it back. The flame seared
her ankle, and she almost dropped the burner in pain, but
she finally managed to aim the heat toward the plastic
strap of the cuffs. For a few agonizing seconds, she waited
for the plastic to melt, pulling the strap tight with her
ankles while grasping the burner with her feet. The tension released suddenly. The flame had cut through the
strap. Her feet were free.

She let the burner loose and leaned forward until she
was on her feet. She quickly repositioned herself, and then
let herself topple to the floor. The chair fell with her,
clattering so loudly that she thought Paolo must have
heard. Using her feet, she pushed her body around until
she could grab the burner with her bound hands behind
her back. This part was easier. She fingered the base of
the burner until the flame was directed at the plastic strap
connecting her wrists. Again, she had to wait while the
flame bit through the tough plastic. But then her hands
were free.

She kicked the chair away and rolled before getting to
her feet. She almost fell to her knees again; her cramped

legs needed time to straighten out. But she recovered as
the blood rushed to her calves.

She quickly returned the Bunsen burner to an upright
position on the lab table. Her eyes raked the room for a
weapon—something heavy to hit him with, if nothing
else. The only possibility was a large bottle of clear liquid
on a shelf behind the lab table. For all she knew, it contained hydrochloric acid, but there was no time to find
out. She grabbed it off the shelf and hid herself behind
the half-open door. Then she waited. She wondered if
Paolo had a gun, and decided that he must. She would
have to steel herself, to hit him as hard as she could. No
holding back, she told herself. No weakness.

After a minute or so, she heard a step on the porch
outside. The door swept open. Paolo was barely inside
when she swung the heavy bottle straight at his head. It
hit with a sickening thud and shattered in her hands. Paolo
dropped to the floor like a bag of sand. A pistol fell from
his hands and spun across the floor. Kate stopped it with
her foot. She grabbed it with both hands and then aimed
it point-blank at the crumpled body on the floor.

She stood still for a few seconds to catch her breath.
She held the pistol—a Glock 9mm automatic—at arm's
length, as steady as she could. The broken plastic cuffs
hung from her wrists like hospital bracelets.

Paolo began to stir. He looked up at her. There was a
mean abrasion on his head where the bottle had hit, and
it was bleeding freely, the blood and the clear liquid from
the bottle coursing down the slope of his left cheek.
"You're trying to make this interesting," he said. He was
still grinning.

"Don't move a fucking muscle until I tell you to," she
said, aiming the pistol straight at his head.

He kept moving, dragging himself to his feet. "You
probably don't even know how to fire that thing," he said.

"Yeah? Try me."

He touched the bloody wound with his fingertips. Then, moving deliberately, he took a step to his left.

"Don't move," she shouted.

Her words had no effect. Maintaining his eye contact with her, he grabbed the cellular phone.

"This is your last warning," she said, squeezing the butt of the Glock in her hands.

He calmly smashed the phone to pieces on the marble countertop.

"You son of a bitch," Kate whispered.

"Now we won't be interrupted," he said. He took a step toward her.

She squeezed the trigger and fired a shot past his head, the noise deafening in the small room. Outside, the dogs started howling again.

Paolo had stopped for just a moment. The smile looked a little strained on his face, but he took another step toward her.

Kate fired again. The shot punched a chunk of cloth and flesh out of Paolo's shoulder. She saw him wince and cover the wound with his wet hand. Little bits of goose down floated toward the floor.

"There were two rounds left in that clip," Paolo said then. "You've just run out of ammunition, lady."

Kate held her position, not letting herself believe this. "The next one goes straight through your neck," she said.

Then, suddenly, he was gone. He bolted out the still-open door into the snowy outdoors. Kate, taken entirely by surprise, fired twice, but much too late. The shots hit the metal door frame. She ran toward the door and saw Paolo's dark form rounding the side of the house. She fired another shot, which split the siding on the corner of the house.

She followed him, hearing the mashing of branches as Paolo pushed through the thick underbrush. There was a flash of movement at her side. A huge gray dog lunged at her, throwing her to the snow-covered ground and knocking the breath out of her. Thinking it would be on top of her in an instant, she rolled, aimed the Glock from a lying position, and fired. One side of the dog's head disappeared in a gush of red as the animal twisted to the snow, a thick choker chain now visible around its neck. The dog was tied up. She saw that now. A few feet beyond it was another huge gray dog, also chained. It threw itself toward her again and again, yanking the chain, strangling itself to get at her.

"Shit Fuck Shit!" Kate shouted, nearly in tears. Paolo was gone now. She could only hope the dog was dead.

She scrambled back to her feet and surveyed the woods around the prefab house. She had no idea where Paolo could be. She made her way to the back of the house, not looking at the first dog, giving the second a wide berth. She kept the Glock out in front of her, ready to fire at the first sign of movement. But she could see nothing moving in the woods. A gentle snow was falling through the skeletal trees, coating the branches of the low pines and wild rhododendrons.

She made a quick circle around the house. An unpaved road led downhill into the woods, the tracks from Duncan's 4-by-4 still visible though quickly filling with snow. There was no vehicle anywhere near the house except a bicycle—a mountain bike with thick tires. It would have to do.

Kate made one last sweep of the woods and then went back inside. Her jacket was draped over a pile of cages. She grabbed it, turned off the Bunsen burner, and then checked around the lab, not knowing exactly what she was looking for. In a desk drawer she found two extra clips for the Glock. She replaced the one already in the pistol and pocketed the other. Then she quickly got into her jacket, zipped it up, and headed back outside.

There was still no sign of Paolo in the woods around

the house. The second dog was barking so fiercely that
she had no hope of hearing any noise he might be making
in his escape. Kate cursed aloud at the dog, but she knew
that there would be no way of making it stop other than
killing it. And this she refused to do.

She made a final check of the area around the road, put
the pistol into her pocket, and then climbed onto the
mountain bike. The road surface was slippery and uneven,
but she managed to keep the bicycle under control. The
road headed downhill as far as she could see. She coasted
unsteadily over the mud and slush as more snow fell
around her. The barking behind her gradually faded away
and then stopped.

She tried to decide what she would do when she
reached the first house. Should she stop, ask to use the
phone, and call the local police? She wondered if Evan
had called the Hampton County detectives before he was
caught. If so, Starks would probably have contacted the
Pennsylvania State Troopers or whoever had jurisdiction
out here. It was possible that a local force was already at
the redwood chalet. Maybe they'd arrested Joel by now—
before he could carry out his plan, whatever it was. Or
maybe Joel and Duncan were dead, killed by some jumpy
SWAT sharpshooter. Even now, the thought of Joel dead
sent a deep shudder through Kate's body. He was still her
husband. She couldn't even pretend not to care.

The dog, flying into her line of vision, hit her from the
left side, its weight and momentum throwing her and the
bicycle into the stiff rhododendrons beside the road.

Pain seared her left forearm as she fell. The dog
clamped its jaws to a place just below her elbow, its teeth
piercing the thick jacket and her flesh. The rhododendrons
absorbed most of the impact of their fall and threw them
back into the road. Breathless from the pain, Kate frantically scrabbled for the Glock with her free right hand.

The dog was pulling now, trying to tear the flesh from her arm.

Her hand found the grip of the Glock in her pocket. She fired through the pocket, hitting the dog at the place where its hind leg met its flank. The sharp grip on her forearm loosened, but didn't release. She fired again, higher this time. Three rounds tore into the dog's torso, imploding its rib cage. Finally, its jaws went slack and it fell away from her onto the snowy road.

Kate gasped for air. Her left forearm pounded when she tried to move it. She got to her feet and looked down at the panting dog. Paolo must have gone back to the house after she left. He must have let it loose from its chain.

The dog's loud breathing stopped then, leaving a hole of silence in the air.

Kate walked back to the bicycle, which lay in a ditch beside the road. The front wheel was bent out of shape, distorted by a six-inch S-curve.

She turned and looked down the road. How far could it be to a house, she wondered.

She'd just taken her first step when the bullet whizzed past her ear, followed by the crack of a shot in the woods above her. Paolo. She dove for the rhododendrons as a second shot rang out. Turning, she aimed the Glock in the direction of the noise, but realized that she had no hope of hitting anything. She got to her feet and ran into the woods.

From the road, the land dropped steeply toward a small frozen stream. Kate stumbled and slid down the incline, her boots skidding on the floor of snow-covered leaves. She almost fell a few times, steadying herself with the injured left arm, the pain a shock each time. At the bottom of the small ravine, she skittered across the slick surface of the stream and turned left, following the slope of the streambed. She knew that her best chance of reaching a house was to go straight downhill, into the valley.

She moved as quickly as she could, swiping away the branches of the creekside bushes as she ran. She couldn't afford to turn an ankle. Once, the end of a branch caught her hair; it pulled out a gluey hank, making her gasp in surprise and pain. For a second she'd thought it was Paolo grabbing her from behind.

After she'd been running for several minutes, she stopped in a heavily wooded area to listen. The forest was mixed pine and deciduous, so the evergreens gave her a good amount of cover. But they also blocked her own view. She listened intently, trying to hear the sound of running footsteps through the wind in the pines, the soft patter of snowflakes, and her own fast breathing.

She edged to a small break in the trees. She could see the road above on the other side of the stream, a wooden guardrail following the edge of a curve. He was up there, on the road, two hundred yards or so away from her. Through the breaks in the underbrush, she could see the upper part of his body moving smoothly down the road. The rifle was in his hands, and his eyes were scouring the woods for her. She lifted the Glock and aimed. But she knew there was little chance that she could hit him from this distance.

She saw him stop on the road, peer suddenly in her direction through the falling snow, and lift the rifle to his bloody shoulder.

Startled, she fired, getting off two hopeless rounds. Then she turned and pushed through a break in the shabby rhododendrons, away from the road.

The slope on this side of the creek was less steep. She climbed up toward the ridge, staying as close to the thick pines as she could. She had no idea how exposed she was to the road, but she couldn't worry about it. Her body was pumping adrenaline now, dulling the pain in her arm and the raw ache in her chest.

She came over the ridge and started going down the
other side. Suddenly, she found herself out of the woods,
exposed, snow swirling all around her. She looked left. A
huge metal tower stood a hundred feet downhill; a sweeping arc of high-tension wires buzzed overhead. She was
in a powerline corridor, a cleared strip of forest running
down the mountainside, about thirty yards wide.

She crossed the corridor and broke through the underbrush on the other side. Here she stopped. She looked
around until she found a good spot—hidden by brush but
offering a good view of the corridor up and down. Paolo
would have to cross the corridor in his pursuit. He'd be
exposed. She'd have her chance for a clear shot.

She sank to the damp ground behind a decaying log.
Bracing her right arm on the snow-laced bark, she held
the Glock as steadily as she could. Then she just lay there,
waiting. She lay like a predator waiting for its prey, as a
weird kind of thrill washed through her. There was no
doubt in her mind now that she would kill this man if she
had the chance. The fear, the anger, had all disappeared,
leaving nothing inside her except this awful determina-
tion. Complexities like compassion and misgiving were
finally gone. She was an animal now, focused, amoral.
She would do anything, anything at all, to save herself.

A minute passed. Then another. Kate's arm started
shaking; a trace of self-consciousness began to infect her.
How quickly this had come back, she thought, this hard-
ening. She realized then that nothing had changed. Nothing *can* change.

The male form materialized out of the gray snow in
front of her and off to the left. It lurched out of the forest
into the clearing, unafraid, oblivious. Kate turned the pistol toward it. She watched as the figure stopped, the rifle
wedged under its armpit, the hands rising toward the
mouth. The man, Paolo, was blowing into his hands,
warming his frozen fingers.

I should shoot to wound, Kate told herself. I'm invisible to him. I'm protected. He can't kill me.

But she aimed straight for the man's chest. Feeling a rush of energy, she squeezed the trigger, firing round after round, until Paolo collapsed onto the wet ground and rolled to a stop against a single twisted sapling in the snow.

22

The snow had tapered off by the time Kate came out of the woods into a small apple orchard. Rows of wildly gnarled trees ran down the hillside in front of her, the lines broken by piles of empty crates topped with a velvety covering of snow. To her left, a few hundred feet down the white hillside, was a house—a tiny frame ranch with a steeply sloped roof and the dried-up remains of a perennial garden in back. A white Ford pickup sat in the doorless cinder block garage next to it.

Kate's ears were freezing by now, and her forearm ached. She ran toward the house.

There seemed to be nobody around. Kate went to the front door and knocked loudly. No answer. She got on tiptoes to look through the glass panels in the door, but she wasn't tall enough to see anything except the cracked ceiling. The panes running down both sides of the doorway were frosted. Frustrated, she tried the lock, called hello a few times, then stepped off the little porch to look in the bay window. The curtains were open, but there was no other sign that anyone was inside. The interior of the house looked more like an office than a home. There were three desks in the room, some file cabinets, and a coffee machine in the corner. On the first desk, closest to the front door, was a telephone.

Kate went back to the porch. She knew that it was time to bring Starks and Jerrold into this. Evan had been caught at the redwood chalet, so it was unlikely that he'd called them. But should Kate notify the local force, too? Would the Karlstadt police believe some stranger calling up and telling them about a dope-pushing murderer in one of those chalet houses outside town? Even if they did, there was no guarantee that they would respond in the right way. They might send a single patrolman to the door, or, worse, the county SWAT team. Either way, somebody would get killed. Probably Evan, the way these things usually worked.

She decided she would call Detective Starks and let him contact the Karlstadt police himself. He'd probably have the locals just watch the house until he and Jerrold and the feds could sort through the jurisdiction issues and get to the scene themselves. That would give her some time.

She knocked again. Then she reached into the pocket of her jacket and took out the Glock. "Sorry," she said aloud, and smashed the grip into the frosted pane nearest the doorknob. The glass tinkled to the bare floor inside. Kate carefully knocked out the rest of the pane, then reached in, unbolted the door, and opened it.

"Hello?" she called again. The interior of the little house smelled musty and airless. And there was no heat on. The house had probably been empty for days or weeks.

She went over to the phone and dialed Detective Starks's number. After three rings, she got his voice mail. She looked at the clock on the wall behind the third desk: 4:25.

At the beep, she started talking: "Detective Starks, this is Kate Baker. I've found your murderer. His name is Duncan Lloyd and he's at a house in southern Pennsylvania, near Karlstadt." She gave him the address and some basic directions. Then she went on: "As far as I know, they have Evan Potter in the house with them, so for God's sake be careful. I'll explain it to you. Just get to the house as soon as you can. And I'd really appreciate it if you didn't shoot me, okay?"

At the end of her message, she pressed the pound key.

"Hampton County Police Department," said a crisp female voice.

"Hi, I'm looking for Detective Starks?"

"He's in the field right now. I can connect you with his voice mail if you like."

"No, I just left him a long message. Can you make sure he picks it up right away? Tell him it's from Kate Baker."

There was a long silence. "Can you hold the line, please? I could try to get him on the radio. I know he wants to talk to you."

"Yeah, I'm sure he does, but I don't have time. Everything I need to tell him is in the message."

Kate hung up the phone. She took a deep breath and looked around the little office. On the wall was a wildlife calendar and a pegboard, where three rings of keys hung from hooks. She walked over and took down all three rings. She recognized the Ford logo on what was clearly an ignition key.

So now you're a car thief, she told herself, pocketing the key ring and heading for the door.

5:45 P.M. For the second time in twelve hours, Kate stood outside the broken garage window of the redwood chalet. Again, it was dark; again, she had a pistol in her hand. The only difference was that this time she had Evan to worry about. How many people were inside? she won-

dered. Duncan had said he was coming here, so that was
one. Joel. Plus whoever it was who was trying to break
into Jin's files. That was three, at the very least. But she'd
been watching the house for ten minutes without seeing
any sign of activity. They, however many they were, were
probably all down in the basement with the blacked-out
windows.

Shivering in the cold, Kate tried to work out her options. Assuming she didn't get shot on her way in, the
worst that could happen if she went inside was that she'd
get caught again. They'd cuff her and throw her into a
room somewhere, maybe even with Evan. If so, she'd just
have to keep Evan and herself alive until the police
showed up—three or four hours at the most.

But if she didn't get caught, she might be able to get
Evan's ass out of there in one piece, before the shooting
started. She also might be able to find out whether Joel,
the man she married, was even remotely worthy of her
trust. Somehow, in spite of all that had happened, she
couldn't bring herself to give up on him yet.

She managed to open the broken window without a
sound and pull herself inside. Glass crackled under her
feet as she crossed the garage. The draped Saab was still
there, surrounded by the drums of chemicals. The door to
the kitchen was closed, but the venetian blinds were open
now. She could see into the kitchen through the broken
pane of glass. She went to the door and peered in. There
was no movement inside, but she could hear the far-off
murmur of voices from the basement.

Praying that nobody had put the alarm back on, she
gently turned the doorknob—it was unlocked—and
opened the door. Then she moved back into the darkness
of the garage and waited, the Glock ready in her hands.
If it was engaged, the alarm would sound after a delay of
a minute or two. She sank to a defensive crouch, trying
not to think about the throbbing ache in her left forearm.

She had been in too much of a hurry to clean and bandage the dog bite back at the house in the orchard, and it hurt badly now. The dog's jaws had been powerful enough to pierce her jacket, shirt, and skin and nick the stringy muscle underneath. Just thinking about the dog made her shiver.

A minute passed, then two, then three. When she was finally sure that the alarm was off, she straightened up and went back to the doorway. She stepped carefully into the stuffy kitchen. The room was dim, the only light a small halogen lamp beside the coffee machine. A half-full pot was warming there on the burner. God, she could use a cup right now. An image jumped to her mind—of herself sitting in the kitchen back at the house in Lewisburg, a weekday morning, Joel across the table with *The New York Times* open in front of him. Kate could feel her throat contract with yearning. That life.

She slowly walked toward the open doorway that led down to the basement, her body tense, prepared for anything.

The first voice she heard was Joel's: ". . . two, three days at the most. We move all the equipment to one of the other labs, and we're fine. We've lost this house and the one in the woods. That's it, Duncan. No big problem."

"Right. No big problem." Duncan's voice.

"You disagree."

"She knows my name, Joel. She knows who I am. To me, that's a problem."

"The cops know your name already, take my word for it. The thing with Don assured it. Any smart detective will check back and start putting two and two together. They'll turn up your name, Duncan. Count on it."

"Look, we'll talk about it later, okay?"

"Duncan, the more bodies you leave behind, the harder they're going to look for you."

A pause, and then Duncan's voice again: "For *us*, Joel,

for *us*. I don't want to hear this 'you' shit. It makes me
nervous. It makes me start to think things you don't want
me to think."

"If I wanted out, I had the perfect opportunity this
morning. Instead, I doped up my own wife for you, shit-
head. Did you forget that?"

"Later, Joel. We'll talk about this later."

Then a third voice, softer. "Shit. Jin was smarter than
I thought."

"What?"

"Wait." There was a long pause, broken by the clattering of a keyboard. Then the third voice said, "This is
going to take a little longer . . ."

"I don't want to hear that, John. I don't want to hear *a
little longer*. I want to hear *now* . . . For all we know his
little broadcast program could be set to pop two minutes
from now."

Another silence followed. Kate was standing rigid in
the doorway. She'd counted three voices. Were there any
more people down there? she wondered. And where was
Evan?

"At this rate," Duncan said then, "I'll fuckin' OD on
Maalox before we're done."

Again, Kate went over her options. It would be hard to
get down the basement stairs without making a lot of
noise. But the only other access to the basement was
through the two blacked-out windows in the back, which
were too small. She *could* wait until somebody came upstairs, but unless all three came up at once, she'd be vul-
nerable. From the sound of it, the third voice belonged to
somebody working a computer—probably the person trying to find Jin's files. He probably wouldn't leave the
keyboard for hours. Not until he had the files he needed.

"The kid asleep?" Duncan asked then.

"You want me to look?"

Kate stood beside the doorway, hoping the answer

would be yes, hoping she'd hear something that would tell her where Evan was being kept.

"Forget about it," Duncan said. "The less he sees of us, the better." She heard a few footsteps. "John, you're smiling. Tell me why you're smiling."

"I got it."

"You got it?"

"I got it. I'm transferring it directly to a disk. It'll take a while. It's a shitload of data."

"He got it, Joel."

"I heard."

Kate knew that she had to make her move. She could roughly guess the position of all three men downstairs. The hacker and Duncan were toward the back, at the computer; Joel was farther away from the bottom of the stairs. She had plenty of rounds left in the Glock. She could probably rush down and get a bead on Duncan and the hacker before they even knew what was happening. But that left Joel. Joel would be across the room. He might or might not be armed. At this point, she had no idea what he would do if he was.

Don't think, she told herself. Do it. It's the only way you'll know.

She was down the stairs in a second.

She had the Glock aimed straight at the chest of Duncan Lloyd. Behind him, a man was sitting at a computer terminal in the back. There was a pistol on the desk beside the keyboard, within Duncan's reach. She couldn't see Joel. He was behind her somewhere, off beyond the lab stations. Nobody had said a word.

Bad judgment, Kate told herself. What she'd just done was the result of very, very bad judgment.

The first person to say anything was the man at the computer. "Hey, lady, I'm just the geek-for-hire. I don't do guns."

"Kate," Joel said, from behind her and to her left.

"Get away from the computer, both of you," Kate shouted.

The man at the keyboard began to move, but Duncan put a hand on his shoulder and just stared back at her. "Joel," he said. "Lift your weapon."

Kate still hadn't turned her head to look at Joel. She knew that if she did, the pistol would be in Duncan's hand in an instant. "I said, get away from the computer."

"Joel," Duncan repeated.

Kate was wavering. She knew she had to take command of this situation. Turning the pistol, she shot two rounds into the screen of the computer, filling the basement with booming echoes and sending the hacker into a fit.

Duncan had barely flinched. "Joel," he said again, "I'll agree to everything we talked about. We leave her behind. The boy, too. Nobody else gets hurt. We cut our losses. But I need your help now, man. She won't shoot you. You're her husband."

Kate kept her eyes fixed on Duncan. "Come around where I can see you, Joel. Come on. It's over now."

"It's only over if you cave, Joel-boy," Duncan said. "You know what's in your best interest."

She heard Joel coming around the lab stations to her right, moving slowly. He came into her line of sight. In his right hand was her own Sig 9mm, aimed straight at her heart.

"I'm sorry, Kate," he said. "I'm not ready to go to jail."

Before she could even take in the extent of this betrayal, Duncan grabbed the pistol on the desk and aimed it at her. "Two against one, Mrs. Baker," he said. "Drop it now, please."

She didn't move. The impulse to shoot—to just mow down all three of them—came and passed. She would die if she tried that. And somehow even dying seemed like too much effort now.

Let the police take care of this scum, she told herself. She lowered the gun.

"That's Paolo's Glock," Duncan said, coming up to her and taking it from her hand. "You are a fucking piece of work, Mrs. Baker."

Joel was staring at her, his eyes unreadable. The eyes of a stranger.

Duncan turned away from her. "Can you connect up a new monitor?" he asked.

John nodded, still looking stunned.

"And is the transfer still going?"

"Should be. She just hit the monitor. Everything else should be fine."

"Good." He turned back to Kate and Joel.

"Duncan," Joel said finally. "If you were lying to me, I'll kill you."

Duncan smiled at him. "I know you would, Joel," he said. "I know." Then he turned to Kate. "Sit down now and tell me how the hell you got past Paolo."

"Okay, we're back in business," John said from the computer. He'd switched monitors and was at the keyboard again. "The transfer's just about finished."

Duncan stared down at Kate for another few seconds before turning away. "Tell me when it's done. Then blitz the hell out of everything in Jin's directories. Whatever it takes. I want Hiroshima, John. Nagasaki. I want every trace of Jin's fucking existence on the system eradicated, got it?"

Kate was still watching Joel. "So you've made your choice," she said to him.

He wouldn't look at her now. "It's not that simple."

"Looks simple to me. Would you really shoot me? If I made a move now?"

He shifted the position of the Sig in his hands. "It's going to work out now. Everyone will be safe."

"Done," John said. He pulled a diskette out of the disk drive and handed it to Duncan.

"Good. Now do what I said." Smiling, Duncan put down his gun and carried the diskette across the basement toward them. "See this? Two men have died because of what's on this diskette. Because of this particular magnetic arrangement of electrons. Amazing what constitutes value in the information age, isn't it? No more gold, no more coal, not even big missiles anymore. It's having the right sequence of ones and zeros." He held the diskette in his fingertips, idly turning it from corner to corner. "And how fragile it all is, too. It takes so little to destroy it." He grabbed something off the lab table then with his left hand and clapped it against the diskette in his right. "It's gone now. All of that valuable information."

It seemed to take a moment for everyone in the room to understand what had just happened. "What did you just do?" Joel said.

"I destroyed Jin's data, Joel. The only copy. It's as if it never existed now. It's as if Jin had never found a thing."

Kate was watching Joel's face. His silence seemed ominous. "What?" he whispered.

Duncan shook his head. "Come on. Think out of the box, Joel-boy. You're a smart guy. You know where our funding comes from." Duncan took a few steps toward them. "These people want to make money, Joel. We're just a tiny blip on their balance sheets right now, a sideline, years away from showing any profit. You can't expect them to take a hit like this right now."

Kate was standing between them now. She understood what had happened. "You find a cure for crack addiction," she said, "and your investors lose their most lucrative market, is that it?"

"Very good," Duncan said, turning to her. "She's quicker than you are, Joel."

Kate felt a wave of disgust. "There's your revolution, Joel," she said. "So much for biochemical utopia."

Duncan shook his head. "Any utopia needs time, Mrs. Baker. Time and a lot of cash flow. And right now, that cash flow comes from people who can't consider losing their best business." He turned back to Joel. "Think it through, Joel. A movement like ours has to be realistic."

Kate caught the movement in her peripheral vision. Joel, still silent, had turned the Sig away from her. Now it was aimed at Duncan.

Kate moved on instinct, running for the Glock on the table. Just as she was about to reach it, she heard a scream—Evan's voice, screaming her name from some-where close by. She hesitated for just a second, confused by the sound.

That's when the windows of the basement came crash-ing in, and the world seemed to crash in with them.

A howling pain in her shoulder spun Kate to the floor. As she fell, she heard shouts and movement coming from the direction of the stairs. She hit the ground and rolled over once on the cement floor, her eyes clamping shut in agony. There was more shouting, gunfire, impossible noise. When she opened her eyes again, a man in black was pointing an assault rifle at her head, yelling something she couldn't understand. The basement was now filled with hooded black figures. She saw the letters on the back of one of them: DEA. Oh God, she thought. Joel. Please, Joel, be all right.

She saw a purple comma of blood swelling on the floor beside her head—getting bigger and thicker until it broke into a rivulet and hurried toward the drain in the floor.

It was silent suddenly, and then, down the stairs, came Detectives Starks and Jerrold, followed by the black over-coat of Lt. Harry Grainger.

Kate thought for a second that she was hallucinating. "How the fuck did you get here so fast?" she asked.

Lieutenant Grainger came over and crouched beside her. "Come on, Mrs. Baker. Give us a little credit."

"The kid's in here," someone shouted from the other end of the basement. "Shit, he looks like he's in shock or something."

Tiny flames were dancing along the edges of everything in Kate's vision. The Lieutenant seemed to be wearing a halo. "I gave up my Thanksgiving for this," he said.

Kate was fading. "Is anybody dead?" she started to ask. She was never sure how much of the question she actually got out before the darkness started to rush in around her head, dragging her down into unconsciousness.

23

"Withholding evidence in a homicide investigation. Assault and battery of a police officer. Endangering the welfare of a minor." Assistant State Attorney Carol Ann Bassett crossed her thin arms in front of her. She was wearing heels and a tight-fitting beige dress that emphasized the blue-black tones of her skin. A powerful woman, Kate thought, sitting across the table from her. Kate's arm was in a sling to protect her healing left shoulder. She felt grateful for the presence of Adrianna next to her.

Bassett's male assistant—a blond kid, barely out of law school, who clearly worshiped her—sat at his boss's side, taking notes on a yellow pad.

"Not to mention the potential charges in Pennsylvania," Bassett went on. "And I'm sure the federal prosecutor will have a few things to add to the list. Counselor, your client is in trouble, if you don't mind my saying so."

Adrianna, looking just as elegant and tough in an all-black suit, stabbed at the tabletop with her pen. "You have evidence of my client's good faith right on Detective Starks's voice mail, Carol."

"For all we know, she already knew the police had traced the rental car when she made that call. She may have been covering her ass."

"How would she know that?"

"Maybe her attorney told her."

"I'll ignore that remark, Carol." Adrianna got up from her chair and took a few steps to the window. Kate watched from her place at the big oak table. She could see that Carol Ann Bassett was watching her, too—calculating, assessing, seeing how far she could push. The clash of the beautiful lawyers, Kate said to herself. Somehow she felt that it wasn't really herself these women were talking about. She was just a spectator here, with only a mild interest in what was going on.

Adrianna turned from the pale light of the window. "It's just as I told you: despite being wounded by a DEA bullet—emphasis on *DEA* bullet, Carol—my client is fully prepared to cooperate in both the state and federal cases, but within the protections allowed her by law. The fact remains that Joel Baker is her husband and any communication between them is legally privileged."

Bassett turned to Kate. "Your husband held you at gunpoint, Ms. Baker. He drugged you with tranquilizers. I don't get it."

Kate shook her head. She didn't get it, either, at least not entirely. She did think Joel deserved to go to jail. She *wanted* him to go to jail. But somehow she didn't want to be the one to put him there. "Have you ever been married, Ms. Bassett?" she asked then.

Bassett rolled her eyes theatrically. "Twice, actually," she said. "And if you ask me, I think both of them deserve to rot in jail. But that's another story."

"Carol," Adrianna said then, coming back to the table. "The fact is, you don't have to understand my client's motivations. The law does. It recognizes the privileged nature of the marriage bond. Besides, you got the indictments without my client's testimony. You can win your case without it, too."

Bassett's searching look was now turned on Kate. "You understand that I can't do a thing to stop Detective Jerrold from pursuing a civil case against you. And I know that he'll be very unhappy if you don't cooperate here."

"Carol, you're treading the line," Adrianna said, softly but ominously.

"Look," Kate said then. "Let me think about this. I need a good sleep before I can decide anything."

Kate saw the two other women exchanging looks. Then Bassett cleared her throat. "We'll talk again tomorrow," she said to Adrianna. Then, to Kate, "We've got hearings for both Joel and Duncan the day after tomorrow. I just want you to think—think *hard*—about one fact: the less you feel you can say on the stand, the weaker my case against Duncan Lloyd. He's got enough family money to hire lawyers by the dozen. If he walks . . ."

"He won't walk, Carol," Adrianna said, putting her hand on the back of Kate's chair, "unless you don't do your job."

"I can't do my job unless your client helps me."

"We'll talk tomorrow."

Adrianna tapped the chair leg with her foot—their signal. Kate got up. "I'll think about it," she said, then followed Adrianna out into the hallway. They said nothing to each other as they got their coats and made their way toward the exit. Then, just as they were leaving the courthouse, Adrianna asked, "Are you going to see him?"

Kate nodded. "Tomorrow morning." They walked down the stairs in bright winter sunshine. At the bottom, Kate stopped. "Do you understand why I'm not sure about testifying?" she asked.

Adrianna didn't look at her, just glanced off toward the

glittering cars in the parking lot. In this light, Kate could see the wrinkles around the woman's mouth and eyes, the signs of wear and tear that were invisible in more flattering light. "I think I do, yes," Adrianna said. She turned back. "But I think the impulse is wrong. Joel is my friend, too, Kate. I've known him a lot longer than you have. But he played false with all of us. He doesn't deserve our loyalty."

"No," Kate said then, pulling her coat tighter around her neck with her free hand. "You don't understand, then." Kate looked out over the parking lot and caught sight of a familiar figure in a black coat—Lieutenant Grainger, standing next to the unmarked Caprice. "We'll talk tomorrow, Adrianna," Kate said. "After I talk to Joel. And thanks."

They hugged and parted, and then Kate walked carefully across the wet asphalt to the Lieutenant's car. "Hi," she said.

He nodded hello, looking a little wary of her, as if he expected her to hit him or steal his car keys.

"I hear you were the one who traced the rental car," Kate went on. "That probably took a lot of legwork. On your own time, too."

He shrugged. "You were smart not to use your credit card. But there aren't that many rental places in this county. And not many pretty, thirty-six-year-old women who come in and put down the security in cash."

Kate smiled at the subtle compliment. "Well, I guess I owe you some kind of thanks. Solid investigative work."

He laughed, rubbing his chin with a gloved hand. "Tell the DEA that, okay? They're trying to take all the credit themselves, as per usual." He pulled his gloves tighter on his hands, first one, then the other. "Besides, you did some pretty good investigative work yourself. How'd you like a job on the Lewisburg force?"

"Yeah, right."

"Well, you don't owe me any thanks. I was out to fry your ass, pardon my French. Still am, in fact."

Shielding her eyes with her good hand, Kate tried to make out the expression on his backlit face. "I'm relieved. I was beginning to worry that I couldn't think of you as an asshole anymore."

"Oh no, Ms. Theodorus-Baker. No cause for that. In fact, if it was me you hit instead of Jerrold, you'd be in civil court this minute."

"Thanks, Lieutenant," she said. "And fuck you."

He laughed again. "You have a nice day, too," he said. "And try to keep your nose clean from now on. If you can manage it."

Elena and Hermann were waiting for her when she got home from the county courthouse. They ran out of the house just as she pulled the Jetta into the drive. By the time Kate stopped the engine and climbed out, they were both all over her.

"How did it go?" Elena asked anxiously. She wasn't wearing a coat and hugged herself to keep warm.

Kate scratched Hermann's neck and then held out the wrist on her good arm. "Still no cuffs," she said.

"As if they'd arrest you. With what you did for them, they should be giving you a parade."

"Don't hold your breath," Kate said. "Let's get inside."

"Coffee?" Elena asked.

Kate raised her eyebrows. "Coffee."

Elena had built a small fire in the fireplace. After they brewed some decaf, they brought their mugs and sat on the floor in front of it, with Hermann lying between them.

"Oh, your brother called while you were out," Elena said.

"Which one?" Kate had forced herself, finally, to call her brothers in Chicago to tell them what had been going on. She hadn't been able to reach any of them directly, so she'd left messages all around.

"Phil. He's coming out here tomorrow afternoon, he says."

"Oh no," Kate moaned. Her older brother coming out to comfort her, to protect her.

"He wouldn't tell me what time, because he didn't want you to pick him up. He says he'll rent a car at BWI."

"So considerate," Kate said. "But you can bet that he'll expect me to have dinner on the table when he gets here."

"Kate," Elena scolded.

"Okay, I'm being unfair. But this is going to be hard. There's only so much I-told-you-so that I can put up with. And you know he'll try to talk me into going back to Chicago to live. I can hear it all now: 'You don't belong out here, Katie. This isn't your place. You're still a Theodorus.' "

Elena stared into the fire. "And will you?"

"Will I what? Go back to Chicago?"

"Well . . . yes."

"Hell, no. I live here, Elena."

"I'm trying not to make any assumptions. You've been through a lot."

"Yeah, I have. But I have a life here—and a job, too, unless David fired me while I was gone. I've got a responsibility to six kids." Then, "Seven. Make that seven."

Elena smiled. "What about Joel?" she asked.

Kate was absentmindedly pressing the bandage over her gunshot wound, pushing until she felt the first twinge of pain. "I'm seeing him tomorrow. I'll see how I feel then."

"He'll go to jail no matter what you decide to do."

"I know." She put her coffee aside and lay back on the rug, her head against Hermann's warm belly. "In a way, what I decide matters more to me than to him."

Hermann thumped his tail against the floor. The fire popped and sizzled.

Kate turned and looked at Elena. "Somehow I feel that one of us should be true to this marriage. Does that sound crazy to you?"

Elena hesitated for a few seconds, but then nodded.

"Yeah, it probably *is* crazy," Kate went on. "But I keep thinking of all those women in our neighborhood when I was a kid. Their husbands would cheat on them, have kids with mistresses, whatever, and sure, they'd make the husbands pay—they'd yell at them and harangue them and sometimes even whop them with a frying pan—but they never divorced them. That part was unthinkable."

"This isn't the same," Elena said.

"No, it isn't." Kate moved her head so that it lay more comfortably on Hermann. The heat from the fire was making his fur give off a reassuring sour smell. "Did you stop loving him?" she asked then. "Alan, I mean. After you found out he was lying to you all along."

Elena thought about this for a while. "Yes," she said finally. "Yes, I honestly did. He made it easy to stop."

Kate stared into the fire, watching the restless yellow flames. "I envy you, I think. That he made it so easy. I'm having a little trouble with that part." She stretched her legs out closer to the fire. "Joel still claims he would have gotten us both out of that mess if he'd had the chance."

"People say lots of things."

"They do, don't they." Kate looked up at the ceiling. "What's amazing is that we sometimes still believe them."

Next morning, Kate climbed the marble steps to the second-floor visiting room of the Hampton County Detention Center. She recognized the smell of the place right away. It was a rank, complicated smell, something she remembered from the jail in Chicago. The smell of perfume, perspiration, and regret.

She took a seat in front of the glass partition of Booth 4 and waited.

Joel was led in a few seconds later. He had a thick
plaster cast over his hand and wrist, and he looked tired
and underfed. As he took a seat on the other side of the
partition, Kate thought he looked younger now than he
did before his disappearance, as if the whole ordeal had
stripped away years of hard experience to show the more
hopeful, less jaded man underneath.

"Hey, you," he said to her.

"Hey, you. How you feeling?"

He shrugged. "Reasonably okay. You?"

"My shoulder hurts."

"You taking anything for it?" he asked.

She smiled. "Nuprin. Just Nuprin."

He looked down at his cast, tracing the curve of it with
his fingers. "I guess you're here looking for some sort of
explanation. Some reason not to hate me?"

Kate shook her head. "I'm not looking for anything,"
she said. "I'm here to see you."

Neither one said anything for a few seconds. In the next
booth a woman began crying quietly.

"I heard about the problems you're giving the state's
attorney," Joel said.

"Adrianna tells me that the legal issue involved is a
little unclear. It's possible they can force me to testify
about everything you told me."

Joel leaned closer to the glass between them. "Look, I
appreciate the gesture. But it'll probably turn out to be
academic. My lawyer is advising me to go for a deal.
They want Duncan a lot more than they want me. So just
tell them you'll cooperate."

"You would testify against Duncan?"

"Kate, he had two of my friends killed. I feel no loyalty
to him whatsoever." He put his hand up and grazed the
glass partition with his fingertips. "I know I have no right
to expect anything at all from you, Kate. But you have to
realize that through all of this I never stopped loving you."

"Shut up, Joel," she said softly. Part of her was starved to hear these words, but she was fighting against it with every bit of her strength. "I can't listen to that."

Joel was nodding faintly. "I understand," he said. "I'll go along with a divorce, if that's what you want. It's the last thing in the world I want, you've got to believe that, but I'll do it if you ask me to."

Kate felt a stab of panic at the word "divorce." "Joel," she said, "what did our marriage mean to you? I just don't get it."

She recognized the look of discomfort in his steady brown eyes. "Marriage is a legal contract," he said. "What meant something to me was you."

"That's bullshit, Joel," she blurted out. "Pure bullshit."

"Number four," a guard said in warning from across the room.

She lowered her voice and leaned in closer. "You held back two-thirds of yourself from me. From the minute we met. That's not a marriage. That's not even a legal contract."

"Kate," Joel said matter-of-factly, "I've let you see more of myself than I've shown to anyone else in my life. As much as I'm capable of."

The comment amazed her, then made her angry. "Well, then, I feel sorry for you and me and everyone else who's ever known you."

"I don't think I'm an exception," he said. "Kate, you can't expect someone to surrender everything to you, not even your husband. No one can live with that kind of exposure. Even with someone you love, you have to leave them some kind of sanctuary . . ."

"Fuck you and your sanctuary," Kate almost shouted.

"Number four, do I have to come over there?" the guard warned again.

"You've made my decision for me, Joel," Kate went on then, in a quieter voice. "We were never really married. I see that now. So the whole legal issue of privileged communication doesn't apply here." She got up from the chair and fumbled for her shoulder bag.

Joel was staring at her through the glass, looking not hurt or sorry but impressed. Even proud. "You keep amazing me," he said.

"The feeling is mutual, believe me." Kate pushed the chair in, took one last look at her husband, and headed for the exit.

"Kate," she heard him say as she left. "Please come back again. After you've had some time. Please. I'll be waiting."

Outside in the lobby, Kate found her way through the busy hallways to the ladies' room on the ground floor. She pushed through the swinging door, found an empty stall, and locked the door behind her. She leaned back against the unstable partition. Her eyes wandered up to the humming fluorescents overhead, and then—for the next fifteen minutes, until someone called in a female cop who started knocking on the stall door—she sobbed out every trace of anger, frustration, pity, shame, and love she could wrench from the pit of her tight, burning stomach.

24

Early on the morning of December 25—an overcast, unseasonably warm day in suburban Maryland—a detailed message of ambiguous origin arrived simultaneously in the electronic mailboxes of the director of the National Institute for Drug Abuse; the editors of the *Journal of the American Medical Association*, the *Lancet*, and the *New England Journal of Medicine*; and the heads of the pharmacology, biomedical engineering, and molecular biology departments of a dozen universities and medical schools in the United States, England, and Japan. The message was from one Jin-Liang Lu, a dead man, and it contained information about a derivative of a drug called "bromolide mesylate," an ergotic dopamine-receptor agonist used experimentally for the treatment of several diseases, including Parkinson's. According to the sender, this particular derivative had shown extraordinary effectiveness in counteracting both the craving and the withdrawal mechanisms of addiction in a small group of crack addicts in Rotterdam. The message, which had apparently been sent au-

tomatically from two of three Internet accounts
maintained by the author before his death, laid out a brief
overview of the research undertaken, and directed interested parties to several on-line bulletin boards where results, experimental data, and other information had been
posted. The author acknowledged that much more research would be required to determine the true efficacy
of the compound over the long term, but expressed confidence that it would eventually represent an important
breakthrough in the treatment of cocaine, amphetamine,
and other addictions.

Kate Baker heard the news from her lawyer. Adrianna
had reached her by phone on the afternoon of December
26, just as Kate was coming back from the airport, where
she'd dropped her brother off for his flight back to Chicago. After the conversation with Adrianna, Kate hung up
the phone and just sat in her living room for a few
minutes, staring at the lights of the pitiful plastic tree that
Elena had brought over earlier in the week. She wondered
what Duncan Lloyd, pacing in his jail cell, would make
of this news. Kate smiled. Jin-Liang Lu had won their
contest after all.

That evening, Kate got into the Jetta and drove to
Franklin, Maryland. She passed through the quiet town
and then headed out toward Kings Mill Road. It was a
dark night, starless and moonless. Any snow that had
fallen earlier in the month had already melted, deepening
the blackness of the woods.

Both Hondas were in the driveway when Kate pulled
in at Evan Potter's house. She parked the Jetta, got out,
and headed up the walk before she could think better of
it. She hadn't seen or spoken to Evan since leaving him
in the Jeep that morning in the Pennsylvania mountains.
After the police raid on the chalet, he'd been taken off in
a DEA van before she regained consciousness. Adrianna
had told her that the boy was in deep shock when they

found him in the oil-tank closet, and that he'd been un-
dergoing treatment for depression ever since finding the
body in the woods.

Evan's mother answered Kate's ring. She seemed to
know who it was before she pulled open the door. The
woman didn't even try to hide her hostility. "You have
nerve," she said, "showing up here again."

Kate had been expecting this kind of reception. "Mrs.
Potter, I know what you must think of me, but I really
am here for Evan's welfare. I really think it would be
good for him to see me."

Mrs. Potter put a hand up, like a policeman stopping
traffic. She stepped out onto the chilly porch and pulled
the door nearly shut behind her, so that nobody inside
would hear. "Evan is in enough trouble without seeing
you again on top of it all. Do you have any idea what
he's been through? What we've all been through? Because
of you?" She hugged herself in the night air. "No, you're
the last person I want him to see. The last person, can
you get that through your head?"

"Mrs. Potter, I think I mean something to Evan. Keeping us apart won't do anybody any good." She was about
to put out her hand, but then let it drop, useless, at her
side. "I think I can help Evan."

"As far as I'm concerned," Mrs. Potter said, her red
hair flying in the breeze, "you're nothing but trouble. And
if I have to get a restraining order to keep you away from
my son, I'll do it." She went back into the house and
slammed the door shut behind her.

Kate nodded calmly at the closed door. What else could
she expect? This was exactly how Kate herself would react if she were in Mrs. Potter's position. Though she probably never *would* be in Mrs. Potter's position, since she
probably never would have a son of her own. It was getting too late for her. Kate had to admit that to herself
now.

She walked slowly back to the Jetta and got in. Then she sat for a while, counting. She reached twenty, and Evan still hadn't come around the corner of the house. She was surprised at how deeply this disappointed her. She leaned forward and turned the key. The engine started with a roar. She was about to shift into reverse when he appeared—surprising her for the second time—beside the car.

She rolled down the window. "Hi," Evan said. He was wearing striped pajama bottoms and a white T-shirt under his leather jacket. His hair was cut short, the little ponytail gone.

"Hi," Kate answered. "You doing okay?"

Evan shrugged. He seemed to want to keep a distance between himself and the car, and kept looking anxiously back at the house. "I guess I screwed up," he said.

Kate stopped the engine. "Evan," she said, "listen to me. *You* didn't screw up. We're both alive, right? And the bad guys are in jail. You did great."

He shook his head, looking sorry for himself.

"I mean it, Evan. It was you who talked me out of running away, remember. And who knows, if you hadn't yelled from the closet right when those cops broke in, I might have taken a bullet in my skull instead of my shoulder."

This seemed to have an effect. Evan's posture straightened. It was a glimmering—the kind of hopeful sign she always looked for when counseling her ghetto kids. "I heard you wasted one of them," he said then. "One of the guys."

Kate had been trying not to think too much about this. "Yeah," she said.

"What was it like? I mean, shooting him."

"Evan," she said, then looked down at her hand on the steering wheel. "Evan," she started again, "I'd like to see you. To be your friend. If your mother will let me." She looked up at him again. "Is that something you would want?"

"I guess." Evan shrugged. Then, "Yeah, I would."

"It could take me a while to convince her. You can help. I don't know, talk to your therapist. It's a woman, right? Give her my phone number."

His nod—if it was one—seemed halfhearted, unsure. "They're gonna keep me out of school, I think. Maybe till next year. They'll send a tutor to the house or something."

"You should study hard, Evan," she said after a pause. She felt ridiculous saying it, like an ineffectual parent. "Really. It's important."

"As important as anything else, I guess."

Kate tried to understand what he meant by this. She stared into his listless, evasive eyes. His enthusiasm of a minute ago was already gone. She wondered if Duncan Lloyd might be right, if someday there would be a pill that could cure whatever problem this boy had. "You like dogs?" she asked then.

Evan shrugged again. "They're okay."

"I have a dog you would like. Maybe you could come over and see him sometime."

"Maybe."

Feeling let down, Kate reached her sore left arm out the window. She took Evan's hand and held it, squeezing the cold flesh and bone. "Thanks," she said. They held hands through the open window for a few seconds—looking away from each other—before Kate finally let go. "Remember what I said. About giving my number to your therapist."

He nodded.

"Is there anything I can do for you? Anything at all?"

A faint smile appeared on Evan's face.

"What," Kate said then, her hopes rising.

"Let me touch your breasts?" he asked.

Kate's jaw dropped, and she felt a hot flush of embarrassment. "Evan," she said. "Of course not!"

His face reddened. He laughed and shrugged awkwardly, then looked back at the house.

"But I'll kiss you," Kate went on finally, relenting. "If you want. A motherly . . . a *sisterly* kiss."

Evan looked back at her nervously. "Okay." He stepped toward the car and leaned over, an expression of intense concentration on his face.

Kate could smell his breath, and see the little spray of acne on his temples. His pale, thin face hovered next to hers, giving off a strange electricity. She kissed him on the cheek as he kissed her, loudly, near her ear.

He pulled away from her. He looked flustered but pleased.

Kate started the engine. " 'Bye," she said. "Take care of yourself."

"You, too," he said.

Kate looked in the rearview mirror as she backed out into the dark road. She shifted into first and then turned her head toward the driveway again to wave good-bye, but Evan was already gone. The spot where he'd stood was marked only by the wet corrugated prints of his Nike sneakers.

That night, sleeping in her own big bed, Hermann lying heavily beside her, Kate had a dream about the animal lab in the Pennsylvania woods. In the dream, the lab was enormous, its domed roof arching impossibly high overhead. There were wire cages piled on every side of her, the interiors hidden by shadow. As Kate moved through the huge room, she noticed a sudden stirring in the cages, a wave of feverish movement that followed her passing like the wake of a ship. The sound bothered her, distracted her. She moved faster, her boots clicking noisily on the cement floor. Someone, she knew, would hear her; someone would find her.

The chimpanzee was out of its cage. The door was broken—it hung by a single twisted hinge. Kate stopped walking. She felt annoyed at first, then afraid. How far could it have gone, she wondered.

She heard the rustling to her left and turned. The animal was there, clinging to the side of an empty cage against the wall, staring at her. It looked wasted by disease, its fur clotted with half-dried blood, its eyes weeping yellow mucus. Kate knew suddenly that she was there to kill it, to put the thing out of its misery. Her Sig was in her right hand. She had loaded it before she came. The job would be easy.

She tried to lift the pistol, but she couldn't move her hand. Looking down, she saw that her wrist was caught on something—a strap or a belt. She couldn't work it free.

She looked back at the chimpanzee. It was in motion now, its long arms and legs unwrapping themselves from the wire cage. Kate began to panic. If the animal bit her, she would be infected, too. Just touching its body would be enough to put her at risk.

Kate tore frantically at her clothing, trying to free her hand, but she knew she was too late. She looked up again. The chimpanzee had already lunged. It hit the cement floor, took one, two, three strides toward her, and then leapt. She could only watch in amazement as it sailed above her, beyond her, disappearing into the blackness overhead.

Acknowledgments

First on my list of thanks has to be the varied group of e-mail correspondents who did so much to keep me going during the past two years of enforced isolation. Some of these people I've never met in person, but all have provided the advice, distraction, bad jokes, and/or moral support that the writing of this book required: Lisa Bergtraum, Alice Bradley, Rick Dooling (whom I came to know, for the record, only after I praised his novel in print), Alice Rose George, Louise Hawes, Eddie Lewis, Rick Moody, Regina Schrambling, Henry Shukman, John Thorndike, Rob Wilder, Robert Wright, and a few others who may become more prompt in their responses now that they realize it can lead to free publicity in someone's book (Laura Barnes, this means you).

Several people were especially helpful in providing professional information. Terry Treschuk, chief of the Rockville, Maryland, Police, fielded my many police-procedural questions for the better part of a year and a half. I'm indebted to him and to the faculty of the Rock-

ville Citizens Police Academy, of which I am a loyal
graduate. My good friends Richard Smith, psychologist,
and Loretta Berger, clinical social worker, taught me a lot
by relating their counseling experiences with children and
adolescents; Richard also provided some valuable editorial advice. Thanks, too, to Steve Koppelman (aka Hat-
less), who kept me relatively honest technologically. All
of these people were generous with their advice and time,
though any lapses in the book in their areas of expertise
are entirely my fault and my responsibility.

I read a lot of other people's books in the course of
researching my own. I'll mention only three that, for various reasons that would probably be obscure to their au-
thors, were most helpful to me: *The Billion-Dollar
Molecule* by Barry Werth, *What Cops Know* by Connie
Fletcher, and *Sudden Fury* by Leslie Walker.

I owe thanks to some other people who offered help,
key ideas, and other feedback at various points in this
ordeal: Lisa Wright; Susan Kamil; my agent, the redoubt-
able Irene Skolnick; Adam Davies; and my editor, Dan
Menaker.

My biggest debts of gratitude, however, are owed to
three people: Martha Browne, who is as excellent a friend
as she is a copy editor; Bob Wright (the flesh-and-blood
version of e-mail correspondent Robert Wright above),
who is my number-one guide to the zeitgeist, as well as
a great chum and a generous provider of editorial advice
and spiritual reinforcement; and, of course, my wife and
perpetual soulmate, Elizabeth Cheng. After reading and
rereading this book, she may want to stipulate that the
two of us spend the rest of our natural lives tethered together at the wrists. I can think of many worse fates.

About the Author

GARY KRIST is the author of two short-story collections: *The Garden State*, winner of the 1989 Sue Kaufman Prize for First Fiction, and *Bone by Bone*, a 1994 *New York Times* Notable Book of the Year. He lives in Chevy Chase, Maryland, with his wife and daughter.